WHAT
SHE
INHERITS

For Margie —
with love +
gratitude!

WHAT SHE INHERITS

Diane V. Mulligan

Worcester, Massachusetts

FIRST EDITION

Designed by Diane Mulligan

ISBN 978-1540362445

This is a work of fiction. Names, characters, businesses, places, events and incidents are either the products of the author's imagination or used in a fictitious manner. Any resemblance to actual persons, living or dead, or actual events is purely coincidental.

For Laura and Tommy, the best siblings in the world.

WHAT
SHE
INHERITS

PART ONE

Chapter One

St. Katherine's College, New Hampshire

IN HER BAG, Angela's phone buzzed and buzzed, but she didn't hear it. She had her headphones on, plugged into her computer, turned up loud. Florence and the Machine made ideal music to work to. Her project was due by the end of class at noon, and she hadn't gotten the effect quite right. The shadows were very realistic and added perfect depth, but the texture was impossible. She could have given herself a simpler task, it was true, but what would be the fun in that? Still, it was 11:35, her eyes were blurry from staring at the computer screen, and she was starting to suspect her recent changes were taking her further from the outcome she sought, not closer. She leaned in close to the computer screen, zoomed in on a corner of the image to isolate a small sliver, and tried again, applying a filter. Better. She thought. Or worse? Hard to say.

A tap on her shoulder and she jumped. Pushing her headphones down she glanced up at her favorite professor, the one she hoped would become her academic advisor when she finally filed the paperwork to declare her major next week. Professor Morgan was tough. She never hesitated to remind students how hard a career in the arts really was, and was therefore always unflinchingly honest in her assessment of students' work.

"Only a few more minutes. Can I see how it's shaping up?"

Angela rubbed her strained eyes and zoomed back out to put the full picture on the screen. The digital canvas showed a white-on-white design with slightly varied textures and tints and careful shadows so that it looked like an image made of layered cut paper, depicting a wintry landscape with sledding children and peeping woodland creatures. It was folksy but also modern and intricate. Angela had been working on it nonstop for two weeks.

"Okay," Professor Morgan said, squinting and cupping her chin with her hand. "Now tell me what you dislike about it."

Angela sighed. What was wrong with it? The tints still needed to be tweaked for the ideal balance. She needed there to be enough contrast but not too much. Also the texture. The texture was driving her nuts. Too smooth and it looked digital, which of course it was, but the whole point was to look real. Too textured it looked too clunky and rustic. She wasn't after kitsch. She said, "It's still not perfect."

Professor Morgan laughed. "Hand it in and live to fight another day, kid."

"But—"

"Angela, it's done. Seriously. It's done and it's fantastic."

A few other students glanced up from their own computers at this rare and unqualified praise. They shot

Angela annoyed or encouraging looks and then went back to their own work.

Unsatisfied but exhausted, Angela submitted the project and grabbed her bag. She didn't open it to see the four missed calls from an unknown number on her phone screen. Instead, she strolled out of the library annex where the design lab was and into the perfect September day, her head tilted toward the sun, letting the breeze wash the tension from her shoulders. Her short, honey-brown hair was greasy with neglect from an all-nighter in the lab, and she ran a hand through it, not caring if it stood on end. On a day so lovely, how could she care what she looked like?

Blue sky, leaves turning yellow and crimson around the stately red-brick college buildings, sun glinting off the leaded glass windows, the midday air warm, but the breeze carrying the crisp scent of fall. Students lounged on the green near the dorms, taking full advantage of the golden day. Already nights in this New Hampshire town were cold. Soon the true colors of the place—the gray and white of ice and snow— would show themselves.

Molly, one of Angela's roommates, had claimed a patch of grass under a massive maple tree whose leaves were bright flame. With her porcelain skin, Molly always chose shade. She called to Angela, who made her way through a game of ultimate Frisbee, past the stoners and their impromptu drum circle, to the blanket where Molly sat with a novel and a pile of snacks. Angela tossed her bag on the edge of the blanket without a thought for her phone, which was buzzing again, unbeknownst to her, another call from the unknown number. Why would she check her phone? It wasn't even noon on a Thursday. Maybe there was a text from Molly saying she'd be on the green, but Angela had already found her, had needed no messages to locate her. Nicole, their other roommate, would soon be done in the chem lab, and she would find them, too. It was no secret that on a postcard-perfect fall day, that if you wanted to find anyone, try the green first.

"Project all done?" Molly asked as Angela flopped onto the blanket.

Angela offered a murmur of assent as she stretched her legs in front of her and folded forward so that her head rested on her knees, her hands clasped around the soles of her feet.

"Show off," Molly said.

Angela was showing off, and she didn't mind at all. A day so ideal seemed to beg everyone to show off, to do their best, to meet the day in its perfection. She sat up and rocked backwards, drawing her legs up over her head and turning a backwards somersault to return to a sitting position, one of those tricks from her childhood gymnastics that was automatic, like riding a bicycle. Molly chucked a cellophane wrapped sandwich at her and rolled her eyes.

"It's the weekend," Angela said, tearing the wrapping from the sandwich.

As juniors, both women understood the importance of selecting one's classes so that the weekend began at lunch on Thursday. Nicole, lab rat that she was, considered them wasteful squanderers of opportunity for discounting every single class that met Thursday afternoon or Friday, but they had learned to ignore her ages ago.

"Want to go to Millers Falls after lunch? Get in one last swim for the season?" Angela asked. Between the weather and the relief of having handed in her project, however imperfect, she was giddy. She needed an outlet for her energy, and Millers Falls was perfect. The clear, cold pool at the bottom of a small but peaceful waterfall within walking distance of campus had never sounded more inviting, even if it was likely to be teeming with other students.

"Glad to see you're feeling better today," Molly said, picking at her own sandwich.

"Do we need to get into that now?" Angela asked. The last thing she wanted to do was ruin her good mood by thinking about the fight she'd had with her mother the evening before.

"What if she follows through, though? Have you even thought of that?"

Of course Angela had thought of her mother's threat to stop payment on her tuition. She had gone back to the computer lab after dinner last night to throw herself into her work because otherwise she'd make herself sick with worry. Her mother did not bluff.

"Look, Nicole and I really think you should suck it up and do what she wants."

Of course Molly and Nicole had discussed her situation without her, and of course they were siding with her mother. Angela suspected she should be bothered by the fact that her best friends, on more than one occasion, had had these little powwows to discuss her problems, but that wasn't the part that irritated her. The real issue was that they insisted on trying to talk her out of making her own decisions, like she was a little kid and they were the grownups who knew best. They meant well, and she loved them, but she wondered if they realized how condescending they were sometimes.

They acted like she was some country bumpkin from the deep South just because she was from South Carolina, but she was from the resort area of St. Nabor Island—not exactly a backwater or broke-down farm region—and was the daughter of parents from Massachusetts. She spoke with hardly a hint of a Southern accent, just the occasional, convenient y'all, and her most Southern traits were a fondness for grits and hush puppies. New Englanders, she'd learned since living here, had something of a superiority complex.

"I already did what she wanted by coming here in the first place," Angela said. She stuffed the rest of her sandwich—most of it; she'd hardly eaten a bite—into the cellophane and got up to throw it away. She had no appetite now. Her stomach was working itself back into an intricate knot.

"Do you want something else to eat? You must be starving," Molly said.

Angela clenched her jaw. It was so Molly, playing mommy again, telling silly little Angela to eat her food.

"It's not like you can't double major," Molly said when Angela didn't respond. "Go ahead with studio art, but then do something practical, too."

"Wait, remind me again, how is your medieval studies major practical? What jobs does it qualify you for?"

Molly's pale face colored, but her Admissions Tour Guide training kicked in, and she answered calmly, ever the good, patient mommy, with her practiced response: "A liberal arts degree prepares students for a wide range of jobs. It teaches us how to think and—"

"Thank you. I read the brochure three years ago,"

Angela said.

Angela was considering leaving, going off to Millers Falls on her own, when Nicole arrived. Nicole didn't have to try to look like a fashion model, with her tumble of thick, glossy curls, her full lips, and startling, bright blue eyes. If Angela and Molly felt plain by comparison, though, Nicole's nerdiness made up for it. She was an unapologetic geek.

"It's a beautiful day. Why so glum?" Nicole said, grabbing a bag of chips from Molly's assortment of snacks.

"Can y'all just not?" Angela said, reaching across the blanket and grabbing her bag. She would bury her face in her phone and ignore Nicole and Molly until they got the hint, and maybe then they could all have a nice afternoon. But when she pulled the phone from her bag, she saw that she had six missed calls and two voice messages, all from an unknown number with a South Carolina area code. If it was a telemarketer, it was a persistent one.

Walking away from Nicole and Molly, she pressed play and listened to the first message.

"Angela, this is Mrs. Porter. Please call me back, honey." Then she slowly listed her phone number, as if she didn't know that Angela's cell phone would store it in missed calls. Mrs. Porter lived next door to her mother on St. Nabor Island, South Carolina. Although they'd lived next to each other for years, they hardly knew each other except to say hello in passing. There was no logical reason for Mrs. Porter to call her. How did Mrs. Porter even have Angela's phone number?

She pressed play on the second message. "Angela, honey, it's Mrs. Porter again. It's very important that you call me back, dear. It's about your mother."

Seriously? Angela thought. Her mother had discussed her with Mrs. Porter? Angela hadn't imagined that her mother was particularly bothered by her empty nest, but if she was striking up friendship with Mrs. Porter, who had to be about ninety years old, maybe Angela had underestimated how much her mother missed her. She walked back to the blanket and dropped her phone back on top of her bag.

"Everything okay?" Nicole asked.

"Who's ready to go swimming?" Angela asked.

Chapter Two

Devil's Back Island, Maine

AS THE BELLS on the door of the Beach Plum Café jangled at Rosetta's entrance, her poodle Bentley at her heels, Casey shoved the piece of paper she'd been studying into the back pocket of her jeans as if she feared it would grow wings and fly into her great-aunt's hands. For two weeks, she'd been avoiding Rosetta, but the evasion couldn't go on forever, not on an island as small as Devil's Back. She braced herself to face Rosetta's uncanny ability to read her mind.

Rosetta tried and failed to flatten her fly-away cloud of white hair as she came in from the breezy afternoon. From the rosy glow on her cheeks, Casey guessed she had just finished her afternoon walk.

"Where is everybody?" Rosetta asked, coming around behind the counter to help herself to coffee.

"Is this the slowest September in memory?" Casey asked.

"Ayup," Rosetta said in an affected Maine drawl. Though she'd lived on Devil's Back since the 1980s, by

Maine standards she was not "from Maine." Thirty years of residency didn't change the fact that she was a Masshole, born and raised, as far as true Mainers were concerned. She owned the island's only hotel, the Wild Rose Inn, and almost never left the island anymore, but compared to third and fourth generation islanders, she'd always be a newcomer.

Rosetta stooped to examine the bakery case and then helped herself to a shortbread cookie, which she took back around the counter to a table.

"Sit with me," she said. It wasn't a request.

Casey sighed but did as she was told. She folded her arms on the table, positioning herself so that her tattoo, which covered her entire left arm, was mostly hidden. She knew Rosetta hated it. Even after all this time, Rosetta's eyes would still drift to the tattoo as if pulled by the magnetic force of the intricate design.

"How long did you think you could avoid me?"

Casey shrugged.

"All right then spill it. What's going on?"

Casey pursed her lips and considered how she might answer. She loved Rosetta, and she literally owed everything she had and was to Rosetta, but sometimes the woman was a pest. Casey was thirty-seven years old. Old enough to keep secrets if she wanted to. But when Rosetta insisted on treating her like a child, it was easy to fall into childish submission. Still, she wasn't ready to talk to Rosetta about what was on her mind. She wasn't sure she ever would be. She twirled a lock of her bright red hair around her finger and studied it, cross-eyed and silent. She made a mental note to order more hair dye and let Rosetta's question go unanswered.

"Is it about that boy you've been seeing?" Rosetta asked. "Because if that's what it is, you should know better. You'll get no judgment from me, even if you are making a damn fool of yourself."

This was a perfect excuse, presented to her on a platter. She didn't particularly wish to discuss her sex life with Rosetta, didn't care for her no-judgment judgments, but it was better than the truth.

"It's stupid, I know," said Casey.

"You got that right," Rosetta said. "For heaven's sake, he's half your age."

"Not half. He's twenty-three."

Rosetta gave a little snort and reached down to give Bentley the end of her cookie.

"We're not exactly serious," Casey said.

"Aren't you a little old for this screwing around?"

Maybe, Casey thought, but what the hell? She wasn't hurting anyone.

"One day you're going to wake up and realize that you're ready to settle down and have a family, and then you'll find out your eggs have turned to dust in there, and how will you feel then?"

This again. If her current life wasn't "settled," no life ever would be, but she had no intention of getting married or having kids. She was fine on her own, here in her safe, cozy bubble away from all the madness of the world.

"Don't you roll your eyes at me. You'll see."

This was Rosetta's own regret, Casey knew. It hadn't been Rosetta's choice to be childless. She and her husband Phil had tried, but it never happened for them. But things had turned out okay for Rosetta. She had been more of a mother to Casey than Maureen, her actual mother and Rosetta's niece, had ever been. Now Rosetta had Casey to care for her. She of all people should understand that you don't need to have children to have family.

"He's great in bed, though," Casey said, flashing Rosetta a wicked grin.

"You'll be the death of me."

Then, thankfully Rosetta changed the topic of conversation to the plans for Halloween Haunting Fest, a scheme she'd concocted a few years ago to push tourist season to the end of October. She had begun advertising the island as "America's Most Haunted Island." On whose authority she made this claim Casey did not know, but she did know that exploiting death stories under the guise of ghost stories was wrong. Did two weeks' worth of travelers truly bring in enough income to justify reveling in morbid tales of loss? Casey doubted it. She hated all the ghost hunting shows that had become so popular on TV, and she hated the tourists who went off on ghost adventures after watching those shows.

Rosetta pulled a glossy brochure from the pocket of her jacket announcing the 5th Annual Halloween Haunting Fest on Devil's Back Island and slid it across the table to Casey.

"These are in every rest area on I-95 from the New Hampshire border to Bar Harbor and still I have vacancies at the inn," she said. "I'm trying online ads to try to target new visitors."

Casey picked up the brochure, which sported a sepia-toned picture of a woman in old-fashioned dress walking on the beach between the massive horn-shaped rocks that formed the geological feature for which the island was named. The woman's dress billowed and some of her hair escaped her Puritan cap. She was looking back over her shoulder at the camera. She was also made to appear somewhat transparent.

"I can't believe you got Barb to pose for this," Casey said, shaking her head.

"Don't start with me. What I came to talk about was catering. I want to have refreshments up at the meeting house for before and after the ghost tours."

"Do I have to?" Casey asked, her voice dipped dangerously close to a childish whine.

"It's good extra business for you. It makes sense."

"Does it make sense to abandon my integrity for a few bucks?" Casey would greet the ghost hunters with as much cheer as she could muster when they came to the café, but she did not want to get involved in the farce of a festival itself.

"This isn't about integrity, it's about entertainment."

Yes, entertaining fiction, Casey thought, because the ghost stories that featured prominently in Rosetta's ghost tours were invented. They were based on historical figures and historical events so that if some sleuth wanted proof, they could at least find evidence to corroborate the normal (as opposed to the paranormal) side of the story, but as for the ghosts themselves, those were made up. Even if Rosetta was serving up real ghosts, though, Casey would not have been on board. The dead should be left undisturbed.

"Do I have a choice?" Casey asked.

"Are you asking me to play the boss card?" Rosetta replied.

Casey shrugged.

"Fine. As your boss, I'm insisting."

After Rosetta left, Casey flipped the sign on the café door to closed—there was no sense in staying open when there were no customers—and went upstairs to her little apartment, where she took the well-worn piece of paper out of her pocket and read it again. When the letter first arrived, the sight of her mother's perfect Palmer script made her shoulders tense. She was past that now. Now it made her head ache, but she couldn't stop reading it over and over anyway. She knew she should burn it and be done with it. She was on her third read when she heard the back door open. Hastily she tucked it into her pocket, just as Jason announced himself. Exactly what she needed. A little distraction.

Chapter Three

LATER, WHEN THE GIRLS returned to the dorm with wet hair and smelling of pond water, they found a note on the door of their room from the RA asking Angela to see her as soon as she got back.

"Oh my God," Molly said. "You don't think your mom has already contacted the school?"

Angela rolled her eyes. It was probably nothing. There were dozens of reasons for the RA to want to see her. Maybe the fire inspector had been in and saw the candle (with a pristine, never-been-burned wick, for the record) on her dresser. Or maybe she wanted to borrow Angela's notes from the history class they were taking together. Or maybe, given her ass-length, unstylish hair, she wanted to ask Angela where she got her fantastic, funky haircut. It could be anything.

"Do you want me to come with you?" Nicole asked.

"It'll be fine," Angela said, leaving her at the door.

The RA, whose name Angela could not remember—

something like Emily or Jennifer, a name shared by a dozen women in their dorm alone—was sitting in her room with the door open. She leapt up when Angela knocked.

"Come in, come in," she said, moving her books around to make room for Angela to sit at the foot of her narrow dorm bed.

"What's up?" Angela asked suspiciously. She crossed her arms and sat on the very edge of the bed.

"Hang on," the RA said. She picked up her landline phone and punched in four digits to call another number on campus. This, Angela realized, was not a good sign. "Madeline? Yes, she just got here."

For a moment, Angela felt both relieved and confused. Whoever Madeline was, she wasn't anyone terribly official if an RA was calling her by her first name. Then the RA held the phone out for Angela.

"Angela? This is Madeline Fontaine, Director of Residential Life."

Angela's heartbeat sped up. Jesus. Her mother had acted fast. The Director of Residential Life was calling to tell her how much time she had to pack her bags, meanwhile she hadn't even filed the paperwork to officially declare a major.

"I'm afraid I have some bad news, and there's really no good way for me to say this," Madeline Fontaine went on.

Angela sat very still, as if she could stop time and prevent this woman from continuing to speak if she just didn't move.

"It's about your mother. We had a call this afternoon. Your neighbor, I think, a—" Angela heard her shuffling papers, "—Mrs. Porter, said she tried repeatedly to reach you."

She wished this woman would come out and say what

she needed to say.

"I got her messages," Angela said tersely.

"You did? Oh. Okay." Madeline sounded much relieved, but then she said, "Um, but you didn't call her back? You didn't speak to her?"

"No. I've been busy."

"Angela, I'm really sorry to have to tell you this, but we've had calls from the St. Nabor Island police and your neighbor, and it seems they didn't know how else to reach you, so I'm afraid I have to give you some bad news. Your mother had a stroke this morning."

Angela felt like she'd had the wind knocked out of her. Last night she and her mother had the worst fight they'd ever had, and then her mother had a stroke?

"Is she okay?" Angela asked.

"I'm so sorry," Madeline Fontaine said. "She passed away. When the paramedics arrived, she was already gone."

Angela set the phone down on the RA's bed and got up and walked as if in a trance back toward her room. The RA caught up with her halfway down the hall and put a hand on her shoulder.

"Can I do anything for you? Is there any way I can help?" she asked.

Angela shrugged off her hand.

"We can help you make arrangements to get home," the RA said. "Madeline said she can come right over if you want."

Angela ignored her and continued down the hall. She didn't need the RA's pity or the Director of Res Life's mothering. She had friends. The RA walked beside her, though, reciting empty expressions of comfort—how it would all be all right, and how her mother was in a better place now.

Molly and Nicole were sitting in their room with the door open. Angela stepped inside and shut the door on the RA's face, and then she leaned back against it and slumped down to the floor. She tried to swallow the sob that had been working its way into her throat, but she couldn't. She gasped and began to cry.

"What happened?" Molly said, crossing the room and kneeling in front of her.

"She's dead," Angela managed to say.

"What?"

"My mother. She died."

Molly leaned forward and pulled Angela into an embrace and let her cry until she ran out of tears for the moment. Then she helped Angela up and over to her bed, where Angela curled into a ball.

Nicole climbed into Angela's bed and spooned her, and Angela began to weep all over again. Eventually, she cried herself to sleep. Nicole woke her up a few hours later to see if she wanted any dinner. She didn't. Molly, meanwhile, had been busy making arrangements. She'd taken Angela's phone and called Mrs. Porter to learn more about what had happened, and she'd arranged for the three of them to fly to Savannah the next morning. Apparently, Madeline Fontaine had visited shortly after Angela fell asleep, and she was going to contact Angela's professors and let them know about the situation. Angela felt numb as Molly explained all of this. Her professors were the least of her concerns.

What she kept thinking was that she needed to call her mother. That's what she did when something big happened and she needed help. She called her mother. Now she could never call her mother again.

"Don't worry, we'll take care of you. We'll take care of everything," Molly had assured her, and Angela had started crying, hysterically, all over again. There was an endless supply of tears, it seemed, and absolutely no words to describe what she was going through.

That night Angela didn't sleep. Gradually the reality was setting in. Her mother was dead. Her beautiful, hard-working, devoted mother. Her pushy, stubborn, stuck-up mother. Her vain, meticulous, short-tempered mother was dead.

Already Angela missed her the way a sailor misses the sea. Her mother was the ocean that buoyed her up, the current that carried her through her life, and the white-capped waves that threatened to drag her under. Without her mother, she was alone on dry land, and the land seemed to move under her feet because she'd been so long at sea. Like a mariner in the desert who understands that she'll never feel the salt spray on her face again, never look out over vast stretches of glistening blue water beneath a clear blue sky again, never walk the deck triumphantly the morning after a gale again, she felt that she suddenly had no idea who she was. Without her mother to guide her, to oppose her, to see her always to safe harbor, how could she survive?

Only recently had their relationship become oppositional. For most of her life, her mother had been her best friend and biggest cheerleader. Yes, she had been stern, had held Angela to near-impossible standards, had been slow to praise and quick to criticize—but Angela knew that everything she did, she did out of love. This Angela never questioned.

Her mother's mission in life was to keep Angela safe and provide her with only the best, and from that mission she did not stray. When she insisted upon early curfews or refused to let Angela go out with kids she deemed too wild, Angela didn't argue. Her parents lost a son before she was born, and she understood that her mother lived with the fear that something terrible might happen to her.

Ryan had been seventeen when he died in an avoidable car accident. Dumb teenagers, driving too fast at night on a road slick with black ice, too cool for seat belts. Angela was born the year after he died. Her mother called her a late-in-life miracle baby sent to draw her parents from their grief. Her mother was forty-four when she born, her father fifty-six.

Had she saved her parents from their grief? she wondered. Perhaps for a time, when she was too young to have a mind of her own. Once she started getting ideas, well... she wasn't Ryan. Her mother wanted a replacement for her golden boy who never could do wrong (except that one time, that one time when he didn't fasten his seatbelt, when he let that irresponsible friend drive), and what she got was a willful girl who resisted most things her mother wanted her to do. Actually, a lot of people, her father among them, teased that the reason Angela and her mother always fought was that they were too alike, and Angela suspected that this was true, but she denied it every time anyway. And though they butted heads over all sorts of things from Angela's choices of clothing to her desire to study art, her mother was her best friend. She could fight with her mother, because she knew they'd always forgive each other. She suspected that she had done more to ease her mother's grief than she had her father's.

Angela wondered if anyone had told her father that his wife had died, and if they had, did he understand? He'd been diagnosed with Alzheimer's ten years earlier, and had lived for the past five years in a nursing home. When he'd been diagnosed, the doctors had said that most patients live only eight years after diagnosis. But then again, he'd been relatively young and fit at the time. Still, what kind of miserable God would take away her mother, who was only 64 and who had always appeared to be the picture of health, while letting her father's body plod on despite the fact that his mind was locked tight against the world?

In the morning, when Molly and Nicole woke, Molly directed them all in a flurry of activity. They were to fly out of the airport in Manchester that afternoon. Angela let Molly tell her what to do, thankful in this instance for Molly's maternal instinct. She was so fully in a daze that it hardly registered to her that Molly and Nicole were both spending money they probably couldn't afford to spend, and missing classes they probably couldn't afford to miss, to stay by her side through her mother's funeral. This only dawned on her as their plane touched down in Savannah. She was so lucky to have such good friends. Her eyes filled with tears again, and Molly mistook this for another wave of grief, but really they were tears of gratitude. Angela let Molly wrap her arms around her and hold her as the plane taxied to the gate.

Grace Crowley, Angela's mother's business partner, met them at the Savannah airport and drove them the forty-five minutes or so to the island. When Angela was a little girl, there wasn't much in Palmetto Landing across the bridge from the island. Then there had been a brand-new outlet mall and a few golf courses, but now the highway was lined with developments of condos and cookie-cutter houses, the sales of which had made her mother a wealthy woman. As they crossed the bridge, Grace rolled down the windows and salt air filled the car. It was a beautiful September day. Blue sky, warm, not too humid, perfect for beach-combing.

Just as development in Palmetto Landing had exploded in the late 90s and early 2000s, so had development on the island. So much newness everywhere. Even though Angela had seen it happen, it still startled her when she crossed the island and saw all the new plazas and housing developments. She thought of the island as it had been when she was a kid, businesses tucked away behind trees, even fast-food signs small and low, not lit up, so that strangers were always having to circle back around, having missed the turns they were seeking. There were still strict rules about landscaping and building styles, but with so many new things appearing, the island no longer felt like an exclusive retreat from the world. Now it was another overrun beach and golf destination.

Still, it was home with all its familiar comforts, and Angela felt the reflexive relaxation she always felt as they passed her favorite old haunts, and then she felt an overwhelming sorrow as they made their way to the far side of the island, to Ocean Pines, where her mother's house was. How long would this be home? Not long, she supposed. She couldn't afford to live here, that much was certain.

Ocean Pines Plantation, on the Southern tip of the island, home to the Jackson Golf Links with its iconic final hole near the Jackson Lighthouse, was one of several gated communities on the island, and if one stayed away from the small, commercial village of Jackson and the touristy Meadows River Marina, it was quiet and peaceful. They passed the gatehouse and made their way along the tree-lined road. Houses designed to blend into the natural beauty of the place were nestled away from the road in cocoons of pristine landscaping.

"You grew up here?" Molly asked, awe in her voice, as they drove. Molly was from Lowell, Massachusetts and had never been outside of New England before, let alone to a resort island like this.

"We moved here when I was eight. We lived across the bridge in Palmetto Landing before that, but this is where my mom planned to retire, so this is where she bought her dream house," Angela said. And now she'll never get to live that dream, Angela thought, squeezing her eyes shut against tears.

The house was near the Meadows River Marina, but not so near that her mother would be annoyed by tourists and their traffic. It was a modern two-story with a two-car garage and a big porch. It was not oceanfront—her mother had been successful, but not quite that successful—but it was only three rows back, and the path to the beach ran alongside the yard between their property and the neighbor's. The landscaping provided screening for the yard and there was a hot tub out on the deck.

Angela wondered if she could manage to hold onto the house as a rental property. Maybe it could pay for itself for now with rental income. Surely keeping such a place in the family was a good idea. She'd ask Grace later, she told herself, feeling guilty for thinking in terms of property when she was about to enter the house where her mother had died.

Grace cut the engine and Angela led everyone inside. It smelled like her mother's perfume and the laundry detergent she used and the scented candles she burned. It smelled like home. Angela had to sit down to keep from falling down. She wasn't ready to face the empty house. She would never be ready. But here she was, and what choice did she have?

Chapter Four

Devil's Back Island, Maine

RATIONALLY, ROSETTA KNEW that there was no way Casey could know what she was up to. Her great-niece could give Emily Dickinson a run for her money in a recluse contest. She almost never left the island, and though she was friendly with year-rounders, she wasn't friends with any of them. She resolutely refused to use the Internet, still placing her orders for supplies for the café over the phone. And yet, as Rosetta's plans were beginning to take shape, Casey suddenly began avoiding her. When Rosetta had gone to the café that day, she'd been fully prepared for an unpleasant confrontation, but it seemed Casey was still in the dark. As she trudged back along the gravel path to the inn, she thanked God for small mercies.

Rosetta had kept her dealings as quiet as humanly possible. No one on the island knew. Even if anyone guessed that she was in bad shape financially, no one would leap to the conclusion that she was selling the inn. The inn was her entire life. But she was selling. If, that was, she could find a buyer, which until a couple of weeks ago had looked hopeless.

She couldn't keep bleeding money to keep the inn (and the tavern, and the café, and the art gallery) afloat. Traffic to the island was down. Despite her best marketing and branding efforts—she was a one-woman tourism bureau and chamber of commerce—fewer people had visited each of the past three years. Once upon a time none of that would have mattered. Once upon a time she could have continued to indulge herself here, let the inn and other businesses linger on as vanity projects into perpetuity. Once upon a time when Phil was alive, doing his magic trick of making money out of money.

The worst part of the whole thing was knowing how thoroughly she'd let Phil down. If he was looking down on her from heaven, he was undoubtedly tearing out his hair at her bad investments. In one stupid, greedy, short-sighted move, she had wiped out the fortune he'd carefully and steadily built throughout their marriage. If only she'd listened to his advice, but he was dead, and the voices of the dead are so easily drowned out by the seductive promises of the living.

Now she could only hope that the developer who was flying out here next week would come through and save her, and that someday Casey would forgive her.

And if Casey didn't forgive her, Rosetta would have only herself to blame. Before her finances dipped to this crisis level, Rosetta hadn't realized how wrong she'd been to enable Casey for so long. Rosetta had given her a fairy-tale life instead of helping her develop a life of her own. At first, when she hauled Casey back here from a life of squalor in New York City, Rosetta's primary fear was that Casey had inherited her mother's fragile psyche, that her chaotic life was due to mental illness. The best thing she could do, Rosetta had thought, was keep the girl close and figure out what sort of help she needed.

But as Casey adjusted to her new life on Devil's Back, Rosetta could see that she wasn't like Maureen in anything except appearances, though Casey had worked damn hard to change that: The awful tattoo covering her entire arm, the ridiculous flame-red hair dye. Whatever had fueled Casey's efforts to escape into a haze of painkillers and booze, it wasn't the mood disorder that had turned Maureen's life upside down.

Now, though, Rosetta could see that her methods for helping Casey get back on her feet had had some serious flaws. After Casey stopped resenting Rosetta for saving her life (and Rosetta had no doubt that had she not gone to New York when she did, she would have soon gotten a next-of-kin phone call), Casey started treating Devil's Back like a life raft. Instead of helping her bring the raft ashore, Rosetta had only fortified it.

It was Rosetta's idea to turn Beach Plum cottage, one of her several rental properties, into a café. Casey had been helping at the inn and had started making homemade goodies for the continental breakfast and afternoon tea. Her concoctions were divine, and so Rosetta gave her a café of her own.

And in doing so, Rosetta had allowed Casey to live as if fairy godmothers did exist. The magic was all over now. The money gone. The future uncertain at best. There'd be no more bailouts from the bank of Rosetta Washburn.

If only there was a way to keep the café. If only she

could keep the café separate from her other businesses; sell off the inn, the tavern, the gallery, some of the cottages, but not the café. Without the other things to worry about, and with some of the money from selling everything else, maybe she could mentor Casey. When Casey was ready to handle the business side on her own, Rosetta could retire.

The inn might be hopelessly out of date and in need of upgrades she couldn't afford; the tavern, with its old fashioned Maine seacoast charm, might be far out of fashion for today's travelers; the gallery, with its displays of work by local artists, might be a total loss because really who wanted another kitschy, ceramic soap holder or amateur oil painting of a lighthouse; but the café—where the bakery cases were full of from-scratch, made-with-love pastries, and the coffee was brewed to rich, smooth perfection—the café was a true twenty-first century business that appealed to everyone from young hipsters who loved nothing more than supporting small local businesses, to nostalgic elderly people who had no patience for trendy gluten-free, ancient grains, sprouted-wheat anything.

Rosetta's legacy wasn't a handful of buildings that would soon belong to someone who was likely to tear them down. Her legacy was her talented niece whose café had become, in a few short years, the best-loved business on the island.

She hadn't expected her walk to clear her head so thoroughly, but as she climbed the inn's front steps that afternoon, she felt as if a burden had been lifted.

Often she lingered in the hotel lounge in the afternoons. She liked to meet her guests and hear their stories. Most days she brought her tarot cards—reading fortunes was a little hobby she'd acquired in recent years, though her knowledge of tarot was academic and not mystical—it was a great way to get her guests to open up. There was something disarming about offering a glimpse into the future. Today, though, she went straight upstairs to her small office on the second floor to take another look at her accounts. She would keep the café. Somehow, she would find a way.

Chapter Five

St. Nabor Island, South Carolina

ON MONDAY, THANKS to Grace's planning and Molly's assistance, there was a small, tasteful funeral for Angela's mother with a mass at the parish Angela had attended her entire life. By then Angela had arrived at a sad but conflicted acceptance of her mother's death. She had visited her father at his nursing home across the bridge in Palmetto Landing, but the staff there told her they didn't recommend that she tell him about her mother's death, so she didn't.

Angela knew she could not speak at the funeral, her emotions were too raw, but when she tried to think of who could give the eulogy, she was at a complete loss. For the first time in her life, it occurred to her how few friends her mother had. She had acquaintances from church. She had coworkers. She didn't really have friends.

In the end Angela asked Grace, who said she'd be honored to make a few remarks. As she spoke at the funeral, though, it was dry-eyed, and most of her reflection had to do with how hard-working and professional Deb had been.

Hers were not the words of a friend. It was more like a letter of recommendation than a eulogy. Angela kept waiting for Grace to at least mention Deb's commitment to her family and how she balanced her career with motherhood, but Grace never did. Angela felt a little bad about that as she glanced around the nearly empty church. The attendees were coworkers, a couple of neighbors, and some old ladies from church who Angela suspected made a hobby of attending funerals. What must they think, hearing her mother remembered in such an impersonal way?

Only a few people bothered to follow the funeral procession to the cemetery, and then it was all over. Her mother was in a box in the ground, and she was back at home with Molly and Nicole, numb and exhausted.

None of them had any idea what to do next. They sat around the kitchen table drinking coffee and staring at the mountains of food people kept dropping off at the house. It seemed that every person who had ever known her mother felt that, whether or not they had been friends, they owed it to her to cook something for her survivors. Angela had no appetite, though. Molly had been sorting things as they arrived, labeling containers, and freezing what could be frozen. Thank God for Molly.

When they'd been sitting in silence for the better part of an hour, Nicole finally said, "Want to see if there's anything on TV?"

This struck Angela as the dumbest question in the world. Of course she didn't want to watch TV. Besides, doing anything normal felt wrong.

"What day are y'all going back?" Angela asked. They had not talked about Molly and Nicole's travel plans.

Molly and Nicole exchanged a look, and then Molly said, "We fly out Thursday around noon."

Angela nodded.

"And you, too," Molly added.

"I think I should withdraw," Angela said, not looking at either of them. "There's so much that needs to be done here. I can't leave."

Grace had told Angela she would help her settle her mother's estate, and in fact she had set up meetings for the two of them with her mother's lawyer and her accountant. It was unbelievable the number of things that needed to be dealt with, particularly when someone died so unexpectedly. Her mother was, in general, the most prepared person Angela had ever met, and yet, incredibly, she seemed to have left no will. Angela had to make all the decisions.

The most pressing need was planning for her father's ongoing care. Now that he'd outlived the doctor's initial predictions, it was anyone's guess how long he might live. Five years? Ten years? And she had to figure out how that would all get paid for.

"I'm sure your professors will understand if you take another week," Nicole said.

Angela shook her head. "It's going to take more than a week to deal with everything. Hell, I have to sell this house."

"You don't need to be here to sell the house. Grace can do it," Molly said.

This was true, but still, it was going to take more than a week before Angela was ready to get back to any semblance of normal. Angela shook her head again. She had already spoken to Grace about the idea of turning the house into a rental, but when they spoke to her mother's lawyer and executor of her estate, they discovered that the house was mortgaged to the max. There was no way they could bring in enough rental income to pay the bills. Apparently her mother had been using the house like an ATM.

"So what? You'll come back in the spring?" Molly asked.

Angela shrugged. Another of her mother's secrets was that there had been no college fund for Angela, as Angela had been led to believe. Instead, her mother was financing her education with private loans. Angela had no idea how she'd ever be able to afford to return to St. Kate's.

"Maybe now isn't the best time to talk about this," Nicole said.

"There will never be a good time to talk about it," Angela said.

"You don't need to make any big decisions right now. You shouldn't. You're grieving and you're overwhelmed. Give yourself some time," Nicole said.

There was no point in arguing, not because Nicole was right, but because in two days Nicole would be back at school, and Angela would be here and could make whatever decision she wanted.

That night, after they all went to bed, Angela heard it for the first time. Nicole was sound asleep on an air mattress on the floor of Angela's room. Down the hall, Molly was asleep in the guest room. While one of them could have slept in Angela's mother's room, they had settled on the current sleeping arrangement quickly and without much discussion. Angela was glad not to be in her room alone, and she also had a strange sort of reverence for her mother's room, as if it would be wrong to disturb the space by sleeping in it. Molly took the guest room because she was a light but enthusiastic sleeper who tended to go to bed before everyone else and to sleep later in the morning. Nicole and Angela were the night owls.

These days Angela was more an insomniac than a night owl. She wondered if she'd ever sleep again. She was wide awake in her dark bedroom, listening to Nicole's slow breathing when she heard the unmistakable sound of footsteps in the hall. She told herself it was her imagination, but her heart thudded. Someone was out there. Someone had broken into the house. But then the footsteps kept pacing back and forth between her mother's room and her study, up and down the hall. What kind of burglar paces?

Reassuring herself that it was Molly, she got up, tiptoed to the door, and peered into the hallway. She couldn't see anyone. She waited, holding her breath, staying as still as possible, and she heard it again. The creak of the floor. But the hallway was empty. She shut the door and crossed the room to the air mattress and grabbed Nicole's arm, shaking her awake.

She came to with a start. Angela hushed her and instructed her to be very still and listen. They waited a few seconds, and when Angela thought the noise wasn't going to make itself heard again, there it was.

"Did you hear that?" Angela asked.

"Hear what?"

"Footsteps."

With a sigh, Nicole threw back the covers and got out of bed. She flung open the door and said, "Come on, boogie man. We're trying to sleep here." Then she went back to bed and got back under the covers. "You've gotta try to get some sleep. You're exhausted."

Of course I'm exhausted, she thought. "I heard footsteps."

"There's no one out there. It was probably Molly getting up to use the bathroom or something."

Angela shook her head, but she slid back down into bed. She agreed—there was no one out there. But there was something out there.

In the distant reaches of her memory, Angela recalled a time when she was very young—four or five at most—when she'd been playing in the yard, and a friendly teenage boy appeared before her and played with her. When her mother came out on the deck to talk to her, he disappeared. When she told her mother this, her mother told her to stop telling tales and not to talk to strangers. Angela had insisted that she wasn't lying, but her mother wouldn't hear it.

It happened again, several times. She'd be outside playing alone and the boy would appear. Those encounters became the basis of her childhood insistence that her big brother's ghost was looking out for her. She didn't have an imaginary friend. She had her big brother's ghost. She told stories about him at school and invented a whole life for him, found evidence of him in all sorts of everyday experiences. It drove her mother nuts.

Eventually, she grew out of it, the way kids outgrow their imaginary friends, and while that memory of the boy who appeared in the yard continued to bother her because she was so sure it really happened, she concluded that there were plenty of logical explanations, most obviously that he was a kid who lived in the neighborhood who wandered into the yard sometimes. It was also possible that he really was an imaginary friend, as her mother had insisted. Her memories of him had faded now and had taken on the cloudy, dull film of all her memories from such an early age. It was impossible to say now if what she recalled of those encounters was hazy memory or pure invention, but she hadn't outgrown her belief in ghosts. She'd never admit as much to her rational, logical friends, though.

There's no such thing as ghosts, she told herself now, listening to the regular rhythm of Nicole's sleeping breath. Ghosts aren't real. But she kept hearing the footsteps, back and forth and back and forth until the sun came up.

Chapter Six

Devil's Back Island, Maine

THE DOWNSIDE TO CASEY'S little arrangement with Jason was that he was always around. She understood that his home situation—crashing at his older brother's house, which meant sleeping on a pull-out couch and being awakened in the wee hours of the night by wailing children—was not ideal for him, but it seemed unfair that he should expect her to shoulder that burden. Now he was staying at her place more than at his brother's, and she was starting to think he was seeing their whatever-it-was as more than a casual fling.

That evening, he'd arrived with a six-pack of beer, a box of pizza, and a baggie of pot, and had settled onto the futon beside her as if he owned the place. He kicked off his stinky sneakers and left them under the coffee table, which he littered with the contents of his pockets and his meager dinner offering, and he grabbed the remote control and turned to the Red Sox game without even asking if Casey minded. It was his third night in a row at her place, and as much as she enjoyed his company beneath the sheets, she was getting sick of him.

"You're quiet tonight," he said, during a commercial break.

How would he even know over the deafening volume of the television, she wondered.

"Just tell me if I'm, like, in the way," he said.

Casey squeezed her eyes shut and did not allow herself to say, "Yes, you are, like, in the way." When she opened her eyes, the commercial break had ended, and he was once again utterly absorbed in the television.

She got up and attempted to tidy up the coffee table. She took the leftover pizza to the kitchen, and grabbed his sneakers—holding them as if they were roadkill—and put them on the back porch. Then she went and got in the shower. She was tired and although it was just after eight, she was ready for bed. The downside of running a café: obscenely early wake-up calls.

She stood under the hot water and tried not to think about the fact that Jason would still be there when she got out, and then, in a turn she probably should have expected, he came into the bathroom, pulled back the shower curtain, and got in with her.

She felt a surge of annoyance—couldn't she have five freaking minutes to herself?—but as his hands slid down her soapy skin and his lips came to rest on hers, she felt herself relent.

He kissed her shoulder, and then left a trail of kisses down her arm, tracing the outline of her tattoo, the intricate vining flowers, birds, and butterflies, which covered her left arm, crept across her shoulder and shoulder blade, and ended at the nape of her neck. She had gotten it when she was seventeen, when she first moved to New York. She'd briefly shacked up with a tattoo artist who seduced her with the enticing idea that she could reinvent herself with ink. The relationship hadn't lasted, but the tattoo was forever. Had she dated him for much longer, her entire body might have been made new under his hand. She didn't exactly regret the tattoo, but sometimes she wished she didn't wear such a huge reminder of what a screw-up she used to be.

She stopped thinking about all of that as Jason's hand slid lower. This was why she put up with his constant intrusions, his Pig-Pen messiness, his remote control dominance. This almost made all of that seem worthwhile.

Casey tossed and turned that night, crowded to the edge of the bed while Jason sprawled, dead asleep and oblivious beside her. She should have told Rosetta about the letter. Rosetta had the right to know that Maureen had died. Of course, if it weren't for the letter, Casey would not know, and she could go on living a life where, figuratively and effectively, her mother had been dead to her for twenty years, and Rosetta could, too. If Casey had the choice to remain ignorant, isn't that what she'd choose?

Although she had on many occasions said the words, "My mother is dead to me," Casey had never thought much about her mother's actual death. When Maureen first kicked her out, she had tried to persuade Maureen to let her back in by suggesting that it would be awful if either of them died and the other didn't even know, but those were just things she said in her naïveté, her foolish belief that reconciliation was possible. And anyway, she had mostly been thinking of herself, how she was likely to die without a mother to mourn her, and not the other way around, because she could never truly envision a world without her mother in it.

And now her mother was dead, and in typical fashion, she hadn't gone quietly. She couldn't have reached out to Casey before she died so they could have seen each other one more time in the flesh and perhaps could have forgiven each other. That wasn't her style. Instead, she wrote a letter, sealed it and signed across the seal, and put it to Eliza to mail it after she passed.

She had probably believed that she would watch from heaven as Casey read the letter and learned of the miserable illness that claimed her life. How did she think Casey would receive this plea to atone for her sins and save her soul in this life so they could meet again in the hereafter? Did she expect Casey to tear her hair and rend her clothing in some kind of Old Testament display of grief? To rush to the nearest church and throw herself upon the altar? To lift her eyes to heaven and thank her mother for showing her the light? It was almost a comfort to know that her mother still had the power to infuriate her, even in death, even after twenty years.

Eliza's accompanying letter suggested that Maureen's dying wishes had vexed her as well. She made it plain that she was the one who nursed Maureen through her fight with cancer. She was the one who made time to make sure Maureen got to her appointments and had her prescriptions filled. Despite her busy life as a mother of three with a full-time job, even though Maureen had never really been a mother to Eliza, who was already eighteen when Maureen and Eliza's father wed, Eliza had been the daughter Maureen needed in her last days. And for all of that, the thanks she got was only half of Maureen's estate, not all of it, as she had expected. For some reason, Maureen had decided to divide her effects between them.

What was particularly shocking was the size of Maureen's estate. Casey and Eliza would each inherit about two-hundred thousand dollars, an unthinkable sum. Casey supposed the money had come from Ed, which must have added to Eliza's sense of insult. After all, Maureen had been unemployable for most of her adult life. Her career as a lawyer ended when she was first diagnosed with bipolar disorder. Casey had only been five or six at the time. Later, Maureen's relationship with Ed helped keep her from dipping too low or swooping too high, but the career she had dreamed of for herself as a litigator was impossible after her first breakdown. The stress of such a job was more than she could handle, medicated or not. She was never the same after that, and she never had a full-time job after that, either.

The fact that Maureen had left any sort of inheritance to Casey was as surprising to Casey as it must have been to Eliza. Did Maureen owe Casey for the way she'd treated her when she as a teenager? Yes. Did Ed owe her for turning her own mother against her? Undoubtedly. But Casey never dreamed her mother would see it that way. Perhaps the cancer had spread to her brain before she finalized her will.

Nonetheless, Casey didn't want the money. She didn't want anything from her mother—it was bad enough to share her genetics—and she would never dirty her hands by accepting something that had been Ed's. The question was should she give it to Eliza? If Eliza did even half of what she claimed she did for Maureen in her dying days, she had earned it. Casey couldn't imagine the patience it would take to play nurse to her impossible mother.

But the Eliza who Casey remembered was so like her father—self-righteous, judgmental, and Bible-quoting, forever finding fault in her young step-sister. What a torment it would be for Eliza to know that there was an account out there full of Ed's money with Casey's name on it, collecting interest and dust, and Eliza would never see a penny of it. There was something satisfying in that. Sometimes wastefulness could be incredibly enjoyable.

Chapter Seven

St. Nabor Island, South Carolina

TWO NIGHTS AFTER the funeral, Angela lay sleepless in bed, watching shadows flicker on the ceiling. Every little noise made the knot of tension in her stomach tighten. The creaking window in the breeze, the intermittent click and rattle of the ceiling fan in the guest room down the hall where Molly was sleeping, the random gurgle and sigh of the plumbing—each arriving in turn whenever her eyelids began to droop, and then she was wide awake again. On the air mattress, Nicole sprawled on her stomach, legs splayed, head half under a pillow, breathing the deep breaths of the darkest reaches of slumber.

If Nicole woke up, Angela wouldn't have to be alone with her fear, but she wouldn't hear what Angela was hearing. She'd insist that Angela's exhausted, over-stressed imagination was playing tricks on her, as if fatigue and grief invalidated her senses. No, it was best for Nicole to sleep. It was enough for her to be in the room where Angela could wake her if she got desperate enough.

As she rolled over and tried to find sleep, a sound caught her ear—a footstep on the squeaky floorboard in the hall near her mother's room. As she feared, the mystery pacer was back. She stayed very still, holding her breath. Nothing. But when necessity forced her to exhale, there it was. Another single footstep.

Doing her best to be silent, she sat up, leaning slightly toward the door. After several seconds, she heard another footstep and the faint yawn of a door opening. Her first thought was that Molly had no right going into her mother's room, but of course, Molly never would. Someone was out there, but it wasn't Molly. Her heart raced.

This was the third night in a row that she'd heard footsteps in the hall in the wee hours of the morning, the second night she swore she heard her mother's door opening. Careful not to disturb Nicole, she slipped out of bed and tiptoed to the door of her bedroom. She opened it slightly and peered into the hallway. Only the door to her mother's study was open, propped with a heavy doorstop.

Whoever had opened the door to her mother's room must have also shut it, and Angela hadn't heard it because she'd been making noise of her own getting out of bed. Moonlight poured through the two-story windows of the foyer and bathed the hallway in light. There was no darkness in which to hide. Angela moved softly toward her mother's door, one hand trailing along the wall as she went. As she stepped into the puddle of moonlight, she heard a voice and froze.

"Angela," the voice said. "Go to sleep, Angela." It was a hoarse whisper, at once quiet and deafening. It seemed to echo inside her head. "Go to sleep, Angela. Go back to bed."

Angela pressed her hands to her ears but the voice continued, "Go to sleep, Angela. Go back to bed."

It had begun gently but was now growing more insistent, repetition after repetition, overlapping like a song in rounds, and Angela clamped her hands over her ears, stretching her fingers through the sides of her short hair. She pressed one shoulder against the wall and slid down into a crouch, curling in upon herself, making her tiny gymnast's body even smaller, a little knot of firm limbs, balled up tight.

"Go to sleep, Angela."

It was a taunt now, a curse. Angela shook her head and whimpered without meaning to. She hadn't realized she was holding her breath until she was overcome with a gasp and the flood of oxygen brought a cascade of tears so sudden she sobbed aloud.

"Stop," Angela said. "Please, stop, please."

At the touch of a hand on her shoulder, she lurched, flattening herself against the wall. The sudden silence surrounding her was total.

"Okay, okay," Molly said, stepping back, as startled by Angela's reaction as Angela had been to her touch.

Angela's chest heaved with labored breath. Her face was soaked with tears. She slumped down, letting her legs stretch before her, her back pressed to the wall. She jammed the heels of her hands into her eyes. When she lowered them, Molly was sitting in front of her, her thick dark hair a messy tangle, her eyes puffy with sleep.

"You heard it, didn't you? Please tell me you heard it?" Angela asked. If ever she needed her best friend to back her up, it was now. Neither Molly nor Nicole had heard anything for the past two nights, but tonight it had woken Molly up.

Finally, Molly would believe her.

"You had a nightmare. It's okay," Molly said.

But I was awake, Angela thought. I was wide awake. You don't have a nightmare when you're wide awake.

"It'll get easier in time," Molly said.

"But she was here. I heard her."

Concern shaded Molly's face. "We talked about this—"

"I know it was my mother," Angela said, wiping her nose with the back of her hand.

"Oh, honey." Molly moved beside Angela against the wall and rested her head on Angela's shoulder.

They sat in silence, and after a few minutes, Angela realized that Molly had fallen back to sleep. Sweet reliable Molly, the best best-friend she could ever ask for, getting up in the middle of the night to care for her while Nicole slept through it all down the hall. But Molly was wrong. It hadn't been a nightmare. What she'd heard was real—her mother's voice, her mother's anger, her mother's frustration. Her mother had been there. Angela knew Molly and Nicole thought she was cracking under the weight of her grief, but they were wrong. Her mother's body had failed, her heart had stopped, and she had died, but she was still here, and she wanted something.

Nicole, with her insistence on science, logic, and reason, and Molly, with her perpetual skepticism, did not believe in ghosts. But their refusal to believe did not change the fact that her mother's ghost or spirit or something was there, in the house.

Angela nudged Molly, who spent a few blinking moments struggling to recall where she was before taking Angela's advice and returning to bed.

Angela went downstairs to the bright, modern kitchen and put on a pot of coffee. When it was ready, she took a steamy mug back upstairs to her mother's study. She sat in the big desk chair and studied the antique roll-top desk where, until only a week earlier, her mother had sat every day, going through bills, taking care of the paperwork for Angela's father's nursing home, writing notes to clients. Angela pushed the top up along its tracks with a swish. The surface was free of clutter. Everything had a place of its own in one of the many drawers. Angela reached up and pulled the knob of one of the small drawers above the writing surface. It didn't move. She pulled again, harder this time, but it was stuck. She tried the one below it and got the same result. She tried one on the other side. They were all stuck. Then she noticed the keyhole in the center of the desk, under the lip of the rolling cover.

It was so like her mother to keep her desk locked up as if it were full of state secrets. Angela tried the file drawers and was not surprised to see that they, too, were locked. Only the shallow center drawer where pens and paper clips were stashed was not locked, because it had no lock. And of course her mother wasn't so obvious as to keep the key in that drawer, which is probably what Angela would have done. Well, she'd have to find the key, wherever her mother had tucked it. She'd be going through everything to get the house ready to sell, and it would turn up. With any luck, it would turn up soon, because there were all sorts of documents she needed to settle her mother's affairs, and every last one was locked up tight in the desk. She rolled the chair back and stood, stretching her arms over her head.

Nicole and Molly weren't likely to be awake for hours yet.

Angela went back downstairs and replenished her coffee. Then she turned to her mother's bedroom. Her mother had been gone for only a week and already a fine layer of dust had settled on everything. Angela swiped her hand across the dresser and brushed the dust onto her nightshirt. She picked up a bottle of her mother's favorite perfume and sprayed it into air, inhaled its familiar sweetness that didn't smell quite right without her mother's flesh beneath it.

At the end of the dresser were two framed photographs—one of her parents and her older brother Ryan, a formal, posed family portrait from when he was three, and one of her parents and herself when she was three. She picked up the older picture and studied it. Her mother looked so young, with her smooth, flawless skin and feathered blond hair. At the time, she would have only been twenty-eight. Her father, twelve years her senior, was already gray, but he was thin, fit, tall, and strong, nothing like the man who now resided at Our Lady of Mercy Nursing Home.

In the second photograph, her mother was forty-seven, her hair still blonde and glossy, but cut in a tidy, chin-length bob. Her father, nearly sixty, had white hair, dark circles under his eyes, and a soft belly. In only a few years, he would be diagnosed with Alzheimer's. Angela wondered if his mind had been going even then.

She wished her brother were here now to take charge of everything. At 20, Angela might legally have been an adult, but she was not ready to be responsible for her mother's household. Ryan would be thirty-six or thirty-seven now, a real grown up. He would understand things like how the sale of a house worked. Angela wondered if her mother and brother were together now, if her mother's promises that Ryan was waiting for them in heaven were true. It was nice to think so, but as Nicole would say, there was no way to prove it. Then again, Nicole would also likely point out that Angela's recent ghost sightings meant she believed in life after death, so why not also believe in heaven and hell? But that last assumption was a leap she'd never been able to make. She could only feel sure some people's souls or spirits or whatever seemed to linger, and others did not. Where those others went was anybody's guess.

Who were you? She asked her brother's picture as she set it back on the dresser. She had asked his picture that question many times over the years, but to date, he'd never answered.

When she was younger and she used to think her brother's ghost was watching over her, he wasn't a very active spirit, just a benign presence looming over her family like a wisp of cloud across the sun. The idea that her family was haunted made an exciting story, so she told her friends from elementary and middle school about Ryan's ghost when they came over and saw her brother's pictures.

"He died before I was born," she'd say. "I never met him, but his ghost watched out for me."

Any time she narrowly escaped danger—the car that swerved at the last moment, the day she was running late and thereby avoiding being caught in a multi-car accident at exactly the time she was usually crossing that intersection— she'd tell herself Ryan was looking out for her. She liked having a ghost-brother. It made her feel safe and special. But where was he now, when she needed him?

Angela awoke in her mother's sunlit bedroom. Down the hall, she heard water running in the guest bathroom. She rubbed her eyes and glanced at the alarm clock on the nightstand. Eleven. She hurled herself from the bed. Nicole and Molly had to be at the airport by noon.

In the hallway, she smelled fresh coffee and toast. The doors to both her bedroom and the guest room were open. Everyone was up and moving. She told herself this was a good thing. She didn't want them to miss their flight. They'd already been here with her for a whole week, missing a full week of classes, which had barely begun when she got the news of her mother's death. They'd be playing catch-up all semester. She knew if she had missed even one of the chemistry classes Nicole was taking, she'd be sunk, and Molly had undoubtedly drained her bank account for plane tickets and would now have to grab as many extra shifts as possible at her work study job in admissions to get by. They were the best, and she could never thank them enough. What was she going to do when they left? How could she stay in this house alone?

She found Molly in the kitchen, her laptop open on the table beside her plate of toast.

"We didn't want to wake you," Molly said.

Angela hated the pity in Molly's eyes. She had heard Molly and Nicole whispering about her the other day, worrying about her mental state. She needed them to understand and believe. Molly had been there last night, in the hallway. How could she still have doubts?

"Listen," Molly said. "Are you sure you're going to be

okay?"

What choice do I have? Angela thought.

"You don't have to withdraw from school. You can come back with us."

This was Nicole and Molly's refrain, urging her to carry on with her life. But she couldn't. There was no one else to sort out her mother's estate, and she couldn't handle all of it from school while also keeping up with classes. Although she'd had a conversation with the financial aid office and the dean of students, she still didn't know if she could afford to finish at St. Kate's.

But if she didn't go back to school, where exactly would she go? What exactly would she do? Her mother's lawyer who was handling her estate had made it clear that she had to sell the house as soon as possible. There were debts to reconcile and her father's expenses to sort out. If she went back to school, at least she wouldn't be homeless. She'd be racking up tens of thousands of dollars in loans that, until a week ago, she hadn't even known about, but she'd have a roof over her head.

It was almost funny. The day before her mother died, she'd been panicking that her mother would make good on her threat to bring her home from St. Kate's, and now here she was. Her mother's threat brought to fruition by her mother's death.

Angela shook her head and avoided looking Molly in the eye.

"Maybe you should go stay with Grace. I hate to think of you alone here."

Actually Angela had had no shortage of offers of places to stay. Acquaintances of her mother, parents of high school friends, her old gymnastics teacher. She didn't have to stay in the house, and even if it sold overnight, she had places to crash. She wasn't really in danger of homelessness, at least in the short term. Couch surfing sounded miserable, though. She wanted to stay here—her childhood home, her safe, comfortable place—as long as possible. If only she could stay in the house and also get a good night's sleep.

Before Angela could formulate a reply, Nicole bounded into the kitchen, well rested and ready for action.

"I wish we could do something fun before we leave," Nicole said, pouring herself coffee. "Do we have enough time to do anything before we have to be at the airport?"

For the past few days, Nicole had been trying to get her to "do something," which meant anything but hang around the house. But it felt so wrong to go out and do anything fun. Her mother was dead! She was in mourning. But, she had to admit, mourning was boring. And she felt bad that her friends had come all the way from New Hampshire and had done little but sit around the house. October was so beautiful in the Low Country. They could have had fun on St. Nabor Island or done something touristy in Savannah if this trip hadn't been for such screwed-up circumstances. All they'd done was take some walks on the beach near the house. Not exactly exciting. But now there was no time. In fact, if they didn't leave right away, her friends were likely to miss their plane. Angela had to face her new life alone sometime, and now was as good a time as any.

Chapter Eight

Devil's Back Island, Maine

AFTER TWO DAYS of relentless rain, Casey feared she'd lose her mind if she spent another day alone in the café. In the winter, she expected and even anticipated solitude, but it wasn't winter yet, not even close, and now she had way too much on her mind to be left to her leisure. She flipped the sign on the café to "closed," locked the door, and, raincoat zipped to her chin, made a run for it along the path to the inn.

In the parlor, a few guests who hadn't canceled despite the miserable forecast sat near the fireplace playing cards. Casey took off her dripping coat and draped it over the back of a chair near the fire and then went in search of her great-aunt.

Now that Rosetta thought Casey had only been avoiding her because of Jason, she didn't need to avoid her at all, which was good, because even a loner like Casey could find the island lonely on weeks like this, and without Rosetta, she had no one to call on.

She found Rosetta in her office. Her desk was a sea of papers, and she was studying receipts and punching numbers into a big old adding machine when Casey knocked on the door.

"Can it wait a few minutes, Lou—" Rosetta started, mistaking Casey for Louise, who worked at the reception desk. But then she saw Casey in the doorway and hastily shoved a stack of papers into a file folder and set them to the side.

Why her aunt would seem so flustered and guilty to see her, Casey could not imagine. Rosetta's desk was normally neat and tidy, and taking in the disarray there, Casey wondered if Rosetta's mind was going. She was seventy-eight years old, after all.

"Everything okay?" Casey asked, sitting in the chair opposite Rosetta's desk and tucking her feet under Bentley's stomach where he lounged on the floor.

"Meeting with the accountant coming up, that's all. Quarterly taxes, you know," Rosetta said, but Casey thought she detected a blush of color on Rosetta's cheeks. Guilt? Annoyance?

"Anything I can help with?"

Rosetta guffawed and moved around a few more piles of paper, tucking everything into folders so that Casey couldn't see what any of it was.

"Shouldn't you be working?" Rosetta asked, taking off her reading glasses and studying Casey.

"I've done inventory, cleaned out the fridge, deep cleaned the espresso machine and the display cases. I'm at my wit's end. Until I have customers, I've got nothing but time."

"We should all be so lucky."

"I can go if you're that busy. I thought you might be in the same boat."

Rosetta waved her off. "I can't look at these stupid things again," she said. Then she stood and picked up the stack of folders. "Cup of tea?"

Casey nodded.

Rosetta took her paperwork and disappeared down the hall, and Bentley, ever faithful, jumped up and followed her, leaving Casey alone in the office. Casey glanced at the computer on the far side of the desk. This was what she was really after. She refused to own her own computer or to have an email account or any other kind of account, but she did occasionally have a use for the convenience of the Internet.

She slipped around the desk, tapped the mouse, and the screen sprang to life. She opened the Internet browser and, after stopping for a moment to peer down the hall to make sure Rosetta wasn't out there, she typed, "Genetic Testing Ovarian Cancer."

According to the search engine, there were over a million hits. Casey let out a low whistle. This was yet another reason she didn't use the Internet. All over the world, at that very moment, people were sitting at computers like this one, searching for information about all manner of sickness, writing blog posts about crazy naturopathic cures, chatting on forums about their symptoms and how hard it was to get a straight answer from a medical professional. Casey wanted no part in it.

She clicked on one of the top links, a government site with a fact sheet about BRCA1 and BRCA2 testing. The page was arranged as a list of clickable questions. Her question was near the top: "How much does having a BRCA1 or

BRCA2 gene mutation increase a woman's risk of breast and ovarian cancer?"

Heart pounding, another glance out at the hallway, and then Casey clicked on the question. She scanned the answer and found the info she sought immediately. According to the website, "39 percent of women who inherit a harmful BRCA1 mutation and 11 to 17 percent of women who inherit a harmful BRCA2 mutation will develop ovarian cancer by age 70 years."

She grabbed a scrap of paper and jotted down "39% - BRCA 1, 17% - BRCA2." Then she closed the browser, stuffed the paper in her pocket, and resumed her seat on the other side of the desk, just in time.

A moment later, Rosetta returned with a tea tray, Bentley wagging his tail as he followed on her heels, eager for a nibble of whatever Rosetta was about to be eating. She spoiled that dog rotten. It was amazing he didn't have diabetes. Dogs are not supposed to eat shortbread cookies.

As Rosetta set down the tray, Casey felt a small pang of guilt for not helping her aunt. She should have been the one to fetch the tea things. But then how would she have managed to use the computer without asking Rosetta's permission? She didn't need her aunt thinking her stance on all things twenty-first century was softening. She liked living like it was 1992. It suited her fine. If time had stopped twenty years ago, she would not have minded one bit. Most of the time she felt like she was still seventeen, whatever the calendar said.

That night, Casey took the scrap of paper and her mother's letter from her pocket and studied them both. Her mother wrote that she had the BRCA1 mutation, and she urged Casey to get genetic testing to learn if she was at risk as well. That, in fact, was the purpose of her letter. It wasn't a deathbed apology. It was a deathbed confession that she may have given Casey bad genes.

Her mother's history gave her a fifty-fifty shot of having the mutation. Without knowing her father's medical history, she could only assume her actual risk could be higher. He had abandoned her and her mother when she was only three and had never even attempted to contact her since. As far as she knew, anyway. She thought that if he had reached out to her when she was growing up, her mother would have told her, if for no other reason than because he owed her thousands upon thousands of dollars in child support, so she would have encouraged Casey to reunite with him. It was possible that he'd looked for her in the years since her mother kicked her out, but she doubted it. Her mother would have told Rosetta.

She had never been great at math, and probability was definitely not her forte, but even she could figure out what this meant. She had somewhere between a 50 and 100 percent chance of having inherited the BRCA1 mutation. If she had the mutation, she had slightly better than a 50-50 chance of living with it without developing cancer.

It helped her to put it in concrete terms. For every one hundred women with the BRCA1 mutation, 39 would get ovarian cancer and 61 would not. The numbers for breast cancer were higher, but she hadn't paid as much attention to those because her mother had had ovarian cancer. She had no idea if the mutation could cause either cancer, willy-nilly, as it wished, but she had decided to believe that she was only prone to what her mother had suffered.

The question, as she understood it from these numbers, was this: How unlucky was she? Was she unlucky enough to have the mutation? Or had she hit the jackpot—the mutation and its ill effects?

The further question was this: If she got tested and learned she had the BRCA1 mutation, what good would that do her? The test couldn't tell her for sure if she was in the 39 percent or the 61 percent. It could only tell her if she was a mutant or not.

No, there was no point in getting the test. Predicting whether or not she'd get cancer was like guessing if a coin would land heads or tails, highly imprecise. Oh, sure, the people guessing would be doctors, with training, who saw lots of patients, and so on, but in the end, they'd still only be guessing.

Casey didn't plan to live in fear due to a guess, educated or otherwise. The hubris of geneticists was, in Casey's admittedly uninformed opinion, likely to be the downfall of civilization. She was willing to be a mutant by nature, but she had no intention of having her ovaries or breasts removed because of a coin-toss's chance that she'd one day develop cancer. Everyone was going to die sometime.

She took her mother's letter and the scrap of paper over to the sink and rummaged in the junk drawer for a book of matches. Time to burn the letter and be done with it. But before she could, she heard the unmistakable thud of Jason coming up the back stairs and tucked the papers back into her pocket. Tomorrow. She'd get rid of the letter tomorrow.

Chapter Nine

St. Nabor Island, South Carolina

ON THE THIRD day after Molly and Nicole had gone, Angela accepted the fact that she could not spend another night alone in the house. She really would lose her mind if she didn't get some sleep. Maybe they had been right— maybe she had already lost her mind and the sounds she heard in the night were products of grief and anxiety and an overactive imagination. She could no longer trust her senses.

Midmorning, she called Grace and asked if her offer was still good, and Grace assured her it was. Angela told her she'd be over around four. She could have called someone she knew better, but the idea of being around a relative stranger comforted her. In front of Grace, Angela could be whatever she wanted, could deal with her mother's death however she wanted, and could pass her days in the company of whomever she chose, because, despite the fifteen years Grace had worked with Angela's mother, Angela hardly knew Grace at all. Grace had no idea what Angela's life was like before her mother's death, no way of knowing if her actions were or were not in keeping with the person she'd been until two weeks ago.

Angela packed some things and went around the house making sure all the lights were off and the windows were locked. She paused in her mother's study. She still had not found the key to the desk. She'd have to get a locksmith in to open the damned thing. What the hell did her mother have in there to warrant hiding the key?

Angela tossed her suitcase in the back of her mother's Subaru. It was only half-past noon. Plenty of time. She steered through the picturesque development where she had spent her childhood, along the winding two-lane road through Ocean Pines Plantation and out to the main highway toward the mainland. Instead of taking I-95, though, she took a rural route, through peach orchards and fields of Vidalia onions, under massive trees draped in Spanish moss. After nearly an hour, she had reached a one-stoplight town where the businesses of the main street were a general store, a diner, a pharmacy, and two grungy bars.

She kept on past the traffic light, through the center of town, and soon turned off the main road into a dirt street marked with a hand-painted, wooden sign that said "Bobcat Lane." The tires churned up a cloud of dust as she passed between farm fields. At last old Spanish moss draped trees sprang up beside the lane, and then, at a sharp right-hand turn, a rusty, leaning iron gate, and the road ended at a dilapidated Georgian house with peeling paint, a sagging porch, and a crumbling chimney. There was a sign in the window to the right of the door that simply said, "Open."

Angela turned off the car, took a deep breath, and then

crossed the packed-dirt yard to the house. When she reached the door, it swung open before she could knock, and three dirty young children regarded her from the hallway.

"Mom!" one of them shouted without taking his eyes off of her.

"Hi," one of the other kids said. Then she stuck her thumb in her mouth and stared at Angela.

Angela wondered why the kids weren't in school.

"We heard your car," the one who had shouted for his mother said. The one who had not yet spoken nodded solemnly.

"I told y'all to stay in the playroom," a woman's raspy voice shouted from somewhere in the house.

At the sound, the children took off, leaving Angela standing on the porch, unsure what to do. She'd been here once before, senior year of high school, with her friend Suzanne and Suzanne's older, world-wise sister Deirdre, when Suzanne couldn't decide what college to choose of the three where she'd been accepted. Deirdre, then twenty-five and the girls' role model of sophistication and cool, said she knew what to do and drove them out here to Lisette LaRoche for a psychic reading.

Deirdre had assured them that Lisette was the best. Deirdre had gone first, and Lisette had greeted her like a long-lost friend. She had returned holding two special candles she was to burn when they got home. Suzanne took her turn next, emerging about twenty minutes later with a small bag that contained a hunk of Himalayan salt, a quartz crystal, and an herbal tonic. Angela had declined to have her fortune told.

She was thinking she might once again leave without

the consultation she'd come for when a woman in a pink sweatsuit appeared on the stairs, making her plodding way down. She had dyed-black hair, wore thick eye makeup, and despite her grubby, stained sweats, wore an array of large rings on the fingers of both hands.

"Sorry about the kids," she said, arriving at last at the door. "These damn teacher in-service things. Really wrecks a mother's day." She stood aside and gestured for Angela to enter.

This was not Lisette. Lisette had been small and gray-haired, with a breathy voice and hippie-meets-gypsy clothing.

"I was hoping to see Lisette," Angela said, standing in the entry hall and taking note of the dust motes heavy in the air.

"I'm her daughter. She doesn't work Wednesdays."

"The sign says—"

"Yeah, I can do a reading for you." Without waiting for Angela's reply, the woman turned and walked toward the back of the house. Hesitantly, Angela followed.

"I'm Belle," the woman said, sitting at the round kitchen table in the big, dusty kitchen. Everything in the room had a worn, gray, faded look, from the 70s-style linoleum floor to the wallpaper with its pattern of folksy drawings of children playing. Angela wouldn't care to eat any food prepared on those scummy looking counters.

"So palm reading or tarot?" Belle asked, tapping a cigarette from a pack on the table.

"I don't know. What's the difference?"

"Thirty dollars," Belle said, lighting the cigarette. She leaned back and blew smoke rings into the air. Then she sat up and considered Angela. "You came a long way. Might as well make it worth your while."

Without waiting for Angela's reply, she picked up a deck of tarot cards from the far side of the table and placed them squarely between herself and Angela. Angela watched her light a candle and wondered how Belle had known she'd traveled a distance to be here. What clues had she seen in Angela that she was using now to fake psychic powers?

"How do I know you won't make stuff up?" Angela asked. After all, she'd come to see Lisette. She'd never heard of this Belle person before.

Belle shuffled the tarot cards, took another drag of her cigarette, and squinted at Angela through the smoke. "You grew up out on the coast, lived there most of your life, but your family's not from the South, which explains why you don't have much accent. Maybe they're from Maine or—I'm getting an 'M'—so Michigan or Minnesota."

This was pretty much true, but it didn't prove Belle was the real deal. The first part was a good guess, and lots of people asked where she was from because she spoke with only a twinge of Southern drawl, not enough to be a true Southerner—a result of growing up with parents from Massachusetts, an "M" state Belle hadn't thought of.

"You're not sure what to do about your boyfriend," Belle said, and Angela nearly laughed out loud. Love troubles were probably what motivated most of the unmarried women who came here. That guess on Belle's part was the safest one she could have made.

"And," Belle added, seeing her skepticism, "you've got some questions about your momma." She cut the deck, crossed her arms and said, "Pick a card."

Angela reached out her hand and then thought better of

it. She sat back and mimicked Belle's pose. She said, "The thing is, my mother is dead, and I don't have questions about her, I have questions for her."

"Your mother is dead?" Belle asked, tilting her head and dropping her bored act for a moment.

"She died a week ago, but I think—" Angela paused, knowing how foolish she was about to sound, "I think she's trying to communicate with me."

Belle stood up and walked to the fridge where she got a liter bottle of Coke, and then she came back to the table. She took a sip straight from the bottle and frowned. "I'm sorry, but I was getting so clearly that you were estranged from your mother. You weren't adopted, were you?"

Angela let out a little snort of a laugh, and then she took out her phone and pulled up a picture of herself and her mother from the summer. A blind person could see the resemblance between them.

Belle shook her head and then shrugged. "I'm not a medium. I'm a clairvoyant."

Angela stuck her phone back in her purse and pushed her chair back from the table.

"I can't talk to your mother, but I can tell a lot about you. I might see something that can help."

Belle was friendlier now, entreating, more eager, Angela suspected, to make a few bucks, than in actually helping. Angela sighed. How could this obvious fraud help? She hadn't come to see Belle. She'd come to see Lisette. She didn't know if she believed in any of this or if it was all nonsense, but she had been willing to trust Lisette because the other time she'd come here, her friends trusted Lisette. Now she had nothing but regret for making the drive.

"Normally I charge $60 for a reading, but let's call it $25. Cut the deck."

Angela wanted answers. That was the problem. She didn't know if Belle had answers, but wasn't it worth a few bucks to find out? She forced all her reservations aside, pulled her chair back in, and divided the deck into two piles.

"Before we begin, I want you to think of a question you want an answer to."

Angela closed her eyes and considered this. She had thousands of questions. Which one made sense for a fortune telling? At last she settled on this one: What should I do next with my life? She opened her eyes.

Belle flipped over three cards from the pile Angela had created and she set them on the table.

"This card is the Lovers."

Angela nearly tsked aloud. She was paying $25 to be given some generic love advice that she could read in Cosmo? She wondered if she flipped over all the cards, would she find they were a dummy deck, full of Lovers to placate the desperate women who came here?

Reading her expression, Belle said, "Don't leap to conclusions. The Lovers, as a card, isn't all about romance. Actually it suggests that you are feeling a deep ambivalence in your life right now. Often The Lovers appear when someone is feeling torn between what their heart is telling them and what their head is telling them, particularly when it comes to work."

Angela bit her lip and tried not to look impressed. Ambivalence. Yes, she felt very ambivalent, not exactly about work, but sort of. Should she go back to college? When she called to formally withdraw, the dean had urged her to take the rest of the semester off as family emergency leave, but not to withdraw completely, and unsure what else to do, she had agreed, so she could go back next semester if she chose. If she could figure out how to pay.

"This card also raises the possibility of a new relationship or reconnection with someone from the past, only this time the bond will be strong, immediate, and long-lasting."

Angela rolled her eyes. That was more like it. More generic, silly, psychic nonsense.

"What, you don't believe in love?" Belle asked.

Angela shrugged.

Belle tapped the second card she had laid on the table. "This is the Ace of Swords. This card tells us it's time to be courageous and take the risk we've been considering. Whatever it is you've been feeling ambivalent about, you really do know what you need to do, and now is the time to be brave and do it. In terms of relationships, it suggests that a new relationship is what you need, and if you are already in a relationship, you may be ready to end it. Cut the ties that bind you and move forward. Does that make sense?"

This was more forceful, directive advice than Angela had been expecting. In fact it seemed dangerously directive. Make the change. Cut ties. Did people really listen to what these cards told them to do? Angela shook her head a little.

"Well, only you can know what's right for you, but if you've been thinking about making a change, this card is telling you to go for it. Find your inner strength and be bold."

Angela nodded.

"And this third card is The Tower, but see how it's upside down? That means it's the The Tower Reversed. This suggests that people you may have relied upon in the past may not be there for you anymore, or at least for the time being, or they can't support you in the same ways they used to for one reason or another. Now, this isn't necessarily as bad as it sounds. It means that things in your life are changing, and you may very well be introducing new relationships into your life to fill the voids left by those that are no longer available to you. That said, when The Tower is reversed, you are likely to have a lot of misunderstandings and arguments with loved ones, or loved ones may be very stressed out and not emotionally available to you. Try not to take it personally, and remember everyone has struggles. For relationships to survive these tough times, you have to work on communication and find ways to compromise or the relationship may be lost forever."

Belle sat back and tapped another cigarette from the pack. Angela cleared her throat and then, assuming they were done, began to open her purse.

"The first thing I notice when taking these cards together," Belle said, "is that you feel like you haven't been being true to yourself. You've been letting other people tell you what you should do and then doing it. What you want and what others think you should want don't mesh. Am I right?"

Angela froze and looked up at Belle. So there was more than a recitation of the meaning of the cards. That was a surprise, and Belle's words rang true, too. She bit her lip and nodded. Belle's description was spot on to describe her college experience so far. She hadn't ever wanted to go to a traditional college. She had wanted to go to art school, but she did what her mother thought best. Once she got to St. Katherine's, the only things she liked were her art classes and Molly and Nicole. Even though she hadn't come here to think about that, she was interested now.

"Maybe," Belle said, "this wouldn't be a problem for some people—some people don't need passion to be content, they can watch TV and go on vacation one week a year and that's enough—but it's not enough for you. Your loved ones have been trying to help and guide you, but they're holding you back. You have some ideas in mind to get on the track you want. You need to take the first step."

Angela shifted in her seat and studied the three cards, trying not to give anything away, because, despite her doubts, she had to admit how accurate Belle's assessment was. Her mother had always pushed her down a safe path, and she'd always felt constrained by it. Molly and Nicole, too, were always trying to talk her out of following her passion and pursuing art professionally. She knew they were acting out of love, but she felt smothered by it. She didn't want to be practical; she wanted to be true to herself.

"The other thing is that you're going to get some help with living your truth. There's a new relationship, or a rekindled one with someone from your past, waiting for you to make the first step forward. I may be wrong, but I do really think it'll be someone you already know but who you haven't seen in a very long time—either an old friend or maybe some estranged family member. Be open to this person. Accept them and see what they have to offer."

Angela frowned. This sounded more generic, clichéd, empty. She had no estranged family, for one thing.

"Do you have any questions?" Belle asked.

"This person, do you know if it's a man or a woman?"

"Give me your hand."

Angela stretched her arm across the table and Belle took her hand, palm up, in both of her own. She closed her eyes and after a moment spoke before opening them. "You have a lot of people around you who care for you and who wish to help you. They mostly mean well. I can't say for certain, though, which of the many the card is pointing to." She opened her eyes and dropped Angela's hand.

Angela shook her head. She pushed her chair back and opened her purse, pulling out two bills. Then she stood.

"So we have these candles," Belle said, gesturing to a built-in cabinet where a display of candles and crystals sat. "I would recommend—"

Angela cut her off. "No thanks. I'm good." She set the money on top of the cards and showed herself to the door without waiting for Belle to rise. That last bit about all the people around her—what total crap. She told Belle her mother just died. Of course there were loads of people offering help at this terrible time, but they were acting out of pity. Most of them hardly knew her. That one bit of the fortune had debunked the entire thing for her. What a complete and total waste of twenty-five bucks and a tank of gas. She was halfway to her car when she heard Belle calling behind her. She turned and saw Belle in the doorway, waving a business card.

"If you want to contact a medium," Belle said.

Angela hesitated. What would be the point of wasting more money on this foolishness? Belle was a phony. How could Angela take a recommendation from her seriously?

Belle came down off the porch with the card outstretched. Angela took it with a sigh. She glanced at the name—Calliope Savidos, Psychic Medium. Below that it said, "Your loved ones are waiting to speak to you." Angela looked back up at Belle, muttered an insincere thanks, and shoved the card in her pocket.

"Sorry if I gave you upsetting information," Belle said.

"No," Angela said, "nothing upsetting. Not much that rings true in my life."

Belle pursed her lips and shook her head. "You know, when you're grieving the truth can be hard to hear."

Angela didn't answer because she knew that if she did, she'd say something rude. How dare this complete stranger suggest her grief was making her irrational? Hell, Belle didn't even know she was grieving until Angela had told her. Some brilliant psychic she was. Angela stalked back to her car and pulled out of the driveway with needless haste, gritting her teeth in frustration. The truth. What did that fraud know about the truth?

Chapter Ten

Devil's Back Island, Maine

WHEN ROSETTA HAD first suggested the idea of opening a café, Casey immediately refused. She didn't know the first thing about running a café, she was no baker, she wasn't fit to be anybody's boss—she could think of dozens of reasons. But there was only one real reason: She didn't want to do something so public.

At the inn, she helped out with housekeeping and busied herself baking little batches of this and that for breakfast and tea time, and she had no interaction with guests at all. That was just as she liked it. She didn't see them, they didn't see her. Her role was entirely behind-the-scenes. If she could be the baker and stay hidden in the kitchen, she could probably be very happy at a café, but that wasn't at all what Rosetta envisioned. She wanted Casey to be the face of the café, the way Rosetta was the face of the inn.

Rosetta, in that way of hers, figured out what Casey's hang-up was and refused to let her hide behind it.

"In over two years here, how many people have you run

into from home?" Rosetta had asked.

"I might have cleaned the rooms of a dozen for all I know," Casey had replied.

"It's not as if your mother will ever set foot on this island again," Rosetta had said.

Casey knew as well as Rosetta did that when her mother made up her mind, however irrational, she didn't waver. She hadn't gone so far as to cut off all ties with Rosetta—she had contacted her every few years to bring news such as Ed's death—but she had not visited Devil's Back since 1991.

Casey had spent that summer with Rosetta, as she had done every year since she was 11, shortly after Maureen had married Ed. Before her mother remarried, Casey had only been to Devil's Back twice, during her mother's stints in the hospital. But Casey and Ed didn't get along. Right from the start, there were problems. Casey didn't trust Ed. Her intuition made him suspect, and, as she would later understand, that intuition was right. Her youthful lack of social graces led her to blurt out her opinions at inopportune times, a habit that put Ed in more than a few awkward circumstances, both because it did not look good for his stepdaughter to call him stingy, stinky, crabby and worse at places like church and crowded restaurants, and because he firmly believed children should be seen and not heard, if they even had to be seen.

Never in her life had she been grounded before they moved in with Ed. She didn't even know what it meant to be grounded. But she learned, and quickly. She was constantly being sent to her room, often without dinner, and God help her if she set foot outside her room again before she was officially released, which was usually breakfast the next day, although a few times Ed "forgot" about her in there and did not let her out even at breakfast time. On several occasions she actually missed school on account of being grounded, because, as Ed was fond of saying, "Grounded is grounded." After the second time she was left in there from afternoon one day until dinner the next, she had started to hide food in her dresser drawers, and after that, it wasn't so bad. She had her own en suite bathroom—Ed's house was new and modern, and every bedroom had the luxury of its own bathroom—and as long as she had a few snacks, a few books, her cassette player and headphones, she didn't mind the solitude.

When Ed realized Casey had come to enjoy being confined to her room, he moved on to other forms of punishment. His favorite was giving her big cleaning projects and then making her redo them over and over until they met his absurd standards. She still recalled the way her arms and shoulders ached and her eyes stung after the weekend she spent cleaning the grout lines in the master bathroom shower. The walls and ceiling were tiled, and though the house was only a few years old, already the white grout was stained and showing spots of mildew. Whatever virtues Maureen had that made her an attractive wife to Ed—Casey suspected it was primarily her relative youth (she was seven or eight years younger than he) and good looks (and everyone agreed, Maureen was stunning)—housekeeping wasn't one of them. Casey scrubbed and scrubbed, all the while wondering if her mother had ever so much as sprayed a cleaner on the walls. She doubted it. When she had scoured every blessed line of grout, Ed had inspected her work, found it lacking, and left her to scrub some more. It took three tries before Ed finally sighed, accepted imperfection, and told her to go to her room for the rest of the day.

In their second summer living with Ed, Maureen, in a rare moment when her meds were well balanced and she was feeling good, came up with the idea to send little Casey, who didn't mean to be a bad girl but who gave Ed so much grief, to Rosetta for the summer. They all needed a break.

The five summers Casey spent with Rosetta were her true childhood. She was free to roam the island, scrabbling over the cliff rock and splashing in the water that was still too cold for any real swimming when it was time to go home in August. She played with the other kids who summered there, rode bikes with them on the gravel paths, held stone-skipping contests in the cove, sat around campfires in the evening watching the fireflies and sharing scary stories. Those were, without a doubt, the happiest days of her life.

But it all ended when she was fifteen, which was when things started to go really wrong with Ed. Maureen had showed up at the end of August to bring Casey home, staying for a couple of nights as she always did. The day they were to leave, Rosetta took Maureen aside, words were exchanged, undoubtedly concerning Casey, and when Maureen left the inn, her face was red with anger. She walked so fast to the pier that Casey had to run to keep up, and once they were on the ferry, halfway to Portland, Maureen told Casey that they would never set foot on the island again. She'd been half right, Maureen never did return, and if it weren't for Rosetta's stubborn insistence, Casey wouldn't have either.

Which was why, in the end, Casey relented and went along with Rosetta's scheme to turn the cottage into a café. Rosetta had always seemed to know what was best for her in the past, so maybe she was right in this, too.

For the first couple of years, Casey was constantly afraid she'd look up to take a customer's order and see someone she went to high school with, someone who would go home and tell everybody they wouldn't believe who they'd seen on their summer vacation, and then word would spread on the Internet, and then... But it never happened. Rosetta was right. Devil's Back was a small, out-of-the-way place, and the odds of any of her old acquaintances stumbling upon it were slim.

And anyway, would anyone from high school even recognize her? Back then she was a scrawny little thing, all elbows and knees but with a soft baby face and chin-length, light-brown hair. She had long since grown out her hair—the short bob had been her mother's idea, simple, low maintenance, flattering to her tiny frame—and for years she'd been dying it red, not ginger red or strawberry blond, not brown with rich auburn tones, but bright cherry red, nothing natural about it. The day she did it, in the filthy bathroom of the apartment of the tattoo artist, she had looked in the mirror and for the first time in a long time felt like she was finding herself. She subsequently lost herself, and only when she returned to Devil's Back did she begin to locate herself again, but the hair color, for whatever reason, was key. And of course there was also the tattoo, the big, beautiful, tough tattoo. Who of those who knew her when she was a teenager ever would have predicted she'd someday have a tattoo like that one? Nobody, which was at least half the reason she got it. And then there were the natural changes of aging—her face was more angular, her figure softer.

For all she knew, some of the visitors to the café were

from her old hometown in Massachusetts, people who had gone to church or school with her, but neither party had recognized the other. She wasn't worried anymore, not most days anyway, that someone would walk through the door of the café and disturb her quiet life here.

When a hipster couple entered the café on that quiet morning in mid-September, Casey hardly gave them a glance. Kim, who worked at the counter part-time as cashier and barista, served them while Casey rotated the items in the pastry case, pulling out day-olds to bag up and sell at a discount, subbing in the freshly baked ones. As she worked, she could feel the woman's eyes on her, but this was not unusual either. Her tattoo drew stares, it always did. But as Casey was taking the tray back into the kitchen to wrap up the day-olds, the woman said, "Do I know you?"

Casey stopped to look at her. She was plump, with long, glossy blond hair artfully fanned around her shoulders in gentle waves, and long side-swept bangs falling over the dark plastic frames of her glasses. She wore a dark plaid button-down shirt with the sleeves rolled to the elbow, a big gray scarf around her neck despite the fact that the day was not cold, dark skinny jeans with a narrow roll at the cuff, and topsiders. Hipster á la J. Crew, manufactured cool. Casey shook her head.

The woman scrunched up her face and said, "I swear, you look so familiar."

"Yeah, I get that sometimes," Casey lied, somewhat absurdly. Who could possibly mistake her for someone else—the hair dye, the tattoo, these were rather distinct.

The man raised an eyebrow. He, like the woman, was in a plaid shirt and dark skinny jeans. He, too, sported ironically geeky glasses, and he wore an ever-so-trendy beard.

"I do know you!" the woman said. "CJ, right?"

Kim, who had been cleaning the espresso machine, turned to look at Casey.

She hadn't been CJ in twenty years. That was what she'd called herself back in high school, a refusal of her given name, a small act of rebellion against her mother. Her birth certificate identified her as Cara-Jayne Seaver. Her mother was a trendsetter in creative spelling and unnecessary hyphenation.

When she started high school, she realized she had a chance to rename herself, so she chose CJ, which struck her as sort of edgy for a girl. There were lots of boys who went by initials; J preceded by any number of other letters: AJ, BJ, DJ, EJ. Why couldn't she be CJ? She had gone to a very small elementary school, so she hardly knew anyone in her class at the big regional high school. It was easy to introduce herself as CJ without being questioned. Even most of her teachers called her CJ.

When she fell in with the tattoo artist and his crowd, she reinvented herself again: from CJ to Casey Jones. In that tattoo parlor, no one used their real names. They all had tough names like Mad Dog and Big G. Her guy went by Montana, although as far as Casey knew he wasn't from Montana. She never even knew his real name. The day she'd walked into the shop in response to the Help Wanted sign in the window, he'd asked her name and then said, "No last names, and not what your momma called you. Your real name. The name that is you."

At seventeen, that struck her as profound. She didn't even have to think about it, "Casey Jones," she said, which was what her best friends used to call her back at school, a name that riffed on her initials and the famous song by one of their favorite bands.

Having christened herself Casey Jones naturally led to everyone in the shop calling her Trouble, after the Grateful Dead lyrics. Everyone except Montana. He called her Jonesy. So she'd chosen a name for herself and nobody called her by it anyway. It was okay with Casey—their names for her were nicknames derived from the name she gave herself, they were signs of affection, signs that she was part of the club. Except, of course, she wasn't. She was the girl who slept with Montana and got paid under the table for cleaning the shop and manning the phone and whatever else anyone asked her to do. The arrangement didn't last long, and when it all fell apart, Casey was inked outside and in. Outside she had the work of art across her arm. Inside she had the name Casey Jones written on her soul. Everywhere she went after that, she introduced herself as Casey Jones without a moment's hesitation. It had taken Rosetta a little while to get used to it, but Rosetta understood the art of self-reinvention, so she accepted it.

"You've confused me with somebody else," Casey said to the woman who was studying her so intently now.

Casey took the tray into the kitchen and let the door swing shut behind her. She set down the tray, rested her hands on the counter, shut her eyes and tried to place the woman, but she came up empty. It didn't matter. What mattered was the thing she'd feared for so long had happened, and she was still standing. The ground hadn't opened up and swallowed her. She hadn't vanished into nothingness at the mention of her name. Someone had recognized her, but it hadn't altered anything. And besides, she'd brushed the woman off with ease. Even if the woman went home and called up other people she knew from school and said she saw someone she swore was CJ Seaver, it wasn't as if people were suddenly going to storm Devil's Back to verify the story. She probably already was a sort of legend at reunions: *Whatever happened to CJ? I heard she went off the rails after you know....* If her legend grew as the result of a possible sighting, fine. Give the people something to talk about. Everybody loves a rumor.

Still, she called the inn, described the couple, and checked to see if they were staying and for how long. Just one night. She'd let Kim manage the counter alone tomorrow morning. No need to test her luck with a repeat encounter.

That night, as Casey tried to stop her racing thoughts and fall asleep, all she could think about was her mother, all the times she flashed her brightest smile, and said, "Hey there, Carrie-Bear, I have a surprise for you."

When her mother was having her good days, she had called her Carrie or, on really good days, Carrie-Bear.

If her mother said, "Hey there, Carrie-Bear," when she came down to breakfast, she knew she could relax that day, because her mother was in an upswing. When her mother was in a downswing, she called her by her full name, Cara-Jayne, or she ignored her altogether. Those were the memories she held onto, that was how she preferred to remember her mother. Angry, irrational, incoherent. She could tell herself she was better off without her, as long as she didn't think about the good days, the chocolate-chip-pancakes-for-dinner, surprise-we're-playing-hooky-and-hitting-the-beach, I-love-you-my-sweet-precious-girl days when her mother had been kind, fun, and spontaneous.

When she thought of the good days, her anger lapsed into grief and sorrow. In her first days on her own, grief and sorrow sometimes led her to call her mother and attempt to reconcile, but Maureen was unrelenting. Eventually she realized her life would be easier if she shut out the good memories and let the bad ones vaccinate her against the childish desire for her mother's approval.

She wished Jason would show up and give her something else to think about, but no, for the first time in days, he stayed away. Without his infuriating presence her mind was full of her mother.

They had had some good times, a million years ago, back before Ed, despite her mother's condition. The thing about Maureen was that when she was in a good mood she was positively high on life, full of energy, ready for adventure, and Casey was her partner in crime. When her mother was happy, she adored Casey, and nothing in the world felt better than having her mother's undivided attention and unconditional love.

Sometimes those upswings lasted weeks, and sometimes less than a day, but they always ended with spectacular crashes into depressive cycles that were every bit as extreme and usually more prolonged, which meant every memory that started good ended badly.

Casey would never forget her ninth birthday. That morning, her mother woke her up before dawn by entering her room with a cupcake topped with a candle, singing happy birthday. Once she blew out the candle, her mother announced that her birthday wish had come true. They were leaving immediately for the airport to fly to Disney World. Despite her half-asleep confusion, she was beside herself with joy. She had wanted to go to Disney since she first heard of its existence from classmates back in kindergarten.

The Magic Kingdom! That place where fairy tales do come true! Somehow in her mind, she had also concluded that a trip to Disney would cure her mother of the demons inside her head that made her act so strange and unpredictable. She was going to meet Snow White and her mother was going to be fixed and they'd come home and her mother would be like all her classmates' mothers. Disney World was the key to normalcy.

The trip to the airport was smooth and easy, the flight was on time, and they arrived in Orlando midmorning to a perfect blue-sky day. Maureen talked excitedly the entire time, telling her about her own childhood trip to Disneyland, in California, the summer her father got laid off from his job and decided to pack the station wagon and drive the family across the country, because if he was going to end up bankrupt anyway, he may as well go in style. Looking back, Casey could see how her mother may have inherited her mood disorder from him.

Maureen had booked them a room at the Contemporary, and Casey could still recall her sense of wonder when she saw the monorail glide through the modern structure. It was like stepping into a brilliant future.

Everything went all right that first day. They checked in, rode on the magical monorail to the entrance of the park, and passed through the gates into Disney's Main Street, the most optimistic version of Anytown, USA ever imagined. The air was heavy with the scents of popcorn and freshly baked cookies, and a horse-drawn wagon clopped up the street, parting the throngs of people milling about. She had her doubts when she saw how crowded it was. Her mother did not do well in crowds. Later, she learned that actually, on that Tuesday in April, when children everywhere were in school, the park had been practically dead compared to how crowded it got in the summer or over Christmas.

Still, crowds and all, her mother's mood was buoyant. They got pictures with the statue of Walt and Mickey and in front of Cinderella's Castle. They rode the carousel, tea cups, It's a Small World, the Pirates of the Caribbean, the Haunted Mansion, Space Mountain. No rides left unexplored. Her mother acted more like a kid than a parent, grabbing her hand and practically dragging her from attraction to attraction. They stayed in the park until the nightly fireworks, and she fell asleep on the short ride back to the hotel. Her mother carried her to bed.

The next day, though, things started to go wrong right away. They went down to breakfast at the hotel, and her mother started complaining about the prices. This, she knew, was not a good sign. As much as she would have loved to order the Mickey Mouse Chocolate Chip Pancakes, she tried to soothe her mother by ordering cereal, which was the cheapest item on the menu. Her mother ordered coffee, nothing to eat, and she knew they were in real trouble. She could see rage simmering behind her mother's eyes as she drank the coffee, and twice she commented that it would be a long time before they had anything else. The day before, she'd offered to stop for snacks at nearly every vendor they'd passed, but today, clearly that wouldn't be the case.

Maureen rallied some as they got back on the monorail to go to Epcot, and Casey thought, despite all past experiences, that perhaps her mother would snap out of her funk and be happy again. As they made their way from one pavilion to another, she tried to impress her mother with her interest in the various nations represented there even though she wasn't particularly enthusiastic about any of them, but her mother, clearly, had no desire to be interested.

Around noon, Maureen announced that they would have lunch at the Mexico pavilion. This might have been a good sign. Her entire life with Maureen was an endless effort to correctly interpret signs so that she could adjust her own behavior accordingly so as not to upset her mother. She tried and tried, but the signs were fickle things. What was a bad sign one day was a good sign the next, and so reading the signs was an imperfect art at best.

The restaurant was inside a building that looked like a Mayan pyramid, but it was made to look like it was evening, outdoors, in a plaza surrounded by a charming Mexican town. The Mexico ride, which was a boat ride, passed right by the restaurant, a little river inside the building. Surely this would cheer her mother up, she thought when they were seated. Her mother told her to order whatever she wanted, another good sign, except that Maureen said it in a harsh whisper.

They ate in silence, a growing knot of fear forming in Casey's little stomach. She found it increasingly difficult to swallow her food as she watched her mother eat in a way that could only be described as vicious. She was shoving food into her mouth and chewing as if she were a conquistador preparing for battle. A few times she noticed Casey pushing food around her plate and told her to stop being so ungrateful and eat up.

The explosion occurred when the bill arrived. The waitress set it on the table, and Maureen, in a forced, toothy grin, opened her purse, put on a show of frantically fumbling through it, her demeanor changing from fake-happy to genuine hysteria in about five seconds. Then she began to scream that her money had been stolen. Casey shrank in her chair, willing herself to become invisible, while her mother shouted and carried on. The waitress came over, and then the manager, and as quickly as they could, which was not very quickly given the state of distress Maureen had worked herself into, they ushered the two of them to an office, where Maureen tearfully explained how she'd brought her daughter for a birthday surprise, and how they weren't wealthy people, but she had scrimped and saved, and she'd had over three-hundred dollars cash in her purse when they arrived that morning, and now it was gone, gone, all gone. She wailed and moaned as if she believed every word she was saying, although Casey knew for a fact there was no three-hundred dollars in her mother's purse, and every aspect of the trip had been paid with credit cards.

The grace with which the manager took all this in was astonishing. He assured her mother they would comb security footage and try to identify the thief. He also, gently, but not gently enough (there was no gently enough), counseled Maureen to consider Traveler's Checks in the future, which were safer than cash, and then he told her that her meal was on the house, and even gave her fifty "Disney Dollars," before suggesting she go back to her hotel and refresh herself.

Maureen pocketed the "Disney Dollars" without a hint of grace or gratitude and stalked away, leaving Casey to scurry along behind her so as not to get separated. They went back to the hotel where Maureen told her to go down to the pool. Casey doubted she'd be allowed into the pool without an adult. At nine years old, she had enough understanding of the world to know that children her age were supposed to be supervised when doing things like swimming, but she put on her bathing suit and left her room without a word. As she expected, the lifeguard turned her away so she wandered around the hotel for a while and then went back to the room.

Thankfully, when she knocked, her mother let her in, and she didn't ask why her hair and bathing suit were dry. Maureen was sloshed. She had ordered champagne from room service and knocked back most of the bottle. She insisted that Casey get into bed with her and cuddle, and then she launched into a familiar old lament about how everyone in the world was out to get her, and life wasn't fair, and it wasn't supposed to be like this, and on and on while Casey tried not to breathe in her stinky booze breath. Eventually her mother passed out, and Casey climbed into her own bed and cried herself to sleep.

The next morning they flew home, and when she went to school, she got called in to the office to explain her absences, as her mother had not alerted the school that she would be out, nor had she returned any of the school's phone calls.

She lied, protecting her mother like she always did, and said that they both had the flu. She knew the principal didn't believe her, but he also didn't really care. She went back to class, and at lunch, instead of making her classmates jealous with news that she'd been to Disney, she stuck by her story, the flu, the flu on her birthday, what terrible luck.

Back then she hadn't understood her mother's condition. She knew only that her mother wasn't like other kids' mothers, and that sometimes she got sick and had to go to the hospital. Casey would spend years thinking of that miserable birthday trip and asking herself how her mother had gone from luxuriating in the happiest place on Earth to raving over the great unfairness of the universe. What had she done, what had she done, what had she done to make her mother so unhappy? They had gone to sleep happy that first night, hadn't they? So why had her mother woken up so angry?

Later, she knew, intellectually, that none of it had been her fault, and that the joyous nature of the first day had been as much a symptom of her mother's faulty brain chemistry as was the disastrous second day, but what she knew and what she felt were two very different things. What she felt was that somehow her mother's misery was her fault. If her mother hadn't wanted so badly to give her a spectacular birthday gift, she wouldn't have spent all that money she didn't have on the trip to Disney, and she wouldn't have been reminded of all the ways her life was a disappointment to her and so wouldn't have had a public meltdown.

When Maureen was medicated, the great big swings flattened out into a steady state of overall apathy. Nothing made her particularly happy or particularly sad. She was just there. Those flat times were calm, and in that way a relief, but also it was as if some essential part of Maureen's nature was missing, and weirdly, Casey found herself missing her mother then almost as much as when she was unmedicated and spiraling downward. It was as if she could not have both a calm life and have her mother, and that was a tragedy she had never gotten over, because she wanted her mother.

How many times had she longed for her mother to hold her and tell her everything would be okay? Who didn't want that? It was the most basic human instinct, and one, it seemed, she had never outgrown, because right now, at thirty-seven years old, Casey still wanted it, but it was no longer something her mother willfully withheld. Now her mother was dead, and there was no hope in this world that she'd ever experience her mother's loving embrace again. As much as she felt like her mother's death shouldn't hurt so much, it did, and there was no escaping the deep ache she felt in her chest.

Since she was a teenager, Casey had lived with the fear that she had inherited her mother's bipolar disorder. Every time she felt unexpectedly happy or sad, she thought, Is this it? Am I going crazy? The last summer she spent on Devil's Back as a teenager, she'd confessed her fears to Rosetta. Right around when she hit puberty, she began hearing things sometimes, like voices or strange sounds, and she thought she was losing her mind. Her friends would tease her that she needed a hearing aid because she was constantly saying, "Did you hear that?"

She'd been terrified to admit to anyone her fears that she was going crazy, but Rosetta had explained that most women in their family heard voices like that, and none of them suffered bipolar but Maureen. Rosetta said the voices were spirits trying to communicate, which Casey found hard to believe, especially since her mother said the same thing, and her mother's impressions generally couldn't be trusted. Unlike her mother, however, Rosetta had taught her to meditate, and with practice, she learned to let the voices pass through her like running her hand through smoke. If she didn't try to hold on to the voices, they evaporated. Rosetta's meditation techniques worked far better than Maureen's suggestion that she talk back to the voices.

As she passed through her twenties and into her thirties, she had suffered losses and had experienced joy, and she had, as yet, not shown any other signs of being anything other than normal. She supposed that if she ever saw a therapist, she could easily be diagnosed with PTSD given the childhood she'd had, but despite that, she was a fully-functioning adult. Not crazy. Not yet, anyway. In fact, she almost never worried anymore that she was showing signs of her mother's mental illness.

How cruel of her mother to give her something new to fear now. Ignorance really was bliss. She would have been so much better off not knowing. But she knew, and once you know something, you can't unknow it. Which was exactly why she had no intention of getting genetic testing done.

After all, there was only one other person in the world to whom it made one bit of difference whether or not Casey had faulty code in her genes, and she could never know about any of this.

Then there was the inheritance to make sense of. Her mother had not said that the money was an effort to make amends, only that she had decided to divide it between Casey and Eliza. Was she sorry or was she trying to make Casey feel sorry? Casey wanted to believe it was the former, but she couldn't shake the sense that it was the latter.

She finally fell asleep sometime after two AM, but she

tossed and turned as her mind continued to dredge up images of her mother and of Ed and of the life she'd had so long ago. It was a relief when her alarm went off at five and she had to get up. Outside rain blew sideways across the bay and slapped against the windows of the café. It would be another slow day, another good day to tackle some big jobs she normally didn't have time for, jobs that would keep her busy enough to shut off her brain for a while.

In the gloomy predawn, she looked around the café and decided she'd redo the chalkboards. It was time to put a fall spin on the decorations anyway. The wall behind the counter was painted entirely in the chalkboard paint. She had to layer on coat after coat to get a smooth, dark surface, but when it was all done, she had concluded it was worthwhile. She created big decorated borders and carefully wrote out the menu by hand in the center, changing the drawings and updating menu items seasonally. For the summer, the border had been blue hydrangea, pink and white rugosa, and butterflies.

As she washed down the wall with a damp sponge, erasing the pretty flowers, she planned her fall border in her head. She would make each side look like the shoreline with pine trees and maples rising up. The bright maple leaves could swirl in the air and scatter throughout the menu itself. Along the top, a few Canada geese. It would take her all day at least.

She flipped on the radio and when the forecast came on, she paused in her sponging. Rain until Wednesday. Four days. She might as well make her chalkboard art intricate, because few visitors would bother to make the crossing during a tropical storm. Really, there was no sense in opening at all until the weather broke. She left the sign on the door flipped to closed, cranked up the radio, put on a small pot of coffee for herself, and threw herself into her art project.

PART TWO

Chapter Eleven

Portland, Maine

BRETT ARRIVED IN PORTLAND in a driving rain that turned the waterfront city into a gray blur and wondered, not for the first time, if this was a mistake. Rosetta had told him that September was the best month of the year on the island, but he'd been watching the forecast, and if this was the best month, the deal was DOA.

The day he had walked into Charlie's office with the proposal for Sweet Water East, he had expected Charlie to laugh in his face and tell him to get his head out of his ass. That's what Brett had wanted to happen, that way he could quit and never look back.

Instead Charlie had listened to his pitch, leafed through the file he'd prepared, and asked how soon Brett could go to Maine to scope it out in person. And now here he was, in a rented Ford, struggling to follow the instructions from the GPS app on his phone to get to his hotel for the night.

He had hoped to board a ferry today for Devil's Back, but when he saw the churning swells in the harbor, he thought better of it. He'd work from Portland tonight and go on to the island when the storm broke. Rosetta had laughed when he phoned to say he wouldn't be arriving that day as planned.

"Land lubber. This is nothing," she had said.

"Call me what you want, but I'd have to be insane to get on a boat today."

"Well, I'm not going anywhere. I'll be here whenever you're ready."

So far in his conversations with Rosetta, he gathered that she was quite a character. When he first called her to see if she was still looking for buyers, the first thing she had done was tell him she could sense his positive aura over the phone, and later she'd asked for his astrological sign. She said it wasn't in her nature to trust people from the West Coast, but she'd give him a chance to dazzle her with an offer.

When he studied the information she'd faxed him about the island, the properties, the businesses she was selling, and her financial situation, he wondered if she was actually insane. None of it made sense. Her businesses had been hemorrhaging money for years, and she'd done nothing to stem the flow. It was nothing short of a miracle she'd managed to keep the place afloat for as long as she had. In fact, if she didn't sell within the next few months, she'd have no choice but to declare bankruptcy.

Once upon a time a situation like this—where he had all the power in the negotiations and could push the seller to rock bottom—would have excited him, but now he mostly felt bad. Whatever he offered, Rosetta had to accept, even if it was barely enough to settle her debts. She probably wanted to come out of this with enough to retire on, but there was no way that was happening. She was about to sell her life's work and walk away with nothing to show. She must be devastated.

Or he was projecting. Maybe—probably—Rosetta would be happy to wash her hands of the mess she had made. She seemed to understand that it was her mess, but she had to be in her late sixties at least, probably older—she and her husband bought the hotel thirty-some years ago—and when Brett thought of her signing away her life's work, he couldn't help but imagine how he would feel in her place.

Maybe he was having a midlife crisis. Nearly forty, he had begun to look at his own life and wonder what his legacy would be. He'd spent his twenties and thirties working sixty, seventy hour weeks, had never married, and despite his best efforts, he had plateaued in his career. His goal had once been to be CEO of Sweet Water Resorts, but he understood now that that was not going to happen. Charlie would promote his sons and nephews over Brett even though they hadn't Brett's skills, foresight, or drive, and Brett would answer to them forever.

He knew he should quit. Charlie had been his mentor, but Brett had long since repaid the kindness Charlie showed him when he was fresh out of college. He'd provided Sweet Water with more value than any other employee including Charlie himself. He could go work somewhere else. He'd read somewhere that the average worker in today's economy will change jobs every two to four years, meanwhile he'd been working for the same company for eighteen years. Maybe it was time for him to stop being an anomaly and embrace change like everyone else.

The possibility of East Coast expansion was enticing, though. He had wanted to move back east for a while now.

If he could make this Maine deal work, maybe he'd finally be looking at a promotion. No one else in upper management would want to move east. He could be president of the East Coast Division and have a whole branch of the company to himself. Even if he still technically had to answer to Charlie, he'd practically be on his own out here, and that might be enough.

His hotel in Portland was waterfront but all the view he had today was of rain slapping the glass. It was hard to give himself a pep talk in the face of such gloom, but he tried. He firmly believed a job worth doing was worth doing well. He couldn't go into this deal half-heartedly. He needed to invest himself fully or call it a day and go home, and as the latter option was off the table, he had his work cut out for him.

He wanted to call Ashley. He wondered if she'd answer if he called or if she would see his number and let it go to voice mail. He hadn't tried to contact her at all since she broke up with him two weeks earlier. Instead he buried himself in getting ready for this trip and tried not to think of her. But now, alone in a hotel room, there was nothing left to do for work until he actually got onto the island and he had nothing else to think about besides Ashley.

To say he hadn't seen it coming would be a lie. She'd been complaining for a long time about how he didn't make enough time for her, how he was too caught up in his work. But he thought when he told her about how Charlie got on board with his idea of opening a resort in Maine and what a big promotion it was, she'd see that all his hard work was worth it. He thought she'd jump at the chance to head east with him.

In Los Angeles, yoga instructors were a dime a dozen,

which meant Ashley was perpetually underemployed, perpetually struggling. But if they relocated to the East Coast, some nice little suburb of Boston or New York, depending on where he decided to establish headquarters for the new division—he was getting ahead of himself, he knew he was, but Sweet Water wouldn't move into a region and only open one resort, Devil's Back was only the start—they could buy an old Colonial and grow vegetables in the yard and she could start her own yoga studio. He could help her. No more waitressing or working retail for her. She could do what she loved, because once they got married, she wouldn't need to worry about money anymore.

In the two years of their relationship, she'd resisted his offers to help her with her cash flow problems, claiming she wanted to be an independent woman, but they'd get married and what was his would be hers. They'd been talking about moving in together, or rather, he'd been talking about her moving into his condo, for months.

Three days after Charlie greenlighted the prefeasibility analysis on Devil's Back, he bought her an engagement ring—antique, sapphire and diamonds, something that wouldn't make her wonder if her gems had funded a bloody war somewhere. When she got home from her evening yoga class, he had a bottle of champagne on ice, a bouquet of flowers on the table, and the ring in his pocket. He did it right—down on one knee like Prince Charming. And what had she said?

"God damn it, why do you have to make this so hard?"

Which didn't seem like an answer to Brett, so he stayed on his knee, waiting for something that more closely resembled yes or no.

She paced back and forth, rubbing her hands over her face for a moment, and then she said, "You're a hopeless romantic. You make these huge gestures like they make up for all the little things. God damn it."

"Ash, come on. I love you. I love you so much. Let's make a life together."

"There's only room for me in your life when it's convenient for you. That's the thing."

He stood back up, the ring box still in his outstretched hand. "At least look at it," he said.

"No. I can't. I can't do this anymore."

She walked back toward the door and picked up her gym bag, but he caught up with her and blocked the door. "Things are changing. I mean it. At work—"

"I do not want to hear about your work."

"I'm going to have my own division. I'll be the boss, and I'll make my own hours."

"You honestly think that taking on more responsibilities will help you work less?"

When she put it that way, it sounded illogical, but he also knew that it was true. The higher ups in the company had middle management to put in the long hours, while bosses played golf and cashed checks. He ought to know. He was middle management. He was the company's number one workhorse.

"This will be a good thing. What we need is a change of scenery. We need to get away from the insanity of this town."

"I'm not moving. I have no intention of moving."

Brett knew he was defeated. All he'd talked about for the past few months was his desire to move back east to be closer to his family, and Ashley had never said a word. Not a single word of objection. She hadn't said anything to lead him to believe she was against such a move, but she hadn't said anything to suggest she'd be willing to go with him either. When she agreed to move in with him, he thought they had a tacit understanding that if he managed to get his wish to go back home, she'd go, too. By living together they would become a package deal. Apparently, she felt otherwise.

"Were you ever going to tell me that?" Brett asked.

"You've been so depressed lately. How could I?"

He felt his frustration rapidly coming to a boil. Yes, he had been depressed. He was at a dead end at the company he'd devoted his life to, he had begun to wonder why he'd ever gotten into real estate development in the first place, and his life had a gaping hole in the middle where his family ought to be. He said, "Did you think I'd slit my wrists if you broke up with me?"

He moved away from the door and put the ring box on the dining room table next to the flowers. Then he popped the cork on the champagne.

"What are you doing?"

"Celebrating." He filled one of the flutes on the table, over-pouring, letting the expensive champagne slop onto the table. He didn't care.

"I thought you were in a bad place, and I was trying to do the kind thing," Ashley said, moving back into the dining room.

Brett filled the second flute and held it out to Ashley.

"What are you doing?" she asked again, stepping away from him.

"Here's to you, kid. You really fooled me. If the whole yoga thing doesn't work out, you should try acting."

"Come on, don't be like this."

"I tried to be what you wanted." He became a vegan for her!

"That's the thing, though. Maybe when it's love you don't have to try so hard."

"Wow. Well, if that's what you think, good luck to you." He raised his glass and took a long swallow.

And she left. Just like that. They hadn't spoken since. And now here he was, an entire continent between them, but he hadn't stopped hoping she'd come around. He needed her to come around. Because she was the only real non-work, non-family relationship in his life, and because his dream for his new East Coast life wasn't a bachelor's life.

He glanced at the clock on his phone. Eleven. Only eight in LA. She'd be getting home now. His finger hovered over her name in his contact list, and after a long moment, he pressed it. She picked up on the third ring, just when he had concluded she wasn't going to answer at all.

By way of greeting, she said, "Are you okay?"

"Of course, why wouldn't I be?"

"I haven't heard from you since, you know, and I don't know..."

"I'm great. I'm in Maine."

"Oh."

Neither of them spoke for a minute, and then Ashley said, "Did you want anything?"

"I wanted to talk to you. I miss you."

"Brett."

"Are you seeing someone?" Brett asked, realizing for the first time that perhaps that was the real reason she'd broken up with him, that she'd been cheating.

"Would it be easier on you if I said I was?"

"No."

"Okay then, no. I am not seeing anyone else and I'm insulted that you would ask me such a question."

"Sorry."

"Listen, I should go. I mean if you don't want anything—"

"I wanted you to know I was thinking of you. That I love you." His voice broke as he said this. What a mistake this phone call had been.

Ashley sighed. "I know you love me. It's just we're in totally different places in our lives. We want different things."

"Yeah, well, I wish maybe we could have talked about that."

"When do you come back?"

"I haven't booked my flight yet. A lot of factors up in the air here."

"Let's get together when you get back, okay? Talk in person."

"Sure, fine."

"Okay, I'm going to go now."

"I love you."

"I know. I'm sorry." She hung up.

What a fool he was. How did he think calling her would help anything? He should have gone down to the hotel bar, had a strong drink, and gone to sleep. He shut off the light, praying that the weather would clear overnight. He needed something to go right for a change.

Chapter Twelve

St. Nabor Island, South Carolina

GRACE HAD A TOWNHOUSE near Colony Beach, one of the two public beaches on the island. Angela slowly drove through the condo complex looking for number 612. It was a corner unit near the back. There was a wreath of artificial fall leaves on the door, the sight of which made Angela miss New Hampshire. Maybe she should have listened to Molly and Nicole. Too late now.

Grace greeted her with a stiff, formal hug, picked up her suitcase and led her upstairs to the guest room, where she left Angela to get situated. Alone, Angela dropped onto the bed and shut her eyes. She was so damned tired. She knew she couldn't hide out for long without seeming rude, but if she shut her eyes for a few minutes...

That night, after a dinner, Angela excused herself to bed early. Despite her afternoon nap, she was still dead tired. But when she lay down on the soft guest bed and shut off the lights, she couldn't sleep. Her mind played and replayed her visit to Belle that afternoon, and the predictions Belle had made for her. Yes, some of it had been vague, and yes, some of it had been wrong, but she had to admit, a lot of it was true. Maybe Belle hadn't been a total fraud.

When she was no closer to sleep an hour after shutting off the light, Angela gave up, got out of the bed and fetched her laptop. Then she dug in her purse for the business card Belle had given her. She took the card and the computer back to the bed and typed the name Calliope Savidos into the search engine.

The top result was Calliope's own website. Below that were Yelp reviews, a Facebook page, and other things like that. Just as Angela was about to open Calliope's website, a result halfway down the page caught her eye: The Low Country Amateur Paranormal Activity Investigators Club. She clicked.

A sleek, professional-looking webpage opened with a black background that looked like a starry sky that was animated to swirl slowly. When Angela clicked the middle of the screen, the star pattern dispersed and revealed a Welcome page.

"We, the Low Country Amateur Paranormal Activity Investigators Club, know there's more to this world than what we can see with the naked eye. We believe that science can prove the existence of a spirit world."

Below this bold declaration were a series of tabs: Events, Field Notes, Membership, and Links. Angela opened the membership page, where she learned that interested persons and the press were invited to drop in at twice-monthly meetings at Third Eye Books to learn more. There was a meeting tomorrow night. She looked up Third Eye Books and learned it was only about twenty minutes away, in one of the shopping centers in Palmetto Landing. There was no reason she couldn't go to the meeting, sit in the back, check it out, and see if maybe they could help her.

Except, of course, that these people were likely to be nut jobs. And did paranormal include stuff like vampires and zombies? Then again, nuts or not, it would be nice to meet people who wouldn't tell her she was "just grieving" if she said she thought her mother was haunting her.

The next night, Angela found herself in the parking lot of Third Eye Books, watching other people enter the store. They looked normal enough. Most of them were men, ranging in age from late teens to advanced middle age, and she guessed these were the ghost hunters, as they all were arriving in time for the meeting. The people entering the shop didn't appear to have any visible satanic tattoos or anything, and only one was wearing a Goth get-up. Not a single one was wearing a cape, much to Angela's relief. She glanced at the clock. 7:03. It was now or never. She took a deep breath and got out of the car.

The paranormal sleuths were gathered in a small room, sitting on folding chairs and chatting amongst themselves. There was harsh-smelling coffee brewing in the corner. Angela lingered in the doorway. As she looked at the backs of the heads of a roomful of believers whom she knew, in light of recent events, she should not judge, she couldn't help but wonder if Nicole and Molly had been right. Maybe she really was suffering from grief-induced insanity, because a few weeks ago she wouldn't have set foot in this bookstore, let alone this meeting.

A young man stood up and walked to the front of the room, and everyone quieted down. He spotted Angela in the doorway, smiled, and gestured toward the chairs. Angela hesitated a moment longer and then found a place to sit near the back.

"Hey, y'all. Big crowd tonight," he said.

He looked familiar. Angela tried to think of how she might know him as she scanned the room and did a quick head count. Eighteen people, counting herself, about a dozen more than she'd expected, truthfully.

"Most of y'all know me," the man went on. "But for those who don't, I'm Randy Davis."

Randy Davis. She knew that name. She studied him more closely. He had a rich, creamy-coffee complexion, big brown eyes, and close-cropped hair. He was average height with a runner's build, lean and lanky. When he smiled, he had adorable dimples. Randy Davis... And then she remembered. Elementary school. He had been shy and nerdy, with glasses. In her memory, she saw him sitting alone at the edge of the playground with his comic books.

"So our top priority tonight is Saturday's investigation," Randy was saying. "Jack and I scouted the Lawton Railroad Bridge, and Neil checked out Marsten Hills, but honestly I'm not sure either will be very exciting."

A man in the front swiveled in his seat to look at the rest

of the group. "Lawton's played out. It might be a fun place for teenagers to go for a laugh and a fright, but honestly, it's not worth the trouble of hauling equipment up there," he said.

Angela had heard urban legends of the Lawton Railroad bridge, some story of a hobo waiting to hop on the train and getting run over instead, or waiting to hop off and misjudging and leaping as the train was crossing the bridge over the ravine, or something like that. If this club took those sorts of lame stories seriously, she was in the wrong place.

"The owner of Marsten Hills says we can send a team," someone else said, "but no more than four people."

"Now, I know we're down to the wire here, so unless y'all have any ideas, we might have to skip this month," Randy said.

Angela watched as people exchanged glances and murmured.

A woman raised her hand. "Since so many of us are going up to Charleston for Halloween next month, I say we skip it."

"Good point, Jen," Randy said.

"Yeah, but what about all of the rest of us who can't afford your little excursion? We aren't all so lucky," a small woman with spiky silver hair said, shooting Jen a dirty look.

"I'm open to suggestions, Krissy," Randy said, shrugging.

There was more murmuring and grumbling, and after a few minutes, Jen said, "I think we should move on to talk about the trip. Obviously no one has ideas. Four people can go to Marsten Hills and the rest of us will skip this month."

Krissy guffawed, but no one else spoke, so Randy invited Jen to come up to the front. Jen was a tiny bird of a woman with hair dyed purple and a face pocked with acne scars. She began going over a list of details such as when and where to meet the bus, who was still looking for roommates if anyone wanted to cut costs, who still owed final payments, and things like that. As she spoke, Krissy got up loudly and left, taking two men with her. Apparently this was a contentious bunch.

When Jen was done, Randy invited everyone to hang around and have some snacks, and like obedient students, everyone queued up at the table of cookies beside the coffee maker. Angela waited a moment and then approached Randy, who was still at the front of the room, deep in conversation with an elderly gentleman. When the man finally walked away, Randy noticed Angela and gave a bright, dimpled smile.

"Hi there. First time joining us?" he asked.

Angela nodded, trying to work out what she wanted to say.

"You look really familiar," he said.

Angela blushed, for no reason she could think of, and said, "I think we went to grade school together."

He furrowed his brow and cocked his head. "I'm terrible at putting names and faces together."

She introduced herself and he opened his eyes wide and gave a little shake of his head. "I would not have expected to see you here," he said. His friendliness toward her seemed to cool a little. When he thought she was a stranger, he was all smiles, but now he was guarded.

"I mean, and don't take this the wrong way, but you were definitely one of those too-cool girls, you know?" Randy said.

Angela winced. What he was saying was that she hadn't been nice. It was true that she'd been popular but she hadn't been cliquey or exclusive. Had she? The mean girl trope was a high school thing, not a grade school thing, right? They'd only gone to school together through fifth grade. How popular was any fifth grader? Could a fifth grader even be too cool?

"Except, I do remember that story you used to tell, about your brother."

She didn't remember telling Randy stories about Ryan. She didn't remember talking to him at all. Maybe she really had been a mean girl if she couldn't even remember ever speaking to Randy, while he recalled stories she'd told him.

"So you still live around here? Are you in school?" Angela asked, hoping to change the subject.

"Yeah, still here. Actually I'm a computer programmer. I maintain websites for local businesses and I'm starting to develop apps." He crossed his arms and said this as if he was now too cool.

Angela nodded. That explained the club's slick website.

"So what brought you in tonight?" he asked.

"What does a site investigation involve?" Angela asked.

They sat in a couple of the cold, metal folding chairs, and Randy explained the logistics of a site investigation. The team usually arrived on site around eight to get familiar with the place. Then they secured the area—which was why they hated outdoor sites like the Lawton Railroad Bridge, so hard to secure—and set up their equipment. Members of the club each brought their own equipment, whatever they had. Generally they coordinated in advance to avoid redundancy and make sure they covered all the basics: infrared cameras, night vision goggles, microphones. They set up a command center in an area of the site where little or no paranormal activity had been detected in the past and shut off lights everywhere else. They used video chat from team members' cell phones to laptops in command center to track the investigation, which lasted until dawn.

He told her all of this in a disinterested way, as if he thought her question was insincere or he was bored with talking to her. What in the world had she ever done to him? she wondered. He had been all welcoming smiles as host of the meeting, and now he was acting like he'd rather be anywhere else. Still, she'd worked up the nerve to come here, so he pushed on. She asked, "How many people to a team?"

"Depends on a lot of factors," Randy explained, "the size of the site, the availability of club members, the preferences of the site's owner."

Angela considered all of this, and then asked, "So y'all's equipment, it would detect stuff that can't normally be seen? Like if a ghost had only ever been seen by one person, even if other people were in the house at the time, you could maybe confirm that the ghost was there?" Her palms were sweaty and her voice shook. She couldn't look him in the eye. She felt so silly saying all of this aloud.

"That's the idea," he said.

"Do you ever communicate with the ghosts, or do you just detect them?" she asked, swallowing the lump that had risen in her throat. She felt color flood her face and tried to will herself not to cry.

"Sometimes. Sometimes it's like they want to talk," he said. "Sometimes we bring a medium along, or come back with one later, if we think the ghost is trying to communicate."

Angela sniffled, nodded, and then sighed. "My mother died a few weeks ago," she said.

"God, that's terrible. I'm sorry," he said, sounding sincere for the first time since she'd introduced herself.

"Everyone thinks I'm nuts, but I know her spirit or whatever is still in the house, and I really need to talk to her." She dropped her elbows to her knees and put her face in her hands.

Randy reached over and put a hand on her shoulder. "Hey, it's okay," he said, and his kindness tipped her over into a fresh wave of sobs. But soon her crying subsided—in the past few weeks she had learned that even when it seems like you might cry forever, the tears do run out eventually—and as her breathing steadied, she felt flooded with embarrassment for this outburst in front of a total stranger.

"I'm so sorry—"

But he cut her off. "Don't apologize. Of course you're upset. Let me give you my number and if you decide you want an investigation—"

"I do," she said firmly. "As soon as possible."

Chapter Thirteen

Devil's Back Island, Maine

CASEY STOOD BY the register of the empty Beach Plum Café, leaning over the well-worn paper of her mother's letter and rubbing her forehead as if to massage away a headache. She had read it enough times that she could do so now without fear of crying. She'd moved past that stage of grief. She was on to anger now. She read it again and caught herself grinding her teeth as she did. She contemplated crumbling the damn thing up and throwing it away, got as far as picking it up off the counter, and thought better of it.

When she heard the sound of the noon ferry's horn bellow through the fog as it approached the pier, she carefully refolded the paper and tucked it into the back pocket of her jeans, shaking her head as if to clear her thoughts. Nothing would be better than a distraction in the form of a few customers. She wondered how many passengers had decided to brave the wet weather that day. September was always slow on Devil's Back—the final, childless tourists enjoying the last warm days of the season before leaving the island until next summer—but the past week, with all the rain, cold, and fog, had been as bleak as November.

"Things'll pick when the foliage starts," Rosetta kept saying, but Casey had her doubts.

Like the entire Maine seacoast, Devil's Back depended on June, July, and August for the income that would carry islanders through the rest of the year. Although Casey kept the café open throughout the winter, it was the visitors of the summer season whose purchases paid her bills. She considered staying open in winter a community service to the year-rounders, since almost everything on the island closed from November through April.

Casey stepped out from behind the counter and walked to the windows to peer out toward the harbor. The fog was thick, turning the other buildings and the boats beyond into ghostly apparitions. She didn't see anyone coming up the lane. No surprise there. Just as she was about to go back to her post behind the counter, though, a flicker of movement caught her eye, and she was startled as a man emerged from the fog to stand on the porch of the café. She had been looking off into the distance, expecting the usual late-season tourists—retirees with slow gaits—and so had not seen this man nearing her own doorstep.

She hurried away from the window and was halfway to the counter when the bells on the door jingled at his entrance.

"Hell of a morning," he said cheerfully, as the door slammed shut behind him.

"Nothing compared to yesterday," Casey said, rounding the counter. "Poured buckets."

"Don't think less of me if I admit that I was supposed

to arrive yesterday, but I couldn't bring myself to board that ferry." He smiled and came to the counter to study the freshly chalked menu on the wall behind her.

He was maybe a few years older than she, Casey guessed, with light brown hair and the tanned complexion of a tennis player or sailor. He wore neatly pressed khakis, a blue and white checkered button-down with the sleeves rolled up to his elbows, and boat shoes. And he had arrived all alone. He was in no way a typical Devil's Back tourist, late season or any other season, and very good-looking.

Most summer visitors to the island were either elderly couples who came to fish, sunbathe, and sit around, or families with young children who came for the peace of mind they could only find in a place with no cars, no athletic events, no shopping malls—essentially a place free from modern life. Single middle-aged men were practically unheard of. Casey glanced at his left hand. Bare.

He wasn't her usual type, which was grungier—artistic she liked to think of it—but he was certainly easy on the eyes. She felt a twinge of guilt as she thought about Jason, who was probably still asleep upstairs. But she and Jason weren't even dating. They were enjoying a convenient arrangement.

"So is the coffee any good here?" he asked after a minute.

"I should hope so," Casey said. Did he really expect someone working in a café to admit she made bad coffee? Her high hopes for him dipped a little.

"Sorry, it's just, so many of these out of the way places I visit, it's like, I find myself wishing there was a good old reliable Starbucks." He flashed a winning smile. "To be honest, when Rosetta said there was an actual café here, I was surprised."

So he knows Rosetta, Casey thought. She wondered what the connection was. Knowing Rosetta was a definite black mark against him as a potential romantic interest. "Well, if Starbucks is your idea of good coffee, you've got another thing coming," she said. "How about a latte? And if you don't like it, it's on me."

"I don't suppose you've got soy milk?" He gave a shrug and an apologetic look.

Casey nearly groaned aloud. He was good-looking, yes, but his flaws were rapidly becoming apparent. Any romantic notions were swiftly evaporating from her mind. Well, she wasn't thinking about romance, she was thinking about sex, but either way, this guy wasn't the one for her. Soy milk lattes—could anything be less appetizing? Of course, she did have soy milk and almond milk and oat milk to cover all the various allergy possibilities, because she needed happy customers. She opened the fridge beneath the counter, produced a carton of soy milk, set about making the espresso.

"So what's the word around here? Anything exciting going on?" he asked, when she placed the coffee before him.

"Couple of weeks it'll be perfect leaf-peeping season," she said, suspecting he was not interested in foliage.

He took a sip of the drink, savoring it and looking contemplatively at the ceiling for a moment before meeting her eye again. "Excellent coffee. What do I owe you?"

Casey punched in the latte on the register, $2.45 for the latte and an extra $0.50 for the soy milk, a price so low the café didn't make a penny on it, but as high as she felt she could charge for a cup of coffee in good conscience. The café's income came from selling the homemade goodies in the glass cases next to the counter.

"Something to go with your coffee?" she asked, gesturing to the displays. They were a little thin that day, because she knew how slow it would be. She couldn't go filling her cases when no one was buying. Still, she had whipped up a batch of her best blueberry crumb muffins and oatmeal scones that morning, along with a couple of kinds of cookies.

He patted his flat stomach and shook his head sadly. "No sweets for me."

Casey bit her lip and willed herself not to roll her eyes. She told him what he owed her for the coffee. He put a few crisp dollar bills on the counter and told her to keep the change, but he didn't walk away. He stood there, sipping his coffee, and taking in the little café.

"How long have you worked here?" he asked.

"This is my café. I don't work here. I..." Casey considered how she might finish that sentence. She couldn't truly say, "I own this place," because actually Rosetta owned it. Still, it was her place.

"No offense," Brett said.

Now he was looking at her tattoo, and Casey drew herself up, squaring her shoulders and setting her jaw. She didn't need this presumptuous, annoying, soy-latte drinker judging her.

"Really, sorry, I didn't mean to offend. I didn't know. You're not, I mean, you don't look like—"

"Like a business owner?" Casey said, cutting him off. What exactly was his problem? He had known her for all of two minutes and had already written her off? She was wearing worn jeans and a tank top, and she had a massive tattoo, and she wore a faded bandana tied around her hair, an outfit entirely suited to baking and serving up coffee. If she had on a floppy white hat and those ugly clogs everyone wore in restaurant kitchens, would he give her a little more credit?

He shrugged apologetically.

"If you don't need anything else," Casey said, nodding toward the door.

He looked around at the empty tables and then back at Casey and raised an eyebrow. "Would it bother you terribly if I sat down? Maybe took care of a few emails?"

Casey pointed at a sign over her shoulder that said "No Wi-Fi. No Cell Phones" and then she crossed her arms.

"You're kidding me. People love to work in cafés."

"This is a place of relaxation and conversation, not a place for everyone to hunker down behind computer screens."

"I guess I've worn out my welcome for conversation," he said.

Casey sighed and turned away from him, moving things around behind the counter importantly, as if there was any reason to do so.

"I'm going to be around for a few days here, so I'll probably see you again tomorrow for another of these excellent lattes."

Great, Casey thought, her back to him.

"I'm Brett, by the way, Brett Campbell," he said. "And your name is?"

Casey turned back to face him. "Casey," she said.

"Casey. Nice to meet you. Do you have a last name or are you like Madonna, first name only?"

"Are you investigating me?" Casey asked, still annoyed by him but also amused by his persistence.

"Maybe."

"Good luck with that. My last name is Jones."

He nodded, thought about it, and said, "Wait, Casey Jones, like the song?"

"You got it," she said, with a smile. Another great bonus of her chosen name was that people who wanted to look her up online were never going to find anything remotely useful.

"All right, well then, Casey Jones, you have a good day," Brett said, nodding and raising his paper coffee cup in her direction.

He left and Casey came around the end of the counter and sat at a table near the window. The fog was still heavy, and he disappeared as soon as he was off the porch steps. Have a good day. Not likely, she thought.

Chapter Fourteen

St. Nabor Island, South Carolina

ANGELA AND RANDY arrived at the house a little before seven. Angela's heart fluttered as she pulled into the garage and shut off the car. She felt both giddy and idiotic, as if she were drunk but completely self-aware. Was this whole thing totally ridiculous? What if Randy and his friends didn't find anything and she was wasting their time? Or, and maybe worse, what if they did find something?

"You okay?" Randy asked.

Angela took a deep breath, nodded, and unlatched her seat belt. Whatever the consequences, it was too late to back out now. Randy followed her into the house and walked from room to room turning on lights.

In the hallway at the top of the stairs, Angela felt nervous sweat on her palms. This was the place where she'd heard her mother's insistent voice so clearly each night between the day after the funeral and the day she'd left to stay at Grace's. Why here? She wondered. Why here and not in her mother's room or study or the kitchen or the garden? Angela sighed and moved along, flicking on lights in every room. The lights made her feel better.

"Wow, that is some desk," Randy said, as they entered the study.

"I'll give you twenty bucks if you can open it."

"What do you mean?" Randy crossed the room and ran his hand along the roll-top.

"It's stuck or locked or something. I can't get any of the drawers open."

Randy slid the top up and bent forward to study the small upper drawers.

"Success!" he said, triumphantly after a few minutes. He turned to Angela holding out a small key.

Angela looked at it dumbly. She could not believe the key had been there all along. How had she missed it? And when did her mother start locking the desk, anyway? It had always been off-limits to Angela, but she had distinct memories of opening and shutting all the drawers, playing at the desk and pretending she was a bank teller. Why she had thought playing bank teller was fun was anyone's guess. Those little drawers had been irresistible. She always thought they must hold some wonderful secrets—love letters, keepsakes, maybe money. She had been bold enough to open the drawers, but not so bold as to riffle through them. All she'd ever seen were documents and boxes of checks and things like that. She'd never moved any of the contents, never so much as picked up a box of checks to see if there was something more interesting beneath. Her mother was so particular that she would undoubtedly have known if Angela so much as slid a piece of paper out of a drawer.

Sitting at the desk, she considered the idea that her

mother had become paranoid about identity theft. She was always sending Angela newspaper clippings about the importance of cyber-security and monitoring one's credit reports. Maybe she wanted to make sure that if anyone broke into the house, they wouldn't have access to any important documents.

"It was taped under the inside of the center drawer," Randy explained.

Angela took the key and turned it over in her hand. She'd never seen it before. "It works?" she asked.

Randy moved aside and let Angela try the key in the lock. It didn't fit. She turned it around and tried again. No luck. It wasn't the right key.

Angela dropped the key onto the blotter and pushed her chair back in frustration. She was no closer to opening the desk, and now she had another mystery: What did the key unlock?

"Damn." Randy crossed the room and picked up they key again, examining it closely. "I guess this could be for a PO box or a safe deposit box," he said.

Her mother got mail at the house and she didn't think there was a safe deposit box, but she wasn't totally certain. If she could get into the bank statements in the desk, she could find out. She reached out her hand and Randy put the key in it. Angela unhooked the clasp of her necklace, threaded the key onto the chain, and closed it again. She knew she was being paranoid, but her mother had hidden that key, and if she didn't keep it on her body, she was convinced it would go missing again.

They went back to the kitchen, and they stood awkwardly at the island. To quell her nerves, Angela fussed in the kitchen, making a pot of coffee, and digging through the cabinets for snacks, suddenly the hostess of a paranormal party.

Randy asked her questions about the house, mostly about the extent to which her mother had used certain rooms, so he could determine where to set up command center. Angela answered his questions distractedly. She couldn't shake the feeling that something wasn't right. Even if her mother was worried about identity theft, why had she hidden the key? Or, at least, why hide it in such a hard to find place? She could have stashed it in any of a dozen equally unlikely places that would have been easier for her to access but no easier for a thief to find. Maybe her mother had been losing it a little. Maybe, like her husband, she'd been developing Alzheimer's and becoming delusional. But she hadn't seemed delusional all summer. She'd seemed fine.

Angela was pulled from her thoughts by the doorbell— more team members arriving. By 8:30, they were all assembled. Rick, probably in his mid-forties, wore a Grateful Dead t-shirt with a dancing bear in the middle of a swirl of faded tie-dye, his gray hair pulled into a long ponytail. When he spoke, he had a soothing, sonorous voice. Bill was younger, a hipster nerd who, Randy explained, was a fellow computer programmer. He would monitor everything from command center.

Krissy and Jen appeared to be on better terms today than they had at the meeting. Jen's hair was dyed blue now instead of purple, and up close Angela could see that she had a small stud in her nose and a thin hoop through one eyebrow. Krissy, despite her silver hair, had a smooth, young-looking face, and wore a velvety moon-and-stars scarf and a long, flowing, old-fashioned dress. Angela wondered if she always dressed like that or if she'd gotten dolled up for the occasion.

Angela led the group around the first floor, pointing out places her mother had most often used, but noting that nothing strange had ever happened to her down there. Then they paraded upstairs, and with a shaking voice, Angela described what she'd heard and felt in the hallway, her face burning red with embarrassment to speak of the improbable sensations.

She should have listened to Molly and Nicole, she thought, as she heard the ridiculous tale spilling from her mouth. She was clearly being driven mad by grief. But no one laughed at her. No one raised a skeptical eyebrow.

When she had finished, they went into her mother's study where the hulking desk sat, and Angela felt the hairs on the back of her neck rise. She didn't know what it was, but something was not right.

She said, "There's something up with the desk, too. I don't know. I just get a feeling."

Randy told her they would pay special attention to it and they went to see the bedrooms. When the tour was over, the team conferred and settled on the dining room as command center. Angela watched the flurry of activity as laptops were arranged, and microphones, cameras, and other mysterious devices were produced from bags and taken to various locations around the house. Angela couldn't begin to imagine what it all was for. Either the strange thing that had happened to her before would happen again and they would all witness it, or it wouldn't. She was watching in a daze, half-seeing, when Randy said, "Y'all have a garage, right?"

Angela looked at him, confused, so lost in her thoughts that she didn't seem to understand the question. He asked again.

"That's where she died," Angela said after a moment. Right there. Alone. On the cold concrete floor. She had been on her way to her car, her purse over her shoulder, going to visit her husband in the nursing home. She'd been at the top of the four steps down to the garage when she had fallen. She had had a massive stroke. What symptoms she may have been having before she fell Angela would never know, only that her mother hadn't understood them, had ignored them, had told herself she was fine, and had gone on with her routine, only to collapse mid-stride. But it probably wasn't the stroke that killed her. It was more likely the fall. Or it was a combination. If she'd been able to reach her phone, she could have called for help, but when her head hit the concrete, it knocked her out cold.

The dining room fell silent. Angela saw Jen and Krissy exchange glances, and she knew exactly what they were thinking. There was no point in investigating this house without including the garage. After all, there was no basement or attic, those usual hideouts for ghosts. But the site of death, that was something.

"Jen, can you set up the infrared camera in the hallway upstairs?" Randy asked, breaking the silence. Then he took Angela by the arm and gently led her from the room. He sat her down on the couch in the den and knelt in front of her.

"You never said she died here."

Angela nodded.

"Look, that's pretty important. I really think we should monitor the garage."

"Nothing's ever happened out there. It's all been upstairs."

"I know that's how it seems, but it could really help us."

"I just—" Angela didn't know how to put into words how she felt. This had all been her idea. She wanted to know what was going on. And yet, looking around for her mother's ghost on the spot where she died felt so intrusive.

"What if we set up a camera and a microphone in there and let it record and the team looks at it later. We won't have them up as live feeds so you won't have to see them."

This was a mistake, Angela thought. Tampering with her mother's spirit. It was so childish and wrong, like playing with a Ouija board. "I feel like we're bothering her or dishonoring her," she said.

"Whatever has been happening in this house, someone or something is trying to communicate with you. You aren't bothering them. They want you to listen," Randy said.

"No, they want me to go away and leave it all alone. The voice, it always said, 'Go back to sleep, Angela.' It doesn't want to talk to me. It wants me gone."

"It's disturbing you, not the other way around. Let's find out why."

Chapter Fifteen

Devil's Back Island, Maine

BRETT PICKED HIS WAY along the gravel path back to the inn, wondering as he went what sort of place this island really was. Rosetta, for all her eagerness on the phone, had had no time for him when he arrived, and now he'd practically been ejected from the only café this side of a boat ride back to Portland. He couldn't scope out the island in this fog—he'd probably fall off a cliff or something—and he could not handle the idea of being stuck in his hotel room all day.

He had meetings the next day with an engineer to work on the environmental impact of development and to determine the carrying capacity of the resort for his prefeasibility analysis report, and he also had meetings in the works with three design-build construction companies, each eager to make a pitch for the project. Eager until they set foot on the island, he thought. The challenges of getting equipment and materials here were obvious and overwhelming, something he hadn't fully understood when researching from afar. He could already see all the objections Charlie was going to have to this location. Everything about his trip had thus far proven inauspicious. Maybe he should leave, tell Charlie the lead hadn't panned out, and ask to be put back on the Cancun team. He could tell Ashley he'd come to his senses and they could work things out.

Reluctantly he went back up to his room, what Rosetta had called a "kitchenette suite," a description that was generous at best. It was a hotel room with a microfridge, a two-burner range, and a two-seat table in the corner. Supposedly it had water views, but he wouldn't be able to verify that until the weather changed.

Unsure what else to do—until he got more input from the engineers, his work was done—he flopped down onto the bed, flicking on the TV. The island didn't have cable, but Rosetta had had satellite installed for the hotel, a smart move, surely, in a place with so few entertainment options. Brett thought he'd lose his mind if he couldn't at least watch some TV. He turned to the History Channel and zoned out for a while. Eventually his restlessness got the best of him, though, and he picked up his laptop and typed Beach Plum Café, Devil's Back Island into his search browser.

He had learned as much about Devil's Back from the Internet as he could to prepare his pitch for Charlie. There hadn't been much. It was named for the humped shape of the island and a rock formation at one end that looked like horns. It had once been a refuge of Quakers fleeing persecution in Massachusetts. Historically its inhabitants were fishermen and lobstermen. On a tourism bureau site, he learned that there were currently two restaurants (a fine dining establishment and a lobster shack that also served pizza), a café/coffee bar, an ice cream stand, a local crafts gallery, and one hotel. Visitors could take scenic boat rides ranging from dolphin cruises and whale watches to sunset spinnaker tours. Kayaks and stand-up paddle boards were available for rental.

There was also a story about the island's "famous ghosts," which he found particularly amusing. The page boasted that Devil's Back was "America's Most Haunted Island." Apparently its author was unaware that Alcatraz was an island. The island's supposed ghosts were clearly an attempt to lure ghost hunters to the island for visits, and the stories seemed ludicrous at best. The wailing woman at Lover's Leap, where the widow of a lobsterman threw herself from a cliff when she learned his boat had been destroyed in a storm. The salty old sea captain whose ghost roamed the second floor of the White Sails Tavern, the oldest surviving building on the island and former home of said sea captain, who lost his wife and children to a flu epidemic while he was out chasing whales. The invisible walker at Rum Runner's Cove, presumed to be the ghost of a prohibition-era booze smuggler who was shot there when a rival gang intercepted his shipment. They were the most overplayed, stereotypical ghosts Brett had ever heard of. He sincerely doubted this information had made ghost enthusiasts do anything but laugh.

He couldn't recall seeing a website for the café when he was doing his research, and as the search results popped up, he saw why. It didn't have a website. Aside from the listing on the Tourism Bureau website, the other results were Yelp reviews and Facebook "check-ins." It didn't even have an official Facebook page. The reviews were all glowing. If Casey leveraged them, she could build a much more robust business. He skimmed through the results for a few minutes, but it wasn't the café he was interested in. It was Casey. He'd been curious the minute he saw her, but when she gave such an obviously bogus name, his interest was fully piqued. He'd hoped searching for the café would lead him to information on her, since the name Casey Jones was clearly a red herring.

He was not used to women reacting so negatively to him. He didn't like to think he relied too much on his good looks and manners to get his way in life, but he also knew that it didn't hurt, and generally when he turned on the charm, it worked. People liked him. Women especially liked him. They opened up to him. In fact, sometimes they mistook his pleasantries for invitations of intimacy he did not intend, which caused awkward problems later on. But they didn't roll their eyes at him. They did not encourage him to go away. The truth was he could not stand for people not to like him. What was there to dislike? He was good-looking, intelligent, polite, and easy-going. He didn't pass judgments. He didn't preach his views or talk politics. He was likable. And he wanted Casey to see that.

How angrily she'd reacted when he'd assumed she merely worked at the café. You'd think someone that proud would boast of her business, and herself, online, but not Casey. He also knew that whatever title Casey claimed over the café, Rosetta owned it. Whatever Casey's deal was, he would uncover it. He enjoyed puzzles. He would solve the riddle that was Casey Jones and win her over. She had clearly issued a challenge that morning, and he couldn't resist a challenge. And if flirting with Casey took his mind off of Ashley, that would be okay, too.

When he shut the lid of his laptop and glanced out the

window, he saw that the fog was finally breaking up and something like a thin, pathetic ray of sun was trying to make its way through. Thank God. He'd take a walk and then try to corner Rosetta so they could talk money. That's what this would all boil down to. If Sweet Water could buy the property cheap enough to offset the difficulties (and accompanying costs) of building here, the deal might have a chance, but that seemed like a big *if* to Brett.

Chapter Sixteen

St. Nabor Island, South Carolina

THE TRUTH ABOUT investigations of paranormal activity is that a lot of the time they are boring. You set up all your stuff, lock yourself in, and wait, and as often as not nothing happens. Nothing but you and your team scaring yourself and each other every time someone hears a noise. But those long boring hours are worth it when you stumble onto something inexplicable.

Randy went into every investigation cautiously optimistic; he knew better than to get his hopes up too high. This investigation was different though. This was the home of Angela Ellis, the girl with the ghost brother.

He hated to think about elementary school. Kids were so mean. He'd never fit in, not from day one. Pretty girls with brand-name clothes—girls like Angela—were the worst. They could pin you down with a look, even as nine- and ten-year-olds. Randy had hated them; everyone who wasn't one of them hated them. And yet, he'd wanted their approval. Everyone did. It was human nature, a grand paradox that governed people's lives from youth through old age.

He hadn't heard Angela's ghost story from her. He'd heard it from a friend he ate lunch with most days, who recounted a story Angela had told on the bus about her ghost brother watching out for her. The conclusion of this retelling was an assertion that Angela was stupid because only babies believed in ghosts. At the time Randy had probably nodded, solidarity of nerds against cool girls, but actually he was intrigued. He believed in ghosts. If Angela also believed in ghosts, they had something in common. Maybe he could talk to her about it. Maybe she'd realize they weren't so different and she'd open the door to a kinder, gentler middle school by bestowing friendship on him.

Except of course she hadn't. He'd tried to talk to her and she'd made fun of him the minute he opened his mouth. He never even got to talk to her about her brother's ghost. Actually, when he thought about it now, maybe it wasn't Angela who made fun of him. Maybe it was one of her mean friends who shut him down before he'd even begun. But either way, Angela hadn't wanted to talk to him, clearly.

And now here she was, asking for his help. The pretty little girl who had grown into a beautiful woman. When she had told him about her mother, when she'd cried right there in the bookstore, he had softened toward her. How could he not? Who could be unmoved at the sight of a beautiful woman in tears? If he was being totally honest, he had wanted nothing less than to take her in his arms, pick her up, and take her back to his place where he could hold her all night long. Still being totally honest, he wasn't sure how much of that was a desire to comfort her and how much was a desire to have proof that he was now, officially, cool enough to get a girl like Angela Ellis. He didn't like that feeling. He preferred to think himself above all that pettiness.

Now, kneeling in front of her in her living room, he felt it again, the desire to be alone with her, to comfort her, to take away all her grief—and then the guilt returned.

She agreed to let him record the garage and they both stood up and went back to the dining room. He led her to a chair at the far end of the table from the computer equipment while he gave instructions for the final set up.

According to the case studies Randy had read over the years, ghost activity was most likely around the hours of noon and midnight, and around the moments of seasonal shift—summer and winter solstice, spring and fall equinoxes. It was only a few days past the equinox, and tonight was a new moon, a pitch black sky. People always thought the full moon was spooky, and there was some truth to the idea that people's inhibitions are lower during the full moon, but spirits were not called forth by the moon. Spirits, it seemed, preferred the darkest nights.

The team had decided that Angela should go up to her room around 11:45. She was to go in and shut the door and turn off the lights, as if she was going to sleep, since all the activity so far had been after she had gone to bed. A camera had been set up in the room and Bill would monitor it from command center, and she had a walkie-talkie to communicate with him.

Jen and Randy would investigate the rest of the second floor, spending time in each room and performing various tests to search for unexplained magnetic fields, air currents, or other energies. Krissy and Rick would investigate the first floor in basically the same way.

He and Jen crept upstairs at 12:30 as planned. First they went to the guest room, where as expected, they found nothing at all unusual. Next, the bathroom, also not a room where anything was anticipated.

At 1:30, they moved on to Angela's mother's suite. They went to the far side of the room from the door and began. First Jen took out her audio-reducer, a handheld box that to the uninitiated might seem like a white noise machine, but which was actually a hypersensitive filter of sound waves that could detect things beyond the capabilities of the human ear and compress them into audible noise. Sometimes, with situations like the one Angela had described, the audio-reducer could pick up and translate the sound from the spirit-world, and with careful listening, one could make out what it wished to communicate.

While Angela reported hearing her mother's voice loud and clear, she had also told Randy that her other friends hadn't heard a thing, but he was hoping the audio-reducer would help him to verify her experience. And if he couldn't verify it? The wounded little boy inside him said that would be okay, too—he was the one with the upper hand here. He could put her in her place. And feelings like that were exactly why he often thought about moving far away from Palmetto Landing. He could move and never run into anyone from his youth and never have to feel those nasty, resentful, vengeful thoughts again. He was above all that, he really was, but sometimes, when face to face with someone like Angela, the old feelings crept in again.

Randy and Jen sat in silence with their backs to the wall, waiting. The audio-reducer gave off its usual, all-normal, static sound. It was just before two when Angela came over the walkie talkie. She had heard footsteps in the hall coming toward her mother's bedroom. Randy and Jen exchanged glances. This was it. Randy put on his infrared goggles and trained his eyes on the bedroom door, which was partially ajar.

"Angela," Randy whispered into the walkie-talkie, "can you go out into the hall?" She had said she only heard the actual voice when she left her room.

"Alone?" Angela asked.

"We're right here. We'll come out the minute you call for us." He hoped she could handle sitting with it for long enough. He wanted to get the voice talking and capture evidence of it, but Angela had said that when her roommate came into the hallway, the voice had stopped.

"Turn that off," Randy said to Jen, nodding toward the audio-reducer.

"But—"

"If the voice starts up, you can get closer to the door and turn it on, but I think the quieter we are the better."

She shut it off.

They heard Angela's bedroom door open.

"We should have left the door open," Randy said. If they had, he'd have a clear view into the hallway where Angela now was, and with his infrared goggles he'd be able to detect anything else out there with her.

"She said she always keeps this door shut," Jen said, defensively. This was true, and they had felt it was important to try to replicate Angela's past experiences as closely as possible.

They heard Angela sob out loud. There was nothing fake about Angela's distress. He could hear that. Whatever she was experiencing, it was real. Randy felt bad for ever doubting her, for ever imagining joy in telling her they hadn't detected anything. She cried out again and Randy leapt to his feet, but Jen caught hold of his hand.

"Wait. She didn't call for us."

Randy looked down at her, and then inclined his ear toward the hallway. He could hear her, out there, whimpering. Jen was right. She hadn't called for them. If they wanted evidence, they needed to see how this would play out.

He tiptoed to the edge of the bed, hoping his view into the hallway would be better, but he still couldn't see Angela. Behind him, Jen got up and, keeping to the wall, crept to the doorway. She set the audio-reducer down on the floor inside the bedroom threshold and switched it on. The static sound competed too loudly with Angela's cries, and Randy gritted his teeth. He didn't like this.

He had never had the slightest hesitation about having someone act as ghost-bait in any other investigations, but it had never been personal before. Usually the suspected ghost and the investigating team were strangers to one another, and the ghosts, however malevolent they might seem to the property owners, were only objects of research to the team, but this was something else.

Angela's voice rose above the noise of the machine. "Go away! Go away!" she shouted, and Randy had had enough. He dropped his infrared goggles on the bed, crossed the room, flung the door open, and went to Angela who was crouched on the floor of the hallway with her hands pressed against her ears. She didn't look up at his approach. In fact, she didn't appear to even notice that he was there. He knelt down and touched her knees. She jumped like she'd been shocked, and then registering that it was him in front of her, she collapsed into him, letting him wrap his arms around her.

He rocked her gently as her breathing returned to normal. He could hear Jen whispering into the walkie-talkie back in Angela's mother's room.

After a minute, Jen brushed by them and stomped down the stairs.

"Y'all didn't hear anything," Angela said softly.

Randy shook his head.

"But it was so loud," Angela said, her voice rising with panic. "It was the loudest it's ever been, and angry."

"What did it say?" Randy asked.

"It said I needed to go back to bed, like always," Angela said. "You believe me, right? You don't think I'm imagining this?" Her lip trembled.

"Of course I believe you," he said, taking her hand and squeezing it gently. "Did it say anything else?"

"It said I was a bad, ungrateful girl. Just once, it said that, right before you came out here. Mostly it was the same as always, repeating over and over that I should go to sleep."

Downstairs, Rick and Krissy hadn't found anything on the first floor. Jen grumbled that she never had a chance upstairs because Randy had intervened before she could pick up anything with the audio-reducer. Bill hadn't seen anything on the cameras, although his attention was divided, and he said he wanted to check some of the footage more closely later. That was it. Nothing. They had nothing. Nothing except Angela's experience that none of them could corroborate.

Randy gave instructions to move some of the monitoring

equipment around and then he sat down beside Bill at the computer. He glanced over at Angela and when he was certain she wasn't watching, he clicked open the live stream from the garage. It was just a garage, with the usual garage stuff in it—trash cans, bikes, Angela's car. Nothing was moving. No strange sights. He closed the window.

The last few hours until sunrise dragged on with no more activity, and then it was six o'clock and they were quickly packing up cameras and microphones and lugging them back out to cars and then it was only Randy and Angela, sitting in the kitchen with fresh cups of coffee, bleary-eyed and exhausted.

"What does it mean?" Angela asked.

"It means that we all witnessed you encountering what you believe is your mother's spirit," Randy said. He wanted to watch the footage from the hallway at the time of the encounter. Until he could see that, he didn't feel that he could make any judgment on the night. Bill said he hadn't seen anything strange, but in the heat of the moment, it's hard to analyze what you're seeing. He would go home, get a few hours' sleep, and then look at it again. There would be something there. He didn't doubt she'd experienced something real and profound. Seeing her in the hallway was all the proof he needed, but he knew she needed more, and he wanted to be able to provide it for her.

"You don't think I'm crazy?" Angela asked.

"Nobody thinks you're crazy," Randy said.

"Jen didn't believe me."

"Jen is difficult." Jen was in many ways a mystery to him. She was one of the most devoted members of the club, but not because she was convinced that a spirit world existed.

Rather, she wanted proof. She needed to see to believe. So far, on all the investigations they'd done, even when everyone else felt they had confirmed the presence of paranormal activity, Jen expressed doubts.

"What am I going to do now?"

"You're going to get some sleep, and then we'll talk more later," Randy said. He would review all the material this afternoon and tell her what he found. He would have some good news for her. He was sure of it.

Chapter Seventeen

Devil's Back Island, Maine

CASEY CLOSED THE CAFÉ at four. The fog had cleared and the sky was a brighter sort of gray, so she went outside for a walk down on the beach instead of going straight upstairs. The problem with working and living in one building was that whole days could pass where she never went outside, which was exactly how the past week had been. Now that the weather was letting up, it was time for fresh air.

But when she stepped off the path onto the coarse sand of the beach by the inn, she saw Brett making his way along the water—thankfully walking away from her—and she turned back. She'd had enough of him for one day.

As she trudged back up the slope from the beach, she saw the light of the TV flickering through the window of her apartment and muttered a curse under her breath. She never should have given Jason a key. Stupid, stupid, stupid. She wanted a long hot bath, a crappy romance novel, and a relaxing evening alone.

She climbed the stairs at the back of the cottage—the

outside entrance to her little apartment—and found the door to the kitchen slightly ajar.

"Jason!" she called, kicking off her shoes and latching the door firmly behind her. "You have to make sure the door actually shuts! Last week after you left, I found a stray cat on my kitchen counter! What if it was a raccoon?" She walked into the TV room and saw him lounging on the futon, remote in his hand, a line of beer cans on the coffee table, and a box with a few slices of greasy pizza on the floor.

"Are there even raccoons on this island?" he asked, turning from the TV to look at her.

She had absolutely no idea. "And anyway, the bugs. I do not need a house full of moths and mosquitoes and whatever else."

"It's not me. The door doesn't catch right."

She wondered if he had ever learned the words "I'm sorry."

He sat up to make room for her on the futon and turned down the volume on the TV. He was watching a baseball game.

He pulled a little baggie from the pocket of his jeans. "If you came home much later, you would have missed out on this. It was really burning a hole in my pocket."

Casey watched him clear a space on the coffee table and dump out the pot. Then he produced a rolling paper and expertly rolled a nice, fat joint.

"I shouldn't," Casey said, sitting back and closing her eyes. Before she started seeing Jason, or sleeping with Jason to be more exact, she hadn't smoked pot in the all the years she'd been on the island. But Jason was basically an overgrown kid, so it didn't surprise her the first time he offered her a puff. The problem was that afterward she always felt foggy-headed and cranky. Pot smoking was for underemployed kids like Jason, not for responsible adults with early-morning jobs.

"Come on," Jason said, nudging her. She opened her eyes to see him waving the joint under her nose. Then he lowered his voice. "Think of how good it was last time."

Casey felt a hot blush rise in her cheeks. Yes, last time it had been very very good. He'd gotten her thoroughly stoned and then they had done things in bed that were astonishing. The thought turned her on so much that she had to stand up and move away from him or she knew she'd cave. She sat down in the armchair in the corner and studied him. That chiseled jaw, those bright blue eyes, that washboard stomach and sculpted shoulders. She felt her resistance flagging.

"Well, suit yourself," he said, lighting the joint and taking a long drag.

Casey glanced over her shoulder out the window to the deserted lane below. Who would care if she smoked a little pot? Who, beside Jason, would even know? It wouldn't hurt anyone, and the last time she probably felt cranky after because she was getting her period. She sighed.

"All right," she said, moving back to the couch.

"'Atta girl," he said, handing it to her.

She took a drag, held it as long as she could, exhaled, coughing like a tuberculosis patient, and then burst into a fit of giggles like a fifteen-year-old girl. Well, not like the girl she had been at fifteen, but the way she thought a fifteen-year-old ought to act. She wondered where she'd be now if she'd had a normal childhood. She doubted she'd have her own café, and she liked having a café, so she had that to be thankful for. Living here on Devil's Back, the café, those things were definitely good. This situation with Jason. This was not so good.

She twisted sideways on the futon and put her legs across Jason's lap. She leaned back against the armrest and had the distinct impression that her head was floating over her shoulders like a balloon. After how tense she'd been all day, it was a wonderful sensation. She closed her eyes and let herself sink down into the futon mattress. She felt Jason pick up her legs and set them back on the futon, and she opened one eye to see him pulling his t-shirt over his head. One look at his firm, youthful body, and she was ready and willing for almost anything. She smiled, closed her eyes, and folded her arms behind her head, as if to say, "I'm yours. Have your way with me."

The futon creaked as he slid one knee in between her legs and the back of the mattress. She felt his hands opening her jeans, and lifted her hips to help him pull them off. His touch on her hips and thighs was electric. He put his lips on her navel and inched her tank top up with his hands as he kissed her stomach, her ribs, the lacy edge of her bra. She leaned forward and tugged her shirt over her head, dropping it on the floor. To his delight, she was wearing a bra that opened in the front. He didn't waste much time with the preliminaries, which was fine by Casey. She liked the salty taste of his sweat as she kissed his neck.

It was late when Casey finally managed to extricate herself from Jason's grasp and get in the shower. Her limbs felt heavy and loose. She was pretty sure she'd pulled some muscles in her groin and her lower back, and as enjoyable as the whole thing had been, she really wished he'd go home so she could have the bed to herself. After all, she had to be downstairs in the café by five-thirty.

For a man who was truly skilled in matters of sex, he was appallingly bad at sharing a bed. He tossed and turned and wound the covers so tightly around himself that she couldn't get them back once he inevitably stole them.

When she came out of the shower wrapped in her big fluffy robe with a towel over her head, he was stretched out in bed, smiling up at her.

"Um, I think maybe I'll sleep on the futon tonight," she said, removing the towel and shaking out her hair.

His expression went from puppy-dog happy to rejected five-year-old.

"It's just that if I'm only going to get a few hours' sleep, I need to actually sleep. Comfortably."

"Well, if you want me to leave," he said, launching himself from the bed, his naked body still beautiful but now somewhat ridiculous too. Big, strong men were not supposed to pout.

He pulled on his boxers and jeans, and Casey knew she was supposed to object. But he had stayed over five of the past seven nights. They weren't even actually dating. They were sleeping together. She'd been very clear on this, and he had said it was cool with him (And why wouldn't it be? Wasn't it every man's dream for a woman to offer a sweet arrangement like this?). And then she thought of his brother and sister-in-law and their three whining, screaming, terrifying little children waking up in the middle of the night to the noise of him banging into the house—and he didn't know how to move quietly, so he would definitely wake them—and her resolve wilted.

"No, I don't want you to leave. I wish I had a bigger bed."

"Hey, no, whatever, I mean, we just had mind-blowing sex, like we do, and you're not the snuggling type, so, whatever," he said. He slid his t-shirt over his head and his beautiful, strong back disappeared from her sight.

"Look, I don't want you going home and waking up your family and everything. I mean, it's really late, and you should stay here, of course."

"I'm not going to stay where I'm not wanted."

Casey wished he had some more of that weed. He got so sulky when his high faded. She got up and put her hands on his shoulders. She pressed her face between his shoulder blades and said, "Please stay."

He turned around and eyed her, his perfect jaw set and his lips pressed together into a thin line. Then his face broke into a smile. "Oh you want me to stay, do you? Because I'm about ready to go again."

Go again they did, and when they were done, Jason fell asleep in two seconds flat, pulling the blankets with him and leaving Casey a small corner of mattress for herself. At four o'clock, she gave up pretending to sleep. She got dressed and went down to the café. She'd make cinnamon buns. Those took hours of rising that she normally couldn't be bothered with, but if she wasn't going to sleep, something nice might as well come out of it.

Chapter Eighteen

St. Nabor Island, South Carolina

BACK AT GRACE'S condo, Angela crawled under the covers, but she felt wide awake. Her mind was racing from the events of the previous night; there was no way she could sleep. Even with all their high-tech, super-sensitive equipment, the ghost hunters had detected nothing at her mother's house, and yet she had heard it, again, as she had every night that she'd spent in that house since her mother's funeral. First the footsteps that seemed to summon her to the hallway, then the voice that told her to go to sleep. It made no sense. Why would her mother wake her only to tell her to go to bed? Why was her mother angry? Or was it all in Angela's head, like Nicole and Molly had thought?

She'd been avoiding their phone calls since they went back to school. It was funny, really, to consider ghosting them—disappearing from their lives—when the issue that was making her avoid them was their refusal to even consider the possibility that her mother's spirit was trying to communicate with her.

Tossing and turning, Angela tried to think of things that might disturb her mother's peace and prevent her spirit from going wherever spirits go after the body dies. Her mother lived such a straightforward, upper-middle-class existence. Sure, there were complications—she lost her first born child when he was seventeen. That had to leave a mark on a person's soul, but wouldn't her soul seek his and not linger here? And then there was her husband, Angela's father, whose early-onset Alzheimer's had effectively taken him from her years too soon. Maybe this all had something to do with him. That seemed as likely as anything.

Angela tossed the covers from the bed. She would visit her father. Maybe he'd have a lucid moment, which she realized was not very likely, but maybe he'd reveal something nonetheless. Maybe today he'd be caught in a moment of his life that could help her.

When Angela visited her father when she first got home the week before, he hadn't known her. He had shouted and carried on when she walked into his room, refusing to let her near him, refusing to let her even talk to him. She had had visits like this with him before, but it hurt more than ever at that moment, as she had realized she was an orphan now, even though her father was still breathing.

In truth, Angela felt like she had never known her father. She had only been 10 when he began to experience symptoms, and by the time she was 15, he had to be put in the home. Her feelings toward him were a complicated tangle. She had no idea, really, what sort of father he might have been had he been well, no idea what sort of father he had been to Ryan before her. There were pictures of her father and brother at baseball games, on fishing trips, and other guy things. Ryan had had a father for all of his seventeen years, but she had only had him for 10, and he hadn't been especially involved. She suspected it was because she was a girl. He lost a cherished son who couldn't be replaced by a little girl who was decidedly girly. In the photos of her with her father, his smile always looked forced to her, an uneasy mask.

Maybe it hadn't been her gender that caused him to hold back but his own age. After all, when she was born, he was old enough to be her grandfather.

She picked up a cup of coffee on the way and fifteen minutes later she was signing in at the front of desk of her father's nursing home. She found him in his room, in a chair by the window. Angela's first thought on seeing him was how unfair that he had outlived his wife. Mentally, he had been lost to this world for a very long time, and yet his heart ticked on. Her second thought was that she'd never visited him alone before her mother died.

"Dad?" Angela said, rapping lightly on the doorframe.

He turned stiffly in his chair to face her, and then he frowned. "Me?" he asked.

"Hi, dad, it's me, Angela, your daughter," she said, nervously stepping into the room.

"Angela." He said her name like he had never put those syllables together before and was testing them for the first time. "I don't remember you."

"I know, it's okay." She took another step toward him. This was better than last time. He was confused, but he didn't seem angry.

"Your mother is Deborah?" he asked.

She nodded. In another circumstance this would almost

be amusing. She was tempted to ask what other woman might possibly be her mother.

"Deborah was here," he said, and he looked around as if Deborah might still be there, might have ducked behind the bed to hide and play a trick on him. He was forming words well today, though, and that was good. Some days when she visited him, he could barely speak, at least in words she could understand.

"She was?" Angela asked, another half step toward him.

"I don't know you. I have one son. That's all."

"That's right, you had a son named Ryan, and me, too. I'm your daughter."

"I never had a daughter," he insisted. "You're a liar. Who are you? Did you come to steal from me?"

Now he was growing agitated. Angela stopped moving toward him and raised her hands as if she were under arrest. She didn't want to upset him. This would be a pointless visit if all that happened was she upset him.

"I'm sorry," she said. "My mistake. I'm... I'm a visitor. I thought you might like someone to talk to."

He shifted away from her and gazed out the window again.

"I'd love to hear about your son, though, if you felt like talking about him," Angela said.

He glanced back over at her and made a tsk sound. "You're too young. What do you know about being a parent?" He sighed and then looked at her again. "You have kids?"

Angela shook her head.

"All kids do is break your heart," he said.

"May I sit down?" Angela asked, gesturing to the chair beside his.

"This place is full of thieves," he said. "You aren't a thief?"

Angela assured him she was not, and he nodded toward the chair.

"Did Ryan break your heart, d—" She stopped herself from calling him "dad" again, but only just.

"Ryan? Ryan is a good boy. Nice day today. I might go to his baseball game."

So today was one of the days when talking to her father would involve time travel. That might be a good thing, Angela thought. She said, "You love him very much, don't you?"

"Of course I do. He's my son."

"Did you ever want to have more kids?" Angela asked.

"Oh sure. Grew up in a big family, always thought I'd have a house full, but my wife is right. One is enough."

Angela's heart thudded in her chest. What did he mean he grew up in a big family? He had one older brother who died before Ryan was born, and that was it. He didn't usually invent a history for himself. "Did you have a lot of cousins around you growing up?" Angela asked, trying to puzzle out what he meant.

"Two sisters and three brothers," he said. "Tons of cousins, too."

"Oh!" Angela said, her surprise genuine. He seemed certain, but he was wrong.

"Marty, he died back in '72, but the rest are all still around, got their own kids, too."

Marty died in 1972 in Vietnam. That was true. Angela had seen his picture and even his obituary, which her mother had saved in a family scrapbook. But where was he coming up with the rest of this stuff?

"They live around here?" Angela asked, her voice trembling.

"All but Mary. Everyone else stayed, though."

"Stayed in Massachusetts?" Angela asked.

"Of course."

But Angela's parents always told her they had no family. All of her grandparents died before she was born, a sad downside of being born to older parents, her father's only brother died in Vietnam, and her mother was an only child. That was what they told her. Although she knew her parents lived in Massachusetts before she was born, and that they raised Ryan there, they never took her there to visit because, they had told her, there was no one there for them to visit. But what if that had been a lie?

"Are you the youngest?" Angela asked, thinking that maybe his other siblings, like Marty, were dead, and that was why her parents never mentioned them. How many dead family members could you burden a child with?

"Second oldest."

Angela was formulating another question, trying to find a question that would help her determine if he was telling the truth or if all of this was some elaborate fiction of his broken mind, when he said, "Who are you?"

"No one, a friendly visitor," she said, standing up. She reached over to pat his hand, longing to be able to embrace him, to have the reassuring arms of a father around her to comfort her. "I'll see you again another time."

As she drove back toward Grace's, she replayed the conversation over and over again in her mind. He hadn't known her, hadn't known where he was, hadn't seemed to know that Ryan was dead, so why should she trust anything he said? And yet, if he thought Ryan was still alive, if he thought he might go see Ryan's baseball game that very afternoon, then it was as if she had dropped in on him in the late 1980s or early 1990s, and why wouldn't he be telling the truth about his life? But why would her parents have lied to her for all these years? Why deny the existence of family?

It would be easy enough to Google a few things and see if she could find anyone who might be an aunt or uncle. She had two names, Martin and Helen. That should be enough to get her started.

As she was pulling into Grace's driveway, her phone rang. Randy.

"How are you feeling?" he asked, sounding chipper.

Her head still full of her conversation with her father, Angela wasn't sure she even wanted to think about the previous night's experience. Distractedly, she mumbled that she was tired.

"Do you want to have dinner? I think we should debrief," he said.

Her stomach rumbled. She hadn't eaten all day. "I don't know. It's so difficult."

"Talking it through might help."

"To be honest, I kind of want to forget the whole thing. I mean, it's obviously in my head. No one else has heard it."

"Okay, but I think I found something," he said.

Angela's pulse quickened. "What is it?"

"Let's talk over dinner." Randy said. "How about Antonio's, 7:00?"

"How about now? I can't wait that long," Angela said, pulling into the parking lot of a gas station to change directions. If she had to wait until 7, she'd lose her mind.

Chapter Nineteen

Devil's Back Island, Maine

BY EIGHT, CASEY was on her fourth cup of coffee. It would have been more, but she forced herself to keep it to a cup an hour. The warm cinnamon smell of her morning baking was heavy in the air, and outside the sun was shining in a cloudless sky, sunlight sparkling on the raindrops still clinging to the trees and grass from the previous day's drizzle. Tendrils of flame-red hair escaped her sloppy French braid and curled around her face in the hot kitchen.

Normally on a day that warm, she would have done the absolute minimum baking to keep the café a reasonable temperature. After the lousy weather of the past week, she hadn't expected it to be so nice. More proof of that old New England saying: *You like the weather? Wait a minute.* Rainy and sixty degrees one day, sunny and eight-five the next.

She hastily opened all the windows, turned on the ceiling fan, and unlocked the front door, flipping the sign to "Open." She stood in the doorway enjoying the breeze for a moment, and then she heard the horn of the ferry. Right on time. She shielded her eyes from the sun and peered out to see a small crowd on the deck. If the morning ferry had that many passengers, the afternoon boat was likely to be completely booked. Hallelujah, finally some customers.

Casey returned to her place behind the counter, forced herself to drink some water instead of more coffee, and waited. Within minutes, the first customers of the day were crossing the threshold, unable to resist the smell of the cinnamon rolls wafting out onto the lane. Despite her exhaustion, Casey couldn't help but think it would be a good day.

Around eleven, though, her mood soured a little when Brett came in, a laptop case slung over his shoulder. He was impeccably dressed again, this time in Nantucket red slacks and a crisp, pale blue, oxford shirt, the sleeves rolled to his elbows. He looked like he had gotten the recommended eight hours of sleep and was ready to take on the world. Despite the humidity and rapidly warming day, he looked cool and fresh.

"Soy latte?" Casey said, grimacing, as he approached the counter.

"Perfect," he said, stepping to the side of the register and stooping to study the pastry case. He tapped his lip thoughtfully and then tilted his head up toward where Casey stood at the cappuccino machine. "Do you have anything vegan?"

Of course he was vegan. He probably also only ate organic, non-GMO foods grown on farms where they played classical music to the crops instead of fertilizing them. She had a case full of delicious, homemade, interesting pastries, and he'd rather have some kind of gluten-free, no-sugar-added, sawdust cookie. He was one of those health-nuts who thinks he's smarter than all of Western Civilization. She gestured to a hutch against the wall where she had a couple of shelves of packaged cookies, bars, and snacks, with cheerful, hand-drawn labels proudly proclaiming, "Vegan!" "Nut Free!" "Gluten Free!" She knew she had to cater to all tastes, but that didn't mean she had to learn to use a whole new set of ingredients to bake for every new fad.

"Thanks," Brett said, winking and walking over to the case. He came back with a granola bar and set a ten dollar bill on the counter. As Casey made change, he asked, "Do I need a Wi-Fi password or anything?"

"We went over this yesterday," she said. "No Wi-Fi."

"Right, you don't share your Wi-Fi, but maybe you could make an exception for me," he said, glancing around the café. "I mean, normally, I'd set up my phone as a hotspot but there's no cell reception here."

This guy was unbelievable. No Wi-Fi meant no Wi-Fi. "I strive to encourage a true vacation, where people can unplug and unwind," Casey said.

"Yeah, well I'm here to work, so." He pocketed his change, dropping the coins in her tip jar.

Cheap, she thought. He should have at least left a one.

"The hotel gives guests Wi-Fi access," Casey said, crossing her arms.

"I work better with some background noise. I want to be around people, get a feel for the place." He ran a hand through his hair and puffed up his cheeks. "Damn. Rosetta may have underestimated the difficulties of working here."

Casey shrugged. She was enjoying seeing his disappointment. He was the type of man who had an answer for everything and who believed he could charm his way through life, but take away his toys, and he lost his cool facade in an instant.

"What you need," Casey said, "is to get back in touch with the finer things in life." Without thinking, she pulled a plate with the one remaining cinnamon bun from the pastry case and held it in front of him. In the back of her mind, a little voice was saying, Casey, what are you doing? But she ignored it. Instead, in her best sultry voice, she said, "Unwind. Take it easy. What do you have to do that's so important, anyway?"

He looked at the pastry and then at her. "Temptress," he said. "You are evil."

"On the house," she said, and then she realized she was actually batting her eyes at him. What had come over her? Fatigue must have been making her delirious.

"Did you make these?" he asked. He looked as if he might actually drool.

"Yes. And they are fantastic." She felt exhilarated and wicked. She was so tired she felt a little drunk. She wondered if she should call Kim to come in for the afternoon so she could duck out early.

"My girlfriend would shoot me," he said, taking the plate.

Girlfriend. The word broke the spell. Here she was seducing a man (whom she did not even like, she told herself) with baked goods and meanwhile his health-nut girlfriend was at home being self-righteously vegan and awaiting his return.

"Yeah, well, enjoy," Casey said, turning away and rubbing her eyes with the back of her hands.

God she was tired. She should have tried harder to sleep

last night. She was never going to make it through the day like this. And what was she doing, flirting with this asshole while Jason was probably still sleeping upstairs? She had to get her key back from him. That situation had definitely outlived its usefulness.

When she turned back toward the counter, Brett was still standing there. He had a mouthful of cinnamon bun and he was studying her.

"Man, that's good," he said, wiping a bit of frosting from his lip. "So what's with the tattoo?" he asked.

"A souvenir of my youth," Casey said, glancing down at her left arm.

"It's interesting," he said, blowing on his coffee and squinting his eyes at her. He leaned over across the counter.

"When did you get it?" he asked. He looked as if he was resisting the urge to reach out and trace his hand along her arm.

"When I was seventeen." Casey pulled her arms in, covering the tattoo as best she could. It was a pose she was used to. The tattoo was engraved on the skin of a woman who had had an utter inability to imagine herself ever being older than she'd been the day she'd first been inked. And even though it had been twenty years since then, most days she still felt like a foolish teenager.

She glanced at the clock and wished Brett would go sit down and leave her alone. She needed to call Kim and get her in here before the noon ferry so she could go sleep. The gust of energy that had turned her into a seductress had evaporated and now she felt raw and vulnerable, as if she had offered him her soul with that cinnamon bun, and all he'd wanted was the tasty treat. She was being irrational, she knew, and she couldn't imagine why she was letting herself get so worked up over a guy she did not even really like.

"I got a tattoo on my twenty-first birthday," he said. He patted his right shoulder with his left hand. "Giants logo. So stupid. I keep thinking I should get it removed or something but you know, who has the time?"

"Anything else I can get you?" Casey asked, thinking that surely he would take the hint.

Instead he said, "Actually, yes. I was hoping you'd be my guide. I want to explore the island, and I'd like a local to show me the ins and outs."

Casey blinked.

"Any chance you're free tomorrow?"

Behind Brett, the door of the café opened and shut and a loud family, parents and two small children, entered. Tomorrow was her day off. Had Rosetta told him? She said, "Oh, I don't—"

"Say yes, and I'll get out of your way," he said, winking. "You're the boss here, right, so you can decide to have the day off if you want?"

Why did men like Brett think they could get whatever they wanted by winking and flashing a smile? And since when could bosses take the day off willy-nilly? For a sophisticated-looking guy, he didn't seem to know too much how life actually worked. But it was her day off tomorrow, and wouldn't Rosetta be delighted to hear she had been spending time in the company of a handsome, age-appropriate man?

"Fine, but don't expect me to bring you any free baked goods," Casey said.

Chapter Twenty

St. Nabor Island, South Carolina

RANDY WENT OVER the video from the hallway three times, pausing it on anything that might be anything, rewinding, replaying, slowing the playback, but the fact was there was nothing there, nothing but Angela shaking, crouching on the floor, crying, pleading with someone or something to stop. He had pinned his hopes on finding some clue in the tape as to what she had experienced. At another investigation a while back, they were able to corroborate the testimony of an eyewitness to an ill-intentioned spirit by catching peculiar and inexplicable orbs on camera.

After the second playback, he had to mute the audio. It was too terrible to listen to Angela's whimpers and cries. And that was a shame, because if he could have isolated and enhanced the audio, maybe he could have discovered an irregularity there. If only she'd been able to hold in her vocalizations, but that was an unfair thing to wish for. She was grieving and afraid. She would have to be superhuman to sit through whatever was happening out there without making a sound.

Flipping through the files on his computer, he decided he could skip the footage from downstairs. Nothing had happened there. That was obvious. Instead, he found the files they'd recorded from the garage. If there was any hope of getting Angela some proof to support her experiences, it was in those files.

There was no time to watch or listen to it all. He started with the video, advancing the recording to about ten minutes before Angela heard the noises upstairs. Sometimes, watching tape of empty rooms in the dark like this, Randy wondered how security guards could work the night shift for years on end, sitting in a room somewhere watching CCTV. Talk about torture. He watched the timestamp on the video, each second an eternity, until he was nearly at the moment when the activity in the hallway began. Then he forced his eyes off the clock and tried to focus on the whole rest of the picture at once.

There was a trick to it. You had to let your eyes unfocus in order to take in the whole screen and not only one focal point in the room, and yet you had to stay alert so that any movement would catch your eye. At even the slightest disturbance, you hit pause, rewound it a few seconds, and then watched again, more carefully this time, trying to make out what had caught your eye.

Randy let the tape play for a full ten minutes beyond the moment he'd interrupted the haunting upstairs. Nothing. Not even a wayward dust mote drifting before the lens. He watched a second time to be sure.

Frustrated and exhausted, he backed up the video again and then he queued up the audio from the garage so that the two were synchronized. Close enough anyway. He listened to the gentle white noise of nothingness and half-heartedly watched the still garage, so still that the only suggestion that it was a video and not a photograph was the time stamp counting the minutes and seconds.

He wanted there to be something, anything, to warrant another visit to the house. There had been too many people. Barely enough recording devices, but too many bodies. Perhaps if it was just he and Angela, the two of them alone, he'd hear it, too. He knew this was ridiculous, though. She had said her friends who stayed with her after the funeral hadn't heard it.

Investigating a ghost of someone so recently deceased had made this feel more urgent than any investigation he'd ever done. Seeing Angela's distress the night before, his old resentment of her had faded. He wanted to help her through her grief, and the investigation could do that.

Every moment he had spent with her, she had become more beautiful in his eyes. She was pretty by any standards, but she was the sort of pretty that at first seemed distant, untouchable. Her grief made her human, and her vulnerability made her irresistible.

At first his attraction might have been about conquest, a desire to say he'd had Angela Ellis, a childish desire to brag on the playground, but not anymore. He had seen enough of her to know that she wasn't some stuck-up, mean girl. Maybe she never had been. Maybe she'd been a follower, which was bad, but forgivable. Whatever the case, she had been nothing but kind and humble since she walked into the meeting last week. And he wasn't a self-conscious nerd anymore, either. He was successful, confident, and good-looking. Why shouldn't he be interested in a girl like Angela?

When he thought of her, he imagined holding her, kissing her, running his hand through her hair, and then he felt guilty. He knew he shouldn't be thinking this way. He hardly knew her. She had just lost her mother. She was in a crazy place in her life. Undoubtedly she was not interested in romance right now. How could she be? And if he did try to turn this into something intimate, wouldn't that be taking advantage of her fragile emotional state? And that was the problem. He was a good person. Good people did not take advantage of the delicate emotions of others.

And yet he liked her. He really liked her. He liked the light, gold-flecked brown of her hair, and the swirly, many-colored hazel of her eyes, and her short, slender arms, and—

A sound on the recording snapped him from his thoughts. His thumb stabbed the keyboard to pause the video and then he clicked the mouse to drag the audio back a few seconds. He brought the volume all the way up, slowed the playback time, and pressed play.

After a couple of seconds he heard it: a sound like air whistling through a loose window casing or a gap under a door, steady, high-pitched (lower in the slowed version, but high when he sped things back up to normal). It lasted only four seconds.

He jotted down the time elapsed on the recording, and then clicked back over to the video. He'd have to use the video time stamp to approximate the time the sound had occurred. He nudged the video back, back, back until the time elapsed was the same as the audio and then checked the time stamp. A little math, some cross-referencing, and he was sure. The noise coincided with the moment he'd gone into the hallway to interrupt Angela's terror.

That was something. Randy slapped his palm against the desk, backed the video up a smidgen more, and then hit play. At exactly the right second, he hit play on the audio so that the time elapsed on each was identical, and then he peered close to the screen, watching and listening and hoping to catch some visual he had missed before that accompanied the whistling sound. He repeated this little game four times, but he found nothing.

Well, he had the audio. That was a start. He would need to listen to the rest and see if it happened again, of course. There was the possibility that it was in fact a breeze coming in around the edges of the garage doors or something, but the time was exactly right. What were the odds that a breeze had gusted up at the precise moment that he turned on the hallway lights and interrupted Angela's encounter with the voice? It hadn't been a gusty night. This was the first piece of proof.

Exhilarated, he called Angela and made dinner plans, but he didn't tell her what he had found. He wanted to tell her in person, see her relief that they were finally getting somewhere.

When he hung up the phone with her, he called Bill.

"I don't know, man, it's a long shot. How long did you listen? It could've been the wind," Bill said, when Randy explained what he'd heard.

"Obviously I have to listen to the rest to rule that out, but I think we've got something here," Randy said, exasperated. He'd expected a more positive response.

"I don't know, dude. I sat there all night and I saw jack squat except for one very freaked out chick."

"You don't believe her?"

"I believe she believes she heard something."

Randy backed the audio up and played it again. Each time he was more certain. Whatever it was, it wasn't natural. It was some kind of paranormal something. The fact was, if he was going to reinvestigate, he needed Bill or he wouldn't have enough equipment to record everything he wanted to capture. "If I go out there again, would you be up for it? Maybe just me and you and her."

"This is because you're into her."

"Come on, don't be like that. She's an old friend, and I want to help her," Randy said, but he didn't like thinking it was so obvious that he was attracted to Angela. If Bill had noticed, everyone must have, including Angela. He hadn't known he was so transparent.

"Send me the files. Let me check them out and then I'll give you my answer."

That was good enough. Randy was certain Bill would agree when he listened to the recording.

That evening, Randy pulled into the parking lot of Antonio's, feeling more nervous than he cared to admit. On the one hand, the sound on the recording was good news—suspicious activity that gave him confidence that something paranormal was happening. On the other hand, Angela hadn't even wanted them to investigate the garage, so finding activity there might feel more like bad news to her than good news. He wanted her to be happy, to be impressed, even, to want to spend more time with him, but he started to realize that her reaction was likely to be far more complex, and certainly thrilled was the wrong word when you were talking about someone's mother's ghost. He sat in the car until he saw Angela pull into the lot, and then he strode to the door in a manner he hoped exuded confidence.

As Angela approached him, he could see that she looked exhausted. Her face was drawn and there were dark circles under her pretty eyes.

"Did you get any sleep?" he asked, once they'd been seated in a quiet corner. He had forgotten how romantic the atmosphere inside Antonio's was and felt a bit self-conscious about the choice. This girl was doing a number on his head.

She shook her head.

"Shit. I'm sorry. Maybe the whole investigation was a mistake. It's too soon," Randy said. But without the investigation, he'd have no reason to see her, so he sincerely hoped she disagreed.

"I have to sell the house," Angela said.

Randy wondered if this was her way of agreeing, as if she was saying, "The hell with it. I'm selling and moving on," but then she went on.

"If I don't figure this thing out now, I'll never know. I mean, I don't hear the voice when I'm at Grace's, so it's not following me around."

Randy smiled reassuringly and reached across the table to take her hand. "Well then, I have some news." He had planned on saving what he'd uncovered for after dinner, but she said that she wanted answers, so why wait?

She looked up at him uncertainly.

"I heard something on one of the recordings."

"You heard her?" Angela's eyes were wide. She looked relieved but also afraid.

"Not the voice, no," Randy said. "I heard a noise, though, and the timing matches up with your experience."

"So there was someone or something in the hallway? You have proof?"

Randy bit his lip. She was excited, as he had hoped she'd be, but now he saw how paltry this bit of evidence was. "It wasn't in the hallway," he said. "It was in the garage. It was right at the moment when I interrupted you in the hallway."

Angela frowned and withdrew her hand from his grasp. She leaned back, looked away, and considered this. "What kind of noise?"

He tried to describe it, to make it sound significant, even though he knew as he spoke that it sounded ordinary and unimpressive.

"So like the wind or something?" Angela said.

Thankfully the waitress interrupted before Randy could reply. She set down glasses of water and rattled off specials, but instead of listening to her, Randy tried to think of what he could say to reassure Angela that it wasn't a breeze.

"If it had been the wind or something, it would have happened more than once," he said when the waitress left. He leaned forward and caught Angela's eye. "It was a still night. No breeze. And the timing. It's too much to be a coincidence."

"So you think what? That she was returning to the garage after you came into the hall?"

He shrugged. That was exactly what he thought. It made perfect sense.

"Are you good at finding stuff online?"

"Sure," he said, wondering how this was relevant.

"I need to try to find some people."

"Look, I really think we should investigate again. Just me and you. And Bill. I need someone to monitor everything."

"I think my parents were hiding things from me," Angela said.

"Like what?" Randy asked. The fact that they were now having two parallel conversations was frustrating. He was trying to help her, but she wasn't focused at all.

"Like other family they never told me about. Like why they really moved here."

"Okay."

"I think my dad has brothers and sisters. If we could find them, maybe I could figure out why my mother is," she paused, considering her words, "not at peace."

She was giving up on the idea of the ghost hunt, Randy could see. She was looking for answers elsewhere. But the answers were right there, in the house, and they needed to pay attention to sort it all out. "If we investigate again, we might get some clarity here. I really think—"

"Just us. I don't want anyone else there. I don't want people like Jen, saying I'm crazy. Just us."

"Yeah, okay. Just us," Randy said. If that was her condition, he could live with it.

As they ate, Angela asked him questions about himself and his life outside of amateur paranormal investigations. When he tried to get her talking about herself, though, she put him off. She was tired of thinking about herself, she said. She wanted a distraction. So he told her about his website design and maintenance company, which he'd started as a hobby in high school, first as a favor to one of his mom's friends for her business selling homemade soaps. And she referred him to someone else, who referred him to someone else, and by the time he finished high school, he was doing enough business that he realized he didn't need to go to college or get a job working for someone else. He had continued living at home and working out of his parents' house until the previous summer when he decided he really needed more space. It was awkward always having to meet clients at coffee shops, and he knew they wouldn't take him seriously if they saw his makeshift home office, so he found a decent two-bedroom, first-floor apartment not too far from his parents' house in Palmetto Landing where he could use the spare bedroom as his office. Meanwhile he'd been teaching himself other coding languages and had started dabbling in app development.

"So you don't think you'll ever go to college?" Angela asked.

"Never say never, but for now it hardly seems necessary."

He had taken a couple of business courses last year at the local community college when he was trying to figure out if he was really doing well enough to move out into his own apartment, but the classes had been too basic. They were for people who had absolutely no experience as business owners, and he found they didn't teach him anything he hadn't already figured out.

They finished their dinners, or rather Randy finished his and most of hers, and got the check, and he followed her out to the parking lot and to her car.

"So when do you want to try again at your house?" Randy asked, trying not to be distracted by how sad but also how pretty she looked in the glow of the street light.

"I know it's kind of late, and you're probably exhausted, but do you think you could help me with that internet stuff now?" Angela asked. She leaned against the car, and Randy felt like she was inviting him to kiss her as she looked up at him from under those long eyelashes, but he resisted. He didn't want to sour the moment if he was reading this wrong.

He glanced at his phone. It was not yet nine o'clock. He didn't have any meetings until after lunch tomorrow. How hard could it be to find some people online? If they existed, surely he could find them in a matter of minutes. Was this an excuse she invented to spend more time with him?

"Have you tried yet? Have you looked them up?" he asked.

"No, I found out all this stuff this afternoon."

"So you want me to go to Grace's with you?"

She shook her head.

He wanted nothing more than to bring her back to his place, but she hadn't slept in God knows how long and she'd had a traumatic day. Even if it was her idea to go back to his place, if anything should happen other than some internet research—and at this point he felt certain she intended for other things to happen—he would feel like he was taking advantage of her.

"Sorry. I shouldn't have asked. You've already done so much for me," Angela said. She put her hand on the car door handle.

"It's not that," he said, stepping forward to block her from opening the door. "Are you sure you want to come to my place? I don't want you to, you know, feel uncomfortable, or..."

"I should go," Angela said, clicking the unlock button on her keychain.

"Look," he said, stooping a little to force her to meet his eyes, "I definitely want you to come over. I want to help you with all of this stuff, and I really like you. I know this is the wrong time, and I probably shouldn't even be saying this, but—"

She tilted her head and pressed her lips to his. When she drew back, he studied her for a minute, and then said, "Okay. Well, I guess you should follow me."

Chapter Twenty-one

Devil's Back Island, Maine

BRETT TOOK HIS PAPER cup of coffee and wandered back toward the hotel, wondering as he went why he had lied about having a girlfriend. The word "girlfriend" had popped out his mouth so unconsciously when Casey started flirting. He was tempted to say it was habit; after all, Ashley was the reason he'd gone vegan, so it was only natural to refer to her when turning down something so obviously not vegan. He suspected, however, that his subconscious was up to something more sinister than a mere Freudian slip.

Casey had gone from seeming tired and wearied by his presence to sultry and playful in the blink of an eye, and he responded with a remark ostensibly designed to put her off. The subtext of the words "My girlfriend would shoot me" was "Your flirting is wasted on me." Except, Brett had noticed, that knowing a man was in a relationship often did not stop women from flirting. If anything, that knowledge made them more interested, as if being in a relationship proved a man was relationship material.

So by telling Casey, who had given every indication of finding him odious until she decided to flirtatiously sway him from his stated veganism (which, let's face it, was not a good sign; what kind of woman so eagerly attempts to make a stranger deviate from his chosen lifestyle?), that he had a girlfriend, he may have actually, subconsciously, been trying to get her to soften toward him, to see him as more interesting and perhaps even a bit mysterious.

He couldn't deny that he wanted her to like him. He wanted her to smile when he came into the café, not to roll her eyes and shake her head as she offered him a soy latte. She was beautiful, intriguing, and also one of the only people even roughly his age whom he'd encountered here. It would be nice to have someone with whom he could be social. He was going to be here for a couple of weeks on this trip, and then, if everything worked out—although he had no reason to believe it would work out—he'd be back to oversee the project.

Even as he thought this, he knew he wasn't being totally honest with himself. A drink with Casey would be nice, sure, but tracing his hand along her tattoo, kissing her pretty lips... He forced himself not to picture pulling off her tank top. What was he thinking? If he wanted to try to reconcile with Ashley, he couldn't go sleeping with someone else.

But he wanted to. It had been a while. Too long. No wonder he was losing his mind. Before he and Ashley broke up, they'd been in a bit of a dry spell. In fact, they hadn't had sex in weeks. And now they'd been broken up for weeks. Who could blame him if his mind slipped under the covers when he saw a woman as attractive as Casey?

She'd said yes to being his tour guide. Even if he'd had to

wear her down to get her to say yes, it felt like a victory. He had to have scored some points by caving to the temptation of the cinnamon bun and then complimenting her so thoroughly (and genuinely—it was the best cinnamon bun he'd ever had).

He needed to scope out the island to work on his prefeasibility analysis, so his tour with Casey wasn't only for fun, but that didn't mean he couldn't enjoy the day. After the past few days, with all his meetings with engineers, architects, department of transportation and ferry authority officers, he could use some fun.

The more he learned about the island, the less likely it was that Sweet Water would move the project forward. The fresh water resources of the island were a major limiting factor to any potential development, and the rocky shoreline—Maine's famous cliff rock—posed problems for building. In a climate like this, with major seasonal shifts, buildings needed substantial foundations, especially to be several stories high, but with the bedrock so close to the surface, the engineers had informed him, they wouldn't be able to have a deep foundation. They advised the hotel be no more than two stories high, which didn't mesh with the typical Sweet Water model at all.

"Think outside the box," an engineer from one of the design-build companies had suggested, when he and the architect who had accompanied him discussed the site and possibilities with Brett.

But Sweet Water liked its box. Its box worked in all its other locations. Also, he was already outside the box by being in Maine. If he was going to suggest they go even further from the box, he was going to have to have darn good reasons. Maybe getting an up-close-and-personal tour of the island, with a charming and sexy tour guide would inspire him.

Realistically, proclaiming the whole project dead right now was probably the smartest course of action. But he didn't want to. Not yet, and not because he had a schoolboy crush on a woman he'd just met. Even if the island wasn't everything he'd hoped, and even if he knew it was going to be a long shot to convince Charlie to move the project forward, this was his chance to prove to Charlie and everyone else that he was an ideas guy who was capable of steering the company into the future. He wanted to think outside the box for his own sake, to prove to himself that he wasn't only a mindless Sweet Water drone. Whether or not he came up with something the company wanted to develop, he had to come up with something he felt proud of.

When he got back to the inn, he sat out on the patio overlooking the beach, sipping his latte, and staring out at the water, willing his mind to let to go of everything it thought it knew about resort development. He needed a beginner's mind—thanks to yoga-teaching Ashley for that concept—if he was going to think outside the box.

Chapter Twenty-two

St. Nabor Island, South Carolina

ANGELA SAT BESIDE Randy at his computer, and within seconds, she was staring at the Facebook page of a Helen Ellis Jenson of Beechmont, MA. She was 63 years old. In her photographs, with a throwback Thursday hashtag, there were grainy, black and white childhood photographs, presumably of Helen and her siblings, two girls and four boys. Only three people were tagged in the pictures: Helen, Mary Ellis Brinkman, and Stanley Ellis. Angela's heart raced. She could hardly breathe. Any of the three untagged boys in the pictures could be her father.

She asked Randy to go to Mary's page, but the security on it was locked down. Not much to learn there. Same with Stanley. They went back to Helen's page and scrolled through more of her pictures until they came across another throwback Thursday selection, a picture Angela had seen before, her father and Marty in the front yard of a post-World War II ranch house. The caption read, "An early Memorial Day tribute: God bless my big brother, Marty, and all veterans who've lost their lives fighting foreign wars."

Her father had the same photo. When she was a kid, it was in a frame on a side table in the living room. Now it sat on his bedside table in the nursing home.

Angela didn't want to cry again in front of poor Randy, who had already seen her cry way too much, but she couldn't help it. There was a picture of her father and his brother on Facebook on the page of an aunt she never knew she had. It was too much. At least she managed to cry silently, for a few minutes anyway, and then she had to blow her nose, and there was no quiet way to get up and find tissues. She pushed her chair back and went to the bathroom.

When she came back, feeling marginally more in control of herself, Randy had another picture up on the screen. It was from the mid-1980s, a crowd of people standing in a semi-circle around a seated elderly couple. In the crowd were Mary, Helen, Stanley, the other unnamed brother, and people who were most likely their spouses. And Angela's father and mother! And children! Angela tallied them up and counted 12, among them her brother Ryan. The caption read, "The last time we had the whole gang together, mom and dad's fortieth anniversary party. The only cloud on that day was Marty's absence."

The floodgates broke. Angela didn't cry silently this time. She wept loudly and messily. Her family! Ryan had known these people. He had grown up surrounded by loving aunts and uncles and cousins and grandparents, and Angela never even knew they existed!

Randy clicked the image and it disappeared, and then he wrapped his arms around Angela, gently pulling her from the rolling desk chair and over to the couch. He sat down and she nestled in against him, shaking with tears. How embarrassing, she thought, as she gradually regained herself. How ridiculous she was being. Randy must think she was the most weepy, unstable person in the world. But he stroked her hair and it felt nice.

When she had stopped crying and her breathing leveled out, Randy said, "So that's them? Your dad's family?"

Angela nodded, her cheek rubbing against his soft shirt.

"That was your parents in the last picture, and your brother?"

She nodded again. His fingertips, as his hand soothed her hair, brushed her neck and lingered there for a moment before gliding on. She closed her eyes.

"God. I'm so sorry," he said.

She shook her head. She didn't want him to talk. She wanted him to run his fingers along her neck again. She took a deep breath and leaned into him a little harder. His hand froze. She drew back and looked up at him. He slid his arm out from around her shoulders and moved away from her a little.

"Angela, I think we shouldn't do this," he said, softly.

Her lip quivered. She thought he was interested. She was sure she hadn't misread the way he looked at her. She needed this now, to be touched, made to forget everything else in her life for a little while.

"I like you too much," he said.

She almost laughed. He was turning down sex because he liked her too much? That was a new one. He had been right. It had been a mistake for her to come over here. She could have found her family on her own. It certainly hadn't been difficult. She stood up.

"I should go," she said.

"You don't have to. I can crash on the couch, and you can have the bed, get a good night's sleep."

"No, you were right, this was wrong, I shouldn't have put you in this position."

She moved to step around him, but he put both hands on her upper arms, gently but firmly.

"You have no idea how much I'd like to kiss you right now and take you to bed with me. Seriously, no idea. But when we do that, I want it to be for the right reasons." He spoke softly, looking in her eyes.

Angela's shoulders slumped. He was right, of course he was right. What was she doing, thinking she could use him for sex to make herself feel better? If a guy had done that to her, she'd have been out the door so fast he wouldn't even see her go.

"I like you, too," she said.

He kissed her on the forehead.

"Would you only lie down with me? No funny business, I promise, but will you?"

He took her hand and led her to the bedroom. They both lay down on top of the comforter, and Angela turned onto her side so he could spoon her. She was asleep within minutes.

Angela woke up to the smell of coffee brewing and sat up in bed, blinking and trying to get her bearings. Then she remembered: She was at Randy's. They had never even gotten under the covers, but at some point Randy had fetched a fleece blanket, which was now draped over her fully clothed legs. She felt better rested than she had in weeks.

In the kitchen, Randy sat at the small table with a mug of coffee and his iPad. He smiled when he saw her, and she felt strangely shy all of a sudden.

"I'm sorry about last night," she said.

"No need to be sorry."

He got up and fixed her a cup of coffee. They sat in silence for a few minutes, and then he asked, "So are you going to contact them? Your family, I mean?"

Angela had no idea. She hadn't gotten that far. She had definitely found her father's siblings, but what she would do with that information, she couldn't quite say. She felt like she needed more information. Maybe she should visit her father again, print out some of Helen's Throwback Thursday pictures and take them to him, see what he had to say.

"I have to catch up on a bit of work this morning for some meetings later, but you're welcome to hang out here," Randy said. "I make damn good pancakes."

Over breakfast, they decided to go back to Angela's mother's house that night. Having agreed to the second investigation, Angela wanted to get it over with as fast as possible. After all, now that she'd found some possible long-lost relatives, what did she really hope to gain from another ghost hunt? She could only send Helen Ellis Jenson a message. But Randy was so excited, so certain that they'd find something, that she didn't feel like she could back out now.

Chapter Three-three

Devil's Back Island, Maine

WHEN AT LAST Casey locked the café at four and began cleaning up for the night, she had run entirely through her second and third winds and was weary to her core. She believed in the importance of doing a thorough job with the cleaning, hoisting the chairs onto the tables, sweeping and mopping the floor, wiping down the counter and leaving the glass front of the pastry case spotless, the handprints of children all erased until tomorrow. But at the moment, she felt unsteady on her feet. Kim hadn't been able to come rescue her that afternoon, and she hadn't even called Barb, because Barb babysat her grandchildren on her free days. Now she looked at the sticky table tops and the crumbs on the floor and felt like crying.

It could wait until the morning while the scones were in the oven. She didn't need to do it now. She climbed the stairs to her apartment, pulling herself along the banister, praying that Jason was not there. She didn't think he was. She hadn't heard footsteps overhead for a while, and besides, he and his brother probably had loads of landscaping to get caught up on now that the rain had stopped.

She threw open the door to the living room and stepped inside. The scent of all-purpose cleaner was overwhelming. She looked around and noticed that the coffee table was spotless, the TV screen was streaky, as if it had been inexpertly dusted, and there were vacuum lines across the rug. She walked into the kitchen to see that there were no dishes in the sink, no messes on the counter, no shoes piled near the door. Apparently, some elf had come to clean her apartment when she wasn't looking. She wondered what favors said elf would expect in return.

In the bathroom, the vanity was wiped down, there was no toothpaste in the sink, no stray hairs near the drain. The toilet bowl was blue with cleaner, as if to ensure that she noticed it had been cleaned. She flushed it and the blue lines where the cleaner had dripped into the water remained.

In her bedroom, the bed had been made up, the pillows propped carefully along the headboard. Everything on top of her bureau had been moved slightly and the surface was dust-free. She hated dusting. She almost never bothered.

If this was Jason's way of saying he was sorry, he'd done good. She pulled back the comforter, ready to call it a day even though it wasn't even five o'clock. The mattress was bare. No sheets.

He had gone so far as to take her sheets to wash them. That meant he'd be back tonight. She climbed under the blankets anyway and closed her eyes for a moment, but then she thought of something and bolted upright. She glanced toward the hamper in the corner. The lid was shut. She never left the lid shut because she was always dangling things like damp wash cloths over the edge to dry so they wouldn't turn all her laundry musty. There was nothing dangling over the edge at the moment. She leapt from the bed and whipped open the hamper. Empty.

It wasn't fear that he'd shrink her shirts or turn her whites pink that worried her. Had he thought to empty her pockets? That was what she needed to know. And if he had emptied her pockets and found the letter that she stupidly left in the butt pocket of her jeans the night before when she'd so foolishly agreed to a stoned evening of delirious sex, had he read it? And if he hadn't emptied her pockets and the letter had gone through the wash... well, it wasn't like a dollar bill. It was more like tissue. It would be an illegible clump of paper at best, a thousand tiny bits of paper stuck all over all her clothing at worse.

She dropped onto the bed and covered her face with her hands, picturing the blue ink, the swooping script in which her mother wrote. She could quote verses from it: *I'm sorry I didn't tell you in person. After all this time, I couldn't face you, but I want to make amends. I want my soul to rest in heaven.*

It doesn't matter, she told herself. She should have thrown the letter out weeks ago. She was only torturing herself by hanging onto it. If it was gone—and it was, because what man thought to check pockets—he had done her a bigger favor than he'd realized. Now she could stop obsessing about the letter, stop reading and rereading it, stop deliberating. Now she could pretend she'd never received it, and she could stop fearing Rosetta would somehow see it.

She curled up on her side and took a deep breath. She was asleep before she could count to five.

When Casey awoke, it was dark in her room, and Jason was sitting on the edge of her bed smiling at her.

"Hey," she said, blinking. Her mouth was dry and her eyes felt scratchy.

"Hey," he said. "Sorry I didn't get this stuff back sooner. Mike had me working till it got dark. Want me to make the bed?"

Casey glanced at the dark outline of the laundry basket on the floor beside the bed, remembered the letter, and felt a flutter of panic. "You didn't have to do that," she said, sitting up, tugging the elastic from her hopelessly disheveled braid, trying to wrestle her hair off her face.

"What time did you get up this morning?" he asked.

"Usual time," she said, rearranging her hair into a quick, sloppy ponytail, and reaching to turn on the light on her bedside table.

"Liar."

Casey sighed.

"Have you eaten?" he asked.

Her stomach answered for her with a loud rumble.

"Come on, let's get a bite and then you can go back to bed on your fresh, clean sheets."

He stood up and held out a hand to her. He was being way too nice. She got up and followed him to the kitchen.

"Let's see," he said. He opened the fridge and came up with a block of cheese. "I make a mean grilled cheese. Actually, that's the only thing I make, but it'll be good."

Casey sat at the kitchen table, watching him wordlessly. He knew. He had to know. He was being too sweet. He wasn't the sweet type. It was one of the things she liked about him.

"Did you wash the jeans I was wearing yesterday?"

she asked, watching his back as he buttered bread on the kitchen counter.

"Yeah, I grabbed everything. Don't worry. I'm good at laundry. It's one of those things my mama taught me."

"Oh. Okay. Thanks." Then surely his mother had taught him to always check the pockets. If he knew her secret, that turned this casual sex arrangement into something more serious, and she didn't want it to be serious. She didn't want him to know her secrets. She didn't want anyone to know her secrets.

The butter sizzled on the hot skillet. Jason took a pot lid from the cabinet and placed it on top of the sandwiches. "The secret," he said, and she felt her heart skip a beat. Was the kid a mind reader? But then he went on, "is you have to cover it so the cheese can really melt without the outside getting burnt," he said.

"Right. Makes sense," she said. She began to bite her fingernail and tried not to meet his eyes.

"Are you okay? You seem a little, I don't know, tense."

"Did you happen to check my pockets before you did the wash?" she asked, trying to sound casual.

"Shit, should I have? I mean, I know my mom always told me to, but I figured you're a girl, and girls think of things like emptying their pockets before they toss stuff in the hamper."

And as he babbled, she knew he was lying. He had checked her pockets, but he was going to pretend he hadn't. Which meant that he had read the letter.

"No worries. I doubt there was anything important," she said, standing up. "I'll just go check."

In the bedroom, she upended the basket of sloppily

folded laundry and grabbed her jeans. She reached into the back pocket and felt the soft square of paper. She took it out and looked at it. She doubted she could unfold it. It had melded together from a normal sheet of paper into a small square of soft, linty meaninglessness. So he hadn't emptied her pockets. She put the now-ruined letter in the top draw of her dresser and went back to the kitchen, feeling shaky and weary.

"Everything okay?" he asked.

"Yeah, great. It was really thoughtful of you to do all that," she said, forcing herself to smile.

He set the sandwich in front of her.

"Looks good."

"Okay, well, I guess I should go," he said.

"Go?"

"Yeah, you were right last night. You deserve a good night's sleep, and I'm not much help with that."

All of this sudden deference was beginning to grate on Casey. Why didn't he just come out and say what he was thinking?

"Don't be silly," she said. "You don't have to go."

He looked her in the eye and then took the key to her apartment, the one she'd given him, and placed it on the table. With one finger he pushed it toward her. "I should go," he said.

Was he breaking up with her? After cleaning her apartment and washing her laundry and making her dinner, he was breaking up with her? He was dumping her? Of course, they weren't really dating, so it wasn't like he was really breaking up with her, and yes, she regretted giving him that key and would be happy to have it back, but still, what was going on?

"Jason," she said.

He raised a hand. "It's cool. I was taking advantage of you, and I think it's pretty obvious that we want different things."

He was? They wanted different things? She had assumed he wanted the same thing she wanted—sex.

"We're just in really different places in our lives," he went on, and she felt her suspicion once again confirmed that he had read the letter. He had read the letter and then tried to cover up the fact by ruining it. She felt a tide of anger rising in her stomach.

"I don't want Rosetta to know," Casey said, interrupting him. "I certainly never planned to tell you."

"Well, I didn't mean to find out," he said defensively. "I was trying to do you a favor."

"You put the letter through the wash!" she said, her voice rising.

"I didn't know what to do! Here I am, trying to be the good guy, and I reach into your pocket and I pull out this letter, and I really think you should listen to her. You need to go get the test. What if you have it?"

"It was private!" How dare he give her advice. He knew nothing about her. Nothing about her, nothing about her mother, nothing about anything.

"I'm sorry. I'm really sorry. I knew you wouldn't want me to have read it, and I thought that if I just pretended—"

"You would be the world's shittiest poker player," Casey said.

"I should go," he said, but he didn't move.

"No, we need to talk about this. Or something. I don't

know. I mean, what are you going to do? I don't know if I can trust you."

"Well, there's not much I can do about that. Unless you're planning to murder me," he said.

Casey rested her face in her hands. She heard Jason pulling out the other kitchen chair and sitting across from her.

"You know, I really like you," he said.

She looked up at him, her eyes rimmed with red, her lower lip quivering. "You don't even know me."

"You're right. I mean, I thought I did, and then I read that letter, and realized that I really don't know you. Apparently, no one knows you."

He was right. She didn't let people in. Even Rosetta didn't really know her. Rosetta knew her minus a gap of about twelve years that she wished had never happened between that day her mother kicked her out and the day Rosetta had dragged her unwillingly away from New York and back to Devil's Back. She didn't need people knowing her secrets, knowing about her past, knowing how much her foolish youth still hurt her every day. She didn't need or want pity. The last thing in the world she wanted was to hear people say, "I totally understand," or to tell their own tragic stories as if somehow sharing suffering alleviated suffering.

"I could be here for you, if you let me," he said, reaching out and touching her arm on the table.

"You are a very nice, very attractive kid, and you deserve to be happy."

"But with you," he said.

"I can't make you happy."

"No one can make anyone else happy," he said. "You call

me a kid, but if you believe that anyone can control someone else's happiness, maybe you're the one who needs to grow up."

"No one can make someone else happy, but one person can definitely make another miserable." She crossed her arms and pushed her chair away from the table.

"Look, I didn't mean to make you—"

"I know. I'm not saying you made me miserable. I'm saying that I would make you miserable. And I'm not up for it."

"Great. So you don't want to be with me, but you also don't want me to leave because you can't trust me."

"Please just promise you will not tell anyone. Not one single person. Not your brother, not Rosetta. No one."

He looked at her as if she'd slapped him. "Of course I won't tell anyone. I care about you."

"Promise."

"I promise."

Casey nodded. She took the key from the table and closed her fist around it. Jason stood up and walked to the door.

"This could have been something good," he said, before he walked out.

No it couldn't, thought Casey.

Chapter Twenty-four

St. Nabor Island, South Carolina

TUESDAY EVENING, ANGELA and Randy drove together to the house. Randy had borrowed some equipment from Bill so that he could monitor everything himself. As Angela helped him set up cameras and roll out wires, a thought occurred to her.

"If the ghost is smart enough to flee when someone other than me steps into the hall, aren't all these things going to tip it off that's something's up?" she asked, watching Randy position a camera in her mother's study.

He stopped and looked at her, considering, and then went back to fiddling. When he was done, he said, "I don't think that's how it works."

Angela had no idea what that meant, but he sounded offended, so she didn't push. Instead, she walked over to the desk and ran a hand along the roll-top. She slid it back in its track and ran her hand over the small, locked drawers.

"You still didn't get this thing open yet?" Randy asked.

Angela shook her head. She'd had other things on her

mind.

"And that key definitely doesn't open it?"

Another little shake of the head.

He came over and tried a few of the drawers again. Then he squatted down to peer under it, and slid it forward to look at the back.

"And you don't think your mom used to keep it locked?"

"I haven't tried to open it years, but when I was a kid I would play in here, and I definitely remember being able to open the drawers."

"But as you got older, she might have started locking it, right? I mean, if your parents were keeping a whole bunch of relatives secret, there might have been stuff in here they didn't want you to read?"

Angela conceded that this seemed likely.

"I think we should pay extra attention to this tonight," Randy said.

Once they had everything set up, this time with the command center in Angela's bedroom so they could both sit in there and wait for the footsteps in the hall, there was nothing to do but watch the clock tick.

Randy had brought a Scrabble set and he beat Angela soundly in back-to-back games before she gave up. Cute and smart. She liked him. No doubt about it.

"How come you don't have a girlfriend?" Angela asked, gathering up Scrabble tiles and returning them to the little velvet pouch.

"Oh, I don't know. Haven't found the right girl yet," he said.

"Oh," Angela said, and then, "Describe the right girl in two sentences or less," and she laughed.

"Why don't you have a boyfriend?" he asked.

She shrugged. "I didn't really like college guys, I guess. But you," she said, playfully, tugging his arm and arranging it around her shoulders, "are not a college guy."

"Look," he said, "I like you." He paused, withdrew his arm from around her shoulder and reached down for her hand, lacing her fingers through his. Then he went on, "But I also get that this is a terrible time for you, so I'm here for you, as a friend. That's all. No pressure. No drama. Just friends."

But I don't want to be just friends, Angela thought, looking at his hand in hers. She wanted him to hold her, and kiss her, and sleep next to her at night, and tell her everything was going to be all right.

He lifted her hand to his lips and kissed her fingers gently. Then he let go.

"I like you, too," she said.

He smiled sadly. "That's good, but here's the thing. I'm not sure you're thinking straight these days, and to be honest, I'm afraid if we act on those feelings right now, I'm going to end up pretty brokenhearted."

"Oh." He liked her enough to fear a broken heart? And here she had thought it was probably just lust. In her brief experience of relationships, lust generally came first, not the sort of deep emotions that could end with a broken heart. But then again, if they were just friends, and she showed up tomorrow with some other guy, wouldn't that also break his heart? Why not just risk it? Life was short, too short to wait around with a head full of what ifs.

She said, "That sounds really pragmatic, but also, I think you're wrong."

"I wish I were."

"Not acting because you think that's the best way to prevent heartache is actually the surest way to end up heartbroken. That's what I think," Angela said. Then she leaned forward to kiss him, and he met her halfway.

They fooled around in an innocent way, kissing, groping one another over their clothes, nothing more.

"I still think we need to take it slow," Randy said when Angela reached for the button of his jeans.

By midnight, they were cuddled in each other's arms on the bed, Randy's laptop beside them showing the video feed from the empty hallway. Angela's eyelids kept drooping. She was nearly asleep when Randy lurched beside her, pulling his arm out from under her and grabbing the laptop.

Angela sat up slowly. She hadn't heard anything. "Did you see something?"

"Shit," Randy said to his computer screen. He was speaking in a whisper. "Come on, show yourself again." After a minute, he pressed a series of buttons and then tilted the screen toward Angela.

"Watch," he said, pointing to the corner of the still image on the screen. He pressed play and Angela watched. A few seconds into the playback, Randy whispered, "There, there," and pointed to something Angela couldn't detect.

He froze the image and said, "Did you see it?"

"See what?"

"There was a blur, like a shadow passing. Here watch again."

He backed up the video and played it again. Angela still wasn't quite sure what he was seeing. He played it a third time, in slow motion, and Angela nodded hesitantly. Yes, she could see some kind of shadow.

"There's nothing out there to make a shadow like that," Randy said.

"Are you sure?" Angela asked, trying to work out if this was true.

"If there were, we would have been seeing shadows pass all night. This is different."

"What do we do?" Angela asked.

"We wait and watch."

Wide awake now, they brought the other laptop with the garage video stream up onto the bed, too. Another half hour passed with no motion, no sound, and then they heard it. Not footsteps, this time, but a gentle rattling sound from the direction of her mother's study. Angela clutched Randy's arm. Randy tapped at his keyboard and switched to the window of the video from the study. They had been recording that room, but not watching it, as nothing had ever happened in there before. Not that they knew. They heard the rattle again, a sound that was like the roll-top being slid in its track but too quiet. The video, however, showed nothing.

"You hear it, right?" Angela asked.

He nodded.

He heard it! She had a witness! Angela could have wept from the relief. She wasn't crazy. Someone else heard the sounds, and saw that there was no physical explanation for them. But her relief was quickly supplanted by fear, because if Randy could hear it, then it was getting worse, wasn't it?

Then they heard a sound repeat three times in succession—the lid of the desk being shut. The slap of wood on wood and the shake of the roll-top, but muted as if it were happening far away or under water. Angela's heart hammered. She felt like she couldn't breathe. She hung onto

Randy's arm for dear life.

"I think we should go into the room, see what happens," Randy said.

Angela shook her head and bit her lip. She couldn't. She couldn't do that again.

"I can go without you."

"No!" she said, speaking above a whisper for the first time since Randy noticed the passing shadow. She couldn't stand the thought of being left alone, even for a minute.

"Shh," he said. "I'll be with you. In the past, as soon as someone else showed up, the voice stopped, right? So if I'm with you, probably nothing will happen at all."

"Then what's the point?" Angela asked. She hadn't realized just how terrifying this would be, coming back again, and with only one other person. Having the whole team here made her feel brave, but now she felt only panic.

"We might catch something on video, some more motion, the shadow fleeing when we enter or something," Randy said. "You can hold onto me the whole time, but I need to bring the camera. Sometimes we can capture images in still photographs that we can't get on video."

He stood up, and despite the perfectly comfortable temperature of the room, Angela shivered. Randy rummaged through his bags, producing a camera which he slung around his neck, and then came back for Angela.

"Your mother wouldn't hurt you, would she?" he asked gently.

Angela shook her head. Reluctantly, she took his hand and got up. Then they went together into the hallway. They inched their way to the study without seeing or hearing anything strange, but they both felt it when they entered the room—a rush of cold air that seemed to drop from the ceiling and pass through them. Unable to contain herself, Angela shrieked aloud.

And then she heard it. The voice again, harsh, shrill, strained, "Angela. Go back to bed, Angela." Repeated over and over, faster and faster, overlapping, filling her brain as if the voice was coming from inside her.

She threw her arms around Randy's waist from behind and buried her face in his back. She didn't know if he could hear it, too, and she didn't care. She just wanted it to stop. Randy extricated himself from her grasp, and then he turned around and took her arms and said, "It's okay. There's nothing here."

"The voice," Angela said, her own voice strangled with fear.

"You hear it now?"

She nodded.

"Right now?"

She pressed her face into his soft t-shirt and squeezed her eyes shut as if that could also block out the sound.

"Okay," he said. "It's okay. It wants you to go back to bed, right? So let's go back to bed."

Randy guided her back to her bedroom and shut the door behind them. He sat her on the edge of the bed, and then he looked around the room, and said, "Shit."

She looked up at him, blinking through her tears. "It's okay," she said weakly. "It stopped."

He pointed to the laptops on the bed. The screens were black.

PART THREE

Chapter Twenty-five

St. Nabor Island, South Carolina

RANDY TAPPED THE TOUCH pads on each of the computers. Nothing. He checked the power cords. They were plugged in securely, but no indicator lights flashed on either computer. They were dead.

"You ever have trouble with that outlet?" he asked Angela, bending to look at it. Maybe they tripped the circuit somehow, although that didn't really explain the lack of life in the computers, because their batteries had plenty of juice to keep them running.

Angela shook her head. She was standing in the center of the room, white as a ghost herself.

"I've heard of shit like this happening before," Randy said, getting up and stepping back over to Angela. "It's okay. I'll sort them out later."

"It's not okay! It's really bad!" Her voice was shrill and Randy could see that she was likely to burst into tears again at any second.

"Let me just grab a few things and we'll get out of here.

I can come back for the rest tomorrow," he said. He gathered up the computers and led Angela down to the car. They didn't need to stay all night. They had all the proof they needed that something was definitely wrong in that house.

In the morning, Randy puzzled over the computers. After a few experiments, he found the problems. The batteries were fried and would need to be replaced, as were the power cords. Once he removed the failed batteries and used a spare cord, he got them both running, but all of the recordings from the night before were wiped.

Until now he had considered whatever was happening in the house to be benign. After all, Angela swore it was her mother, and she had a good relationship with her mother, but sending a surge of electricity to blow out the computers was a clear threat.

They had to get into the desk. That much was obvious. They had to get into the desk in the daytime. Angela said even when she was home alone nothing ever happened in the daytime. But something about the previous night's events bothered Randy. The sounds they heard from the desk—those weren't warning sounds. Those sounds seemed to beckon them, as if something wanted them to open the desk. But then when they got into the room, Angela heard the voice again, telling her to go back to bed. It didn't make sense for the thing—whatever it was—to lure her out only to scare her away. If it weren't for the sounds—last night from the desk, the other nights of the footsteps in the hall—she never would have gotten out of the bed at all.

What if, he wondered, there were two spirits at play here? If the voice, with its anger and frustration, was her mother, then maybe the other thing was someone else, perhaps her brother. She said that she hadn't felt his presence in a long time, but now she was effectively an orphan, so maybe he knew she needed him.

Randy thought back to the pictures they'd seen on the Facebook pages of Angela's lost family members. Her brother had been in some of them. Maybe he was tired of the secrets their parents were keeping from her.

They had to go back to the house. They had to investigate again, but this time, no computer equipment. This time, they needed help from someone who could communicate with the dead. They needed Calliope Savidos.

Randy expected Angela to resist his request that they go back to the house again, but she didn't. She agreed, and she said the sooner the better. For the second night in a row, they drove together in the evening to the quiet street full of big homes tucked back from the road, a home so new that no one would imagine that there could be any lingering ghosts there.

Angela looked like she hadn't eaten in days. In fact, Randy hadn't seen her eat anything in the many hours they'd spent together in the past week. Tonight, he knew, would be the game changer. Tonight she could get some closure. When he thought of the way she'd kissed him the night before, he felt the strongest urge to gather her up in his arms and take her out of here. The way he felt around her—he had never felt such a crushing desire to protect someone in his life.

He'd spent all of his middle and high school years

protecting himself against the casual cruelty of pretty, popular girls like Angela and had a well-developed sense of suspicion that kicked in whenever a girl like her approached him, even now, even knowing he was no longer that scrawny little nerd with the big ugly glasses and braces and comic books in his back pocket. He rejected girls who exuded the confidence of high school prom queens in advance, so they never had a chance to reject him. And now here he was, head over heels for a girl who represented everything he hated—phoniness, superficiality, pettiness. Obviously, Angela wasn't really those things, but he still had moments of doubt when it felt like this was all some elaborate practical joke.

And then he saw the fear and vulnerability in her eyes when she turned to him for reassurance and he knew, she wasn't faking anything. This was no prank. She trusted him, and she needed him to trust her. Still, they had to take things slowly. There was no reason to rush the relationship and every reason to take their time. The ghost investigation, though, that was time sensitive.

Together they went around the house and gathered up the cameras and microphones they'd left in place the night before. Then they sat in the den watching TV, not really talking, just waiting.

Calliope arrived at eleven and greeted Randy with enthusiasm. She was a tall woman with wild black curls, gaudy makeup, and flowing clothing. She wore a ring on every finger, bangles on her wrists, several necklaces around her neck. In others words, she fully fit the stereotypes her customers had of psychic mediums. Randy had known her long enough to expect her theatrics, but he also knew she was the real deal. People saw her and their expectations fell because she looked like a cartoon character, but then they witnessed her at work and they became believers.

The first thing she did upon entering the house was to embrace Angela, pulling her in so that Angela's head nestled between her substantial breasts, and holding her close for several minutes before letting Angela go.

"Do you hear ghosts often?" Calliope asked.

Angela frowned and shook her head. Why would she hear ghosts often? What other ghosts could possibly want to talk to her?

Calliope asked for a tour of the house, and they showed her around, detailing what they'd witnessed so far. As Randy had done the night before, she explored the desk, but she was slower and more methodical about it, placing her hands flat on the roll-top and closing her eyes as if the desk might communicate to her, peering at the drawer-handles up close, getting down on her knees to look into the space where the chair fit. If she gleaned anything from this, she didn't say.

They went back downstairs to the kitchen and sat at the table. Calliope needed to ask Angela questions to prepare. Randy could see that Angela was hesitant to reveal anything, but he reassured her. This wasn't like having one's fortune told. Calliope needed to know about the people she would be communicating with. She wasn't going to spin the details Angela gave her to pretend she could talk to the dead, Randy reassured her. Reluctantly, Angela spoke. She explained about her father's illness, her brother's death, her mother's perfectionism, and her recent discovery of relatives she never knew she had.

Randy hadn't yet told Angela of his theory about two presences in the house. In fact, he had tried not to talk about the investigation all day in the hopes that she'd be able to relax a little. Now, though, he had to speak. Calliope needed to know what he thought. He cleared his throat.

"I have a theory to run by y'all."

Angela looked at him, surprised. Calliope gestured for him to speak.

"I think there are conflicting spirits at work here. One, maybe her brother, who wants Angela to know something, and one—her mother, I think—who wants to make sure she doesn't find out what."

As he explained his idea, Calliope nodded agreeably, but Angela stared at him, slowly shaking her head.

"That can't be it," Angela said, when he'd finished.

Randy thought he had explained it all clearly. It was hard to see what she might be objecting to. "It makes sense, though," he said.

"I don't know," Angela said. She bit her lip. She looked like she wanted to say more, but then she just shook her head, shrugged, and looked away.

"Well, my dears, isn't that what y'all brought me here? To find out? Randy's theory is nice, and if it has any truth to it, I'll find out." Then she stood up, gathering her notes, and said she needed some things from her car.

Alone in the kitchen, Randy tried to get Angela to look at him, but she was obstinate in her refusal.

"All that stuff about Ryan," she said, "I don't know. I used to say his ghost watched over me, but that was so long ago. It's like I can't trust those memories. What if I made it all up?"

And Randy thought he understood. Angela doubted her own stories of her brother's ghost. Of course she did. She had been a kid when all that happened, and now looking back her mind wanted to find logical explanations. That was only natural. Faith was always tested by doubt.

"It's okay," Randy said.

"I just wanted people to think I was special, you know? Everyone else had brothers and sisters, and I didn't, but if I was going to be different, I could at least be special, right?"

Randy made a face to suggest that she was being silly. She had never need to prove she was special, she was born a cool kid.

"I didn't mean to lie," she said. "I mean, I don't know now if something happened, and then I embellished it, or if I told the stories so many times I started to believe them, or what." She looked pathetic and cute.

"All that was a very long time ago, and anyway, kids are very intuitive. Maybe you should give your memory more credit."

A look of relief washed over her face. "I feel like no one ever believed me," she said, and then she let out a sad little laugh. "My life isn't usually this melodramatic."

"The thing is," Randy said, "we need to figure out what's happening now, and whatever happened in the past, I really think it's not just your mother in the house, because I heard that stuff last night, too. I haven't heard the voice that you hear, but I heard the desk. I saw the shadow."

Angela nodded solemnly.

"Come here," he said, drawing her in. He rested his cheek on the top of her head. He could smell the fruity scent of her shampoo.

They heard Calliope open the front door and dropped their embrace like kids who had just been caught by one of their moms.

"Interrupting, am I?" Calliope asked. "Let's get started then."

Chapter Twenty-six

Devil's Back Island, Maine

BRETT SAT AT the desk beside the open window of his small hotel room, watching the sun dip behind the mainland across the bay. He wanted the deal to work out, for his own sake and for Rosetta's, but he would have to start from scratch in designing the resort and conference center, because the usual models just wouldn't work here.

Most Sweet Water Resorts sat on wide, flat beaches with long stretches of sand, but here the beach was a small cove nestled in cliff rock. Usually, Sweet Water properties were large, high-rise hotels with fine dining restaurants surrounded by condo villages with their own pools and snack bars. To do anything like that here, they'd have to buy the whole island.

How could he interest Charlie in doing something so unlike their typical set up? He was way out on a limb here, and it seemed like the branch might break at any second.

But the island was gorgeous. There was no denying that. It was pristine, quiet, and timeless. Those were the features he would have to use to his advantage. This wouldn't be the typical beach-and-golf arrangement. For one thing, there was definitely no room on the island for a golf course. But they could cater to the sailing and deep-sea fishing set. Offer chartered sailboat cruises, dolphin cruises, fishing excursions, that sort of thing.

And entertainment. They'd have to have a steady stream of live entertainment. Or maybe they could package it as a couples resort. Adults only. That might work. All people wanted at couples resorts were big beds, soft sheets, swimming pools, and places to sunbathe. They could do that here.

Brett scrawled some notes and then sighed. This might be a hopeless mission.

But the fact was that Rosetta wasn't even beginning to scratch the surface of possibilities here. The hotel, which her brochure described as having "Old-Fashioned Sea-Side Charm," was so hopelessly outdated that he couldn't believe she had managed to stay open this long. The rooms were tiny, with hideous wallpaper, threadbare carpets, and old creaky beds. Everything had a musty smell. Only a handful of rooms had air-conditioning, and although Brett knew that air-conditioning was only a necessity here for a small part of the year, travelers sought comfort, and sweating it out on a hot night in this tiny room was anything but.

And the bathroom. It was like something from a horror movie. Cracked titles on the floor, rust-stained toilet bowls, shower stalls with cheap vinyl sides. It looked clean, or as clean as something so old and worn could look, but that did not really improve matters.

If they put up a new, all-amenities hotel, they could pack

this place all summer, and with a few special promotions they could keep the traffic flowing throughout the off-season, too. They'd done it in other "summer" places, and with great success. You just had to find the right gimmicks to attract a young crowd with deep pockets. At the moment, it seemed the median age of island guests was 65. Not Sweet Water's target audience.

That bakery, though. That was something. They'd have to cut a deal with Casey, hire her on to run the hotel's coffee shop. They could offer her a better salary than she was making now. She could have charged him double for the lattes he'd gotten there and he wouldn't have blinked. She was underselling herself.

But they could change her life. They could give her security, better pay, and more help. That morning she had looked exhausted. She had still been stunning—her bright red hair (which suited her, even though it was obviously dyed), her big hazel eyes and full lips, her slender arms, that tattoo. She was absolutely beautiful. And not his type at all.

He didn't go in for angsty alterna-chicks. Not anymore. Twenty years ago (okay, ten years ago), though, she would have been irresistible to him. Ah, the mistakes of youth. He used to be drawn to the deep, romantic, damn-the-man types back in the day. The problem was that once he got to know them, they were never that deep, their down-with-the-mainstream attitudes were just posturing, and what seemed like a romantic disposition at first usually turned out to be more like a mood disorder.

And why was he even thinking about this at all? He should be thinking about Ashley. She wanted to meet up when he got back to Los Angeles, and he needed to figure out how to win her back. The fact that he really didn't want to return to Los Angeles was beside the point. If he could make this deal work, and if he could convince his bosses to relocate him here to see it through and get it up and running, if he could convince Ashley to come with him, they could have a great life. She would love it, if she'd only give it a chance.

He glanced at the clock. 8:30. Only 5:30 in L.A. Ashley would be teaching her evening class. There was no point in calling her for the reassurance of hearing her voice, and anyway that hadn't gone great the last time. He grabbed his wallet and hotel room key (This place still used actual keys! How ridiculous! He hadn't been to a hotel with actual keys since he was on vacation at the Jersey shore with his parents back when he was a kid!) and headed for the White Sails Tavern, the island's "upscale" bar and the only "fine dining" on offer.

The decor—fishing nets, harpoons mounted to the walls, lobster traps hanging from the ceiling—didn't exactly scream fine dining, nor did the menu: Baked haddock with a Ritz cracker crust, scallops baked in a cream sauce and topped with Ritz cracker crumbs, baked stuffed fish rolled in (you guessed it) Ritz cracker crumbs. Apparently Ritz crackers were the height of sophistication here on Devil's Back Island. There was no beer list full of interesting micro brews, no cocktail menu full of exotic drink possibilities, and the wine list had exactly three options in red and three in white.

Actually, when he was done guffawing about it, Brett sort of enjoyed the novelty of it all. When was the last time he ate at a place like this? Probably when he was visiting his grandparents as a kid and they'd taken him out to their favorite restaurant where the bread basket featured slices of white, store-bought bread (Wonder Bread, perhaps?) and little packets of cold, hard butter.

He ordered a Miller Lite, and when the bartender slid the drink in front of him, he also offered a basket of pretzels, which Brett happily accepted. It was kind of fun being away from all the phoniness he was used to, everyone philosophizing over their beer, describing the character of the hops and the floral notes of the whatever. What was wrong with just having a regular old beer, nice and cold, with some plain old boring pretzels?

Sitting at a bar alone led him into a philosophical frame of mind. What was wrong with a nice, simple restaurant like this? Did every restaurant in the nation need to serve parmesan truffle fries and artisanal cheese slates? Over the years, he'd grown used to the shiny surfaces of everything Sweet Water. When he first started working for the company, he was in awe of the polished splendor of it all. Then he'd begun to take it for granted. And then later, he'd gotten acquainted with the underside of all that glitz, and that had led him to develop a conscience that kept nagging him about his current career path.

For one thing, the environmental toll was outrageous. The carbon footprint of people flying all over the world to escape their lives. The water needed for the daily laundry for a massive hotel. The fossil fuels burned to generate the electricity required to keep hotel rooms a comfortable 68 degrees in tropical climates. The mountains of trash hauled away from a hotel each day.

Then there was the actual impact on local people. Yes,

Sweet Water offered jobs, but they were unskilled positions with low wages. The people who worked in the resorts had excessive wealth paraded in front of their faces daily, while they were barely making enough to feed their families. However glowing the surface of a Sweet Water property was, the truth underneath was toxic. The glow wasn't heavenly light; it was radiation. But what else could he do? He'd devoted eighteen years to keeping that poisonous surface prosperous, and he didn't know how to walk away.

He was starting to feel downright melancholy when he glanced down the bar and saw Casey wander in. He motioned to the bartender for a refill and brushed away thoughts of the economy of exploitation in which he participated. This was his chance to show Casey he wasn't just some jerk trying to take up space with a laptop. It was show time.

Chapter Twenty-seven

St. Nabor Island, South Carolina

CALLIOPE WAS NOT at all what Angela had expected. Randy swore the woman was the real deal, but when she showed up in her flowing black dress, utterly decked out in layers of costume jewelry, Angela had to stop herself from rolling her eyes.

But when they set up for the—Angela wasn't sure what you'd call what they were doing. Was séance too middle-school cliché? What had Randy called it? Another investigation, she supposed—it started to feel real.

Calliope brought a large round cloth, like a tablecloth, with writing and symbols on it, which she spread on the floor of Angela's mother's office. She set two candles on the top of the desk and one in the center of the cloth, and then she asked Randy and Angela to sit on the floor. She sat, too, so that they were forming a little triangle at the edges of the cloth.

Calliope closed her eyes, said something so softly that Angela couldn't make out the words, and then leaned forward, making a sort of circling gesture over the candle's flame with her hands, as if she were ushering the light or smoke or scent of the candle up toward her face. Then she opened her eyes and dropped her hands to her knees. She looked like an oddly dressed yoga teacher, cross-legged on the floor like that, back straight, first finger and thumb of each hand touching while her other fingers were relaxed.

They sat in silence for what could have been five minutes or fifteen. Angela's feet went numb, but Calliope and Randy were both remaining so still that she wasn't sure she was allowed to adjust her pose, so she tried to ignore it.

And then the candles—all three simultaneously— flickered as if someone had tried to blow them out. Calliope raised her hands like a priest at church, palms up, and took several long, slow breaths. She closed her eyes, cocked her head, nodded, as if she were in conversation with someone. Angela couldn't hear whatever Calliope was hearing, but she could hear sounds, a low rumbling like an engine in the distance or distant thunder, except the sound was inside her head, the way her mother's voice was when Angela heard it in the night.

At last, Calliope opened her eyes, looked at Angela, and smiled. "It's your father," Calliope said. "There are things he needs you to know."

Angela frowned and shook her head. "My father is alive."

"He's in a nursing home," Randy added. Angela thought she detected a hint of concern on his face.

Calliope was utterly unruffled by this news of her failure. She closed her eyes again, listening to something only she could hear. When she reopened her eyes she said, "He says he's your father. He says you need to find your mother."

Randy grasped Angela's hand and squeezed it and then said, "You've got it backwards. Angela's mother recently died. Her father is still alive."

Calliope pursed her lips and shrugged.

"Cal, Angela visited her father just the other day, and just a couple of weeks ago, she buried her mother. You're wrong on this one."

Behind Randy, the candle on the desk flickered out. All three of them turned to look.

"This is no time for playing games," Randy said.

Calliope raised her hands as if she were under arrest and shook her head. "No lies, my friend. I tell y'all what the spirits tell me. This spirit says he's her father."

Angela felt a lump rising in her throat. Her parents had lied about so much. They had hidden dozens of relatives from her. Could they have lied about this, too? And what had Belle, the so-called psychic, said? She had thought Angela was estranged from her mother. She had been surprised when Angela said she was dead. "It's okay, Randy," she said. "Ask him his name."

But just as Calliope began to do the deep-breathing thing she did while communicating with the spirit world, the doorbell rang. At the sound, Angela, who had been expecting the angry voice to fill her head again any moment now, leapt, knocking over the candle on the floor. Calliope snatched it up before all the wax could spill, before the cloth could catch fire, and Randy jumped to his feet.

"Who's that?" he asked, looking at Angela.

She had no idea.

"Do you think it could be Grace?"

She shook her head. Grace seemed not to have noticed

that for the past several nights Angela hadn't come home, returning instead in the morning to shower and change. She was the most hands-off host imaginable. There was no way she'd come out in the night looking for Angela.

"Maybe it's," Angela paused, swallowed, felt her hands tremble, "Maybe it's like the computers the other night, an electrical fault or something."

Calliope shook her head. "That's no ghost ringing the bell." She began gathering up her things. Apparently the investigation was over.

The bell rang again.

Randy took the lead and went downstairs and opened the front door. As it swung open, Angela found herself face to face with her mother. Then she passed out.

Angela came to on the sofa. Randy was kneeling beside her, patting her hand. As her eyes focused, she didn't see anyone else in the room, but when she recalled the sight of her mother in the doorway, her heart raced, and she sat up and looked around. Randy gently pressed her back down against the sofa and offered her a sip of water.

"Did you see her?" she asked.

"Yes."

Angela hadn't expected that answer. She blinked and waited for him to say something else, but he didn't, so Angela said, "You saw my mother?"

"She says she's your aunt," Randy said.

"You saw the pictures of my aunt," Angela said, struggling to follow what he was saying. The woman at the door had been her mother—her mother's eyes, nose, chin, height, but not the hair. Her mother's hair was blonder, tidier.

"Not your dad's sister. Your mom's sister," Randy said.

"My mother's sister?" Angela repeated, feeling stupid and confused and exhausted. Her mother had long-lost siblings, too? How far did her parents' trail of lies go?

Chapter Twenty-eight

Devil's Back Island, Maine

CASEY WAITED UNTIL she was sure Jason was gone, and then she stood up, scraped the grilled cheese sandwich into the trash, and grabbed her wallet. She couldn't possibly sit around alone in her apartment all night. Instead, she went to the closest thing Devil's Back Island had to a night spot, the bar at the White Sails Tavern.

The tavern, like her café, was in a house that had been converted from a private residence to a restaurant. Unlike the café, which had been a cottage, the tavern was a large salt-box. It was the oldest remaining building on the island, built in 1822. That was half of its claim to fame. The other half, regrettably, was not the food, but the lore of the tavern ghost. Casey had no interest in the history, the food, or the ghost, on that early fall evening. She was interested only in the bar.

She waved to Michelle, the hostess, and passed through to the bar, which was in the part of the house that had originally been the kitchen. The original fireplace, where the women would have cooked over an open fire, had been restored, and on chilly evenings, there was always a welcoming blaze, but tonight the weather was warm, the fireplace was cold, and the restaurant was crowded. The bar ran along the back wall, and as Casey approached, she noticed Brett sitting at the far end near a window. Just her luck. She stood up a little taller, took a breath, and then walked up to the other side, hoping to escape notice. She ordered a beer, and as she awaited it, she felt Brett looking at her. She glanced in his direction, and he waved and gestured for her to join him. Just what she needed. A night of making conversation with Mr. Charm. She decided she'd say hello, finish her beer, and then go home.

"I thought you'd be resting up for our big adventure tomorrow," Brett said, as she climbed onto the barstool next to his.

"Tomorrow?" she said, taking a swig of her beer.

"Don't tell me you forgot! You don't seem like the forgetful type." He smiled and she wondered how he kept his teeth so white. They practically glowed.

She blinked. Tomorrow. Tomorrow was Tuesday. No, tomorrow was Wednesday. Her day off. Her day off on which she'd agreed to take the preppy vegan on an island tour. And as she remembered that promise, she also remembered that she'd left the café in a state of disaster, when in her exhaustion she failed to recall that the next day was her day off. Shit and double shit.

"Sorry," she said. "Long day. What time tomorrow?"

"Actually I was hoping you'd tell me."

"Why?"

"I thought we should take some kayaks out. That will

give me the best sense of it all."

"You know the water is freezing cold, right?"

He smiled his charming, white-toothed smile. "I bet it's warmer now than it was for half the summer. I hear the water in September is as good as it gets."

She leaned over the bar and waved to the bartender. "You got a tide chart around here?" she asked.

He returned a moment later with the Island Advisor, a seasonal bulletin put out by the tourism bureau, which was basically just Rosetta. Low tide tomorrow was at eleven-thirty in the morning. She considered how long it would realistically take for them to get around to the other side.

"You kayak much?" she asked.

"Actually, I've never done it before," he said.

Great. She'd have to teach him to kayak in addition to guiding him.

"It looks easy enough. I work out a lot, so I'm sure it'll be fine." He said this as a simple matter of fact, without any irony or boastfulness, as if he thought whatever workouts he did at his fancy gym at home would qualify him to be a natural in a kayak.

"I guess, to be safe, we should leave at nine," Casey said. Her one morning of the entire week to have a slow start was officially ruined.

"Rosetta said that the ghost sightings at Lover's Leap have all been at low tide."

Casey let out a little derisive laugh. Ghost sightings. For heaven's sake. Casey could think of few ghost stories that were more clichéd and suspicious than the ones Rosetta cooked up for tourists. Was there a cliff in the universe that hadn't been dubbed Lover's Leap?

"What?" Brett asked.

Casey took a huge sip of her beer before looking back at him. "You're a smart guy. You don't believe those stories?"

"Seems like the closest thing the island has to a tourist attraction."

"Oh, God," Casey said. She finished her beer and set the glass heavily on the bar.

"Besides, there are loads of things that are beyond explanation," Brett said. He waved to the bartender and ordered them each another beer. "I have seen some freaky things in my travels, stuff that would make a believer out of anyone."

Casey rolled her eyes. She did not disagree that there were loads of things beyond explanation. Actually, she had no doubt that ghosts existed, but she was certain they weren't anything like what Rosetta invented for her Halloween Fest, and Rosetta knew it, too. That said, she wasn't in the habit of discussing her family's talent for talking to spirits. Growing up, she'd been so embarrassed by her mother's obsession with paranormal activity. She'd seen it as a sign of mental illness, until she, too, experienced it. It wasn't something to boast about. It was one more thing to hide.

"But it's fun, isn't it?"

"If morbidity is fun, sure." People didn't get what it was like to actually encounter the spirit of someone who had died. If they did, they would know to leave the dead alone.

The bartender came back and set the beers in front of them. Brett waited for him to move away before he answered.

"Don't try to hide behind me if we see the ghost tomorrow," he said, tipping his glass to her before taking a sip.

Casey shook her head and rolled her eyes. Ghosts. One of the things she liked about living on Devil's Back was how few ghosts lingered here. Rosetta was full of shit.

And then, somehow, Casey found herself on her fourth beer. In the haze of alcohol, Brett seemed funny and not nearly as ridiculous as he had sober. He was handsome, too. Maybe a little too put together, which was not her usual type, but still, he was an undeniably good-looking guy.

"You know, the vegan selection on the island is appalling," he said. "I might have to adopt a 'when in Rome attitude' for this project. I've heard the clam chowder here is fantastic."

"Are you hungry?" Casey asked, remembering suddenly that she had not eaten lunch or dinner. The room swayed, and she knew she absolutely needed food before she attempted to stand up again.

"I could eat," Brett said.

They ordered a plate of fried calamari and two cups of clam chowder, good heavy food to hold the beer down. They ate in companionable silence and when they were finished, Casey noticed how empty the bar had become. She glanced at the clock behind the bar and saw that it was nearly eleven o'clock, closing time at the bar on the early-bird island.

"Well, that was worth it," Brett said, putting his napkin on his plate and pushing it away from him. "You know, I don't mind skipping meat and even dairy, but there's nothing like some good seafood."

"Why are you vegan, anyway?" Casey asked. Her pre-meal giddiness had settled down. She still felt drunk, but not fall-down drunk.

"The things we do for love," he said, shrugging.

Casey made a face. In her experience, when people

said they were doing something for love, what they really meant was that they were acting out of fear. When people actually did something for love, it wasn't something they had to explain to a stranger as an act of love, because it was so obvious. Giving up two food groups sounded like an act of desperate approval-seeking to Casey.

"What about you? You have a significant other?"

"Significant other?" she asked, raising an eyebrow. Around here, no one bothered with politically correct questions. She couldn't imagine any islanders using the words significant other. "Where are you from?"

"I live in Los Angeles, but I grew up in upstate New York."

"Vegan. Significant other. I should have guessed California. That's all a little New Age for me."

"Soulmate?" he said, smiling and raising an eyebrow.

"Gentleman caller?" Casey said, enjoying his banter. "No. I do not. Pickings are slim around these parts." She thought about Jason, the wounded look on his face just hours earlier. He was a nice guy, and good in bed, but he was so young. And a pothead. It wasn't as if she'd broken his heart.

"I have noticed an age gap," Brett said.

Casey shrugged. "I'm not here looking for love," she said, draining the last of her beer and deciding that she must not order another, though she was tempted.

"Oh come on. Everyone's looking for love."

"Okay, Mr. Romantic." Casey stood up and had to reach for the bar to steady herself. The food had taken the edge off her drunkenness, but she was by no means sober. "We can discuss this more in the morning." That early wake up call for a morning of kayaking was going to be miserable. Her punishment for how she'd treated Jason.

"Calling it quits already?" he asked, glancing at his watch.

Casey was suddenly flooded with a feeling of exhaustion. Her afternoon nap had not been enough to make up for a string of sleepless nights. She wavered a little on her feet. Had she been sober, she probably would have made a joke about how he was on West Coast time, but she couldn't manage any quips at the moment.

"I'll walk with you," Brett said, slapping a few bills on the bar and standing up.

Casey realized he was paying for her, but she didn't object. Her head felt heavy and fuzzy. She hated the way alcohol hit her in waves. One minute she was having a fine time and the next she was utterly dysfunctional. "It's fine," she said, her tongue feeling thick in her mouth. "I'm fine. It's only a short walk." She waved him off and turned to walk away, wobbling. For a moment, she was afraid she was actually going to pass out, and when she felt Brett's hand on her arm, she knew that resisting his offer would be a mistake. She actually might not make it back to her place if she struck out on her own.

"Come on, lightweight. Let's get you home."

Outside, the warmth of the day had faded, although the humidity still hung in the air, thick as a blanket. In the morning, there'd be fog. Casey liked going out on the water in the fog, even though she knew it was dangerous. She loved the sense of being the only person in the world, just floating on the nothingness of a glass-smooth bay with nothing to look at and no one looking at her.

"I live above the café," Casey said, leaning into Brett a

little. Then she hiccuped and burst into hysterical laughter, which she quickly suppressed, realizing that it was late, that the windows of the cottages they passed were probably open in hopes of catching the evening breeze.

"I think I owe you an apology," Brett said. "I may have influenced you into drinking a few too many beers."

Casey snorted. She had gone to the bar with the express purpose of getting drunk. She'd be stumbling in the dark alone now if Brett hadn't been there. She knew better than to do this to herself. She really did. But knowing and doing are two different things. "I don't usually drink this much," she said.

"Yeah, I'm getting that impression," Brett said, catching her as she staggered sideways on the gravel path.

"I'm sorry. Rough day is all." She didn't know why she felt like she owed him an explanation, but she did. She always felt like apologizing, that was her problem. Why did she always feel like she'd done something wrong? Everyone gets drunk sometimes.

"We've all been there," he said.

He was being so nice. Just like Jason. So nice. It would be so much easier if he'd act annoyed. Then she could be annoyed that he was annoyed. Instead, she felt like crying.

They arrived at the café and she led him around to the back stairs. She gripped the railing and stepped out of his grasp.

"Thanks," she said.

"Maybe I should help you up."

If he hadn't professed his deep love for his vegan girlfriend just an hour before, Casey would have been suspicious of this offer. She didn't think he had any untoward designs. Actually the offer was sort of insulting. She wasn't that drunk. The walk had sobered her. For heaven's sake, she could make it up the stairs.

"No, I'm fine," she said, firmly. She pulled herself up the stairs, but she noticed that he was standing at the bottom watching her, not walking away. She got to the door and struggled to pull the key from her jeans pocket. She leaned her forehead on the door and fumbled with the door handle. She just needed to lie down. If only she could get the damn key in damn lock.

"How about I help with that?"

She hadn't even noticed that Brett had come up the stairs to stand beside her. He took the key from her hand and opened the door. Then he put a hand on her back and escorted her into her apartment as if he owned the place. He walked with her to the bedroom, where she dropped onto the bed, a dead weight.

Brett picked up her ankles and swung her legs over onto the bed. She felt him hovering over her. Her eyes flickered open, and she felt a little flutter of fear. What was he doing? She glanced up at him and he smiled. "You have an alarm clock? I don't want you to be late tomorrow."

Casey groaned and turned her face into the pillow.

"You going to be okay?"

She could hear a note of concern in his voice. He was probably imagining her asphyxiating in her sleep.

"I promise I'll sleep on my stomach," she said.

"Sweet dreams," he said. He reached across her and pulled the blanket over her, and then she heard his footsteps as he showed himself out.

Chapter *Twenty-nine*

St. Nabor Island, South Carolina

MARILYN HADN'T MEANT to show up at twelve-thirty in the morning unannounced, but nothing that day had gone as planned. Starting around eight o'clock that morning, she had begun trying to reach her brother-in-law and her niece, right after she checked her email and got the Google alert to her sister's obituary. She'd set that Google alert years ago. It had been so long since it turned anything up, she'd forgotten all about it. And then that morning, there it was. Deb was dead. She couldn't begin to believe it.

First she called the number for her sister's office, but no one there would give her any information, not surprisingly. After more sleuthing, she discovered that Angela had been enrolled at St. Katherine's College in New Hampshire, so she called there, but again, only dead ends. In a stroke of inspiration, she called the parish the obituary had listed in the funeral information. After explaining who she was to the secretary, she'd been passed on to the priest, to whom she explained her long estrangement from her sister, and he revealed that Richard was in a nursing home and that Angela was living at home for now. And then, gem of a man that he was, he gave her the home phone number and address. Marilyn left a voicemail message, but when she didn't hear back after an hour or so, she was too antsy to keep waiting. She did what anyone would do: She drove to the airport. She couldn't just sit there and do nothing.

Having made up her mind to take action, however, the universe conspired to detain her. First she'd had to wait around at the airport for hours on standby to get a flight. Then, once she'd been assigned a seat on one, severe thunderstorms delayed take off from JFK. She kept calling her sister's house and leaving messages, updating her plan and ETA. At last, her plane departed from New York, and it should have been a short flight, but backups at the Charlotte airport, where she had a stopover, had caused the plane to circle for an hour before landing, which caused her to miss her connection, and of course, she couldn't call to offer more updates or check to see if Angela had ever returned any of her calls when she was in the air. When she landed in Charlotte she raced to the ticketing counter and got rebooked onto the last flight into Savannah. She had to race to get on the plane and never had a chance to call.

When at last she got off the plane in Savannah, she was exhausted and emotionally drained, and all she wanted was to go to sleep. It only then occurred to her that perhaps she should have made hotel arrangements. But, she reasoned, Angela was a kid. Kids stay up late. She would just go to the house. Enough of this waiting game. She'd waited twenty years to know her niece, and she wasn't going to wait any longer.

She was somewhat dismayed that Angela hadn't returned any of her phone calls, but then again, weren't her friends always complaining about how their children never responded to their messages? And if Angela's reason for ignoring her was not just typical young-adult laziness, if it had to do with the fact that Marilyn and Deb had been out of touch for the entirety of Angela's life, then better to face Angela as soon as possible and get it over with.

Marilyn found a cab willing to drive the 40-odd miles to St. Nabor Island, and they pulled up at half-past midnight. The house was dark, but there was a car in the driveway. She could see lights in one of the rooms upstairs, too. This was it. She was here. She was almost too tired to be nervous as she pressed the doorbell.

And the handsome young man opened the door. And the lovely young woman—Angela—fainted like a Victorian lady. And the gypsy woman looked on in a bemused but unsurprised way. And Marilyn realized that she had probably acted in haste, flying down here like this.

The gypsy woman, who turned out to be a psychic medium named Calliope, of all ridiculous things, took Marilyn into the kitchen, while the handsome young man took care of Angela. Calliope briefly explained that they had been trying to communicate with some spirits that had been troubling Angela in the house since her mother's death. Marilyn half-listened, but she was so overwhelmed to be in her sister's house, to be surrounded by her sister's beautiful possessions in her perfectly decorated home, to pay much attention. When she did pay attention, she understood that she should be concerned for her niece if she thought she was being haunted, because ghosts weren't real.

Eventually the young man came to the kitchen and told Marilyn that Angela wanted to see her. Calliope declared that she would send him a bill and headed for the door. Marilyn followed the young man, who introduced himself as Randy, to the living room.

Angela was sitting up now. She didn't appear to have suffered any injuries in her fall, thank God. Marilyn supposed the expensive-looking oriental rug in the entry was plush. Marilyn sat opposite her, a coffee table between them, and Randy sat beside her. Angela resembled Deb, and by extension herself. Marilyn could see that now. That must have made Deb's lies so much easier.

"You look like her," Angela said.

"You do, too," Marilyn said. Then, as Angela sat silently, expectantly, Marilyn realized Angela wasn't going to ask questions or make this easy. It was up to Marilyn to explain herself, which seemed entirely unfair since it was Deb's fault that she hadn't been a part of Angela's life.

She cleared her throat and said, "Your mom and I were only a year apart," Marilyn said. "She was my little sister. For a long time, my best friend."

"She said she didn't have any siblings," Angela said, accusingly.

"We had a disagreement, before you were born."

"And now she's dead and you thought you'd just show up?"

Well, yes, Marilyn thought, something like that. But she said, "You and I are family." She thought she saw Angela's cold facade melt a little at the word family. "I was so lucky that I got to watch Ryan grow up," Marilyn said, and as she spoke the words began to tumble out of her. "He was such a good kid, smart and funny and handsome. The only thing I hated about living in New York was that I didn't get to see him more often. I loved him so much. My God he would be proud to see you now—" Marilyn stopped when she noticed the strange look on Angela's face. "I'm sorry, did I say something wrong?"

"Why did my parents lie to me?" Angela asked. "Why didn't they tell me about you and about my dad's siblings?"

Marilyn shook her head, wondering if she'd done the right thing coming here. Why had she come? For closure, she supposed. For some kind of proof that her little sister was really dead. But if that's what she wanted, she could have just gone to the cemetery and then flown back home. She had been drawn to Angela, she had been pulled here with a sense of purpose, and, if she was honest with herself, she knew exactly what that purpose was: To tell her the truth. But to what end? What good would it do Angela to know the truth now? She would never be able to look back on her childhood again without seeing it through the haze of the lie, and if this beautiful home were any indicator, the girl had had a very nice life so far.

"Your mother and I disagreed about you," Marilyn said.

"And my dad's siblings did, too?" Angela asked, looking at her dubiously.

What could Marilyn say? No lie she could invent would be big enough to cover her sister's lies.

As far as Angela knew, Deb and Richard were her parents, but biologically, they were not her parents. And that was the reason Deb and Rich cut off all ties with the rest of the family. That was the reason they moved to South Carolina. That was the reason Marilyn had lost her little sister and best friend. Marilyn hadn't approved of the deception, but she had sworn that she'd go along with it, if only Deb wouldn't leave, but Deb knew better. She knew that if they stayed, the truth would find its way out. Too many people would know. Too many people for it to be a secret.

Actually, some part of Marilyn had believed that by now Angela must know the truth. Adopted children always seem to find out, one way or another. They have the wrong blood type to be their parents' biological child, or they see a birth certificate and something on it doesn't make sense, or someone accidentally lets the truth slip. Rich had a big family. In all this time, had none of them ever sought to reconcile with him? Apparently not. So now it was up to her. Tell the truth that tore the family apart, or let Angela keep her family story as she knew it. Before Deb could make up her mind, Angela spoke again.

"Am I adopted?" Angela asked.

"Yes," Marilyn said.

"And you didn't think my parents should adopt me?"

"No. I mean, we were happy for them to bring a new child into their lives after Ryan's death, but your mother told me she wanted to pass you off as her own child, and I didn't think that was right," Marilyn said.

"So my parents took me away."

Marilyn nodded.

"And they never spoke to you again?"

"I tried a few times over the years, but your mother wouldn't."

"Why?"

"I guess she thought I'd tell you the truth." And, it seemed, Marilyn silently conceded, that Deb had been right.

First Belle had been so sure her mother was alive. Then Calliope had been so insistent that her father was dead. As Angela put those things together with the fact that her parents had hidden their actual pasts and families from her, there seemed to be very few logical conclusions she could reach. Either Belle and Calliope were frauds who were in cahoots or her parents were not her parents at all. But she looked just like her mother. Everyone said so. They couldn't coincidentally look so alike, could they? Then again, that a mother and her adopted daughter might look alike was at least as likely as hearing the voices of ghosts. When she had asked Marilyn if she was adopted, she had hoped, deep down, that the answer was no, but she knew it would be yes.

Still, she hadn't been prepared to consider what the answer meant and how much it mattered to her. So what if someone besides her mother had given birth to her? Her mother had raised her. The woman who gave birth to her had no claim over her as a mother, because she had chosen to abandon her, and the woman she'd always known as mother had loved her as if they were flesh and blood.

Her parents lost their beloved son and were too old to have another child of their own, so they adopted her to fill the void in their lives. They saved her from a sad, unwanted life. It made sense. As Angela began rewriting her history to create a new narrative that included this truth, she began to feel better, calmer. Her parents were good people. They'd done their best by her.

She supposed that this was what her mother's spirit

had been trying to keep from her, and she was certain that in unlocking the desk, she'd find some sort of proof. Her mother's spirit didn't want Angela going through the house and discovering it. But now she knew the truth, and she wasn't sure what was going to happen next. Would her mother's spirit go to wherever spirits are supposed to go? Would she have peace?

Sitting in the living room with this stranger who was her aunt, Angela had more questions than she could keep track of. She sifted through them in her mind and finally said, "Here's what I don't get. Why did you think it was so bad for them to let me think they were really my parents? If they had me since infancy, and I know they did because I've seen the pictures, why not just let us be a regular family?"

"Because I knew your biological parents."

Angela's mouth formed the shape of an O but no sound came out.

"Maybe we should all take a pause here," Randy said. "Maybe we should wait until morning to talk more. Angela, you don't have to listen to this. You don't know this woman."

"Look at her," Angela said. She was pointing to a family portrait on the side table. "Marilyn is obviously my mother's sister."

"That doesn't mean she isn't lying."

Angela shook her head and sighed. "Will you go get a crowbar from the garage?"

Randy gave her puzzled look.

"Let's open the desk."

Marilyn assured Angela that she would leave if Angela wanted her to, but Angela told her to stay. Randy returned with the crowbar, and the three of them went back to the study.

"I might damage it," Randy said as he tried to work out where to go at the desk first.

"Bash it to pieces for all I care," Angela said.

She felt numb. She hadn't even begun to take in the night's events. All she wanted now was some concrete proof that she was adopted, and once she had that, she'd listen to everything Marilyn had to say. With a splintering of wood, Randy pried open the lower desk drawers, and Angela pulled them fully from the desk and dumped the contents on the floor. She knelt down and began sifting through them. As she did, her mind was flooded with sound, more of the now-familiar but still unbearable noises that seemed to come from inside her own head but that were not part of her. There were no words now, though, just hissing and rumbling, and she wondered if she was actually losing her mind, but she gritted her teeth and shook her head against the noise, silently telling it to leave her alone. Whatever it was, whoever it was, she wasn't its plaything. She wanted it gone.

Marilyn, lingering in the doorway, said, "What are you looking for?"

When she spoke, the sounds in Angela's mind evaporated. The silence that remained rang in her ears. She shook her head again and said, "Proof."

Angela heard Marilyn's footsteps retreating down the steps, but didn't stop her or ask where she was going. She wasn't going far—she'd arrived by cab. A few minutes later, Marilyn returned with her purse. She sat on the floor beside Angela and pulled out a faded snapshot of Ryan and a girl. He was wearing a Chicago Bulls Jersey—a throwback to the era of MJ—and baggy jeans and his arm was around the girl's shoulder. Both of them were grinning as if they'd been caught mid-laugh. The girl was short and slim with long golden-brown hair, and she wore an oversized painter's smock.

"I don't need proof that you're my aunt. I believe you," Angela said, handing the picture back, and turning back to the piles of paper on the floor. Apparently her mother had never gotten rid of a single piece of paperwork in her life. Bank statements. Appliance warranties. Angela's elementary school report cards.

"Those are your parents," Marilyn said, thrusting the picture back in front of Angela.

Chapter Thirty

Devil's Back Island, Maine

ROSETTA KNEW THAT Brett had made plans with Casey for her day off, and had he been nearly any other man, she would have been thrilled. That girl needed to get out there and date, find a nice husband, and enjoy her life. She was entirely too serious and too gloomy. She needed someone who could provide a nice life for her. Brett was certainly a good foil for Jason, but Rosetta couldn't have Casey getting close to Brett.

Anyway, when Jason showed up at Rosetta's the night before and told her about the letter, he had shown remarkable judgment. Sure the kid was a stoner, but maybe Rosetta had underestimated him. Casey shouldn't jerk him around like that.

Cranky from a sleepless night of worrying, she trudged along the gravel path to the café with Bentley. Kim was behind the counter when Rosetta pushed through the door. She got two big cups of coffee and then went back outside and around the back to the steps to Casey's apartment. The door was locked. Sighing, Rosetta set down one of the coffees and fished her keys from her pocket. Pushing open the door, she sent Bentley in ahead of her.

"Go get her, boy," she said.

The dog wagged its tail and took off through the apartment. Rosetta followed at a leisurely pace, giving the dog time to pounce on the bed and wake Casey up so she wouldn't have to. When she heard Casey's startled shrieks, Rosetta went into the bedroom with the coffee as a peace offering for the rude awakening.

"Good God, girl, you reek," Rosetta said, setting the steaming drink on the side table. Maybe she'll be canceling her date with Brett without my intervention, Rosetta thought.

Casey was frantically trying to untangle herself from the sheets and shove Bentley off. At last she managed to get free and ran to the bathroom. Rosetta could hear her retching, but she didn't offer any kindly gestures like holding her hair off her face. Served the fool right. Instead Rosetta went to the living room and settled in on the futon to drink her own coffee.

Casey came back a few minutes later, wiping her face with a washcloth and looking no less green for having lost her dinner.

"What are you doing here?" Casey asked.

"And good morning to you, too," Rosetta replied, crossing her legs and sipping from her paper cup.

"It's my day off. It's my one day to sleep," Casey said.

"Whining is unbecoming. Besides, don't you have a date this morning?" Rosetta asked, raising an eyebrow. "You really need to give Kim a few more lessons. Her coffee isn't half as good as yours."

Casey pressed the washcloth against her eyes and

dropped back into the armchair.

"Honestly, I don't think you should see Brett today. Not in the state you're in."

"Jesus, Rosetta. You're always after me to date more."

"Well, he's not really the right sort, is he?"

"He has a girlfriend. I'm not going on a date with him."

Damn it, Rosetta thought. She needed Casey to stay away from him, and there was no way to tell her that without revealing more than she wanted to. She sighed and changed subjects.

"I had a little chat with Jason last night," she said, setting her cup on the coffee table and calling Bentley over to sit at her feet.

Casey dropped the washcloth and looked warily at Rosetta.

"He was worried about you."

Casey rolled her eyes and then tilted her head back and draped the washcloth over her face.

"Looks like he had good reason to be," Rosetta said.

"I'm a big girl. I can get drunk if I want to."

"Were you going to tell me about your mother?"

"Damn it," Casey said. She grabbed the washcloth and flung it across the room. It smacked the far wall wetly and thudded to the floor.

Rosetta had tried to hide her surprise when Jason told her about the letter he'd found among Casey's things, but she had been shocked. Rosetta had given up reaching out to Maureen after her last entreaty was met with the question, "Have you accepted Jesus as your Lord and Savior yet?" That had to have been at least three or four years ago. Casey hadn't spoken to her in much longer than that. Still, it was impossible to grapple with the fact that Maureen had gotten sick and died without either of them knowing. There should have been some kind of psychic connection between them. But no. Neither of them had had any idea that Maureen's life had come to a close. Here, they'd both assumed she was out there being a do-gooder, saving the world by picketing abortion clinics and whatnot, but actually she had given up the ghost.

"Well?" Rosetta said. "Is that all you have to say?"

"He shouldn't have read it."

"That may be, but he did. And he probably shouldn't have told me, but he did."

Casey stood up, glowering at Rosetta, and went to her room to get the coffee that Rosetta had brought for her and what remained of the letter. She came back and threw the melded blob of paper at Rosetta before sitting back down in the armchair.

"What's this?" Rosetta asked.

"Oh, he didn't tell you how after he read my rather personal letter he put it through the wash?"

Rosetta put the lump of paper on the coffee table and sighed. Jason had told her that the letter was from Casey's mother; that it said if she was reading it, then Maureen was dead; that it was an apology of sorts; that it said Maureen's cancer was the result of a genetic mutation that Casey might have inherited. In fact, he had offered so much mind-boggling information in a ten minute conversation that Rosetta was still reeling. And of course all Casey wanted to talk about was how Jason was an idiot.

"She was dead to me a long time ago," Casey said, when Rosetta was silent.

"You need to talk to a doctor, Casey," Rosetta said.

"Why would I do that?"

"You need to find out what your risks are, what you can do—"

Casey interrupted her. "Everyone's going to die some day. Do I really need a countdown timer?"

Rosetta felt her face flush with frustration. Why couldn't Casey see that genetic testing could give them both of peace of mind? It wasn't a foregone conclusion that Casey had inherited the mutation. She could get tested and learn that she was no more at risk than anyone else, and they could breathe a sigh of relief. Or she could learn that she was at risk and she could do things to minimize that risk. Take vitamins or start eating seaweed or any number of things that could supposedly prevent or reverse cancer.

"Don't be stupid. It's the twenty-first century, not the dark ages. There are things they can do," Rosetta said.

Every time Rosetta learned about some new breakthrough in diagnostic technology, she thought of Phil, and she thought of all the other people who wouldn't have to watch their loved ones die miserable, early deaths thanks to new, early detection tools. He'd only been 57 when he died. If there was one thing Rosetta didn't understand, it was how young, smart people like Casey thought they could take their health for granted. If Phil had gone to routine physicals each year, they might have caught his cancer in time. He might still be with her now.

"I've made up my mind," Casey said. She closed her eyes and leaned back in the chair.

Rosetta reached down and ruffled Bentley's fur behind his ear. Then she studied her great-niece, who was beautiful despite her hungover state, despite that massive bruise of a tattoo on her arm, despite the ridiculous color she dyed her hair. Then again nothing she did could diminish her beauty to Rosetta, even if Rosetta would never say as much to her. But if only she let her hair be natural, if only she covered up the tattoo—she would be stunning. A little bit of mascara maybe, some blush, a dress, perhaps, in place of her uniform of jeans and tank tops. She could be breathtaking. She would also look like her mother, which Rosetta supposed was the entire point of the changes she'd made to her appearance.

Rosetta could remember Casey as a skinny preteen, her light brown hair streaked with golden highlights from the summer sun, showing off her back dive at the Wild Rose Inn's pool. By her last summer on the island, she wasn't such a little kid anymore, at least physically. She turned heads everywhere she went, and she hated it. She wore baggy t-shirts and long shorts that summer, walked with her shoulders slumped. Rosetta supposed it was normal, the awkwardness of a girl growing into a woman's body, but she blamed Maureen and that born-again, Jesus-freak, second husband of hers, too. They criticized Casey too much, made her afraid to be herself. They should have let her continue to summer on the island. Rosetta could have balanced out their particular brand of insanity. Maybe she could have prevented whatever it was that caused the final rift between Casey and her mother.

Even now, all these years later, Rosetta knew there was more to the story, more to explain how Maureen could kick her seventeen-year-old daughter to the curb without two pennies to her name. Maureen had her struggles with mental illness, it was true, but Ed was a smart, educated man. He should have helped her and supported his step-daughter. He should have stopped Maureen's righteous nonsense. Although to hear Casey tell it, Ed was the real reason her mother kicked her out. Dirty bastard.

Well, now they were both dead. Maureen had written Rosetta several years back to say that Ed had passed, and all Rosetta could think was good riddance. Maureen's death, though, that one was harder to make sense of. As a child, Maureen was a good girl. Rosetta had always been happy to the play the role of the fun, childless aunt, spoiling her niece and doting on her. But by the time she got the diagnosis of bipolar, Rosetta couldn't deny the signs that had begun to show themselves when she was still in her teens. Looking back, recalling the temper tantrums and mood swings Maureen had been prone to as a child, she only wished she'd recognized the problems sooner. Poor Casey, growing up with a mother who could barely care for herself, let alone for her child.

Rosetta suspected that Casey had been living for years with the fear that one day she'd start to show signs of bipolar disorder herself, that she had inherited her mother's mental illness. That, Rosetta assumed, was the reason the girl insisted on closing herself off from the world. But here she was—sound of mind—and as far as they knew sound of body.

"It could be worse, you know," Rosetta said.

Casey let out a derisive snort.

"You don't have any children, so you don't have to worry about having passed it on."

Casey opened her eyes and looked hard at Rosetta, and Rosetta raised her hands as if to say, "Don't shoot." Casey had always been very clear: She had no intention of becoming a mother. Rosetta hadn't brought up her childlessness as a dig. But as Jason had recounted the contents of the letter, he'd said something that didn't make sense. He said Casey's mother urged Casey to consider her child. Why had she written that? Casey had no children. Rosetta supposed Maureen was writing hypothetically, covering her bases or taking into account that Casey might have become a mother in the years since Maureen had last seen her. But the idea kept tugging at Rosetta. She hadn't pressed Jason on that point because she had had so many other things to think about, but now she thought of it again. She'd always hoped Casey would have a family someday. It would bring her so much joy to be a mother, and if anyone needed joy it was Casey.

She said, "I mean, if you think you're ever going to have children, you should find out, because you don't want to pass on—"

"No, you're right. If I had children, this would be much worse," Casey said, standing up. She walked to the kitchen and Rosetta could hear the water running in the sink, the sound of a cabinet being opened and closed. She came back with a couple of aspirin and a glass of water. She sat down beside Rosetta, sideways on the futon to look at her, and said, "But since I have no kids, I have even less incentive to get the test, don't I?"

"As Shakespeare said, my dear, 'At length the truth will out.' This time you get to decide when and how the truth comes out."

The look on Casey's face changed then, and she swallowed hard. At last she sighed and said, "I have to tell you something. I had a baby when I was seventeen."

Chapter Thirty-one

St. Nabor Island, South Carolina

THE DESK HADN'T contained any documents to corroborate Marilyn's story, but it had contained the information about her mother's safe deposit box, so when Randy went home in the morning to catch up on some work, Angela took Marilyn to a hotel—the woman might be her blood relation, but she was also a total stranger—and then drove to the bank. She brought with her all the paperwork regarding the safe deposit box, as well as a copy of her mother's death certificate.

She was the first customer in the door that morning, and she wasted no time in explaining her circumstance to the clerk, who seemed skeptically sympathetic. A manager was summoned, and she repeated her case—her mother's sudden and unexpected death, her need to access certain missing documents, and so on. The manager nodded politely, sighed sympathetically, and then said that only the executor of her mother's estate could access the box in these circumstances as there were no signatories on the account aside from her mother.

Angela was not the executor; her mother's lawyer was. Astonishingly, given her father's circumstances, and the fact that her lawyer was a family friend who should have advised her on the matter, her mother had left no will, so the lawyer was now making sense of her parents' affairs. When she met with him last week, he had confided that, upon seeing her mother's finances, he thought he understood why she hadn't made a will. Perhaps, he had guessed, she was embarrassed by how house-poor she was, and how little she had to bequeath to anyone.

Frustrated and exhausted, Angela drove to the lawyer's office, and when his assistant insisted he had meetings all morning, she sat obstinately in the lobby, refusing to schedule an appointment, demanding she be seen immediately. Finally the assistant relented and alerted him to her presence, and he appeared in the lobby.

"Were you aware that my mother had a safe deposit box?" Angela asked, when he asked why she was there.

"Let's go to my office," he said, reaching out a hand to guide her.

Angela didn't care where she discussed her mother's business. Her mother was dead! She didn't want to walk down the hall and discuss things calmly. She wanted answers. Now.

"Did you know about the safe deposit box?"

"I learned about it last week," he said. "Now, if you'll just—"

"Were you going to tell me?"

"Of course, but I don't see what the rush is. I thought we'd go over everything once I made all the arrangements.

Will you please follow—"

"I need to get into that box," Angela said, crossing her arms and standing her ground.

"Miss Ellis, this is really not the place to discuss personal matters."

"I would like you to accompany me to the bank right now," Angela said. She was so tired. If she could only get the contents of the box, maybe she could go home and get some rest. But first she needed answers, and the box was the only place left for her to seek them.

"That won't be necessary," he said.

How dare he refuse her! He worked for her. She opened her mouth to protest, but he spoke before she could.

"I have already emptied the box. The contents are in my office. So if you'll please follow me," he said softly, and then he turned and walked down the hallway.

In his office, he told her to sit, and this time she complied. He moved a stack of file folders on his desk and produced a slim folder.

"I'm afraid there wasn't much in there that'll you find useful. No secret treasure, no family jewels."

He handed her the folder and then leaned on the edge of his desk as she opened it and flipped through. Birth certificates, social security cards, the title for her mother's car, her parents' marriage certificate—it was ordinary records. Angela had expected more than this. She turned back to the birth certificates—her mother's, her father's, Ryan's, and her own.

She took out her birth certificate and studied it. On the line for her mother was her own mother's name: Deborah Ellis. On the line for father, Richard Ellis. They really were her parents. The birth certificate said so as clear as day. Date of birth: May 7, 1992. Nothing was amiss here.

"May I have this?" Angela asked, closing the folder, but keeping her own birth certificate on top.

"Certainly. It's yours. You can keep the entire file."

"Okay," Angela said, standing up.

"I'll be ready to go over the estate plans with you next week."

Angela nodded. She didn't care. All she cared about now was finding out why Marilyn had lied. She was no closer to solving the strange happenings at her home now than she'd been two weeks ago, no closer to understanding why her parents had kept her from their families all these years.

"I'm afraid I won't have much good news," he said, as she was walking to the door. "I'm going to have to put the house on the market immediately."

Fine, she thought. Sell it and its ghosts. She didn't need to solve the mystery. She could walk away.

Marilyn studied the birth certificate Angela held out for her. She couldn't explain it, but the document was wrong. The date was right, but Angela had not been born to Deborah and Richard. About that, she had no doubts. For one thing, Deb had had her tubes tied several years before Angela was born. She shook her head and handed the birth certificate back.

Angela said, "I don't know what's going on here. I believe

that you really are her sister, you look exactly like her. But I don't get why you're lying any more than I get why they lied all these years."

There was nothing Marilyn could say that she hadn't said the night before, and part of her wanted to shake the girl to wake up and listen, but the poor kid looked exhausted. She was way too thin, her cheekbones sunken, her eyes ringed with dark circles. Her hair was a mess, and she hadn't changed her clothes since the day before. She needed sleep, a good meal, and a long hot shower.

"Honey, I've told you everything I know," Marilyn said. The only proof Marilyn could offer was the photograph of Ryan and his girlfriend, CJ, that and her own testimony, and she thought Angela would realize that she was right, if she'd calm down a little.

Angela ran her hands through her hair, rubbed her eyes, and sighed.

Marilyn asked, "Do you want to know more about Ryan and CJ?"

Angela met her eyes for a minute and then looked away. Then she gave a little nod.

Marilyn told the story as best she could. Ryan and CJ had been picture-perfect high school sweethearts. He was a handsome, popular, smart athlete. She was pretty and thoughtful, although Marilyn suspected she was something of an outsider. She was artsy, loved to draw and paint, and she wanted to be an artist, which Marilyn found charmingly naive. Deb didn't like her, though, and it wasn't that Deb would have disliked any girl Ryan brought home. It was about her home life. Marilyn didn't know all the details, but she had inferred that it was a wrong-side-of-the-tracks situation. Even in the few times Marilyn met her, she had been able to tell there was some unspoken tension regarding her parents. But she and Ryan were adorable together. They had been dating for a year—an eternity for high school students—when CJ got pregnant.

"Your mother called me crying," Marilyn said. "She went on and on about how Ryan's whole future was ruined and his life was over." She left out the part where Deb called CJ a money-grubbing whore.

Marilyn didn't really know how Ryan and CJ had felt about the whole thing or what their decision-making was like. She only knew what Deb had told her. She couldn't even imagine being seventeen and discovering she was going to have a baby, even if she did love the father.

She did know, however, that CJ's mother was every bit as unhappy as Deb, or maybe even more so, because she kicked CJ out, and Deb, infuriated though she was, took her in. By Christmas, when Marilyn arrived for the holidays, the decisions had been made: CJ would have the baby, and she and Ryan would raise it, and apparently they'd live with Deb and Rich until they were able to support themselves, which could take God only knew how long.

The kids seemed happy. They had their own little world. CJ had confessed to Marilyn that she and Ryan wanted to get married, and that they planned to go the justice of the peace as soon as they were both eighteen. For her part, Deb had confided that she was trying to convince the kids to let her and Rich legally adopt the baby. Despite this quiet scheming, it had been a fairly cheerful holiday. That was the last time Marilyn saw Ryan. Soon after, during a night out with some friends, Ryan died in a car accident.

"He wanted to be your father," Marilyn said. "He was happy and excited. So was CJ."

Angela had tears in her eyes. She wiped them away and sighed.

"After Ryan died, Deb moved forward with her plan to adopt you. She told me that CJ had agreed, and to be honest, I was stunned, but I thought it was for the best, all things considered, until she told me that she planned to raise you fully as her own, to let you think you were hers. I thought CJ should get to be part of your life, but Deb was dead set against it. And that was it. She began making plans to move away, and as soon as you were born, they took you away and didn't leave any way for any of us to reach them. They literally disappeared in the night."

"What happened to CJ?"

Marilyn shook her head. She had no idea, and why would she? She wasn't anything to the girl, there was no reason for CJ to keep in touch with her.

Angela picked up her birth certificate again and studied it.

"Then how do you—" She let her question trail off and brought the paper closer to her eyes. "This says I was born in Palmetto Landing, South Carolina."

Marilyn shook her head. "You were born in Massachusetts."

Angela frowned and Marilyn reached over and took the piece of paper up again. City of birth: Palmetto Landing, SC. Then she noticed something else in the top corner: The date filed. December 11, 1992.

"I don't think this is your original birth certificate," she said, pointing to the date.

"What does that mean?"

"I don't know," Marilyn admitted, but she could make a guess: Somehow her sister had had Angela's birth certificate changed.

That afternoon, after Angela recounted Marilyn's story to Randy over the phone, he asked the only logical question, "What are you going to do?"

Angela knew that the first thing she had to do was see if it was possible to have someone's birth certificate altered after adoption. The second thing would be to contact her father's sister and see if her story matched Marilyn's. And then... and then she didn't know what.

"Will you contact your birth mother?" Randy asked.

"I don't know," Angela said. And she really didn't. What would she accomplish by contacting this woman who had walked away from her the moment she was born? Her mother was her mother. She couldn't make her brain think of the woman who raised her, the woman she now believed was actually her grandmother, as anything but mom. This CJ person wasn't her mother any more than Ryan was her father, whatever their role in her conception and birth. Anyway, she'd be hard to find. Marilyn hadn't known her full name—not what her initials stood for or her last name.

But then there were all sorts of questions she still had about the situation. Why had CJ given her up? Yes, she had only been seventeen, younger than Angela was now, but if she had loved Ryan the way Marilyn said she did, how could she abandon his child—the only part of him that was left after he died?

CJ had wanted to be an artist. So that's where Angela got it. What else had she inherited from this stranger? As much as Angela wanted answers to the questions swirling in her head, she also realized that whatever answers she got might not be satisfactory, and in that case, what was the point? She had never before appreciated the saying that ignorance was bliss. She already understood that whatever she decided about meeting CJ, she would never again be able to think of her parents without thinking of their deception, and that loss, on top of the death of her mother, was crushing.

"Maybe you should try to get some sleep," Randy said, "or eat something. Or both."

But Angela was wired and she had no appetite. Instead she turned to her computer. After a brief internet search, she learned that birth certificates could be amended. It was actually common for the birth certificates of adopted children to list their adoptive parents. This fact felt like a personal insult. Things like birth certificates were supposed to preserve a record of facts for posterity. Hundreds of years from now, a record of her life would be maintained in the official public record of birth and death certificates. But her birth certificate was a record of lies. She could understand that in the case of an anonymous adoption, the birth parents' names had to be withheld, but it should be clear whether or not the parents listed were biologically her parents, shouldn't it? She looked at her birth certificate again. The filing date was the only clue. Without that, there'd be nothing to suggest that Deborah Ellis hadn't given birth to her.

That clue and Marilyn's story were proof enough, though. She searched again for her father's sister and opened a window to send her a private message, but with the cursor blinking in front of her, she wasn't sure what to say, how to even begin. Did her father's family even want to hear from her? And then she thought, Who cares if they do or don't? She typed:

Dear Helen,

I believe you are my aunt. My father is Richard Ellis, and my mother was Deborah. My parents always told me we had no family, and my father let me believe his only brother, Martin, died in Vietnam. Now, however, I have learned that they were not telling me the truth. If you are my aunt, as I believe you are, I would very much like to talk to you.

She left her phone number, signed her name, and before she could second-guess herself, hit send. Afterward she didn't know if she felt good or not. All she could do was wait for a reply.

Chapter Thirty-two

Devil's Back Island, Maine

ROSETTA WASN'T SURE what to say. She knew there had been more to the story of Maureen and Ed kicking Casey out, but frankly this wasn't the more she expected. She thought maybe they'd caught Casey stealing money—they treated her like a seventeenth-century indentured servant, and Rosetta wouldn't have blamed Casey if she had helped herself to a few bucks from Ed's wallet; or perhaps Ed had taken too much interest in his beautiful, developing step-daughter and Maureen's jealousy had gotten the best of her. Casey had suggested that Ed had untoward intentions toward her, although she had never said or implied that he had acted upon those intentions. But a baby? How could Casey have had a baby without Rosetta's knowing?

"I had a boyfriend, Ryan, his name was, and we adored each other," Casey went on.

Ryan. That Rosetta remembered. When she had tried and failed to change Maureen's mind about sending Casey back to the island for her sixteenth summer, Casey had assured her that it was okay, because she had a boyfriend and she didn't want to be away from him anyway. Rosetta should have insisted. She should have told Maureen that letting a sixteen-year-old make decisions based on not wanting to miss her boyfriend was idiotic.

"We had been together for over a year when I found out. It was an accident, obviously. I mean, we weren't stupid. We used protection, most of the time anyway. It just happened."

Rosetta let out a little snort and shook her head sadly. In her mind, she was picturing teenaged Casey—she was still CJ back then—so sweet, so pretty, so full of promise despite the hardships of her young life, sitting in the bathroom with the pregnancy test and struggling to comprehend what came next.

"I was freaked out, I mean, I was totally terrified, but I was also secretly happy. I was going to be a mother and have a baby that I loved and that loved me. Me and Ryan and the baby were going to have our own little world, a universe of love. Ryan was happy, too. He knew it would make things harder, having a baby so young, but he loved that baby the minute he learned it existed, like I did."

"But?" Rosetta asked, because there was obviously a but. Where was Ryan now? Where was the baby—the baby who would now be twenty? Could that possibly be right? For the first time in a long time, Rosetta felt every one of her 78 years.

"But nothing. When mom and Ed kicked me out, I stayed at Ryan's parents' house. They weren't happy, not like we were anyway, but they at least understood what family is. They were going to help us. They promised to see Ryan through college and to help take care of me and the baby.

They wanted us to have a good life."

Where did all that love and happiness go? Rosetta wondered. She didn't want to interrupt Casey now that she'd finally told her after all these years, but the suspense was unbearable. She knew better than to rush Casey, though. She didn't want her to change her mind and cut the story short.

"And then," Casey said, sighing, "Ryan died. Car accident."

"Jesus," Rosetta said. What did fate have against the poor girl? Couldn't the universe give her a little bit of goodness without always snatching it away again?

"His mother convinced me that it would be best if I let them adopt the baby. They would pay for all my medical expenses, take care of me through the end of my pregnancy, and in return, I would let them raise their grandchild as their own. I was grieving, distraught, alone in the world. I did what she asked."

"I don't understand," Rosetta said, squinting at Casey as if she could see into the past by doing so. It sounded as if Ryan's parents had done the right thing. They had had the resources to raise the baby, and Casey had had nothing. But at what point did they cut Casey out of the picture? Or did she remove herself from her baby's life? Where was Casey's child right now?

"They didn't want me. They only wanted the baby. They agreed to adopt her if I agreed to let them raise her as their own. Once the baby was born, I was not to have any further contact with any of them."

How had Casey ever agreed to such a thing? It was insane. "That can't be legal," Rosetta said. "How can it be?"

Casey shrugged.

"And that's it? You gave birth and walked away?" Rosetta was surprised by how angry her voice sounded as she spoke. She wanted to be sympathetic to Casey, but she simply could not understand what Casey was telling her.

"Why didn't you call me? Why didn't you ever tell me?"

"How could I tell you? You were the one person in the world who believed in me, and then I went and got pregnant and I knew my future, the future you always talked about back when you wanted me to go to college and be the next Georgia O'Keefe or some crazy shit like that, was over. Your disappointment would have been worse than my mom's in some ways. Hers was par for the course, but to disappoint you—I couldn't."

Rosetta wilted as Casey spoke. "What I've always wanted for you was happiness."

"Yeah, well, I was on my way to becoming a single, homeless, teen mother, which I think we both can agree is not a recipe for happiness."

"I would have taken care of you!" Rosetta said. "And the baby."

"I know that now," Casey said, throwing her arms around Rosetta. They were not huggy people, didn't demonstrate their feelings physically under normal circumstances, but Casey clung to Rosetta like her life depended on it now. "I was scared and stupid and I hadn't seen you in two years. That's a lifetime to a kid."

Rosetta nodded but she held onto Casey for a moment longer before letting go. Then she thought of something. "But the baby would be legally an adult now. You can contact her."

"How could I do that to her?" Casey asked. "Suppose she knows she's adopted. The Ellises could have told her about me and she could have found me, but that hasn't happened. So either she doesn't want to know me or she doesn't know she's adopted."

"She has a right to know."

"It's too late. It won't do any good."

"You have to get that test," Rosetta said.

"No, I don't. Just because medical science has made something possible, I am not required to use that science. I don't want my future told by some geneticist. I want to live my life." Casey got up, rubbed her eyes again, and stood as if waiting for Rosetta to get up and leave.

"But what if you gave it to her?"

Casey sighed and crossed her arms. "I can't think that way. I can't. I would have been better off not knowing what happened to my mother, like she is better off not knowing about me. Now if you'll leave me alone, I have to get ready. Brett'll be here in a minute."

"You aren't still going out with him today?" Rosetta asked. She'd come here to prevent Casey from this date and instead she'd learned that her niece had lived a life of secrecy for twenty years. Apparently secret-keeping was a family habit.

"Of course I am. I said I'd go and I'm going."

"Do you really think that's smart?"

Casey rolled her eyes. "Nothing's changed. I'm not going to sit here all day."

"I don't know about Brett," Rosetta said, getting up to leave. "Watch yourself around that one. Those business types can't be trusted."

Chapter Thirty-three

St. Nabor Island, South Carolina

RANDY BROUGHT A COUPLE of boxes of pizza over to Grace's, and they went down to the beach. When they sat down on a blanket on the sand, neither of them spoke. It was a lovely fall day, crisp blue sky, smooth blue sea, gentle rollers breaking in the distance, and big gulls circling, eager for crusts of pizza. Angela had never felt less at ease on the beach in her life. She was too confused to appreciate the serenity of it, but she didn't feel like talking, either. Angela had already repeated Marilyn's story. They could sit around and speculate all night about what CJ had been thinking when she'd agreed to let the Ellises adopt her baby, but what was the point?

They talked a little about how all of this fit in with Angela's ghost encounters. Randy felt the answer was fairly obvious. In fact, it was exactly what he'd already surmised before the last investigation: Ryan's ghost was trying to help her discover the truth, her mother's ghost was trying to keep it from her.

"Now that I know, do you think it's over?" Angela asked.

"We don't know one-hundred percent for certain what your mother wants," he said.

Angela felt tired and frustrated. They'd solved the mystery, so now life had to get back to normal. No more ghosts. No more huge family secrets. She wanted it all to be over.

Randy said, "Maybe you should try again. See if Calliope can communicate with your mom and put this all to rest. We didn't get very far—"

"I'm starting to think there never were any ghosts, okay? It was my subconscious or whatever telling me something was wrong, and now I found out what was wrong, so it's over," Angela said, her voice tense. This wasn't what she thought at all, but it was what she wanted to think. Maybe, if she told herself none of it was real it would stop. She got up and collected their paper plates and pizza boxes and took them to a trash can near the lifeguard chair.

"Two things," Randy said, when she sat back down. "One, I think I know how we can find out about CJ, and two, I think we should go back to your house tonight."

Somewhat against her will, Angela listened to Randy's explanations. First, his idea to find CJ was to seek out classmates of Ryan's from high school. If anyone could tell them where to find CJ, they could. After all, the two of them had been high school sweethearts, so they must have known the same people. Angela had to admit, that was a pretty good idea, even if she wasn't sure she actually wanted to find CJ.

Then again, Helen hadn't replied to Angela's message, a fact Angela was trying not to read into. Helen's past posts to Facebook were scattered, often with several weeks in between updates. If Angela wanted to find proof to back up Marilyn's story, and she didn't want to wait weeks and weeks for Helen to notice her message, Randy's idea might be the way to go.

His second idea, to go to the house, was based on the logic that if, as Angela claimed, there would be no paranormal happenings now that Angela knew the truth, then there was no reason not to go spend the night there.

"Your mother's spirit is restless, right? But now that you know the truth and there's nothing she can do about it, maybe she needs help going wherever spirits go," Randy said. "I really think we should bring Calliope back. Through her, you can assure your mother that you still love her and help her let go of whatever is keeping her here."

"I'm sure Calliope is busy tonight," Angela said. She was tired of the house, of the drama, of the confusion and questions. Yes, she still wanted answers, but so far she'd found more answers outside the house than inside.

"No, I texted her. She said she's up for it," Randy said.

She could see how much he wanted this. They had been really getting somewhere before Marilyn interrupted the night before. Maybe this, on top of everything else she'd learned, would finally bring her some closure. "Fine, one more," she said, and then she added, "We're bringing Marilyn, too."

Chapter Thirty-four

Devil's Back Island, Maine

BY THE TIME Brett knocked on Casey's door, she had gotten herself together. Mostly. She had showered despite the fact that she'd get salty kayaking, dressed in her nicest cut-off jean shorts, favorite black tank top, and least-stained hoodie, even put on a little makeup, if only because the puffy circles around her eyes were dead giveaways that something was wrong.

All this time she had kept the truth from Rosetta. So many times she had wanted to tell her, especially in that first year when Rosetta brought her back here. She knew she owed it to Rosetta. It was no exaggeration to say that Casey would be dead by now if Rosetta hadn't come to New York to find her.

Rosetta, God bless her, hadn't asked any questions. She showed up with an empty suitcase, crammed as many of Casey's things in it as she could, and got her the hell out of that flea bag apartment. Not that Casey had gone willingly. In fact, on her first attempt, Casey had literally kicked and screamed. Rosetta had left, and when she returned an hour later it was to say that the cops would be raiding the apartment on a drug tip in matter of minutes, so unless Casey wanted to be arrested, she would need to get in the car.

Casey never found out if that was true. She hadn't spoken to any of the people she'd known in New York since she left. She had never really known them, anyway. They were people she somehow found herself living with, people she got high with, people who would steal from her if she didn't hide her money and her valuables, people who were even more lost than she had been.

From ages 17 to 29, Casey's life had been like a slow-moving natural disaster, and if Rosetta hadn't stepped in when she did, it would have met its logical conclusion long ago. She didn't know how Rosetta had even found her, and it took her the better part a year to be grateful that she had.

Rosetta had given her a blank slate. She had never once held those lost years of Casey's life over her head, never reminded her what her life would have become without her intervention. No, Rosetta always focused on exactly one thing: The Future. The big, bright, bold future that had everything in it. She dreamed a life for Casey, and Casey eventually started to share that dream, and now here she was—running a café, doing something she loved on this beautiful island where most days she could forget where she came from.

And on the days when she couldn't forget, the days when she wanted to confess everything to Rosetta and get her advice, the days when she showed up at Rosetta's door in tears, Rosetta hadn't let her. No pity parties, she would say. We've all had troubles, she would say. You mustn't look back, she would say. And now it had been so long...

"I always suspected there was more than you had told me," Rosetta had said that morning when Casey finally let go of her secret. She did not exclaim at the injustice of it all or offer empty condolences. She just sat there, scratching the dog's head and nodding as if it all made perfect sense. Then, when the conversation was about finished, she had said, "I think this means you have to get tested, Casey."

Casey knew that already. She had known it the minute she read her mother's letter. If Casey had inherited her mother's genetic defect, then she could have passed on that genetic defect to the baby she gave away when she was seventeen years old. But even if Casey got the test, she wasn't allowed to contact her daughter. She so seldom let herself think that word. Daughter. Usually, she thought Baby, but that wasn't right. She had been born twenty years ago! Twenty! It was inconceivable.

Casey had agreed to all of Deb's requests. She had signed the papers and had never so much as held the baby after she was born. She wasn't supposed to know the gender, but a nurse let it slip. She didn't know what Deborah and Richard had named the baby, but she knew who they were. If she wanted to, she could find them. Which was why it was so perfect for her living here on Devil's Back where she had no cell phone reception, no internet connection. She avoided the temptation of finding her child by never going online. It was so easy to shut the world out by living here. In New York, she'd had to use drugs to do it. Here, she could pretend that this island was all there was to the world.

"You could cancel your date, you know," Rosetta had

said when Casey said she had to get dressed.

But Casey didn't want to. She wanted distraction. If she canceled her date, she would sit here all day thinking about her mother and her baby and the likelihood that her genetics left her disposed to die an early death from an aggressive form of cancer. That didn't sound like anybody's idea of a day off. Besides, the only thing that had changed since she agreed to spend the day showing Brett around was that now Rosetta knew everything Casey knew.

So she'd pulled herself together and when Brett knocked, she even managed to smile as she opened the door.

"You look fresh as a daisy," Brett said, offering his trademark grin. He was dressed impeccably, like an actor going kayaking in a movie—cheerful board shorts, one of those sunscreen swim tops, fancy athletic sandals, expensive sunglasses.

"You sound surprised," Casey said, stepping out onto the porch and pulling her apartment door shut behind her.

"I half-expected you to cancel on me after last night."

"I wasn't that bad," Casey said.

He raised an eyebrow and she said, "Okay, I was. But here I am now."

They strolled along the gravel path that led back toward the Wild Rose Inn. It was another beautiful day, the sort of ideal autumn day that late-season visitors flocked to the island to enjoy.

Casey led the way to the boat shed and selected two of the newer kayaks and paddles. She hoisted hers and told Brett to do the same. Behind her, she could hear him fumbling with it. She set hers on the beach and went back for life jackets.

"I can swim," Brett said.

"Tell it to marine patrol," Casey said. "You have to have it in the kayak. You don't have to wear it." She tucked hers into the straps on the front of the kayak, and Brett imitated her with his.

Casey kicked off her flip-flops and put them in the boat and dragged it into the shallow water. It was cold. The sun-warmed late summer water was losing out to the cool fall nights. She sat and pushed her paddle gently on the beach to move forward, free of the sand. In a few quick, sure strokes, she was well away from the shore. She swiveled around as quickly as the boat could manage and saw Brett still hadn't gotten situated. He had tried to get in without getting his feet wet and was beached. She laughed out loud. Maybe today would be fun after all.

As they paddled around the island, Brett got the basics pretty quickly. He could mostly keep pace with Casey. He couldn't maneuver very well, which led to a lot of laughter each time he tried to follow her into a narrow cove, but he was doing all right. When they paddled side by side, he talked to her, revealing more about himself, his life in LA, his childhood in upstate New York, and his desire to move back to the East Coast. He was a good storyteller, charming and self-deprecating, good with a punchline. Casey couldn't help but laugh at his jokes. She hated to admit it, but it was hard to dislike him.

After the better part of an hour, they came to the formation of rocks that gave the island its name. Casey steered toward a pebbly cove where they could pull the kayaks up and then got out and climbed up over several boulders to sit looking out over the water.

Behind her, the cliff rock formed a sort of terraced slope rising fifteen or twenty feet. The profile of the cliff was like the spiky back of a dinosaur. In front of her, two pointy boulders jutted up from the water—the horns of the devil emerging from the depths.

"This is why they call it Devil's Back," she said, as Brett picked his way over the rock to sit by her.

"Not hard to see why."

"Now, sure, but at high tide those points are almost totally submerged. Despite the buoys, every few years a boat wrecks itself on them."

"The devil will get you," Brett said, lightly.

"Yeah. It's always rich bastards in fancy yachts who don't know how to read charts," Casey said.

"I have to admit, I did wonder about the name. It's not exactly friendly."

"It's mysterious," Casey said, turning to look at him.

"Yes, mysteries abound here."

He was flirting with her. She decided that she wouldn't mind at all if he kissed her. Except that he had a girlfriend.

"How's your girlfriend feel about moving east?" Casey said, looking back out to sea.

"She'll come around," Brett said, the flirty tone gone from his voice.

Casey got up and went back to the boats. They might as well keep moving along. The tide was almost slack.

Along the seaward side of the island, the cliff rock was steep. They paddled along the coast now with nowhere to pull up for a break. As they passed under the highest point, Casey stopped paddling to point out Lover's Leap, the supposedly haunted cliff. Brett looked up at the stark rock wall and gave a low whistle.

"Wouldn't want to fall from that height."

Casey agreed.

"But you don't think it's haunted."

"I think what haunts most people is their own pasts," Casey said, and then she resumed paddling and he had to hurry to keep up.

They continued along with the jagged rock face to their right and the wide blue-black sea to their left until they rounded the curve into the sound. Here the island was covered in tall pines and Casey turned into a narrow inlet. She heard Brett cursing behind her as his kayak bounced off the side of the rocky entry. This was one of her favorite places on the entire island, accessible only by a boat. In the spring, a small stream trickled down a stony bed between fragrant pines and emptied into the sea. Although the entry to the cove was narrow, once inside, a small beach opened up. Now, in the fall, the stream bed was dry, but the cove was still lovely. The gentle lapping of the water on the sand, the breeze in the trees, the smell of sun-warmed pine needles— to Casey it was heaven. She hadn't intended to show it to Brett. It was her special place, after all, but as they had paddled up to it, she found she couldn't resist. And she didn't mind sharing it with him, either. She had misjudged him when they met, had thought he was too preppy, too stuck up, too business-like. But actually he was nice, thoughtful, maybe—given how he'd taken care of her last night—a real gentleman.

Casey got out of her kayak and dragged it far up onto the sand out of the reach of the incoming tide. They wouldn't be able to stay long. As the tide rose, it would erase the beach here.

"My God, this is beautiful," Brett said, as his kayak scraped into the sand.

Casey sat on a smooth flat rock and leaned back to tilt her face to the sun. Brett came to sit beside her. They should have brought lunch, Casey thought, as she soaked in the warmth of the early afternoon. Her stomach rumbled.

"Look at that," Brett said, and she opened her eyes.

On the pebbly beach near the water's edge, she saw a flicker of movement, and then another and another. Hermit crabs. Hundreds of them, ranging in size from as small as a sunflower seed to as large as a teacup, all scuttling in the same direction, light reflecting off their various shells and off the trickle of water around them, streaming toward some unknown destination for some unknown reason. It was strange, and strangely breathtaking. Casey had often seen fiddler crabs at dusk popping in and out of the holes they dug on the beach by the hotel, dozens at a time, in and out, in and out, but she had never seen hermit crabs congregate this way.

"Why do they do that?" Brett asked.

"I have no idea," Casey said.

When he took out his phone to take a video of the parade of hermits, it took all of Casey's restraint not to knock the stupid thing from his hand. Why wasn't it enough for people to participate in the moment? Why did everyone feel the needed to record everything now? They never lived anything. They only recorded things for posterity, but she doubted any of them ever bothered to look back at what they recorded.

But they were having a nice day, nice enough that she didn't want to ruin it, so instead of saying anything, she stood up and walked along the edge of the water, picking up smooth stones and skipping them across the water. She had set a personal best at eleven bounces when a stone whizzed by her and bounced a respectable seven times before sinking. She glanced over her shoulder and saw Brett poised to skip another. He wasn't so bad for an uptight, city-type.

"Let's see that tattoo," Casey said, dropping the rest of the stones from her hand and walking back to where they'd been sitting.

"Only if I can see the rest of yours."

Casey wasn't wearing a bathing suit. She had to think for a moment about what bra she had put on and whether or not taking off her shirt would constitute an act of seduction.

"Come on," Brett said. "I know you're only going to make fun of mine, so it seems only fair that you at least let me see yours."

"Right, I show you mine, you'll show me yours. I feel like I'm in middle school."

Brett took off his sunglasses and set them on the rock and then he pulled off his shirt to reveal his tanned and toned stomach and chest. Then he stepped close to Casey turning so she could look at his shoulder.

She bit her lip and resisted the urge to laugh. "It's cute," she said, reaching up to trace a finger along the outline of the design. "Still a Giants fan?"

"Till the bitter end," he said.

"I guess you have no choice as long as you've got that tattoo."

"Your turn."

"I didn't agree to your little plan," Casey said, crossing her arms.

And then Brett did the most surprising thing. He turned and kissed her. He had swept in so quickly that she hadn't had time to even think of resisting, not that she wanted to resist. She leaned in to him, smelling the salt and sweat mingling with cologne on his skin. Briefly she thought about his girlfriend, but hell, he had initiated this, so what did she have to feel guilty about?

His hands slipped to her waist and then his fingers found their way under her tank top, sliding up her back. She withdrew her mouth from his long enough to tug the tank top over her head and then resumed kissing him. His mouth dipped to her neck and then he turned her around so he could see her back. He ran his hand over her inked skin, leaned down to kiss her between the shoulder blades, and then put his hands on her waist and drew her against him, her back to his chest, and kissed her earlobe gently.

"It's beautiful," he murmured.

Casey stepped out of his embrace and turned around to face him, her conscience getting the better of her. It was wrong to let this happen.

"You have a girlfriend," she said.

He sighed. "Okay, you caught me. I lied. She broke up with me when I told her I wanted to land this development deal and relocate to the East Coast."

"So you don't have a girlfriend?" Casey said, crossing her arms.

He shook his head and smiled apologetically.

"And you lied because?"

"Because you looked like trouble."

She had heard that one before. She almost laughed, but then she rewound his words. Development deal. His girlfriend dumped him over a development deal. What exactly was he doing here, on her island? "So you're here working on a development deal?"

He gave her a funny look. "Rosetta must have told you."

Some scheme orchestrated by Rosetta. Of course. But Rosetta hadn't said a word to her about development. She shook her head.

"I'm sorry. I figured that you're her family, and I thought you knew."

From the way he was hedging, Casey understood that this wasn't just a deal, it was a big deal.

"She's selling the hotel. I work for Sweet Water Resorts," Brett said, stepping toward her and reaching out a hand.

Casey took a step back and shook her head. Rosetta would never sell the hotel. It was her life's work. She and Phil had bought the hotel in the early 1980s. The place had been condemned. It was a rundown wreck of building. And they restored it and turned it into a quiet family vacation spot that they had loved. After Phil died, Rosetta threw herself into her work at the hotel as if the only way to honor Phil's legacy was to make sure the hotel succeeded. Rosetta would want to keep it in the family. Casey had always assumed the hotel would be hers someday. She hadn't especially wanted it and all the responsibility that came with it, but she had been certain Rosetta's plan was for her to have it. Never in a million years would she sell it to some resort company.

"I'm sorry, I thought you knew," Brett said, trying again to close the gap between them.

Casey evaded him again, hurrying back to her kayak. She wanted only to get away from him. She needed to talk to Rosetta.

Chapter Thirty-five

St. Nabor Island, South Carolina

THIS TIME CALLIOPE suggested they gather in Angela's mother's room, since it was only her mother they wanted to speak to. She had brought a new assortment of props this time, which she arranged around the room, explaining that the goal for tonight would be to free Deborah's spirit from the house.

"What do you think your mother feared most in the world, Angela?" Calliope asked.

Angela shrugged. Her mother put up a tough front. She wasn't afraid of anything.

"She'd already lost one child," Marilyn said. "I'm sure she was terrified that she'd lose you, too."

Angela gave a half-nod, half-shrug. She had agreed to go through this again, but that didn't mean she had to like it.

"And when she died, did it happen quickly? Did she suffer?" Calliope asked.

The doctors had told Angela that it had been swift and that she hadn't been in pain, but Angela hadn't believed them.

If her mother had been able to call for help, she probably would have gotten to the hospital in time to save her life. Instead, she died alone on the cold concrete floor.

"I don't know," Angela said.

"Pain leaves a residue on the place where the suffering occurred," Calliope said. "We need to soothe your mother's pain so she can move to the next world. We need to help her feel loved, and reassure her that you are okay and will be okay without her. Even what she said to you, 'Go back to sleep,' that's the sort of thing a mother says to a fussy child, right? You see, mothers always think of their children as being young and helpless, and it's usually not until a mother becomes a grandmother and sees her own children become parents that she can see her children as adults. Your mother didn't get to have that, so to her spirit, you're still a child, and you need her. She needs to understand that you still love her, even though you no longer need her."

But I do need her, Angela thought. I need her to help me figure out what to do with my life, and to go shopping with me someday for my wedding dress, and to hold my hand when I have babies of my own. She's my mother, and I will always need her. Angela had been so angry at her mother for lying to her that she'd had a brief reprieve from missing her, but as Calliope counseled her now, she found that she didn't care about the lies. She cared only about the loss.

"And how do we do that?" Marilyn asked, clearly skeptical.

"We listen, and then we talk, and then we pray."

Pray? Calliope's whole psychic medium thing didn't exactly seem compatible with religion, Angela thought. But her mother had been a religious woman. Her mother would want her to pray, so if that's what Calliope said they should do, they would do it.

Calliope asked Angela to gather some of her mother's favorite things, and then she used them to make a sort of altar on her special blanket. Again, she lit candles around the room, and then she instructed everyone on exactly where she wanted them to sit. She had Angela sit in the very center of the blanket, facing the makeshift altar, and then she took the blanket from her mother's bed and wrapped it around Angela's shoulders.

"Now, we're going to begin. I need y'all to understand that things might happen during our communication, but I need y'all to stay where still, and to stay quiet. Do not speak unless I ask you to. Understand?"

Angela could feel Calliope behind her, hovering over her. She glanced at Randy and Marilyn sitting along the wall to her right. They all nodded. Angela wanted to ask what sorts of things might happen. Things like the candle flickering as it had the night before?

Then she heard Calliope doing her deep breathing, and then she began to speak, addressing Deb directly, inviting her to join them.

When her incantation was done, she began to walk slowly in circles around the blanket, waving incense and repeating some sort of chant over and over. She was on her third lap when there was a sound of breaking glass behind Angela. Everyone jumped. Angela looked around for the source of the noise and saw that the the picture frame holding the family portrait on her mother's dresser had fallen over.

"Thank you for joining us, Deborah. I understand you're

hurting and you're upset, but we want to talk to you," Calliope said, freezing where she stood.

In response, the decorative, antique perfume bottles that lined the back her mother's dresser fell like dominoes. Angela drew her legs to her chest, drawing the blanket tight around her to keep from trembling.

"You have our attention. You don't need to resort to these childish displays," Calliope said. She sounded like a bored kindergarten teacher.

All the candles except those at the edges of the altar went out, and Angela realized she'd been holding her breath.

"Your daughter is here, Deborah, and you're frightening her. You aren't the sort of mother who scares and intimidates her daughter, are you?"

Angela felt a gentle pressure then, as if a big soft animal was resting gently against her back, and she gasped. Calliope turned to her and indicated that she needed to be quiet.

"Something's touching me," she said in a strangled whisper.

Calliope nodded and resumed circling the blanket.

"Your sister Marilyn is here, too. They're here because they love you and because they don't want you to go on suffering this way."

Angela stuck the edge of the blanket into her mouth and bit down hard to suppress a scream as she felt the distinct sensation of hands running through her hair. At first the hands combed through it gently, playfully, but when Calliope said *Marilyn*, it was as if the hand closed in a fist, grabbing a handful of hair and yanking hard. Angela's own hand shot out to her scalp. There was nothing there.

"Deborah, we have to insist that you play nice, or we

can't continue. You're very unhappy, I know, and we want to help you so you can find peace."

And then Angela heard the voice, ringing in her head again, saying, "You should have listened to me. You should have listened."

"Listened to what?" Calliope said, and Angela looked up at her in astonishment. Calliope had heard it, too! Even though the voice seemed to be inside Angela's own brain, Calliope had heard it.

"We were happy. We were a good family," the voice said.

"Of course you were," Calliope answered.

"We only did what was best," the voice hissed.

"Of course. And now you have to let us help you," Calliope said. "You did everything you could, but you shouldn't be here any more. This isn't a good place for you. What can we do for you?"

Angela couldn't believe how calm Calliope was. Randy was right. She was the real deal.

"We only did what was best," the voice said again, and then again, faster and faster, rising in intensity at it had in the past when it was telling Angela to go back to bed. She clamped her hands over her ears and pressed her face into her knees.

Calliope knelt in front of Angela and lifted her hands prayerfully. "Dear Lord, we pray today for the repose of the soul of Deborah Ellis, the mother of Angela and Ryan, sister of Marilyn. She was a good woman taken too soon from the bosom of her family. Please help her to find comfort in your arms and to know that not a day passes that her family doesn't remember her with love."

As Calliope prayed, the voice continued to echo in

Angela's ears. She didn't know how Calliope was managing to talk over it. Then she felt Calliope tap her hand, which was still covering her ear. She opened her eyes and saw that Calliope had gestured for them all to join hands. Angela did as instructed, holding Calliope's hand on one side and Marilyn's on the other. Then Calliope began to pray the Hail Mary, and they all joined in. As Angela spoke, the voice gradually faded. By the third repetition of the Hail Mary, it had gone completely, but they continued praying until Angela completely lost count. At last Calliope squeezed her hand as they reached the end of another Hail Mary, and then Calliope said amen, and they all let go.

Calliope got up and turned on the lamp on the bedside table, and they all blinked in the light. Angela looked at the dresser and saw that the glass in the picture was intact, and the perfume bottles were all standing up in a row as always. She looked back at Calliope, confused. She had seen and heard the broken glass and toppling bottles. All of them had jumped at the sound. What had happened?

"Why don't y'all go downstairs while I clean up here, and then we'll debrief, okay?" Calliope said.

The three of them stood and went slowly back downstairs, each and every one looked dazed and frightened.

"That was the craziest fucking thing I've ever experienced," Marilyn said.

"You heard it?" Angela asked.

"Calliope's weird chanting?" Randy asked.

"What language was that?" Marilyn asked.

Angela looked back and forth between them to see if they were joking. She'd understood every word Calliope had said. She'd been speaking English.

"My mother," Angela said. "I could hear her, and Calliope could, but could you?"

Randy shook his head. Marilyn shrugged.

"Did you hear me, when I said something was touching me?" Angela asked.

"I heard you make this strange sound, but you didn't really speak," Randy said.

But she had spoken. Calliope had told her to stop.

A few minutes later, Calliope appeared in the kitchen with her box of enchanted artifacts. She sat at the head of the table and said, "I can't say for certain that she won't be back. I think we soothed her somewhat, but she's angry, and anger is a powerful emotion. Honestly, you might want to consider having a priest in to bless the house, and you might also keep a rosary on you when you're here."

Marilyn let out a snort of a laugh. "That is some superstitious nonsense if ever I heard it. Tell me this, how did you make that glass-breaking sound? And the candles, how did you get them to go out like that?"

Calliope studied Marilyn, rolled her eyes, and turned to Angela. "I think she's afraid that you'll end up resenting her, that you'll lose sight of your happy memories. When you pray, be sure to say prayers of gratitude for her. Pray for her soul so she can get to heaven. That's all you can do."

Then Calliope pushed back her chair and stood. "Call me anytime, sugar," she said, blowing a kiss to Randy, and then she took her things and left.

Chapter Thirty-six

Devil's Back Island, Maine

SITTING IN HER OFFICE contemplating the tale Casey had told her that morning, Rosetta did the only thing she could think of: She set about finding Casey's daughter. She didn't have a lot of information to go on, but she figured that the Internet would turn up something if she was persistent.

Rosetta refused to be one of those old ladies who cringes at the sight of a computer, who listens to young people describing new technologies and says, "Gosh, that all sounds a bit too complicated for me. I'm no good with these newfangled whatsits." No, thank you. She might be old, but she wasn't dumb. She had kept up with the technological times. She ran the website of the hotel and the tourism bureau and kept a Facebook page for each as well. She had drawn the line at Twitter, which she could never quite understand despite her best efforts, but in general, she considered herself savvy enough to get done whatever needed doing online. Still, the task of finding a person about whom she knew so little was daunting.

The first problem was that she didn't know Ryan's parents' first names or what they'd named the baby. Ellis was a very common last name, but she knew that Ryan had died in 1992, so she started there. She found his obituary right away. All she needed was his name, year of death, and the town where he lived, which she had guessed was the same town where Casey grew up, Beechmont, Massachusetts. She almost couldn't believe how easy it was. And of course the obit named his parents: Deborah and Richard Ellis.

Next she searched for Richard Ellis, but that turned up nothing that seemed relevant, at least not in the first few pages of results. Richard Ellis was too common a name.

At first she thought Deborah Ellis would similarly prove a needle in a haystack. Three of the results on the first page all led to a Deborah Ellis from South Carolina, some real estate maven, and Rosetta would have completely dismissed those as the wrong Deborah Ellis if it hadn't been for a picture of Deborah and her daughter that came up from some small town newspaper.

The picture was from a high school awards ceremony. In it, Deborah had her arm around her daughter, identified as Angela Ellis, who was holding up an award plaque. The picture was a couple years old, which made the girl about the right age. Rosetta clicked on the picture and it opened up in its own window. She zoomed in and studied the girl's face. Was it her imagination or did that girl have Casey's eyes, Casey's cheeks, Casey's chin? Could that be her niece's long-lost daughter?

Rosetta saved the picture and then turned back to the results, opening up the other returns on Deborah Ellis. The first was for her real estate firm. Deborah was gym-thin, perfectly coiffed, wearing a prim business suit with a silk scarf around her neck, her too-white smile beaming from the page's header. Aside from the picture, there was no real information about her.

The second result stopped Rosetta cold. It was another obituary. Deborah Ellis, mother of Angela and wife of Richard, had passed away two weeks earlier. Wife of Richard. How many Deborah and Richard Ellises with twenty-year old daughters could there possibly be? This had to be them. Why and when they'd left Massachusetts was anybody's guess, but Rosetta was certain now that she'd found Casey's little girl.

After saving the article, Rosetta tried searching for Angela Ellis, and this time she narrowed it down to Angela Ellis from St. Nabor Island, South Carolina. The search took her to a Facebook page, but when she clicked on it, she got a message saying the page was private and asking her if she wanted to "friend" Angela. She closed the window and sighed.

It was that easy, after all this time, even with so little information. A few minutes' work and she had uncovered what Casey had kept secret all that time. No wonder Casey refused to use the Internet. How could she have avoided the temptation of looking for her baby?

Rosetta thought the news that Deborah Ellis was dead might be enough to change Casey's mind about attempting to contact Angela. Certainly that information was important. Why should Angela believe herself motherless when in fact her biological mother was right here, where she'd spent most of her adulthood regretting the decision to give her baby away?

Casey dragged the kayak up to the shed, but she didn't bother putting it away. One of Rosetta's peons could do that. She needed to confront her aunt and find out what was going on. When she thought of the way Rosetta had manipulated her that morning, her insistence that she only had Casey's best interest in mind, fury rose in her chest. How dare Rosetta pretend she cared about what was best for Casey when she was selling the hotel to a resort developer. What Casey needed was for the island to stay as it was, a perfect hideaway from the world. If Brett planned to turn it into some kind of tourist trap destination, it would be ruined. The one good thing she had would be gone and she'd have nowhere to go.

She found Rosetta in her office going through a stack of paperwork. The documents pertaining to selling the hotel? Casey wondered.

"You're selling out?" Casey asked by way of hello.

"Sit down, Casey," Rosetta said, gesturing toward the chair opposite her desk. She got up and shut the door. When she came back to the desk, she said softly, "You aren't the only one who has made mistakes."

Casey listened as Rosetta explained the dire financial situation she was in. She wasn't only selling the hotel. She was also selling the cottages and the White Sails Tavern and the craft gallery. Basically, she was selling everything she owned on Devil's Back except the Beach Plum Café. Casey was stunned. Rosetta had never so much as hinted at financial hardship. Phil had been an investment banker back before they bought the hotel and opted out of the fast lane for island life. Even after he'd changed his business focus, though, he had invested for them, and as Casey understood it, he had known how to get a serious rate of return. When he died, he did so on a large pile of money, plenty for Rosetta to continue with her comfortable lifestyle and to keep running the hotel.

"I don't understand. How did things get so bad?" Casey asked.

Rosetta blinked and Casey saw tears in her eyes. Rosetta picked up a framed picture of Phil from her desk and smiled at it sadly. Then she set it down and looked back at Casey.

"Phil would never forgive me," she said. "I made a bad investment decision, and I went all in."

"It can't be that bad," Casey said.

"Bernie Madoff."

Casey couldn't believe what she was hearing. Surely she was too smart to fall for a Ponzi scheme.

"I can't keep operating in the red, and at my age, I can't take out loans. This is a young person's game. I have to sell. That's all there is."

"But they'll ruin it," Casey said. It couldn't be as bad as Rosetta was saying. How much debt had she racked up? And then Casey had a thought: How much of the debt was on account of the café?

"I think Brett understands how special the island is."

"He took a video of hermit crabs!" Casey said, louder than she intended to. Someone who couldn't enjoy a nice day in nature without videotaping it couldn't possibly get how special the island was.

"That hardly seems like a crime," Rosetta said.

"That letter from my mother," Casey said. "There was

more than what Jason saw. There's money. She left half of her estate to me. I wasn't going to take it, but I can, for you. It's not millions, but it's about two-hundred thousand. Would that be enough for you to turn things around? You can have it all."

"And by this time next year, we'll be right back where we are, looking to sell, and you will have lost your inheritance," Rosetta said, shaking her head. "I'm sorry, Casey. I've failed you, and I've failed Phil, but this is the only way."

"But what does that mean?" Casey felt panicked and short of breath. This couldn't be happening.

"I'm going to retire. That's all."

"It's not supposed to be like this."

"I was going to have to retire someday. I can't keep running myself into the ground over this place forever. This is a little sooner than I'd planned. Nothing's going to happen to the café, though. I've made sure of it."

She couldn't believe Rosetta would betray her this way. She could have told her about her financial problems and what she was thinking of doing. Casey could have found a way to help before things got so out of control.

"The resort will have its own coffee bar. I'll be out of business in months," Casey said, as if what she cared about most was business.

"They won't be able to compete with your baking," Rosetta said.

Why does everything I love get taken away from me? Casey wondered.

"Listen, I did some research after we talked this morning—" Rosetta said.

Casey interrupted her. "I have to go. I can't be here right

now."

"But it's about your—" she faltered. Daughter. Casey's daughter. The idea was still overwhelming to her. "It's about the baby. Your baby."

"I don't have a baby. I gave birth to a little girl and I gave her away. That's all in the past. I never should have told you."

"But she's out there, she—"

"Of course she's out there!" Casey felt her rage turning into a ball of words that she knew she'd regret so she tried to swallow them.

"Don't you want to know—"

"I can't know! I can't!" She stood up and walked out of Rosetta's office without another word. There was nothing to say. She'd spent twenty years trying not to think about the daughter she gave up, twenty years in which not a day went by that she didn't wonder, that she didn't see a little girl of about the right age without feeling a stab of regret and loneliness. Still, it was better to wonder what she missed out on than it was to know.

When Brett got back to the boat shed, Casey was long gone. He clumsily lifted his kayak onto an empty space in the boat rack, and then he put away Casey's, too, since she'd left it in the doorway. He couldn't believe she had no idea about the development deal. But then again, she had never asked him what he was doing here, and he had never said. He assumed Rosetta had told her.

It was a big deal, and he understood that. If all went according to plan, his company was going to transform the island completely, although he hoped he could find a way to retain the spirit of the place, because for the first time in his 18 years with Sweet Water, he'd found a location that he didn't want to sanitize and standardize.

Most of the Sweet Water properties he'd worked on were truly improvements to their settings, replacing dilapidated beach shacks and trashy fried food stands with attractive, clean, well-maintained, all-inclusive resorts and providing at least slightly better jobs for the locals than they'd had before. Tourism was an economy of exploitation, no matter where the tourism was taking place—rich tourists making other rich people richer on the backs of impoverished locals. At least Sweet Water resorts looked good in the process. There were worse developers out there.

And the fact was, even on this beautiful little island that he was coming to appreciate more and more each day, a Sweet Water resort would constitute a benefit to the local economy. If the hotel and restaurant went out of business and weren't quickly replaced by something else, how long could the year-rounders realistically afford to stay here? They relied on that commerce. And would the summer people want to keep their pretty little cottages if all the businesses faded away? Locals might not initially like the idea of a resort, but if they wanted to stay on the island, they'd come around.

Paddling with Casey that morning, he'd finally come up with an idea that he thought might work for everyone. He always had his best ideas when he was working out. Kayaking proved to be both good exercise and good inspiration.

He would scale back the development plan from a

three-hundred room hotel complex to clusters of two to four bedroom condos, none more than two stories high, designed to blend attractively into the surroundings, and with every attention to the best in green building practices and long-term environmental sustainability. There would be fewer beds available that way, but the rental value of each condo would be triple that of a hotel room, and anyway if the idea was to sell privacy, peace, and quiet, condos made far more sense than a hotel. Where the inn currently stood, they'd make a community center with a big pool and hot tub, exercise facilities, a convenience store, a coffee shop, a bar, banquet facilities—all the typical resort amenities. It would be a best-of-both-worlds arrangement: The entertainment, comfort, and ease of a hotel-resort, the privacy of an exclusive island escape. He had a conference call with Charlie and some of the other top execs scheduled for that evening. He'd go draw up some plans and get ready to pitch it to them.

He'd been hoping to talk to Rosetta about the café, though. It was the one property she wasn't selling, aside from her own home, and it was in a prime location, up the path from the pier. Sweet Water needed that location to make an island welcome center. As much as he hated the idea of hurting Casey's business, he knew for a fact that Sweet Water could offer her more than what she had now. He could transform her life.

Given her reaction to the news today, however, he understood how steep a climb he would face to bring her around to the idea. With Rosetta's help, though, maybe he could make her see that the changes he wanted to bring were not only not bad, they were essential to the island's survival. He needed to talk to her, calmly and rationally, to make her see.

The way it had felt when he kissed her. That kiss was more than lust. He didn't just want to sleep with her. He wanted to know every single thing about her—her likes and dislikes, her past and her dreams for the future. He wanted to press his body against hers not merely for pleasure but as if to absorb some essential part of her through his skin. He wanted to see her smile and to comfort her when she was sad.

As a generally sensible person, Brett understood how illogical the intensity of his feelings was. He'd only known her a week, had only spent a few hours with her, and for half of those, she'd been roaring drunk. He understood the basics of the pheromones that people give off and the way attraction happens as a result of hormonal reactions, so he understood that what he was feeling might be explained away by body chemistry, but if this was indeed his hormones taking over his senses, he was willing to give himself over to them, because when was the last time he'd cared for anything or anyone this much? He'd never felt this way about Ashley.

What would it take to get her to give him a chance? Short of going back in time, quitting his job, and then magically finding his way here as a mere tourist, was there anything he could do?

He could abandon the project. He could go through with quitting this time and move to Maine and see where things went with Casey. In the absence of a time machine, a fresh start was the only option he had. He could get away from the corporate insanity that had been his life since college, do something quiet and easy like work in a bookstore or something. It wouldn't even matter if he suddenly found himself scraping by, paycheck to paycheck—not if he was happy.

But if the deal failed, the entire local economy would collapse, and Casey would lose everything and have to leave this island where she so clearly belonged, which meant that, even though it might make Casey hate him, Brett had to make the deal go through.

He went back to his hotel room to perfect his pitch. He had to get his bosses on board tonight.

After Casey left, Rosetta pushed aside the account statements she'd been going through and buried her face in her hands. Casey was right that she was selling out. She was a failure. She'd been a failure for a long time now, but she'd been able to keep up the facade. No longer, though. Even if she didn't sell the hotel, she'd have to close for good at the end of the season. It was over. She'd had a long run and now it was time to face defeat.

Since the whole Madoff scandal exploded, she'd been treading water and she was exhausted. The timing of it. In retrospect, she wished she'd started running low on cash sooner. Maybe she could have gotten her money out before the whole scheme collapsed. Instead, she'd been running in the red for years, assuming she had that big payoff to count on, and when she was ready to draw on it—poof. What a dark magic trick it was. Four years later and she still hadn't gotten back so much as a penny. Maybe she never would, or if she did, it would be too late to save her legacy.

She could no longer keep her head above water, but thanks to Brett, she had a lifeline. She wasn't going to drown after all. And anyway, she was far too old for this. She was seventy-eight years old, for God's sake. She deserved a quiet retirement, and she needed money to make that happen, even if it meant letting Casey down. She couldn't hold Casey up forever.

Still, when she considered Sweet Water's initial offer, as big as the number sounded, she could see that when all was said and done, she'd need to be frugal moving forward. She hadn't had to be frugal since the day she married Phil, over fifty years ago. It would be a hard change, but even hard change didn't have to bad, she knew. She had lived long enough to know that one must adapt or die, and she certainly was not ready to die yet.

She got up from her desk and called Bentley, and together they went out to the hotel's patio overlooking the beach. It was a beautiful day. The sun glittered on the water, and the air, though warm with the midday sun, carried the crisp smells of ripe apples and fall leaves. When was the last time she actually got to enjoy a day like this, instead of running herself ragged keeping this place from falling apart?

A few more concessions from Brett, and then she'd sign and be done with it all. She was ready.

Chapter Thirty-seven

St. Nabor Island, South Carolina

RANDY HAD DRIVEN them all to Deb's house for the séance or whatever you wanted to call it, and once the ridiculous charade was over, they climbed in his car to go home. As he drove, Marilyn wondered how worried she should be about Angela. Had she unwittingly walked in on a Shakespearean tragedy here? All this talk of ghosts was unsettling to say the least. The kid seemed way too smart to go in for smoke and mirrors and voodoo magic tricks, but Angela had clearly believed they had made contact with the spirit realm tonight. The most frightening thing that Marilyn had experienced all evening was seeing how convinced Angela was that she had heard her mother's voice.

They pulled up at the hotel and Marilyn asked Angela to walk her to the door. She needed to talk to Angela alone for a minute.

"Why did you want me there tonight?" Marilyn asked.

"I thought you might want closure," Angela said, not meeting her eyes.

Marilyn did want closure, but the evening's air of Ouija board foolishness had only put her further away from it.

"You know that was all a lot of nonsense, right?" Marilyn said, hating how condescending her words sounded. She meant to sound concerned, but it hadn't come out that way. She had no practice talking to kids, even twenty-year-old kids.

"I don't know what I think."

"And all that stuff about calling a priest. Look, I may be a lapsed Catholic, but I wouldn't go mentioning all this ghost hunting stuff to any priests if I were you."

"But the Hail Mary's helped. She quieted when we prayed," Angela said.

"Honey, if prayer helps you, then pray, but chasing after ghosts?"

"What about purgatory? I mean, don't we pray for the souls in purgatory?" Angela asked.

Marilyn struggled to think of an answer that would make sense to Angela, who had been a Sunday school student much more recently than Marilyn had. At last she shrugged and said, "I don't know about purgatory, but I do know that when we die, we die."

"Yeah, well, I guess it doesn't feel that way to me," Angela said. She brushed her hair out of her eyes and gave Marilyn a weary look.

"I'm leaving tomorrow," Marilyn said. "My flight's at three." When she'd booked her flights, she figured forty-eight hours was enough. Enough for what? She didn't know, as she hadn't exactly had a clear-cut plan, but she had to get back to work, anyway.

"Tomorrow?" Angela asked, a furrow creasing her brow.

"I can change it if you want. I don't have to go right away," Marilyn said.

But Angela had regained her cool composure. "No, don't trouble yourself. You have a life to get back to."

"Look, I don't want this to be the end for us. I want to get to know you."

"Yeah, sure. We'll keep in touch," Angela said, in a tone that suggested she knew the words were a lie.

"Let's have lunch tomorrow before I go, okay? Just us?" Marilyn said.

Angela agreed to meet her at the hotel, and then Marilyn watched as she went back to Randy's car. He seemed like a nice kid, aside from the ghost business. Marilyn hoped he was good to Angela.

It was late. She was way too old for this. It was nearly two a.m., for heaven's sake. She was cranky, too. She would have loved for someone to explain to her why Calliope's absurdist theater had to take place at midnight.

She tried to sleep, but exhausted as she was, sleep wouldn't come. She wondered if she should try to see her brother-in-law in the morning, see if he was really as bad off as Angela had led her to believe. If he was, then she couldn't leave Angela here to fend for herself. She might be legally an adult, but she still needed guidance. Hell, she was going to need a place to live, and Marilyn didn't think she'd be crashing with her mother's business partner long-term.

Marilyn knew she should talk this over with Jeff, but it was the middle of the night now, and he'd be at work in the morning before she woke up, if she ever went to sleep. Anyway, talking it over with him would only be a courtesy. He'd never disagree with her on this. Family was too important. Would he be surprised if she showed up with Angela and said Angela would be living with them for a while? Yes. Would he refuse to allow it? No. Would he be unhappy about it? Probably not. They'd never had children, but they'd always been devoted to Jeff's nieces and nephews—everybody's favorite aunt and uncle. And Angela was nearly grown anyway, so it wasn't as if they'd be doing any diaper changing or hand-holding. They could provide her with stability and help her determine the course of her future. Jeff couldn't say no to that.

He hadn't wanted Marilyn to fly down here, that was for sure. He had never forgiven Deb and Rich for their disappearing act—and people say men don't hold grudges!—but he couldn't hold her sister's actions against Angela. Jeff was a reasonable and fair man. He'd see that the right thing to do was to take Angela in.

Randy lay on his side, his head propped on his elbow, his free hand resting on Angela's smooth, flat stomach. She was wearing one of his old t-shirts. They had both passed the point of being too tired long ago and neither could sleep. He wanted to understand what she had experienced during Calliope's ritual. He had felt something electric in the room as Calliope had passed around her inscribed cloth, and he had heard the sounds of breaking glass and toppling perfume bottles, but the sounds Calliope made hadn't even seemed to be words to him until the Hail Mary's at the end. He wished he had set up some of his equipment. There had definitely been some strange magnetic field activity. He could have detected it.

Angela seemed calmer, though. Whatever Calliope had done, it had eased Angela's mind, and he was glad for that. And he was glad that she was here now, tired but more content than she'd seemed at any point since the night she walked into the paranormal investigators club meeting. He leaned down and brushed his lips against her forehead.

She smiled up at him, and then she drew his mouth down to hers. This was dangerous, he knew. It was his choice that they hadn't yet had sex, and God, how he wanted to, but he still wasn't sure what was going on in her head. If they had sex right now, it would undoubtedly feel amazing, and probably afterward they'd both be able to sleep, but how would Angela feel when they woke up in the morning? Would she be glad they'd done it, or would she push him away?

And to be honest, as much as he desired her, he had no idea if they had any future now that all the investigations were over. Besides this ghost hunt, did they have anything in common? She wasn't exactly interested in becoming become a paranormal investigator; her ghost interest, he understood, was wholly selfish, and he was fine with that. There was more to him than his paranormal hobby, but he couldn't help but thinking that without these extraordinary circumstances, she never would have been interested in him in the first place.

But then again, she was here now. She was here, and she was kissing him, pressing her body against his, God help him. He pulled away.

"What is it?" Angela asked.

"I don't want either of us to get hurt."

"I don't plan to hurt you."

"So you want to be me with? You want to—"

Angela giggled. "Are you asking me to go steady?"

Randy couldn't help but smile. "Yeah, I want to give you my varsity jacket."

"I accept," she said, pushing herself up so their lips met again.

Sometimes, Randy thought, refusal is futile.

Chapter Thirty-eight

Devil's Back Island, Maine

CASEY KNEW IT was a mistake to go looking for Jason. She knew and she did not care. What difference did anything make, now? She was going to lose her business, she was going to have to leave the only place where she'd ever been happy, she didn't know how she'd ever look Rosetta in the face again, she was probably going to die an early death from the same cancer that had killed her mother, and basically, her life was pointless and empty.

She found him at the bar at the Lobster Shack, where he went after work on those rare days when he did work. She sidled up to the bar beside him, and he registered her presence with little surprise.

"Got any plans for this evening?" she asked, turning sideways to rest one elbow on the bar.

"Yeah," he said.

Behind him, his brother and another guy laughed. Casey felt her face color.

"That's too bad," she said, lowering her voice. "I was

thinking maybe you could come over."

Jason picked up his beer, peered through the dark glass of the bottle, assessing how much was in there, and then drained it in one long swig. With a nod to his brother and not so much as a word to Casey, he started for the door. Hating herself for it, Casey followed him. She practically had to jog to keep up with his long stride as he stalked up the gravel path.

"Are you seriously running away from me?" she said, when she was close enough that she could make herself heard without yelling.

He whirled and faced her, crossing his arms.

"I—" Casey wasn't sure what she wanted to say to him. How about, *I want you to come home with me and sleep with me so I don't have to think about my life?* Or, *I was seriously hoping you had some more of that pot, and I am willing to have sex with you to get some?* Or, *You are the only person in the entire world I can turn to right now so please don't make me beg?*

"What?" he said. "You miss me?"

"I do, as a matter fact," she said.

"It's been all of two days. You haven't even had time to miss me."

"I'm sorry. I shouldn't have come here. I'll go. You can go back in and I'll leave you alone." She stepped around him and started up the path, struggling to hold back tears.

"Casey," he said, calling after her.

She didn't turn or stop. She couldn't. She'd already humbled herself by seeking him out, and he'd made a total ass of her, thereby proving what she already knew: It was a mistake to go looking for him. She'd learned her lesson and she wasn't turning around now. She shoved her hands into the pockets of her hoodie, kept her head down, and walked as fast as she could without breaking into a run. She hadn't made it more than a dozen steps when her toe snagged on a stone and she tripped, stumbled, and fell to her knees on the sharp gravel of the path. There was no holding back the tears after that.

She heard footsteps behind her as she knelt where she'd fallen, crying and struggling to breathe, and then hands on her upper arms, helping her up, pulling her into an embrace.

"It's okay," Jason said, holding her close.

When she'd calmed down some, he walked her home, keeping his arm around her shoulders the whole time. Her skinned knees stung and trickles of blood rolled down her legs as they walked. Without Jason's support, Casey didn't think she would have been able to muster the energy to walk up the slope to the cottage. He wasn't a bad guy. She could do worse. So what if he was only twenty-three? Men dated younger women all the time, so why couldn't a woman date a younger man? In terms of maturity levels, they were probably about even, if she was being perfectly honest.

They rounded the café to the back stairs to her apartment, and Jason stopped short. Casey, who had been letting him guide her along with her eyes trained on her feet, looked up. Sitting on the bottom step, looking handsome and contrite, was Brett. He stood as they approached.

"Who are you?" Jason asked, the same moment Casey said, "Brett."

Brett looked back and forth between them, clearly confused, and Casey could imagine what he must be thinking: Here she was again, the arms of a man around her, being escorted home, and though she wasn't drunk this time—only hysterical—she probably looked inebriated, stumbling up the path beside Jason with her bloody knees and tear-streaked face.

"Casey, I thought we should talk," Brett said, stepping forward.

"You know this guy?" Jason asked, tightening his hold on her shoulder.

So here she was, caught between a sweet but too-young man who did stupid things like put the last letter her mother would ever send her through the wash and a handsome, age-appropriate man who seemed nice enough until she remembered that he was the type of capitalist whose every action was designed to destroy her way of life.

"Are you okay?" Brett asked.

Of course she wasn't okay! And he wasn't exactly the reason for it, but he was certainly part of the reason.

"I think you should leave, guy," Jason said.

"Look, I don't know who you are or what's going on here, but I'm pretty sure you don't get to tell me to leave," Brett said, puffing up a little.

Men actually did that, Casey thought with a sense of mild amusement in spite of everything. They actually puffed up their chests when walking into a conflict. It was so silly. In the end, they were all big babies. Brett should have been old enough to know better, but here he was, planting his feet in front of Jason. Though Brett was fit, anyone's money would be on Jason, whose job involved physical work and who had never in a million years even considered wearing a pink Vineyard Vines button-down, as Brett was doing right now. The little whale insignia took away from his posturing.

Jason let go of Casey and shifted so he was partially in front of her, his hands balled into fists.

"Kid, you really don't have the first clue. Why don't you go on back to the playground," Brett said.

Jason moved fast, swooping in and punching Brett in the face before Brett could even raise his hands in defense. Clearly Brett had no experience with manly stand-offs actually coming to blows. He fell back against the wooden stairs, catching himself on one hand and bringing the other up to his nose, which was gushing blood. Jason sprang back, fists up, ready to strike again.

Casey threw herself between them, letting out a string of expletives as she crouched in front of Brett, feeling the scrapes on her knees open up as she did. They were making enough noise now that a few people had come out onto the the porches of the cottages up the hill from the café. This was turning into an actual scene.

"Get out of here," Casey said, looking over her shoulder at Jason. "Go on!"

He looked at his knuckles, which were spattered with blood, shook out his hand, shrugged and walked back toward the Lobster Shack. Casey helped Brett to his feet, and instead of trying to climb the stairs, she led him in through the back door of the café into the kitchen, where she sat him at a stool inside the door while she went to get some towels and ice.

She had Brett tip his head back and rest a cloth full of ice on the bridge of his nose. His beautiful nose. It was impossible to tell right now how badly Jason had gotten him, but that nose was broken for sure.

"Do you want me to take you to the hospital?" Casey

asked, sitting on the floor in front of him and dabbing blood from her own wounded legs. They looked like they'd been through a war.

"There are no more ferries tonight," Brett said, sounding like a kid with the worst cold of his life.

"I know, but Rosetta has a little motor boat and she keeps a truck at the marina," Casey said. The ferry was great, but they couldn't be solely dependent on it to get on and off the island.

"What the hell was that?" he asked.

It was strange to see cool, calm, charming Brett unnerved, strange and also appealing, despite the hideous red blossoms of blood across his expensive shirt. He was always so put together that he had seemed somehow unreal to Casey, but now here he was, laid low and cursing about it like anybody else.

"He's sort of my ex," Casey said, hating to describe him as "ex," but deciding it was better than booty call.

"You're kidding me. How old is he? Twenty?"

Casey sighed. "Twenty-three."

"You've got to be at least thirty-five."

"Thirty-seven," Casey said, a little hurt that he'd guessed so close. People always guessed her age much younger than she was, although she could see how this week of all weeks she might look her age. Being bludgeoned by piece after piece of bad news will do that to you.

"I did not take you for a cougar," Brett said, lifting the ice so he could look at her. He had the beginnings of two black eyes. Jason had clocked him good.

"Are you making fun of me?" Casey asked.

"Yes I am."

"I think we should get you to a hospital. What if you have a concussion?"

Brett shook his head a little. "I didn't hit my head. I'll be fine. I'm a man. Sometimes men get hit in the face."

Casey couldn't help but laugh. "That is the dumbest thing I've ever heard."

"Spoken like a true woman."

"But your nose. It was so straight and nice. You need to have it looked at."

"Oh, so you like my nose, huh?"

"I did, but who knows what it'll look like now. Come on, let me take you to the hospital."

Brett took the ice from his face and looked at her, all traces of joking gone from his face. "I want to talk to you. About my work, about the hotel stuff. It doesn't have to be bad."

Casey was halfway to standing, but she dropped back onto her butt on the hard tile floor and sighed.

"If Rosetta doesn't sell to us, she will have to sell to someone else. I'm going to make this project a good thing, though, I promise, and someone else probably wouldn't care half as much."

"Why do you care so much?"

"I don't know."

"Put that ice back on your nose," Casey said. Then she got up and moved around the kitchen, making herself a cup of tea. She didn't offer one to Brett. She knew he was right. Rosetta had clearly made up her mind to sell, and one way or another, she was going to. Rosetta was to blame here, not Brett, who was only doing his job, but Casey didn't have to like his job, either. As the tea steeped she realized that once again she hadn't eaten all day. She took the last muffin from the case and put it on the plate, and then she sat on the floor in front of Brett again.

"I'll tell her to sell the café," Casey said.

Brett shifted the ice so he could see her with one eye, but he didn't say anything.

"I mean, it'll go out of business anyway, so she should sell it. My life here is over."

Brett dropped the ice and leaned forward to look at her more closely, but when he did, his nose started gushing again, dropping angry red blood onto this crisp khakis. Casey picked up the ice and gently pushed him back to lean against the wall. As she pulled away he grabbed her hand and squeezed it.

"Come work for me. Run the café at the resort," he said.

Casey let out a snort of a laugh. "I hate those types of resorts and I hate the people who stay at them. No thank you."

"Don't say no until you've seen the plans. I don't want this deal to hurt you."

"I don't need to see the plans."

"The way I felt when I kissed you this afternoon, I've never felt that way before," he said.

Sitting on the floor, Casey studied his chin, which was all she could really see of his face. It had been a nice kiss, she couldn't deny it, but she was pretty sure it wasn't a sign of true love.

"You don't even know me," she said, gently.

"I want to."

"I am not a good person. In fact my life is a total disaster right now, so believe me, you don't."

"Maybe my life is a disaster right now, too," he said.

Casey shook her head. He was in the middle of making a business deal that had to be worth millions. How could that be called a disaster? "Can I take you to the hospital now?"

"Could I crash on your couch for tonight? If it looks terrible in the morning, I'll go to the hospital. I don't think I can handle a boat ride right now."

That was fair enough. Bouncing over the chop while trying to keep his head tilted back in a small aluminum boat probably wouldn't improve his current situation much in the short term.

Casey helped him upstairs and got him arranged on the futon, and she brought him a big glass of ice water and some aspirin, and then she realized it wasn't even seven o'clock at night. What a ridiculous day it had been.

"Are you hungry? Can I make you something?" she asked.

"I think it'll hurt to chew," he said.

"I can make you a smoothie."

He agreed, and she went back down to the café and whipped up a big strawberry smoothie.

"Will you sit here with me?" he asked when she handed the drink to him. He sounded all of eight years old.

"Brett."

"Please."

So she sat at the end of the futon and let him rest his legs across her lap. She flipped on the TV and Brett said, "I think it's time for *Jeopardy!*"

He sounded so sincere that she bit back a snide remark and switched channels until she found it. All Jason had ever wanted to watch were sports, horror movies, and porn, so this was a change of pace. Despite his broken nose, Brett managed to call out answers to most of the questions. He was usually wrong, but this didn't dampen his enthusiasm. Casey watched him, amused, not bothering to chime in with the answers she knew, which were surprisingly numerous. He was a college-educated businessman, and she was a high-school dropout baker, and yet, if they had been keeping score, she'd be kicking his butt. She decided to chalk it up to the fact that he'd just been punched in the face.

After *Jeopardy!*, Casey found some stupid sitcom that Brett liked, but within minutes he was asleep and snoring. She wondered if he always snored, or it if was because he couldn't breathe through his nose right now. She carefully lifted his legs from her lap and got up. She might as well go to bed, too. She had to work early in the morning.

Before she turned off the light, she stood in the doorway, watching him sleep. He was a good man, even if he worked for some evil corporation that turned nice places into big, ugly resorts. Would it be so bad to get to know him better? Would it be so bad to kiss him again and see how it felt? And as quickly as she thought this, she forced herself to shake the image of Brett kissing her from her head.

Everything was one big perfect mess. That was all she could be sure of.

PART FOUR

Chapter Thirty-nine

IN THE MORNING, while Randy worked, Angela checked Facebook to see if Helen had responded yet—she hadn't—and then she decided to try his idea to find CJ. She found a group for Ryan's high school class—Beechmont High School, Class of 1993—and then struggled to compose a succinct explanation of who she was and what she wanted.

I'm looking for friends of Ryan Ellis, a classmate of yours who died during your junior year. I'm his younger sister, and I never got to know him.

She reread her words. If these people went to school with Ryan, they probably didn't need to be reminded about his death, because the death of a high school classmate is traumatic, and also they likely knew that his girlfriend had been pregnant, because as far as Marilyn knew, CJ had stayed in school until she had Angela, so maybe she should be honest? She erased the words and tried again.

I'm Ryan Ellis's daughter. He died before I met him and I was raised by my grandparents. My grandmother died recently, and I find myself asking a lot of questions about my family. I'd like to talk to more people who knew Ryan.

Well, that was truth, she thought, watching the cursor blink. She couldn't drop all of that on a bunch of strangers via Facebook. She erased it again.

She hadn't expected this to be so hard, and she wondered why she felt compelled to explain herself. These people didn't need to know everything about her or about why she was asking. Maybe later, when people responded, she'd need to tell them all the details, but not now.

I'm looking for classmates of Ryan Ellis. If you'd be willing to talk to me about Ryan, please send me a private message. Thank you.

Angela wasn't sure if that was better or if it made her sound like a cop or a private investigator. She added that she was a relative of Ryan's, a fact that her own last name could corroborate, and hit "Post."

Although she hadn't yet admitted it aloud, she had made up her mind: If she could locate CJ, she was going to go meet her. She had to. The only person who could add clarity to the situation was CJ, and if Angela was going to have closure, she needed clarity.

All morning she checked Facebook. Every few minutes.

Refresh, refresh, refresh. Nothing, nothing, nothing. She thought thirty-somethings loved Facebook. Peers in her own age group kept their accounts only because they used Facebook to log in to a zillion other things online, and also because it was a handy way to reach people who weren't really your friends but whom you sorta-kinda knew and might want to connect with sometime. But thirty-somethings hadn't moved on to other social networks. As she understood it, they used Facebook to flirt with old flames and share a thousand pictures a day of their children and pets.

She had also discovered that Randy had all the graphic design software she had used in her classes at St. Kate's, software she'd never purchased herself because it was way too expensive. At school, she'd relied on the design lab. She'd been so wrapped up in her grief and confusion these last few weeks, she hadn't had time to miss creating art, but now she opened a blank canvas and begin to compose a design—a beach-scape using the same technique she'd been using for her project at school where she mimicked the look of layered cut paper. She'd draw for a minute, and then check Facebook, and then draw for a minute, and then check Facebook. She wanted to throw herself wholly into this new art project, but her heart wasn't in it, and after a while she stopped flipping back and forth and just stared at Facebook, waiting.

She was staring at her post, with its absence of responses, when she felt Randy's hand on her shoulder. He gave a little squeeze, leaned down, and kissed the top of her head.

"Give it time. People are at work now," he said.

Angela nodded.

"Can I see what you were working on?" he asked,

reaching around her and tapping the mouse, opening the design program.

"It's nothing yet," Angela said. "One drawing can take me forty or fifty hours. I'm just setting up a flat design, sort of like an outline, right now."

"I'd love to see some of your work."

"Yeah?" she asked, swiveling around to look at him.

He nodded. She went back to the web browser and opened her cloud storage account where she'd saved all her projects from school in a virtual portfolio. She opened the first one and slid out of the way so he could look. Some of them were school assignments, but the more recent ones, the ones that showed off her skill with texture and her interest in playing with traditional folk art styles were pretty good, if she said so herself.

"These are all yours?" Randy asked, clicking from picture to picture.

Angela smiled and blushed. He sounded surprised. He hadn't expected her to be a digital artist. She liked taking people by surprise in this way.

"These are really good. This kind of intricacy—you could really sell these."

"Oh, I don't know—"

"Um, I do. I do design work for people. Nothing like this, though. With these sorts of skills, you could be making people logos and things like that and selling work like this on one of those sites that does paid downloads."

Angela thought of what she did as fine art, not graphic design, and she cringed a little at the thought of designing logos.

"I'm serious," Randy said. "You should go look at some

of those stock photography sites. They sell digital designs and drawings too. It's not all photographs."

"Yeah, maybe," Angela said, and she knew she sounded unconvinced.

"I mean, if you're learning this kind of stuff at college, what do you plan to do once you get a degree? You can make an okay living in graphic design if you're good at it."

Angela sensed that she'd hurt his feelings by showing so little enthusiasm for his idea, as if the fact that she wasn't sure she wanted to work in graphic design was an insult to him in his chosen career, but it was totally different. He wasn't an artist. He was a programmer who built and maintained websites. What she did was nothing like what he did.

"Totally, that's definitely something I have to look into, especially if I decide not to go back to college," Angela said, hoping to sound more appreciative of his suggestion.

"Or what, you thought you'd go get a job at Pixar or something?" he asked.

Actually, she kind of had thought that. She shrugged.

"College girls dream big," Randy said.

"Why shouldn't I?" Angela asked. She didn't know what was the matter with him. Did he expect her to decide right now to be a freelance graphic designer and work here, out of his apartment, like he did?

He sighed. "Sorry. I'm tired. Anyway, we should get you back to Grace's."

Angela glanced at the clock. Eleven. Just enough time to get to Grace's, shower and dress, and meet Marilyn at the hotel. She wanted to sit here, greasy hair and dirty clothes, and make Randy see that she hadn't meant to offend him.

And watch the computer screen until somebody answered.

"It'll be good for you to go out for a while," he said. He reached around her to shut the screen of the laptop.

Angela tried not to pout. He was right, of course, but she was still not caught up on sleep, and was so wired with conflicting emotions that she wasn't about to concede as much. Grudgingly she followed him to his car and let him drive her back to Grace's.

It was strange sitting across a table from Marilyn. She looked so much like Deb, although her style was completely different. Where Deb had been prim, proper, matchy-matchy perfect, Marilyn's style was funkier, messier, more lived-in. But they had the same eyes, the same face-shape, the same heart-shaped lips. Their voices were similar, too. Angela thought that if Marilyn called her on the phone, she wouldn't be able to detect a difference between her voice and Deb's— except for the accent, of course. Deb's years on St. Nabor had given her a hint of a Southern drawl, and she was prone to using the ever-convenient pronoun "y'all," whereas Marilyn spoke with the hard, clipped tones of a Northerner.

Angela still didn't know how to feel about Marilyn's appearance in her life, let alone how to feel about the fact that she was already leaving. She had arrived at a moment of such turmoil that they hadn't even gotten to know one another at all.

When the waiter came with the bread basket, Angela

realized that for the first time in days, she was actually hungry—no, starving—and felt relieved. Maybe the insanity really was over now. As she buttered a piece of bread, she noticed that Marilyn was watching her intently and felt a little self-conscious.

"I'm sorry you have to go so soon," Angela said.

"Are you?" Marilyn asked.

Was she that transparent? Angela wondered. "Well, I feel bad. I wish we could have met under some other circumstances."

The fact was that thanks to the lies Angela's parents had spun for all those years, there were no good circumstances under which they could have met, but still, she did wish she could have a do-over for her introduction to Marilyn. She should be happy to discover that she had long-lost family and that she wasn't all alone now, instead of being suspicious and confused.

"I shouldn't have shown up like that," Marilyn said. "I did try to contact you, though."

She had said this when she arrived, too, but honestly Angela thought the handful of voicemail messages (which she listened to only after Marilyn's arrival) didn't constitute much of an effort. Any normal person would have waited for a response before getting on an airplane.

"I was wondering, have you worked out where you'll live? Until you go back to school, that is?" Marilyn asked.

Angela shook her head without looking at her aunt. Instead she pulled the bread apart and rolled it into little soft pieces.

"Will you go back next semester, do you think?"

Angela glanced up at her. She knew where this was

going. Marilyn was going to urge her to go back to school and finish her degree and act like she had the right to counsel Angela on her life, which she did not, as they had known each other for exactly two days.

"I'm worried about you. You're so young to be dealing with all of this, and I would hate for you to make decisions now, during this difficult time, that you'll regret later."

"Well, thanks, but you really don't need to worry about me," Angela said, sweeping the little doughy balls of bread up into her paper napkin and setting it on her bread plate. Just like that her appetite had vanished again.

"Yes, but how well do you know Randy? It seems like things are pretty serious between you, and I have to say, all the ghost talk," she paused and shook her head. "Are you sure he's the right sort of person?"

Angela was ready to get up and leave. Marilyn could have lunch alone and get a cab to the airport. Who did she think she was, prying this way?

"I'm afraid he's giving you funny ideas about things. You know ghosts aren't real," Marilyn said. She reached out to put her hand over Angela's, but Angela pulled hers away.

"I went to Randy for help. He isn't giving me wrong ideas." Angela crossed her arms and scanned the room for the waiter. She needed to cancel her order and get the hell out of there.

"Angela, I don't know what you thought happened in that room last night, but you've got to see how it might look to other people. I mean, it seemed kind of crazy. I feel somehow responsible for you now that Deb is gone, and I really am very worried."

"Why did you come here?" Angela asked, struggling to

keep her voice down.

"Why? I—" Marilyn looked uncertain.

"You knew you were going to tell me the truth about my parents, right? That's really why you came."

"I came because I needed to see for myself. Reading the obituary, it was like it couldn't possibly be real," Marilyn said.

"So why did you bring that picture of Ryan and CJ?" Angela asked. She doubted Marilyn happened to carry it around in her purse day in and day out.

"I hoped I could finally meet you, and, yes, I thought you deserved to know the truth, and then I showed up and walked into a séance! What was I supposed to do?"

Angela started to slide out from the behind the booth, but this time Marilyn managed to get hold of her hand.

"Look, I think you should come live with me and my husband for a while, until you're ready to go back to school. It isn't healthy for you to be here all by yourself trying to deal with all of this," Marilyn said, her tone low and insistent.

Angela shook her head and pulled her hand free. "You are a stranger, and I'm hardly alone here," she said, and she walked out of the restaurant as fast as she could.

After Angela left, Randy thought about how she'd acted when he'd said she could make money as a graphic designer. She'd had a look on her face like he'd spit in her eye. This was exactly what he had been afraid of—the ghost investigation was over and now she was thinking of herself as above him again.

He could also detect this attitude of entitlement that sometimes crept into what she said. She'd never had to work hard for anything. She kept saying how she was totally broke now because her mother's finances were such a mess, and yet she showed no sign of doing anything about it. She talked about transferring to art school, maybe in Savannah, but today was the first time he'd seen her artwork. He knew she was grieving, but he wondered if she was ever going to start making a plan for her future.

And what sort of spoiled rich girl doesn't even know how her parents are paying for college? When she told him she hadn't been aware that her mother had taken out loans for her tuition--to the tune of nearly forty-thousand dollars a year—he could hardly believe it. They came from different worlds. His own parents worked maintaining the homes and lawns of people like Angela. When he'd driven her by the house where he grew up the other day, she had stared at the tired-looking little ranch house like she was touring a third world country.

He couldn't help but wonder if he'd made a terrible mistake letting things get so serious between them. He had to walk on eggshells around her, and that was no way to be, but it was also an impossible situation because he couldn't talk to her about it without upsetting her. He either had to be okay with possibly hurting her feelings or keep walking on eggshells while ignoring his own feelings. But that wasn't fair either. It wasn't that he was afraid to upset her, but rather that she had so many other things on her mind. If this was a normal situation, he'd be honest with her, but nothing was normal about her life right now. Which was exactly why he never should have let the ghost investigations turn into something romantic.

And as he sat there, it occurred to him that he needed to break it off with her. He'd been so obsessed with her, with helping her through this stuff with her mother, that he'd fallen way behind on work. He'd been acting like her, like a person without responsibilities, but he had a life, and he couldn't neglect it forever.

But she wasn't so bad, was she? She was beautiful and sensitive and she liked being with him. She was a computer geek, like him, and he had to admit, he found that kind of sexy. Most girls he met seemed skeptical of him when he told them what he did, like they assumed he was one of those guys who'd rather play computer games than have a conversation, but Angela understood that there were other reasons for a person to get lost in a computer screen than games.

Why couldn't they have met some other way than because of her mother's death? The timing made everything so complicated. They'd definitely been spending too much time together. He needed space to get his feelings in order. He needed to work up the nerve to tell her so, even if it meant saying things she didn't want to hear.

Chapter Forty

Devil's Back Island, Maine

CASEY TIPTOED PAST the futon in the morning on her way to the bathroom. She hated that she had to work so early. She didn't want to disturb Brett. As she passed, he said, softly, "Hey." She cursed herself for being too loud.

"It's okay, I've been awake for a while," he said. He still sounded congested. Casey didn't want to turn on the light. She didn't want to see how bad he looked.

In the dim, early morning light, she saw him kick off the blanket she'd thrown over him the night before. As he sat up, he brought one hand to his forehead. No doubt he had quite a headache.

"I know you have to work, but could you come here for a minute," he said, patting the futon beside him.

She sat down, the fresh scabs on her knees tight and uncomfortable as she bent her legs, and was surprised to realize how nervous she felt. About what? In the past week, she'd gotten sloppy drunk in front of him and had a temper tantrum, and he had been knocked on his ass and had his nose broken because of her. What could he possibly have to say now that could be more embarrassing than all of that?

"Look, I know you don't really want to talk about it, but I think we need to," he said. "After I talk to my bosses today to finalize a few things, I'm presenting Rosetta the formal offer, and then I'm going back to California and put things in motion, and when I come back, it'll be to oversee the project as construction gets underway."

Casey sighed. She wished she didn't like Brett. She wished he were an ugly, old asshole that she could dismiss with a snide remark and, if he said something misogynistic enough, a slap across the face. But he was nice in his dopey, mainstream way. At least he wasn't a hipster.

"I know you don't want things to change around here, and honestly I don't think Rosetta does either, but she's in a bad position. She has no choice."

Casey nodded. She had woken up feeling surprisingly well-rested, but now she was weary. Why bother opening the café today for a small handful of late-season visitors? Why not stay in bed? Why open the café ever again? Why not put up a sign that said closed forever and disappear? She'd disappeared from her life twice before now. She could do it again.

"I know how special the island is," Brett said. "It's beautiful and unspoiled, and I'm going to do everything I can to honor that."

"How?" Casey asked, turning her head to look at him. How could he possibly honor the spirit of the place *and* put up a luxury resort?

"We've scaled back the plans, for starters. A condo village instead of a big hotel. We'll design the buildings to suit the environment and do everything the greenest way possible. We'll sell it as a quiet place to escape from it all and get in touch with nature."

He became more animated as he spoke. He really believed what he was saying. Casey could see that. He didn't seem to get that there was no environmentally friendly way to build here, a fact he really should have picked up on.

"We're going to appeal to a new clientele—young and liberal. The socially, economically, and environmentally conscious crowd," he said.

Casey laughed. "And rich. Do you really think they'll want to come here and not, I don't know, Mexico or Ibiza?"

"I do," he said earnestly.

Casey shook her head. This was a place where middle-class New Englanders came because it was one of the cheapest places to get a rental with a water view. They gave up the tourist attractions of Bar Harbor or Ogunquit in favor of the ability to afford an entire week's vacation someplace where they could easily walk to the beach.

"I want you to work for me. I want you to run the coffee shop and bakery in the resort. You'll make more money, you'll have more help, and you'll have more customers."

"I like the customers I have now," Casey said.

"You don't need to decide right now, of course, but think about it, okay? I wish I could tell you that your café could stay as it is and survive the development, but I can't lie to you."

She felt a flare of anger, but it passed quickly and turned to dread. She was losing her café and her home all in one swoop.

"What am I going to do?" Casey said, more to herself than to Brett.

"Come work at the resort," he said.

She shook her head.

"Casey," he said. "I really like you. I want to—" he paused, formulating his words, "I want to give us a try."

Casey stood up then. It was ridiculous for him to say such a thing. There was no "us" for the two of them. They might have been able to have a nice fling for a while if she hadn't learned what he was actually doing here, but she had, and however attractive and nice he might be, there would never been an "us."

"I have to get downstairs. Feel free to take your time up here. I really think you should go see a doctor about that nose, though," she said coldly.

When he got back to the hotel, it wasn't even seven o'clock yet. There were still two hours until the first ferry, two hours until he could take his wrecked face to a doctor. He should have gone to the ER last night. He should have let Casey take him. Too late for that. He had two black eyes, he couldn't breathe through his nose, and he had a headache that throbbed from the crown of his head down through the bones of his face and into his teeth. He helped himself to an empty ice bucket from the housekeeping closet near the ice machine and filled it before going on to his room.

As he sat on the bed, arranging a hand towel full of ice for his nose, he noticed the message light blinking on the room phone. He followed the instructions on the card beside the phone and listened:

> *Brett, this is Charlie, here. We need you to hold off*
> *on that deal. We love the whole eco-tourism thing,*
> *but you and I need to talk. Do not move forward*
> *with the offer. I'll be here tonight another hour or*
> *so, or call me first thing in the morning. I'll be in by*
> *nine, I mean nine, my time.*

The message had been left at ten o'clock the previous evening. Brett didn't like that "you and I need to talk" business. He knew what it meant. It meant that this deal was dead. He lay back on the bed and set the ice pack on his face.

At the stroke of noon, he dialed Charlie. He'd taken enough ibuprofen to kill a small animal and his head felt moderately better. He'd taken a hot shower, and he could now sort of breathe out of one nostril.

Charlie's secretary picked up on the second ring, and after a couple of minutes on hold, Charlie came on the line. Brett didn't bother with pleasantries.

"What the hell is going on?"

"What's the matter with you? You got a cold or something?" Charlie asked.

"Why are we delaying the offer?"

"Look, I probably should have reigned you in sooner on this one," Charlie said. "We've decided to move forward with that site in Costa Rica instead."

Costa Rica? Brett gritted his teeth to prevent himself telling his boss where he could put his Costa Rica development.

"We're going to do it your way, though—the whole ecotourism thing. It's your concept, kid, through and through."

Charlie went on, trying to convince Brett that the fundamental alteration of his plan in moving it to a tropical country was a good thing. Finally, Brett cut him off.

"I don't get it. Why did you let me scout this location if you knew you wanted Costa Rica?" he asked.

Charlie sighed heavily into the phone. "Look, why don't you get yourself on the next flight back here and we can talk."

"Let's talk now," Brett said. His head had resumed its pounding.

"You know how much we value the work you do, right? You're an important part of our team."

"That's great. I feel really valued on this wild goose chase right now."

"I was doing you a favor, you know. The past year or so, anyone could see you weren't happy, and your work was suffering, so when you wanted to look into branching out into new markets and new locations, I thought, all right, let's see what the kid's got. Honestly, I had my doubts before I even let you fly out there. I mean, come on, what the hell does Sweet Water want in a location where winter lasts from October to May? But you know, you've worked for me for a long time. If what you needed to get your groove back was a change of scenery, fine. And once you got there, you sounded so damn happy, like it was Christmas fucking morning, for God's sake, and so I waited to see what you came up with. And good thing, too. This ecotourism stuff is big, and it's time for us to get in on it. As far as I'm concerned, your trip there was money well spent, and now it's time for you to get your ass back here—"

"Will you be putting up a big hotel in Costa Rica?" Brett asked.

"What? Yes, of course."

"Not a condo village built using sustainable practices."

"Obviously we're still working on the details."

"Tell me how my idea for a smaller-scale, more exclusive, more environmentally friendly and socially conscious resort fits into your plans for Costa Rica," Brett said, his voice flat and low.

"We're still working it out, but I can assure you, we are taking your ideas seriously."

"Yes, I'm sure you are."

"Laurie checked flights for me. How far are you from Boston? We can get you on a flight this afternoon at four-fifteen. Can you get there by then?"

"No," Brett said, and hung up the phone.

He found Rosetta out on the patio overlooking the beach. She smiled as he approached, but when he got close enough that she could see his face, she leapt up and hurried to meet him. She moved fast for an old lady. He explained away his battle scars as his own stupid fault, stumbled on the cliff rock in the dark the night before when he was out walking, he said. She seemed suspicious but let it pass and led him back to the table where she'd been sitting.

There were a few other patrons enjoying the warm, breezy afternoon, but they took little notice of Brett and Rosetta. This is it, he thought. This is the last season for the Wild Rose Inn. And then he realized that that would have been the case if the deal had gone through, too. But he would have kept the spirit of what Rosetta had done here.

He would have tried.

"You don't look like you have good news for me," Rosetta said.

He shook his head.

"How low are they going now? Can I afford this deal?"

"No," he said, sighing. "There's no deal. My bosses have changed their minds."

Rosetta looked at him with narrowed eyes for a moment, and then nodded. "Well, we tried, didn't we?" she said, turning her gaze out toward the water.

"I'm sorry. I wanted to help you. I—"

She waved him off. "To be honest, I have no head for business at all. I've been running this place steadily into the ground since my husband died. All that's happened here is we've arrived at the logical conclusion."

"So you'll declare bankruptcy?"

She nodded.

He felt like he might cry. It was so wrong that she would have to see everything she'd spent a lifetime building come to nothing.

"You're a nice man. None of this is your fault," she said. "You going to see a doctor about that face?"

He forced a smile. "I'm fine. I'm going to stay a few more days, though, okay?"

"Suit yourself, as long as you pay your bill," she said, winking.

"What does it mean?" Casey asked.

When Brett had walked into the café with his black eyes and a splint on his swollen nose, she felt a strange surge of happiness at the sight of him, which she quickly squashed by reminding herself that he represented the enemy.

But then he had said that the deal was dead and she didn't know what to think. Just that morning, he'd assured her it was moving forward, and now he was saying his bosses had backed out. They sat at a table near the open window, with two steaming mugs of coffee. There were no customers, and she had been planning to close when he arrived.

"The court will step in and negotiate a plan to settle her debts. Most likely they'll liquidate her assets."

Casey looked at him like he'd started speaking in tongues.

"They'll sell off anything she owes money on."

"I offered to help her. I recently came into a little money. I offered it to her, but she said it won't change anything."

"Her debt burden is pretty big," he said.

Casey watched him trace the pattern of the wood grain on the table top with his finger.

"Did you do this? Did you stop the deal?" she asked.

He looked up at her and shook his head.

"The deal was going to save her, give her enough money to pay off her debts and retire. Now, I don't know. When all is said and done, she's not going to have much."

"And this is bad for you, too, right? I mean, wouldn't it be better for your job if it had gone through?"

He gave a sad smile and a little shrug. "I was thinking of quitting anyway."

"Oh yeah? What'll you do?" she asked.

"Do you ever regret not getting married, having a family, all of that?" he asked.

Casey made a face. "How old do you think I am? Is it really all over for me?"

"Sorry," he said. "I mean obviously you could still get married and stuff, but—and don't take this the wrong way—as you get older, isn't it harder to have a baby? More risky and all that?"

Casey looked out the window and didn't answer him. Whether or not she wanted to get married and have a family was really none of his business, and entirely irrelevant to the topic at hand.

"I didn't mean to pry. I'm thinking about myself. I never wanted to settle down before, but now, I look at my life and think, what have I been doing? What have I accomplished? I have a nice condo, I make good money, I travel to beautiful beaches for my job, but it all feels kind of meaningless."

She turned back to face him. "I stopped looking for meaning a long time ago. There is no meaning."

"I don't believe you."

She shrugged. He could believe what he wanted. She shouldn't be sitting here shooting the breeze with him. She should be going over to see Rosetta and find out what exactly she was planning to do next. But then again, what good would it do? Brett had already told her that Rosetta had a lawyer who had been working on the bankruptcy even before he came in with his initial offer.

"If there is no meaning, how do you get up every morning?" Brett asked.

"Because I'm alive. Because I have to pee or I get

hungry."

"I need to learn from you. I need you to be my guru."

Casey looked back out the window again. She didn't like it when he said things like that, as if there were some future for them.

"Casey," he said softly, "I think I'm falling in love with you."

"You don't even know me," she said.

"I do, though."

"You know this can't work. You live in California. I live here, for now anyway. We are from different universes. And seriously, you don't even know me."

"What do I need to know about you, then?"

She rolled her eyes but didn't answer.

"I got punched in the face for you. I feel like the least you could do for me is tell me something about yourself."

She pursed her lips and studied him, and then she said, "Okay. You want to know about me. My mother, who recently died, disowned me when I was seventeen because I got pregnant. Do you want to ask me again if I regret not having a family?"

"I'm sorry. I didn't know."

"How could you? But that's what happened. I had a baby and I gave her up for adoption." It was weirdly easy to tell him this. Maybe it was because she was annoyed or because her emotions had been on overdrive for weeks or because having already told Rosetta, she had opened the floodgates, but for whatever reason, she told him, just like that.

"Do you ever get to see her?"

"I agreed to give up all my rights," Casey said. He didn't need to know how screwed up the circumstances had been.

"Well, it sounds like you took the mature, responsible route," he said, kindly.

"I wanted to be a mother. I loved that baby, and I loved her father. That's how I know what love is, and that's how I know that whatever you feel for me, it isn't love," she said, standing up. She had let this conversation go on long enough. He needed to leave the café, leave the island, go back to California, and let her figure out what she was going to do now.

"You were a kid," he said.

"Kids know what love is. Adults, not so much." She carried their mugs to the kitchen, and to her dismay she heard him follow her.

She set the mugs on the counter, and she felt his hands on her waist. He rested his chin on the top of her head and gently pulled her back against him.

"Would it be so bad to see if we could love each other?" he asked.

It felt good, leaning against him that way. It felt easy and comfortable and warm. And yet, in her gut, she knew it was wrong. How could he even talk about starting a relationship when he was thinking of quitting his job with no plan for what he was going to do next, and when she was about to lose her job, with no plan for what she was going to do next? She stepped out of his grasp.

"Both of our lives are in chaos right now," she said, turning to face him.

"Who cares? If we were kids, would you care?"

"We aren't kids."

"You said kids know what love is. So think like a kid. If you were a kid again, what would you do right now?"

She shook her head but didn't answer.

"Maybe we can help each other get through the chaos. Have you ever thought of that?" Brett asked.

She wanted to kiss him. Black eyes, swollen nose and all—she wanted to kiss him. And normally, when she wanted to kiss someone, she did, but normally the people she wanted to kiss didn't use words like "love."

He took a step closer to her and put his hands back on her waist again. She had to tip her head back to look at his face. And then he leaned down and kissed her, gently, innocently on the lips before pulling away. She put her hands on his back and squeezed, burrowing against him, and he laughed a little.

"Sorry," he said. "I don't think I can give you the kiss I want to give you right now. It hurts too much."

She laughed, too, then, and said, "Talk about romantic."

He set his chin back on top of her head and wrapped his arms around her. "You got that right."

Chapter Forty-one

St. Nabor Island, South Carolina

WHEN ANGELA GOT back to Grace's after lunch, the first thing she did was see if there were any answers to her messages. It was as Randy had said: She stopped watching Facebook for a couple hours, and the responses started rolling in. Several people commented on her post about Ryan, writing comments about what a good guy he had been, gone too soon, rest in peace, and so on.

Then she opened her private messages and saw that she had four: One from Helen Ellis Jenson, one from somebody name Lindsay Wilcox, and one from Nicole and another from Molly.

She had ignored every call, text, and Email from Nicole and Molly for a week. She couldn't deal with them telling her she was acting irrationally, that she needed to calm down and think things through, but she couldn't avoid them forever.

She opened Molly's message first. It was brief:

Where are you? Why aren't you answering your phone? Please call me.

Angela hated the thought of Molly worrying about her, and yet she needed to put her own needs first for now. Molly didn't understand what she was going through, and that was okay, but Angela needed to distance herself until she could sort things out. She deleted the message.

Nicole's message was similar:

Please let's talk. I'm always here for you. XO

Instead of feeling sad or guilty at Nicole's words, Angela only felt annoyed. If Nicole and Molly were really always there for her, they wouldn't have tried to talk her out of her belief that her mother's ghost was trying to communicate with her. They should have tried to understand.

She was too nervous to read Helen's reply, so she clicked the other message instead.

Hi Angela,

I saw your post about Ryan. When I saw your post and profile picture, I knew right away you had to be his baby. I didn't know your parents well. We weren't friends. That said, everyone knew when CJ got pregnant. And then, when she was getting close to her due date, after Ryan's death, she disappeared. I don't think anyone heard from her at all after that.

I guess kids today would say she ghosted us. I always hoped she took her baby away and raised her Gilmore Girls style in some adorable little town somewhere where she could start fresh and be a great mom and also her daughter's best friend. It's possible that I watch too much TV. Anyway, I hadn't thought about her in a long time, and then a couple of months ago I ran into her when I was on vacation. She didn't recognize me, but I've always had a thing for faces, and I remembered her right away. She was working at a place called the Beach Plum Café on Devil's Back Island, Maine, but maybe you already know that?

Even though we weren't friends, as a I said, I always liked your parents. I hope you find what you're looking for.

Lindsay Wilcox

Angela stared at the screen for a long time, deliberating whether or not she should look up the Beach Plum Café. After a few moments of indecision, she opened Helen's message instead.

Dear Angela,

You have no idea how much I've hoped and prayed that one day you would reach out to me. I knew Richard would never go against Deborah's wishes. That's the kind of husband he was. But the day he disappeared from our family, taking you with him, it broke my heart. All these years, I have held out hope that one day he would see that it had been wrong to run away like that, and that he would come back. And now here you are, writing to me, and I see that my prayers have finally been answered. I fear I must infer from your note that your mother has passed on. I will not pretend she and I were friends, but for your sake, and for Richard's, I am sorry. Does my brother know that you have contacted me? I tried to reach out to your parents many times in the early years after they left, but they never responded. It would bring me so much joy to have my brother in my life again. Please call me as soon as you can.

Love,

Your Aunt Helen

Angela looked at the phone number at the bottom of the message. She couldn't believe it had been so easy to find her long lost family. She couldn't believe her parents had kept such massive secrets from her and she had never even guessed that the secrets existed, let alone the nature of all they were hiding.

With shaking fingers, she dialed. A woman answered

on the third ring and introduced herself as Helen Jenson.

"This is Angela, your niece," Angela said. On the other end, the woman burst into tears.

Angela confirmed Helen's inference about her mother's death and broke the news about her father's illness. Helen had had enough time since getting Angela's message to develop high hopes for seeing her brother again, and Angela felt terrible as she dashed those hopes. She waited while Helen absorbed this news, and then she took a deep breath and explained to Helen how she had learned about her parents' lies. She left out the ghosts and stuck to documents in her mother's desk and safe deposit box as an explanation—no need to have two long-lost aunts fretting over her mental state.

"I've met my mother's sister, Marilyn, and I was wondering if you could maybe tell me your side of things, why they did what they did," she asked.

Like Marilyn, Helen said that the whole family had been shocked to learn that Ryan's girlfriend was pregnant, but they liked the girl, and anyone could see that the kids were in love. With Deborah and Richard's help, they thought the kids could raise the baby. It wasn't ideal, but they planned to get married once they turned eighteen, and at least they had a support system. After Ryan's death, when Deb decided to adopt the baby, everyone agreed that that made sense, but, Helen said, she was worried about CJ, who had been kicked out by her own mother and who had now lost Ryan, too. Deb never told her in-laws about her plan to raise the baby as her own, though. They hadn't learned about that until after, after Deb and Rich were gone and no one could find them. They sought out Deb's family, and Marilyn confessed Deb's plan. That was it. The only difference between Helen's story and Marilyn's was Helen's obvious loathing of Deb and her insistence that Deb had cajoled Richard into going along with such a duplicitous scheme.

"Do you have friends there, dear? Do you have people to help you through this hard time?" Helen asked, as the conversation seemed to be winding down.

Angela assured her that she did.

"Do you think, maybe, you would like to meet us someday?"

As angry as she'd been at Marilyn, she had no hesitation in her response that she would absolutely like to meet her father's family sometime soon.

After she hung up the phone, and before she could talk herself out of it, Angela looked up the Beach Plum Café, Devil's Back Island, Maine. The café did not appear to have its own website, but it was listed on the island's tourism website, with a picture of a charming little cottage and the café hours: May 1 - Columbus Day, Monday-Thursday, 7AM to 4PM; Weekends, 7AM to 7PM; Mid-October - April, Thursday-Sunday, 8AM to 3PM. She glanced at the clock. The café was open right now. She could call and maybe talk to her birth mother this very minute.

She punched the number into her phone, and then, before she could hit dial, she chickened out. She wasn't ready yet. She needed a strategy. She needed to think this through. Her stomach rumbled. She needed a meal and a good night's rest. And then she would make the call. She needed to hear CJ's side of the story.

Chapter Forty-two

Devil's Back Island, Maine

BRETT WASN'T A BLANKET-STEALER like Jason. In fact, he was a perfect gentleman even in sleep. He didn't hog the bed or insist on keeping their limbs entwined or encroach on Casey's pillow. Waking up beside him felt like the easiest, most natural thing in the world.

For the past four nights, he'd stayed with her instead of in his hotel room. They both knew he was going to have to leave eventually. He had a life in California—a life he planned to walk away from, it was true—but a life nonetheless. A job, a condo, a car, friends. And what if when he got back there to the perpetual sunny summer of LA, he realized that he didn't want to abandon his whole world? Because now that she had let him into her life, she wanted him to stay.

"That's a pretty serious face for this early in the morning," he said, rolling onto his side and studying her. His black eyes had faded to an ugly greenish yellow, and the swelling of his nose had gone down. He sounded normal again.

"I didn't realize you were awake," Casey said, giving him

a smile.

"What do you think about taking the day off today?" he asked, taking hold of a lock of her hair and twirling it around his finger.

On the one hand, Casey thought it was pointless to open the café at all. On the other hand, she had to make the most of her final days at the Beach Plum Café.

"Why?" she asked.

"I want to go up to Weldon. I want to show you something."

"Can you show me tomorrow?" she asked.

"It's kind of time sensitive."

"Because you're leaving?"

He furrowed his brow and then said, "No. I mean, sort of. I'm planning to fly out Wednesday, but that's not why I want to show you this today."

"You're leaving on Wednesday?" Casey asked. It was Saturday. Wednesday would be here in the blink of an eye.

"I'll be back as soon as I can," he said, leaning down and kissing her.

She wanted to believe him, but in case he never came back, she decided she'd better go with him.

They took Rosetta's motor boat to the marina up the bay where she kept a pickup truck, and in a nod to chivalry, Brett drove. Casey always liked Weldon. It was a cute little town with an old-fashioned Main Street lined with shops and restaurants. Brett parked in front of a vacant storefront, got out, and opened the door for Casey. He led her up to the door of the storefront, and a woman opened it to let them in.

"What is this?" Casey asked, standing in the dusty, empty space. The floor was battered old black and white linoleum, the walls a hideous, too-bright, blue. The ceiling was intricate pressed tin, although someone had painted it neon green.

"It's the perfect place for your new café," Brett said, turning a circle with his arms out like Julie Andrews at the end of *The Sound of Music*.

"I'm Lisa," the woman said, holding out her hand to Casey.

"Brett, what is going on?" Casey asked, not shaking Lisa's hand.

"Well, while you were working yesterday, I was scouting locations for you. It's kind of my thing. It's what I'm good at." He sounded very proud of himself.

"Lisa, could you leave us alone for a minute," Casey asked.

Lisa took her polite perma-smile and stepped back out onto the sidewalk.

"What's wrong?" Brett asked.

"What are you doing? I didn't ask you to do this." This, Casey thought, was exactly the problem with men like Brett, men who had their lives together and thought rationally about financial security and the future. They thought women like her needed tending and fixing.

"I know you didn't, but you said it yourself—the café can't stay in business on the island without the hotel."

"I can't buy this place, or rent it, or whatever. I have no money. Look at this place. It's a dump. Does it even have a kitchen?"

"It does," Brett said.

"Yeah, well there's no way I can afford it. I might as well start applying for barista jobs in Portland because there's no way—"

"You said your mom left you some money."

Casey kept forgetting about that. The idea that there was a whole pile of money sitting in an account somewhere waiting for her was hard to incorporate into her world view. She looked around the room again and then shrugged. "I'm sure it's not enough."

"How much do you have?"

"About two-hundred thousand," she said, looking at the filthy floor and scraping at a wad of something or other with her shoe. She wondered what her checking account balance was. Probably more than she thought. She never spent money on anything.

"That's enough to get you started, if you manage your finances right."

She wondered if he was right. It sounded like an impossibly huge sum of money to her personally, but in business terms it sounded like nothing.

"Yeah, well, I doubt I'm any better at managing money than Rosetta is, seeing as she's the closest thing to a mentor I've got."

"What if I was your business partner?" Brett asked, closing the distance between them and taking both of her hands in his. "What if we go in on it 50-50? I have savings, too. We can renovate it ourselves, and you can be in charge of the cooking and I can run the business side of things." His enthusiasm had returned. He was excited and happy and hopeful. It was enough to make Casey crack a smile.

"Do you know anything about running a restaurant?" she asked.

"I know a lot about business."

"And you're handy with tools and paint and DIY projects?"

"There's only one way to find out."

"This might be the worst idea you ever had," Casey said.

The fact that Rosetta seemed to think it was a good idea for Casey and Brett to go into business together gave Casey pause. For tons of reasons, it was a really bad idea. She sat there, listing them for Rosetta—

1. It's a bad idea to go into business with the person you're sleeping with.

2. Their relationship was ridiculously new and therefore precarious.

3. Brett had no experience running a restaurant.

4. Restaurants are incredibly risky and most of them fail.

5. She'd have to take the money from her mother, which went against her vow to herself to never have any dealing with her mother again...

"Let me stop you right there," Rosetta said. "Your mother is dead. You aren't dealing with her. Be like Mother Theresa. Dirty money is washed clean when put to good use."

"Really? Mother Theresa?"

Rosetta shrugged.

"What about the whole sleeping together thing?"

Rosetta made a disapproving face, but then she said, "Who was my business partner when I started this place?"

"Phil, but you were married. You already had been married for years," Casey said. She couldn't believe Rosetta was defending Brett's insane idea and using her own life experience to back it up. Rosetta should have been talking her out of this.

"And what? We weren't sleeping together?" Rosetta asked, raising an eyebrow.

"You know what I mean."

"Here's what I know: When you reach a certain age, it's easy to know if you've found the right person for you. When you're a kid, you have to take your time because you know you're going to do a lot of growing and changing and that might tear you apart. But you're not a kid, he's not a kid. You both know what you want. Who cares if you hardly know each other? Hell, if you eloped tomorrow, I'd only throw you a party."

That was crazy talk. Rosetta was clearly going senile saying things like that. But the part about them not being kids anymore, that was true.

"I'm looking into one of those retirement communities. My sister-in-law thinks there are spaces available at hers," Rosetta said, changing the subject.

"But that's in Florida," Casey said.

"They tell me it's a great place to retire. Bentley would like the warm climate." She reached down and gave the dog a pat. "I'm too old to keep living out here. I need to be someplace where if I have an emergency I can actually get to a hospital."

"You're perfectly healthy," Casey said. Rosetta liked to play the old lady card when it suited her, and then to act indignant any time anyone treated her like an old lady.

"I'm also 78 years old. If I have a stroke, I'll be brain dead before the paramedics ever get here."

"Okay. Right. So I'm going into business with a man I've only known for a couple weeks and who I'm now sleeping with, and you're moving to Florida. Good talk," Casey said, pushing back her chair.

"What's the worst thing that could happen if you open a café with him?" Rosetta asked.

"It might tank."

"And then?"

"I'd be broke."

"And then?"

"I don't know."

"Would you be any worse off than you are right now?" Rosetta asked.

"I might get my heart broken, too," Casey said after a minute.

"Your heart is already broken. Everyone's heart is broken by the time they're—how old are you now? Thirty-six?"

"Thirty-seven."

"Right. Well, there you have it."

Rosetta tried to tell Casey about what she'd found online when she looked for the Ellises. She tried over and over, but every time, Casey cut her off and refused to let her speak. She'd even gone so far as to clamp her hands over her ears and shout "lalala" at the top of her lungs.

Rosetta considered contacting the girl herself, but then she came to her senses. She didn't generally have a problem meddling when she thought she might be helpful, but even she could see that contacting Casey's daughter would be a step too far. As Casey had pointed out, there was no way to know if the girl knew of her adoption or not, and there were too many variables in how she might react.

Still, it pained her to know that the girl was out there, her great-great niece, and she'd never know her. But Rosetta knew when to call it quits. She had other battles to fight, anyway.

After encouraging Casey to move forward with Brett's crazy scheme—and it was crazy; the two of them hardly knew each other, but what else was there for Casey to do?— she set out for her appointment in Portland with her lawyer. She had to think of her own future, too. She had to accept that Casey was a grownup who could (and would have to) take care of herself. Rosetta the fairy godmother could do no more magic for her. Now she could only be her doddering old auntie.

Chapter Forty-three

St. Nabor Island, South Carolina

"ARE YOU BREAKING up with me?" Angela asked. She was sitting on the deck at Randy's apartment. She'd shown up, unannounced, a few minutes earlier, giddy to tell him about the messages she'd gotten. He hadn't seemed happy to see her. Then he'd had her sit down and had started talking, and now she couldn't make sense of what he was saying.

"No, but, can't we take it slow? I mean, this is all so intense," he said.

Whose fault is that? she wanted to say. Whose idea was it to keep going back to the house for investigation after investigation? Yes, it was intense, but if it had been up to her, she'd have dropped the whole ghost-investigation thing after the first one. She could have found all the answers she needed without delving into any more paranormal activity.

"Look, you're going through a lot right now," he said. His eyes looked tired and sad. "This isn't the right time to start a relationship."

"So you're really breaking up with me." She couldn't

believe it.

"I need time to think, okay? I think we both need some space to figure things out."

But Angela didn't want time or space. Without Randy, she had nobody here. Without Randy, what was she doing on St. Nabor? She suddenly missed her friends. She needed her friends, and it was obvious to her now that Randy was right. They were being too intense. She'd been turning to him for all the support she felt she hadn't gotten from her friends. She'd only known him a few weeks (not counting the fact that they'd gone to grade school together, because that really did not count), and she was clinging to him and relying on him for everything. She didn't want to admit it, but he was right. Under any sort of normal circumstances, she would want to take things slower, too. She stood up.

"You don't have to go," he said. He looked miserable.

"I think I do."

PART FIVE

Chapter Forty-four

Weldon, Maine

Casey had to hand it him. When Brett made up his mind, he really knew how to get things done. The Monday after first showing Casey the storefront, after she impulsively told him to go for it, he had negotiated a lease agreement and they had signed and officially become business partners. The man was sexy in action—setting up a bank account, filing paperwork to incorporate, applying for whatever kinds of licenses they needed to open a café—all kinds of things Casey knew not the first thing about. All she had to do was walk up and down the aisles of the home improvement store, making decisions about paint colors and fixtures.

He had left Wednesday afternoon, though, back to California to take care of things there, and he wasn't certain how soon he'd be able to get back. No later than Halloween, he had promised. He promised he'd be back for the last hoorah at the Wild Rose Inn for Halloween Haunting Fest. He gave her daily, sometimes thrice daily, updates on his progress by phone.

He hadn't succeeded in getting her to cave in and get a smartphone (or a tablet, or a computer—he had tried and failed). He wanted to be able to Skype and see her face every day, but she had convinced him that there was more old-fashioned romance in relying on phone calls, and maybe even snail mail. He'd taken her up on the latter. In three weeks, she'd gotten eight handwritten letters. He had sent the first one from the airport.

He had tried to convince her to go with him, drive back across the country together, but there was so much to do here. It was a good thing she hadn't gone with him. They'd never be ready for their target opening day if she had. As of last night, he was still in LA, still sorting out the sale of his condo, he said, but it was October 24, and Casey was starting to panic. The only thing that could keep her calm was working, so every day from the minute she woke up until she dropped asleep exhausted at night, she was working on getting the new café ready. Painting, cleaning, planning, shopping. It kept her from thinking.

Tomorrow, though, she had to get back to Devil's Back to open the Beach Plum for the Halloween spectacular Rosetta was throwing. After Sweet Water backed out, she had gotten to work. If this was the end of the line for the Wild Rose, she was going out with a bang. She'd gone into marketing overdrive, contacting practically everyone who had ever stayed at the inn to let them know that this was it, the last rodeo before old Rosetta rode into the sunset. She'd managed to pack the place. No vacancies. The festivities would start Friday and go through November 1 and then everyone would go home and she'd close the inn forever.

Casey was glad there would be enough customers to

keep her busy for the week because otherwise the occasion would be too sad. This was it. The end of the best era of her life so far. Her years at the Beach Plum Café had transformed her into someone she never knew she could be, and she had Rosetta to thank. She didn't want to leave her beautiful island, and yet, every day at the new café, which they had decided to call The Perk, but which Casey could not think of as anything other than "the new café," she felt excited. She was doing this. While she wasn't on her own, Brett was her partner fifty-fifty on the whole thing, she felt strong and independent. This wasn't Rosetta swooping in, saving the day, and calling the shots. Now Casey really was her own boss, and she thought she and Brett could make the café a success.

They had decided to set up a take-out counter with a bakery display case right up front, and to have a little area to sell knick-knacks and crafts. That was Brett's idea. Even from the other side of the country, he was making phone calls and reaching out to people, lining up local crafters who might want to sell things there, with the idea that they would send their friends in to see their goods, and that would bring more business.

The new kitchen equipment had been delivered earlier in the week and the place was starting to shape up. Casey had spent the better part of the week lamenting the state of the ceiling. What idiot had painted it that hideous color? There was no stripping it, no chance of restoring it. She'd never get that glowing shade out of the details of the pattern on the tin. The only option was to paint over it. After that, the other work was easy if time-consuming. She had given the walls a nice coat of a fresh latte-colored paint and washed the windows. She had redone the floor—all by herself—with click-together linoleum tiles, a classic checkerboard pattern, but with chocolaty brown and beige squares, not black and white.

For furniture they'd decided on artfully mismatched pieces, so she'd scoured local flea markets and Goodwill stores buying tables and chairs, which she brought back and painted to match the coffee colors of the café. She was actually running out of things to do at this point. Brett had suggested she use her free time to try out some new recipes and get the menu ready, but who would eat what she baked? Besides, she didn't need new recipes.

They were planning to open the weekend before Thanksgiving and be in full swing in time for the little town's holiday festivities, especially the Buy Local Saturdays in December. Brett might never have run a restaurant before, but he definitely had good ideas about timing and attracting customers. He was already scheduling musical groups to play on weekends. He also said they'd use the Halloween festivities on Devil's Back to spread the word, handing out flyers and coupons.

She was sitting at one of the tables near the front, trying to catch some of the thin late-October daylight and sketching out designs for the new chalkboard menu when the door opened with a jingle of bells. She looked up with a start—she wasn't expecting anyone—and there was Brett, a massive bouquet in his hands, grinning like he'd won the lottery.

Casey was on her feet and in his arms in seconds. She didn't give him a chance to even set the flowers down. She could feel the blossoms tickling her scalp as he embraced her. She pressed her face into his chest and squeezed him close and was shocked to realize there were tears in her eyes. She had missed him more than she had dared to admit.

"Now see, if you'd let me get you a smartphone, you could have had one of those apps that let you see exactly where I was the whole time I was driving back here and—"

Casey shut him up with a kiss.

"I can't believe you're here," she said. If having a smartphone meant living in a world where she didn't get surprises like this, then she had made the right decision in resisting.

He set the flowers on a table and kissed her again. Weeks of nervous anticipation, weeks during which she had nearly convinced herself that he wasn't ever coming back, that despite his investment, despite their partnership, any minute he was going to call and say it was all a mistake—and now here he was. She kissed him with hungry desire, and when at last they pulled away from one another, she said, "Go lock the door."

His silly grin was replaced by a knowing smile and he happily complied, locking the door and following her into the kitchen, where she made love to him like he was a soldier home from war.

"That," he said, when they were spent, "was a hell of a welcome."

"You're not allowed to go away like that again for a long time," Casey said.

They got Chinese take-out and walked back to the little apartment Casey had rented a few blocks from The Perk. Weldon was a nice little place with an old-fashioned Main Street and a lot of small-town charm. Thanks to the tidal river that formed the town's northern border, it had long been a center of shipbuilding. Most of that industry was gone now, but it had been replaced by a museum commemorating Maine's maritime history, and that drew in tourists who, Brett knew, were going to love The Perk. It was also close to beaches, so there were always people passing through, picking up goodies for beach picnics. They were going to adore Casey's baking.

"Welcome to the servant's quarters," Casey said, as she led Brett up the narrow back stairs from the side porch up to her place.

It was the third floor of an old Victorian that had been converted into apartments, and likely the top floor really had once been servants' quarters. The walls sloped under the mansard roof and the window sills were only inches from the floor. Just a galley kitchen, a teeny-tiny bathroom, a small living room, and a little bedroom with a laughably small closet.

While Casey set out the food and some paper plates, Brett picked his way through the place stepping over all her unpacked boxes, checking it out. He came back a moment later and gave a thumbs up.

"It's small," Casey said, spooning lo mein onto her plate. She seemed shy and self-conscious, which Brett found adorable, given the steamy greeting she'd offered back at the café.

"It's so New England. It's great," Brett said. It was

the opposite in every way of the condo he'd sold back in California, and he loved it.

"It's probably nothing like what you're used to," Casey said, stepping over boxes to take her plate to the living room. Brett hastily scooped some food onto a plate and followed her to the futon, the one box-free space in the living room.

"You forget, I grew up in upstate New York. I always loved the rambling old houses."

They hadn't actually discussed living arrangements, and Brett worried that perhaps he'd overstepped a boundary by speaking as if the apartment was to be his, too. He hadn't intended to be so presumptuous. The fact was, in the rush to move his life forward, he hadn't given any thought at all to where he'd live once he got back here. He watched as Casey took a bite of her food and set the plate down on a nearby box. She leaned back against the futon cushion and closed her eyes, and Brett wondered how badly he'd screwed up with his casual comment. He knew she scared easily. He knew he had to tread carefully.

"Hey," he said, setting down his own plate and placing a hand on her arm. "You okay?"

She opened her eyes and tipped her head to look at him. Then she smiled. "I can't believe you're here. I haven't had a good night's sleep since you left."

He moved over and wrapped his arms around her, pulling her against his chest. She wasn't mad. She was content. He almost laughed at himself for his own overactive nerves.

"We are crazy, right?" she asked.

"Oh yeah, for sure."

They snuggled like that for a minute and then Casey sat

up, revived, and picked up her food again. As they ate, she updated him on all that she'd done at the café. He couldn't even believe it. She was a DIY wonder. He couldn't have done half of what she had done. He wouldn't even know how.

"I got some stuff done, too," Brett said when she'd run through her list of accomplishments. "I set up a website, Twitter feed, Facebook page, and once I can get in there and take some pictures, I'll set up Instagram, too."

Casey's face darkened as he spoke.

"Don't worry. I'm not going to make you use any of it. I'll handle it."

He got up to refill his plate and when he came back, he found her still scowling.

"Come on, don't be like that," he said, sighing. "This is good business."

"I didn't have to do any of it at the Beach Plum."

"No, but you had a captive audience on the island. Here people have choices and we want them to choose us."

Casey chewed in silence and Brett let her think this over. He knew this was going to be a point of contention, but he also knew that he was right and she'd come around. After a few minutes, he said, "You know, back when we first met, I tried to check you out online."

She gave him an amused look. "Oh yeah? Did you find me?"

"Nope. Not a trace. As far as the Internet is concerned, you do not exist."

This fact had been nagging at him since the day they'd signed the lease on the café. He felt like he knew her. He believed, as cheesy as it sounded, that they were soul mates, and yet, as they had signed the lease together, he couldn't help but consider the fact that he hardly knew a thing about her. When she had to tell him her legal name for all the paperwork, he could see her hesitation. She was ready to back out to avoid revealing her true name. He'd had to swear that he'd keep it secret before she finally told him: Cara-Jayne Seaver. That evening he'd searched the Internet for Cara-Jayne Seaver, as he had searched for Casey Jones of the Beach Plum Café back in September. Again, he found nothing. At that moment, when he had looked at her name spelled out on paper—a pretty name, a name that was unique, just as she was—he felt afraid. What if she wasn't who she said she was? What if this, too, was a lie? On a personal level, in terms of his feelings for her, he didn't think it mattered. But in terms of business, it definitely mattered.

"How is it even possible for a person to be invisible online in this day and age?" Brett asked.

"I made a choice. I want to live in the real world," Casey said, as if it were that simple.

"Okay, but I have to say, it's pretty weird. I mean, are you in the witness protection program or something? Are you some kind of secret agent?" He was only half-joking. These were possibilities that actually crossed his mind when he tried to comprehend the fact that she had no cyber-presence and lived under an assumed name on a remote island.

She laughed and shook her head. "Why be normal?"

Brett felt slightly panicked by her evasions. "Casey, be serious for a minute. I really need you to explain this to me."

She sighed and curled her knees up to her chest. She rested her chin on her knees and looked at him and her eyes held no trace of laughter.

He put his hand on her feet and said, "Please tell me.

Whatever it is, just tell me."

"I already told you."

He didn't know what she meant. She had never told him why she hated the Internet so much. She had said she didn't have any Wi-Fi at the café because she wanted people to relax there, but that didn't explain her overall aversion.

"It's like, when something is too tempting and the only option is to avoid it altogether," Casey said. "Like how a recovering alcoholic can't even be a social drinker."

"So you were addicted to the Internet?"

"No. I never really had the Internet. I mean, people were only starting to get dial-up connections when I was in high school, and then I dropped out, and I never went to college, and I just never had a need to use it."

This all made sense, but it also didn't make sense. She was too young and too smart to be a total Luddite. So she hadn't grown up with the Internet. Everyone around her had smartphones. They had access to the World Wide Web in their hands every minute of the day. She couldn't be immune to that influence.

"I know what would happen if I went online," she said.

"I'm not following you."

"Please don't make me spell it out," Casey said. She bit her fingernail and avoided looking at him.

"I only don't get what you think would happen."

"I know what would happen. I would find my—my—" She stopped and rubbed eyes, shaking her head.

He waited for her to continue.

"I told you," she said. "I had a baby, a long time ago."

Brett struggled to connect the dots. Of course he remembered what she had told him about giving up her baby for adoption as a teenager. "But you said it was all private and you gave up all your rights."

She got up and got a roll of paper towels. She tore one off and used it as a tissue. "I don't want to talk about this," she said as she struggled to compose herself.

Brett reached out to embrace her, but she slid further away from him. "Casey, please. You can tell me. There's nothing you can say that will change the way I feel about you, certainly nothing from when you were only a kid. It's okay. I love you."

She sniffled and shook her head.

"Please. I want to understand. I want to understand everything about you." It was torture to see her beat herself up over something that happened twenty years before.

"You can't," she said, and she got up and went to the bedroom and shut the door.

Casey slumped down to the floor with her back to the door. There were some things she couldn't say out loud. If he couldn't understand that, he couldn't understand her at all. This was the reason she'd avoided relationships for all these years. This was the reason she didn't let people into her life. She knew that love required trust and honesty, but how could she be honest? Who would love her if they knew what a selfish coward she'd been, if they knew she'd let her baby go without a fight, if they knew she'd let the one chance she had at unconditional love—both giving and receiving it—slip from her life?

She'd let this thing with Brett spiral out of control and now here she was, tied up with him in a crazy business venture that had them both utterly out of their depths. Just because she found him attractive, just because her body hummed in his presence, she'd tugged the wrapping off the corner of her secret, and she couldn't cover it back up again, but she couldn't tear the rest of the paper off either.

A sob escaped her chest and she gasped for breath and for control of herself.

"Casey," Brett said from the other side of the door.

She didn't answer.

"Open the door. Please."

"No," she said, swallowing hard and trying to regain herself.

"I can't help if I don't know what's going on."

"You can't help," she said, and she realized how dramatic she sounded but she didn't care.

"It's okay that you want to find your baby. It'd be pretty damn weird if you didn't," Brett said.

Casey sobbed out loud. Every feeling she had tried not to feel for twenty years was forcing itself to the surface now. Brett's kindness sliced right through her to the place where she was still raw and tender, still seventeen, alone, and terrified and desperately in need of love.

She heard the handle of the door turning slowly and instead of protesting, she moved so she couldn't fall when the door swung away from her back. Then she felt Brett's hands taking her under the arms and pulling her up to her feet. He wrapped his arms tightly around her and shuffled her over to the bed, where he nestled in behind her. She found his hands and twined her fingers in his, grasping them tightly. Neither of them spoke. Entwined like that, she cried herself to sleep.

When she woke up, daylight was pouring through the windows and the smell of coffee filled the apartment. Her eyes felt swollen and her tongue thick, as if she was hungover. After a confused, sleepy moment, the events of the previous day—Brett's return, her hysterical breakdown—came back to her and she burned with shame and nervousness. She sat up in bed and wrestled with the elastic snarled in her disheveled hair. As she tried to force her fingers through the tangles, Brett appeared in the door with two mugs of coffee. He smiled.

"You're up," he said. He set both mugs of coffee on the nightstand, sat on the edge of the bed, and leaned over to kiss her on the cheek.

She waited for him to say he was leaving. That was what would happen next, she was sure of it. Who would want to spend another minute with a basket case like her?

Instead he reached out and tucked a stray strand of hair behind her ear.

"I'm sorry," he said. "I shouldn't have pushed you last night. You have your reasons and I should have respected and trusted that."

Casey studied him, dumbfounded.

"Coffee?" he asked, picking up one of the mugs and holding it toward her.

She nodded and accepted the mug gratefully.

"I wasn't sure how you take it, but I found half and half in the fridge and guessed," he said, blushing. "Usually you're bringing me coffee."

She took a sip. He must have put three heaping tablespoons of sugar in, but she smiled and said, "It's good."

"I promise, what happened last night, I won't do that to you again," he said, turning serious. "You don't owe me an explanation."

In the bright morning light in the as-yet curtainless room, Casey studied this kind, patient man and wondered where on earth he had come from.

"I want to explain," she said, holding his gaze.

"You don't have to."

"I know I don't," Casey said. She wanted to explain her feelings to him, and even though she didn't believe he could ever really understand, she knew he would respect her feelings and he wouldn't try to talk her out of them.

"I had this really messed up childhood," she began. And she told him about her mother and how her father had abandoned them. She told him about Ed and how he turned her mother against her because he knew she'd never let him touch her the way he wanted. And she told him about Ryan.

"It sounds crazy now, when I think back," she said. "We were only seventeen. But I think we would have made it. I think there is such a thing as soul mates."

Casey looked at Brett with tears on her eyelashes, and he took her hand and squeezed it and said, "Me, too."

Casey took a deep breath. "And then he died. I was pregnant, and he got in a car accident, and he died."

When she looked at Brett, she saw that he had tears in his eyes, now. She forced herself to smile a sad smile and said, "It's okay. It was all a really long time ago."

"I can't imagine. My God. Two of my four grandparents are still alive and relatively well and they're in their nineties.

I've never lost anyone, really."

"Yeah, well. And Ryan was dead, and my mom had kicked me out, and I had nothing and nobody. His parents let me stay with them, and his mother started talking about how she could adopt the baby and provide for it and give it this great life—we didn't know if it was a girl or a boy—and anyway, the more she talked about it, the more it made sense, but then she started saying how kids who are adopted have all these complexes and whatever and wouldn't it be better if the baby thought she was its mother? After a while I started to think she was right. The best life that baby could have was the nice upper-middle class one that she and Ryan's father could give it. And they would love it. I knew that. They may not have liked me, but they adored Ryan, and they would give that baby everything. So I agreed. I signed the papers. I gave up all rights and privileges and they paid all my medical bills and gave me ten-thousand dollars when the baby was born."

Brett took this in for a moment and then said, "So all you'd have to do to find the baby is look up Ryan's parents."

"Yeah."

"That is quite a temptation."

"It's better to believe that they gave her a great life and try to move on with living my own. I mean, if I let myself, I'd be a cyber-stalker. That's no way to live."

"So you don't think she ever learned the truth?"

"How would she have?"

"Other people had to know."

Casey shrugged. Of course other people had known Casey was pregnant, including Ryan's extended family, and when a baby showed up, they'd know Deb hadn't been pregnant, but Deb had been resolved to raise the baby without any of the complications of having her know she was adopted. Deb was stubborn. She knew how to get her way.

"What if she found out about you? What if she wants to contact you?"

Casey shook her head. She had often thought of the possibility that she should make herself visible online in case her daughter ever sought her out. But there was a flip side to that. What if her daughter learned about her and never sought her out? If Casey went online and set up a Facebook profile or something, she'd spend all of her days waiting for a message that said, "I think you might be my mother." No, it was better to be a living ghost. She was thinking of this when Brett started to laugh.

She cocked her head and looked at him and tried to imagine what could possibly be funny.

Seeing her expression, he said, "Sorry. When I was younger I used to date these women who thought they were deep, misunderstood artists, you know? But really they were suburban rich kids whose biggest problem was that one time daddy found their bag of pot."

"Let me guess. They had tattoos and funky dye-jobs and wore a lot black," Casey said.

"And piercings."

"Ah-ha. So you saw me, with my tattoo and my hair, and I was your type."

"No. I thought you were the type I should avoid. I learned my lesson with those posers back in my youth. But you, Cara-Jayne Seaver, are not a poser. You are the real deal."

"Next time you call me that, you're a dead man," she said, but in truth the name sounded nice when he said it.

Her stomach fluttered nervously. She had bared the worst chapter of her life to him, and he still had plenty of processing to do. He might think over the whole sad tale and head for the hills.

He leaned forward and kissed her lightly on the nose.

"So?" she said.

"So what?"

"Aren't you going to say something?"

"No? I mean, what is there to say?"

Another unexpected reply from this unexpected man. She didn't want him to offer platitudes or tell her it was going to be okay. She didn't really want him to say anything. And he wasn't. How bizarre.

"Look, what happened to you, all of that is awful. I can't stand the thought of you going through all that suffering alone. And I'm so thankful that you told me, that you trusted me. I promise to live up to that trust." He picked up her hand and kissed her knuckles.

What a ridiculously perfect thing to say. In return, she was speechless.

It was a beautiful fall day, the temperature rising into the upper sixties and the sun shining and you could trick yourself into believing winter was still far away. Casey and Brett boarded the ferry to the island with all the supplies they needed for a week of camping out at the Beach Plum. She'd moved all her furniture already, so it would be a week of sleeping on an air-mattress, but when they weren't sleeping, they'd be plenty busy. Brett was going to be her helper at the café since her summer employees were gone for the winter.

The minute they got off the ferry, they saw that Rosetta had been hard at work. The pier and the path to the inn were lined with jack-o-lanterns and bundles of hay tied up with festive orange ribbons. The porch of the Beach Plum was adorned with scarecrows, pumpkins, big fake spiders and gauze cotton spread out to look like massive webs.

Inside the café on the counter, Rosetta had left a list of the Halloween-themed names she wanted Casey to use for her menu for the week. She really was going all out. As Brett set about opening windows, Casey looked around her little café.

"You gonna be okay?" Brett asked.

As sad as it was to think of this being the final days of the Beach Plum Café, Casey mostly wanted to get it over with. She'd made peace with it all and had begun to move her life forward. Once Halloween was over, she could begin her new life in earnest. She nodded and said, "Lots to do. We'd better get to work."

Chapter Forty-five

St. Nabor Island, South Carolina

CALLIOPE RAN HER business out of the front room of her house. It was a small ranch with weathered shingle siding, tucked away in a quiet part of the island on the sound, nestled between tall trees draped with moss. Angela sat in a wicker chair at a glass-topped table in the small front room, waiting for Calliope to return with tea. The room was decorated in typical beach-cottage style, with pale, slightly distressed furniture and bowls of seashells. Angela had expected something gothic and strange, but this was as normal as could be. Calliope returned with two steaming mugs.

"It's good that you came. I was hoping you'd call me," Calliope said, smoothing her skirt as she sat opposite Angela. "So many people don't seek out a mentor to help them, so they never learn how to control their abilities."

Angela shook her head. Mentor? Abilities? She didn't know what Calliope was talking about. She'd come because she had some questions about the last séance. She wanted to know why Randy and Marilyn hadn't understood what Calliope had been saying. It had been a month since that night and still the question had nagged at her, so finally she'd come seeking answers.

"How long have you known you could communicate with the dead?" Calliope asked. Then, taking in the look on Angela's face she said, "That is why you're here, right?"

Angela half-shrugged, half-shook her head, and then she said, "I wanted to understand what happened that night, when you talked to my mother."

"Let me ask you something," Calliope said. "Do strange things ever happen to you? Like maybe there's a light bulb that always flickers when you're in the room, but it's fine when other people are there, or you walk into a room and get the chills for no reason?"

Angela bit her lip and thought about it. Nothing like those two examples had ever happened, but she often heard things that other people didn't hear. Molly and Nicole used to joke that Angela had conversations with the breeze, because she was always saying to them, "Did you say something? Did you hear that?"

"Probably started right around when you hit puberty, right?" Calliope asked.

"I don't think so," Angela said. Actually, it had started much earlier than that. She'd always heard things. And the backyard ghost encounters—those had been when she was only eight or nine, long before puberty.

Calliope nodded, she said, "The minute I met you, I knew you had the gift. It didn't surprise me at all that you were hearing spirits in your mother's house. You were so raw and vulnerable."

"So you're saying that other times, when I thought I heard things and no one else did, that wasn't my imagination?"

"That's right," Calliope said, studying her.

"But—" Angela tried to object, but she had no words. Calliope was suggesting that she wasn't just being haunted by her mother and brother but that she could actually talk to spirits. That was crazy.

"When your emotions are so close to the surface, it's easy for the spirits to make contact," Calliope said. "Spirits latch onto emotions, they feed off of them."

"So I can talk to other spirits?" Angela asked.

"You can. You'd have to be willing to make yourself available to them, though. You have to learn to open up and offer them your feelings. It takes practice."

Angela was stunned. These weren't the answers she'd been expecting. "So this is why I could understand you but Randy couldn't?" she asked after a few minutes.

Calliope nodded. But it still didn't make sense. Calliope seemed to have heard more than Angela did that night. And the time before, Angela hadn't heard Ryan at all when Calliope said she did.

"Why couldn't I hear Ryan? Why couldn't I hear everything my mother said to you?"

"Two things. First, spirits attach themselves to places and objects. I'm guessing there are very few objects of Ryan's in your house, and he never lived there, so you had a hard time hearing him, but there must have been something of his in that desk, so I could hear him. Your mother, on the other hand, is everywhere in that house, surrounding you, so she was hard for you not to hear. Second, you haven't learned how to communicate with spirits yet. You could hear as much as you did because you have the gift, but like any talent, you have to learn to use it. When we were at your house, your emotions were like a gaping sore, but you were trying hard to keep them in check. If you had let go, if you had let yourself fall into your emotions, you'd have been able to communicate with your mother yourself, instead of only hearing her."

Then Calliope described a meditation she used to tame her emotions so she could use them in her work. Emotions, she said, are like wild horses. They have to be coaxed very gently and gradually into trusting the conscious mind to care for them. You have to build a pen for them inside you and provide them everything they need. And then, once they know they not only can trust you but also need you, you can let them out of the pen and know that you can always get them back in.

As she listened Angela's brow furrowed. Visualize her emotions as wild horses? She couldn't visualize how such a visualization would work at all.

"If you want to learn to use your gift, I can teach you," Calliope said. "If you don't want to learn, that's fine, but you can't go out there and dabble without some instruction. It's dangerous. It can tear you apart."

Another question occurred to Angela. "How does a person get this gift?" she asked.

"You inherit it from your mother," Calliope said, matter-of-factly. "It's passed down mother to daughter."

"No men ever get it?" Angela asked.

"Sometimes, but it's very rare."

Angela knew what Randy would say if he were here. He'd say that she had to learn. They were having dinner together that night, and she could talk to him about it then, she supposed. She also knew what Molly and Nicole would say. They'd tell her to run for her life.

"So my mother, my birth mother, she had it, too?"

"I have to assume so. That's how it works."

"Can a person have it and not ever know?"

Calliope nodded. Angela thought that made sense. If it hadn't been for her mother's sudden death, she never would have known she had it. She wondered if CJ knew, and if she did, what she felt about it. Another question for her missing parent.

It had taken Angela three days to work up the nerve to call the Beach Plum Café, and when she did, there was no answer, no answering machine. It rang and rang and rang, even though, according to the Internet the café should have been open. She kept trying the number for a couple of weeks, but she never got any answer, and finally two days ago, her call reached a message saying the number was no longer in use.

She had been living with the truth about her family for a month, and she was no closer to understanding if it mattered. Suppose she had lived her entire life not knowing, had gone to her grave believing herself the late-in-life child of Deb and Rich Ellis, their miracle baby sent to help them recover from the loss of their beloved son. Would her life have been incomplete if she died thinking that? Was there any good reason she needed to know the truth?

Learning about her parents' lies seemed to change everything and nothing all at once. The woman who raised her, the woman she would always and forever think of as "mom," was still dead. The father who had spoiled her as a little girl and who had forgotten her as a sick old man was still locked in his own mind. Knowing the truth didn't erase the car crash that killed Ryan. It didn't alter the fact that her parents had given her a comfortable, even luxurious, upbringing and as much love as they could muster, which was all any parents could do. If she now understood better why her mother had been so protective of her, why she had so often looked over her shoulder, that understanding didn't change the fact that she was grateful for all the advantages her parents had given her, advantages, she was gradually realizing, that she was going to need to act upon.

She couldn't keep living off others. She needed to get a job and make a plan for her future. Grace kept telling Angela to stay as long as she wanted, to take her time, not to worry about a thing. That was sweet of her, but Angela was starting to feel like she had overstayed her welcome. She also had to admit, she missed college. She missed the routine of it, but more importantly, she missed the environment. She'd been talking to Professor Morgan and one of the deans about coming back next semester, but there were so many details to sort out. It was overwhelming.

The question of what role her newly discovered family was going to play in her life was still hanging over her head, though. She certainly wasn't going to go live with any of them, although Marilyn had called several times to repeat her offer, and now Helen had gotten in on the action, too. But she didn't want to live in New York City, and she didn't want to live in some little western Massachusetts town. She wanted to go back to St. Kate's, she also wanted to stay here. This was home, after all, with all its familiar comforts, and the essential new comfort of Randy's bright eyes, dimpled smile, and strong arms around her.

After they had decided to slow things down, they had started over, and Randy's romantic nature had proven a nice surprise. He liked taking her on real dates. He bought her flowers and left her sweet little notes. They'd slowed down the intimate side of their relationship, too, at his request. He wanted to know her as a person without letting lust get the best of them. This was not what Angela was used to from guys. The dating scene in college had been driven entirely by lust as far as she could tell. Randy, however, was not like those partying college boys. He went to church on Sundays with his parents, and he loved babysitting his nieces and nephews, and while he wasn't immune to Angela's physical charms, he was clear-headed enough to see that a relationship needed to be about more than sex.

Angela also wondered if he knew how much all the waiting turned her on. Finally, two nights ago, she'd slept over at his place for the first time in the weeks since their dating do-over began, and it had been totally worth the wait.

"Do you have other questions for me?" Calliope asked, calling Angela back from her wandering thoughts.

"How do you go through life like this?" she asked. The idea of being bombarded by the voices of spirits everywhere she went sounded exhausting. She didn't know if she wanted to learn to use her gift, but she definitely had to learn how to cope with it.

Calliope laughed. "Honestly, there are some places I simply avoid because there's too much paranormal activity there, but you can learn to control it and to close yourself off from the spirit world, kind of like putting your cell phone in silent mode."

"And you can teach me that?" Angela asked.

With that, Calliope began her first lesson.

"How would you feel about taking a road trip with me?" Angela asked that night over dinner. They had gone back to Antonio's, the restaurant where they'd met to talk about the first investigation. This time Angela could actually enjoy the ambiance and the food.

Randy raised an eyebrow. "What do you have in mind?"

"I have to go get the rest of my stuff from school," Angela explained. Molly had packed up her clothes and shipped them to her, but she had other things there, taking up space in what was now Molly and Nicole's room. Thankfully they hadn't been assigned another roommate, although they might have one for the second semester.

"Do you think you'll meet the rest of your family while you're in New England?"

Angela nodded. She couldn't go all the way and not meet them. Beechmont wasn't even two hours from St. Kate's. Anyway, she wanted to meet them. She and Helen had spoken on the phone several times, and it was clear that Helen was eager for her to visit. She thought she might also visit Marilyn. After all, she'd never been to New York City, and anyway, she felt bad about how she'd treated Marilyn when she was here. She'd taken her frustration with Deb out on Marilyn, and that wasn't right.

"What about CJ?" Randy asked.

She shook her head. Angela had corresponded with Lindsey Wilcox and had gotten CJ's full name: Cara Seaver. Lindsey hadn't been sure what the "J" stood for, but she knew CJ's first and last names. Having her name, however, had not brought Angela any closer to finding her.

"What if you went to Devil's Back Island? You could go to that café and ask questions."

Angela bit her lip. She didn't want to barge in on CJ the way Marilyn had barged in on her. She wanted to contact her first. Except she couldn't figure out how. Anyway, if the café's phone was cut off, how likely was the café to be open?

"I mean, once you've driven all the way, you'll be so close," Randy said.

Angela took a big bite of pasta and didn't answer.

"Also, small world, but I got an email today from a paranormal investigator listserv I'm on with information about a big Halloween festival," Randy said.

Angela didn't see why this information needed the "small world" preface. She didn't see how it was relevant at all.

"Guess where the festival is taking place?" he asked, grinning.

Honestly, Angela had no idea and she hated guessing games.

"Devil's Back Island!"

Chapter Forty-six

Devil's Back Island, Maine

THE PHONE AT THE Wild Rose Inn had been ringing nonstop since Rosetta began her marketing blitz. Where were all these people during the regular season? she wondered. One weekend of heavy traffic wasn't enough to change anything, but at least she wasn't going out quietly. She was about to change the message on the inn's answering machine to say there were no vacancies when the phone rang.

"Greetings from the Wild Rose Inn. How may I help you this fine day?" Rosetta asked.

"I, um, do you have any rooms for Halloween?" a youthful, nervous female voice asked.

"I'm sorry to say we're booked. I can add you to the waiting list, though, in case we get any cancelations. Always have people change plans last minute."

"Oh. Right, well, never mind," the girl said.

"You don't want the waiting list?"

"I'd be coming from too far away to wait until last minute

to know if I had a room," she said.

"I hate to disappoint travelers from afar. Where you calling from?"

"South Carolina, actually," the girl said, and Rosetta's heart skipped a beat. Obviously South Carolina was a huge state full of young women who might be interested in a trip to Maine for Halloween. There was no reason to get excited over a phone call. Still, there were no other guests coming from so far away. Not even close.

"That is far. Have you ever stayed with us before?" Rosetta asked.

"No, but I, my boyfriend, he got an email about your Halloween festival."

Rosetta was cheered to think that news of her celebration had made it as far away as South Carolina but disappointed to hear that the girl, or her boyfriend, anyway, was just a ghost hunter.

"Tell you what, why don't you give me your name, and if we know of any openings by Monday, I'll let you know," Rosetta said.

"I don't want to waste your time," the girl said.

"Don't be silly. What's your name?"

The girl paused like she was taking a moment to make up her mind and then said, "My name is Angela. Angela Ellis."

Rosetta almost dropped the phone. She was practically jumping up and down with excitement, but she kept her voice calm, "Angela, what a nice name. And your address?"

And the girl rattled off an address that concluded St. Nabor Island, South Carolina. Rosetta had to hurry her off the phone so she could get a grip on what had happened.

Angela Ellis of St. Nabor Island, South Carolina, Casey's daughter, had called to see about visiting the island! Rosetta wanted to call her back right away and say she realized she did have a room available. She didn't actually have a room, but she'd figure it out. Someone would cancel. Hell, the kid could stay in Rosetta's own apartment and she'd go sleep on the floor at the Beach Plum. She'd do anything if it meant getting the girl here, but she had to tell Casey first.

She put up a "Back in 5" sign at the registration desk, called Bentley, and went as fast as she could to the café.

"You have to sit down," Rosetta said, bursting through the door of the café like a gale force wind. Bentley, caught up in Rosetta's excitement, pranced around her feet, waiting for whatever exciting thing was going to happen next.

"I'm a little busy," Casey said. She was piping frosting onto cupcakes. She had to be ready to open the doors at 7 AM tomorrow, and there was still so much to do.

"Please, sit down."

"I can do that," Brett said, reaching out a hand for the pastry bag. He was wearing an old apron over his crispy pressed khakis and button-down shirt.

Casey shot him a dirty look. "You stick to the cookies," she said. She set down the pastry bag and came around the counter to sit at a table.

"I have to tell you something, and you need to listen," Rosetta said.

Casey crossed her arms. If this had to do with her daughter again, she was going to scream. How many times did she have to tell Rosetta she couldn't know. It wasn't about what she did or did not want. It was about what she needed. She needed not to know.

"I got a phone call," Rosetta said, "from a girl in South Carolina."

Casey made a hurry-it-up gesture.

"It was from an Angela Ellis."

Casey pushed her chair back to stand up. She'd heard enough. There were zillions of people with the last name Ellis. If Rosetta freaked out every time she met one, they were going to have a big problem on their hands.

"It's her," Rosetta said.

Casey shook her head and pursed her lips.

"It's her. I know it is because I found her weeks ago, which is what I've been trying to tell you."

"How? How in the world could you possibly have found her?" Casey refused to believe it. This was all absurd.

"Well, Casey, there's this magical thing called the Internet, I don't know if you've heard of it—"

"Stop it! I told you to stop!" Casey shouted. Nothing about this was okay. Rosetta had violated her wishes and contacted her daughter and what was she supposed to do now? "I have begged you not to look for her, and now you're telling me she's calling you? Are you leaving out the fact that you called her first?"

Brett came out of the kitchen and looked back and forth between them. Rosetta motioned for him to go away.

"I swear to you on my life I didn't reach out to her in any way. I found her, and I've been trying to tell you, but you won't listen. I didn't think it was my place to contact her."

"So she up and called you out of the blue?" That was awfully convenient.

"She wants to come to the festival. Is that so hard to believe?"

"Um, yes," Casey said. She rubbed her hands over her face. "How sure are you that it's her?"

"I'm pretty sure."

"Pretty sure or actually sure?"

"I'm sure."

"Jesus."

"Can I tell you the rest?" Rosetta asked.

"There's more?" Casey said, grimacing. What more could there be?

"Deborah Ellis is dead, Casey," Rosetta said. "She died back in September. That's what I've been trying to tell you."

Casey felt her eyes fill with tears and tried to blink them away. "And you think that means I'm free to contact my daughter now?"

Rosetta gave her a look that said she did think so.

"The inn is totally booked, so I put her on a waiting list, but I can call her right now and tell her I found her a room. She could be here in a matter of days," Rosetta said.

"And then what? I walk up and say, 'Hi, I'm your mother'?"

"All I know is that it's like the universe wants you to meet. That's what I think."

"Do not give me your tarot card bullshit."

"What if the real reason she's coming here is because she wants to find you? Don't you think you should give her the chance to find you?"

"How would she know to look for me here?" Casey said, suspecting again that Rosetta must be orchestrating this whole thing.

"Well, if her parents told her who you are, she could have traced you here."

"How?"

Rosetta shrugged, and then Casey remembered that day in the fall when the hipster couple came into the café and the woman had recognized her.

"Okay, tell her you have a room for her," she said softly.

"Are you sure?"

"Are you really asking me that now?"

Rosetta stood up and pulled Casey into a hug. "This is the right thing."

Casey wasn't sure, but there was only one way to find out.

Chapter Forty-seven

I-95 North

ANGELA AND RANDY had a few tense moments criticizing one another's driving, but for the most part the journey had been smooth sailing. They stayed with Marilyn for a night, and she gave them a whirlwind tour of Manhattan, and then they continued on to Massachusetts. When they arrived at Helen's house, they were greeted with a surprise party. Helen had gathered all of her siblings and most of their children to meet Angela. The whole scene was vaguely terrifying for a person who had spent a lifetime thinking she had no extended family. Fortunately Randy was from a big family, so he helped Angela navigate the celebration.

They stayed for two days and two nights, two days and nights of awkward, getting-to-know-you conversations, but her father's family proved to be kind, open, and loving. Helen was an incredible cook. She took one look at Angela's skinny arms and legs and vowed to fatten her up. Helen showed Angela old family photos, everyone told stories, and Angela soaked up this new heritage that was hers. It was so hard to reconcile this great big, happy family with her withdrawn father. Even before he got sick, he had never been an effusive person. When Angela was old enough to draw conclusions, she decided it was a generational thing, but now she thought maybe he had been protecting himself, that losing this family had made him withdraw.

Before they left, Angela promised to keep in touch, and she meant it, but she also knew that these lovely people weren't suddenly going to be a part of her daily life, a fact that made her sad. But they lived here, and she didn't, and everyone was busy. Helen said she was going to come visit Rich, even if he wouldn't know her, and Angela decided that the occasional phone call or holiday greeting might be enough. That was what most people seemed to have with their extended families, and now she was going to have it, too.

From Helen's they drove north into New Hampshire to St. Kate's, which sat on the Connecticut River. Even though the trees were already winter-bare, the campus was beautiful, the leaded-glass windows in the old brick buildings glistening in the sun. Angela was nervous to introduce Randy to Molly and Nicole, but she quickly realized, she was worried for no reason. They loved him instantly. They loved his southern accent and good manners, and they loved how he looked at Angela, like he'd never seen anyone so beautiful in his life.

Angela's things were piled in boxes in a corner of the room, and it almost felt like she was arriving for the semester, not like she was here to take her things home forever. She hadn't realized how much she missed her friends until now, sitting with them on the floor of their room, eating pints of ice cream and catching up on gossip. Now that she was back, she wished she didn't have to leave.

On Monday morning, she had a meeting with the

financial aid office. She'd spoken to a woman there on the phone several times in the past couple of weeks, and there was a chance that they could get things sorted out for her to come back next semester. While Angela had never had to cope with a sudden change in her financial circumstances before, the folks in financial aid seemed used to crises like this. She hadn't told Randy yet. She didn't want to upset him if it wasn't a sure thing.

The meeting was early, and Randy was still sound asleep when Angela crept out of the dorm room. Nicole was up, though, and walked her across campus.

"Randy's sweet," she said, hooking her arm through Angela's as they walked.

"He really is," Angela agreed.

"How's he going to feel about you coming back to school?"

Angela shrugged. She didn't want to talk about this now. She just wanted to have a nice time.

"You shouldn't quit school for a boy, you know. That's a terrible idea," Nicole said.

Angela stopped short. "Nic, I love you, but you have to stop babying me," she said. She had let Molly and Nicole treat her like a kid since the day they met. When she'd first been paired up with them as roommates first year, they had both seemed so much more worldly than she, and certainly they were better students than she, so she'd quickly fallen into a habit of deferring to them, and they'd developed a habit of treating her like their little sister. But in the past few months, she'd grown up and realized she didn't need her friends to tell her how to live her life. This part of their friendship she had not missed.

"I'm not—"

But Angela cut her off. "You are. You and Molly always do this. You two may be taller than me, but that doesn't mean you get to talk down to me like I'm a little kid."

"Whoa, I don't even—"

"I don't know what Randy will say if I decide to come back here, but what I can tell you for certain is that whether I come back or not, it'll be one-hundred percent my decision, not his, and not yours or Molly's, okay?"

Angela couldn't recall a time when she'd stood up for herself like that. It felt good. She felt taller.

"Okay," Nicole said, and then she took Angela's arm again and they finished their walk across campus.

An hour later, Angela went back to the dorm with her emotions swirling inside her like creatures in an aquarium. Calliope might envision her emotions as wild horses, but Angela's emotions were sharks, whales, and dolphins. She didn't have an equestrian pen inside her. She had an aquarium. And right now, every fish and mammal in there was swimming in a different direction.

It was official. She was coming back to St. Kate's in January. All she had to do was tell Randy. But not right now. She wasn't ready yet. She'd tell him later, when the time was right.

Tuesday afternoon, they hit the road again, east this time, toward the coast.

"I don't know if this is a good idea," Angela said when they crossed the state line into Maine. She didn't want to meet CJ by sneak attack, the way Marilyn had done to her.

"If we find her, you can always decide not to tell her who you are," Randy said.

They stopped for lunch in the touristy, beach town of York, where almost everything was closed for the winter, and bought salt-water taffy at a convenience store. They stood for a while on the small sandy beach watching the waves crash and the gulls circle and then they kept driving.

When they got to Portland, they walked along the harbor, though the breeze carried hints of winter and the trees were bare of leaves. They had ferry tickets for the next day and had booked a room at the Wild Rose Inn.

"I could live in New England," Randy said, as they walked hand in hand along the waterfront. The moon was low on the horizon over the water in the darkening sky and boats bobbed gently on their moorings.

"You could?" Angela asked, surprised.

"Yeah, when I was a kid, I was fascinated with the Revolutionary War the way other little boys were about dinosaurs. I always thought it would be amazing to live in Boston."

"Not Philadelphia, birthplace of the nation?"

"Paul Revere was sort of my hero."

Angela smiled. "Winters are cold." Her two years in New Hampshire had been a major adjustment. It was so cold, and the snow! So much snow! She had liked it, though, once she had gotten used to it.

"So you get a warm coat," Randy said, and Angela realized he was being serious.

"This is something you've really considered? Leaving St. Nabor?"

"Hell yes. I mean, I love my family, but I've always felt like at some point I would have to leave, go out on my own in the world."

He had never mentioned any of this before. Angela wasn't sure what to think. "What about work?"

"I've been getting more and more into freelance app development. I can do that anywhere."

Angela stopped walking and tugged on his hand so he stopped, too. "Why are we talking about this right now?" she asked.

He leaned forward and gave her a little kiss and then said, "Because I want you to know that I'm up for adventure. I know my life seems settled, but it's not. Not really."

"Oh. Okay."

"Also, you seemed really happy at St. Kate's with your friends, happier than I've seen you since we met. I don't want you to stay in South Carolina because of me."

"Randy, I—"

"And if you wanted to move up here and be closer to your family, I totally understand that."

"But what about us?" Angela said. She liked to imagine her future with Randy, dream of her wedding dress and all of that, but if he was talking about relocating for her, that was terrifying.

"I love you, Angela," he said, and he kissed her. "I love you, which is why I want you to do what's right for you. If we have to make due with long distance, that's what we'll do for a while."

"Long distance never works," Angela said, fearing she would cry. She had finally gotten the crying thing under control. She did not want to start weeping now.

"Never say never," Randy said. "We'll figure it out."

"I am going back to St. Kate's," Angela said. "Next semester."

He took both of her hands and looked her in the eye. "I know. I saw the paperwork."

"Oh, I wasn't trying to keep it secret, I just—"

"It's okay," he said, wrapping his arms around her and kissing her.

In the morning, they caught the ferry. It was a gray day. It was Halloween, and a storm had swept up the coast, bringing wind, rain, and clouds, as if conjuring Nathaniel Hawthorne's Gothic New England before their very eyes. At any moment a band of angry Puritans might have appeared and set up a gallows and Angela wouldn't have been the least surprised. It was cold enough that they ventured out onto the deck for only a few minutes before retreating back into the warm cabin.

At last, they disembarked on Devil's Back Island and walked up the pier toward the little village nestled into the slope of the island. The very first building they passed was the Beach Plum Café. The smell of coffee and fresh cookies wafted out onto the lane.

"Let's go in right now," Randy said, tugging Angela's arm.

"No! Not yet! We'll go to the hotel first and then we'll see." She had to work up the nerve first. She was here, but she wasn't ready. Not yet.

Chapter Forty-eight

Devil's Back Island, Maine

AT THE INN, Angela and Randy went to the registration desk. Initially the clerk said she couldn't find any reservation for them, and Angela thought it was a sign. They should turn around and get back on the ferry before it left. But then the clerk came back and apologized and said their room wasn't ready yet, but that they could check their bags at the counter for now and she'd have the room ready in a few hours. She gave them a brochure detailing the Halloween festivities and, unsure what else to do, they went to sit by the fireplace in the lobby.

"You know, these ghosts sound pretty phony," Randy said, studying the brochure. "I'm awfully glad I didn't haul any equipment out here."

He'd skipped the trip to Charleston with the paranormal investigators club for this, Angela thought, with a twinge of guilt.

"On the upside, there's a lot happening tonight. Apparently there are going to be bonfires on the beach and food tents and music from sundown until ten." He held up the brochure as if Angela had asked for proof.

"You're awfully quiet over there," he said.

She shook her head. She was nervous. She had nothing to say.

At five o'clock the front-desk clerk found them in the lobby and apologized again. The room still wasn't ready. Angela was starting to wonder if there was a room.

"The hotel owner sent these for you," the clerk said, handing Angela two coupons that turned out to be vouchers for free food at the festival.

With nothing else to do, they took the vouchers and made their way to the beach. It was still cold and breezy but the rain had stopped. Three fires were burning on the sand, and the small beach was crowded with people. A band was playing on the hotel patio under a tent. Randy and Angela walked past smaller tents where local crafts were on sale and finally arrived at the food tents.

Angela glanced at the vouchers. "These are weird. I don't know how to use them," she said.

Randy took them from her and read them. They were a little ambiguous. All they really said was free food, with no information on how to redeem them. He handed them back to Angela.

"I guess we can ask somebody," she said. "As long as it's free, want to get lobster rolls?"

Randy agreed and they went to the stall selling seafood. Before ordering, Angela showed the vendor the vouchers. He called out to another vendor, and after a moment's confusion, a white-haired woman appeared, a dog at her heels.

"Angela Ellis?" she asked. "I am so sorry for the

confusion over your room. Go on and order anything you like. It's on me."

"Who are you?" Angela asked.

"Rosetta Washburn, proprietor of the Wild Rose Inn."

Angela looked at Randy, who shrugged, and they each ordered a lobster roll and fries.

Once they'd ordered, Rosetta said, "Will you join me over there when your food is ready?" She pointed to a table on the edge of the patio.

"Okay," Angela said, uncertainly. After Rosetta walked away, she turned to Randy. "This is weird, right?"

"Yep, super weird."

Nonetheless, they took their food to Rosetta's table and sat down. Angela took a big bite of her sandwich, and as she chewed, she noticed that Rosetta had a stack of tarot cards on the table.

"Are you a psychic?" Angela asked.

"A little," Rosetta said. "Should I tell your fortune?"

"Oh, I don't—"

"Come on, it's fun," Randy said, nudging her.

Rosetta shuffled the deck and studied Angela. Then she set the cards down and said, "You're here to find someone. Is that right?"

Casey sold out of cupcakes, cookies, and coffee by seven o'clock. Rosetta had been right earlier in the day when she said they should have made more. Then again, now that their work was done, she and Brett could relax. Well, relax might be the wrong word. All day, Casey had been waiting for someone named Angela Ellis to appear and introduce herself. Rosetta said Angela hadn't canceled the reservation, so either she was here somewhere or she'd changed her mind without the courtesy of a phone call to say so. Casey and Brett were packing up to haul things back to the café, when Rosetta appeared at their tent.

"Don't tell me you told me so," Casey said, stooping to load the last of the trays onto a cart.

When she stood back up, Rosetta stepped aside and Casey saw the girl who was with her. The entire world stopped. As she took in the girl, little electric currents seemed to shoot through her. She resembled Ryan, and more so Ryan's mother. The likeness was strong enough to be eerie.

The girl stayed where she was, studying Casey, and Casey stayed behind the table in the tent, studying the girl, until at last Rosetta broke the silence.

"Look who I found washed up on the beach."

In the glow of the bonfire light, Angela took in the sight of the woman she'd come all this way to meet. She looked young. Too young. How could she be anybody's mother? She looked like some kind of biker chick or punk rocker.

After a long moment of strained silence, Rosetta managed introductions.

"Angela, this is my great-niece, Cara-Jayne Seaver, formerly known as CJ, known to everyone around here as Casey Jones, aka Trouble," Rosetta said.

Trouble. Yes. She looked like trouble.

"And Casey, this is Angela Ellis." Angela was glad Rosetta hadn't said, "your daughter." This woman may have given birth to her, but the words daughter and mother didn't make any sense to describe their relationship.

Casey remained mute. Her eyes were wide and she looked lost. Angela understood that feeling. This was why she hadn't wanted to ambush Casey. But when Rosetta had insisted they go find her right that moment, there had been no way to refuse. After all, they'd come looking for her, and here was someone who knew where to find her.

If only there were a script for this type of thing, Angela thought. For the past month, she'd had a head full of questions for Casey, but now that they were face to face, she couldn't think of a single one.

"When did you find out about me?" Casey asked at last.

"About a month ago," Angela said.

"How?"

Angela had anticipated this question and had rehearsed a succinct response. She didn't feel she should go into the whole ghost story yet. She said, "My mom—Deb, I mean—passed away. I was getting the house ready to sell, and I found out."

"I'm sorry," Casey said. Although she had recovered the ability to speak, she still looked and sounded dazed.

"Thank you," Angela said. What she mostly felt as she watched this woman who had given birth to her was not the anger she had expected to feel. She had no desire to ask indignantly why Casey had abandoned her, why she had given her up for adoption. No, what she mostly felt was sorry. She had altered the rotation of Casey's world in the very same way that news of Casey's existence had rocked her own, and now she saw that perhaps she had been selfish to go along with this. This woman had been only seventeen when she was born, three years younger than Angela was now. Angela certainly wasn't ready to be a mom at the age of twenty. It was no wonder she had given Angela up, especially since she had known Angela was going to a good home. She was allowed to move forward and have a life. She didn't deserve to be intruded upon this way.

"No. I'm sorry," Angela said, "We shouldn't have come. This was a mistake."

She turned to walk away but Casey called after her.

"I have thought about you every single day."

Casey and Angela walked together up the slope to the café while Rosetta and Bentley took Randy for a tour of the beach and Brett finished packing up the tent. Casey couldn't believe this was happening. She couldn't believe her baby girl was here, beside her. Since the only furniture upstairs was an air-mattress, Casey took Angela into the café and they sat at a table near the window.

"I didn't want to burst in on you like that," Angela said. "I tried to call you."

"It's okay." Casey said. She wondered if she should

admit that she had known Angela was coming. But if she did, Angela would want to know why Casey hadn't tried to contact her. She bit her lip.

"I don't want anything from you, okay? I didn't come here because I want something. I wanted to meet you."

Casey nodded.

"I mean, my parents will always be my parents, you know, even if they are technically my grandparents, which is weird. I can't think of them that way," Angela said. She was toying with the zipper of her purse now, and she seemed much younger than her twenty years.

Twenty years. Casey couldn't believe it. Twenty years, and now here she was, a full grown, beautiful woman. "Were they good to you?" Casey asked, when Angela didn't say anything else.

"They were. I miss my mom a lot."

"I wish you didn't have to go through all of this," Casey said. Part of the reason she had given in to Deb's demands and agreed to give up all custody was to prevent Angela from ever having to experience unnecessary hardship. When Deb offered to raise the baby as her own, Casey had wanted to believe that Deb was right, that the baby would be better off if she never knew. But Angela found out anyway, and maybe it was even worse for her to find out now. Instead of having incorporated information about her birth parents into her identity as a child, she had grown up believing a set of things about herself that she now knew were false. At twenty years old, instead of growing more confident in her identity, she had just had it pulled out from under her.

"They should have told me," Angela said.

"We all did what we thought was best at the time."

"You and Ryan loved each other, didn't you?"

"We did." And she would always love Ryan. He was the one person who had never hurt her, except when he died. She knew it was unfair to keep him on a pedestal. He hadn't been perfect, nobody is, but that was the one upside of death, wasn't it? Those who were left behind got to hold onto whatever parts of their loved ones they chose.

"You were so young," Angela said.

So young. God, how could twenty years have passed since then? But she had wanted to be a mother. She had wanted to know the unconditional love between a mother and baby. She wanted to start a family that would be hers forever. She wanted to prove that she was nothing like her own mother. And then Ryan died.

"Will you tell me about my birth?" Angela asked.

"Sure," Casey said. "You were born at 5:03 AM. I had been in labor for about twenty hours. Deb and Rich were there with me. Deb cut the cord. She held you as soon as you were born." Casey left out the part about how she wept when she wasn't allowed to hold her daughter.

"When I asked my mom about my birth story, she always told me that people are too interested in the gory details these days," Angela said.

"They probably are."

The two of them shared a smile. Casey felt the pit of tension in her stomach loosening slightly.

"My aunt said my parents didn't like you," Angela said, and then she apologized. "Sorry, that wasn't very tactful."

"It's okay. It's true. They thought I was the wrong sort of girl for Ryan."

"Were you?"

Casey wondered how to answer. The Ellises were solidly upper-middle-class people with a big, new suburban home, and nice new cars. They vacationed on Martha's Vineyard and belonged to a country club. She grew up with a mentally ill mother who couldn't hold down a steady job and a Jesus-freak stepfather. But Casey had been a good kid. She did well in school, she never got in trouble, and she loved Ryan.

"No," she said at last. She saw Angela eyeing her tattoo where it showed on her arm below the pushed up sleeve of her sweatshirt, and said, "I didn't have any tattoos back then. I didn't dye my hair. After you were born, I guess you could say I went through a rebellious phase."

"And you never tried to find me?" Angela asked.

"I couldn't. You have no idea how hard it was not to, though." It had taken years of drug use followed by years of self-imposed banishment on this island, she thought, but she didn't think this was the right moment to get into all of that.

"I keep trying to picture what my life would be if he hadn't died," Angela said.

Casey understood that feeling perfectly. But the thing was, he had died. Hypotheticals were no good for anybody, and however much Deb and Rich had messed Angela up with their lies, she and Ryan would have messed her up in other ways. All parents mess up their kids.

"It's no good to think that way. Believe me, I know," Casey said. "And anyway, if Ryan hadn't died, we would have had a tough road ahead of us. We were so young. Who knows how we would have managed."

Angela nodded, but Casey could see she wasn't convinced.

"Seriously think about it. We didn't even have high school

diplomas yet. We would have had to support ourselves and you. Life is hard. Who knows if our relationship could have stood up to it? How many people stay together with their high school sweethearts?"

For some reason, Angela started to laugh.

"What's funny?"

"I was thinking something like that myself, about me and Randy, that's all."

"So it's pretty serious with you two?"

Angela nodded and said, "But we aren't high school sweethearts. We've only been dating a little while."

"Well, as long as he's good to you," Casey said.

"Do you think that you would want to see me again? Do you want us to get know each other?" Angela asked.

"More than anything." In fact, the idea that she might never see Angela again was so painful, that Casey's throat constricted at the thought of it and she had to swallow a sob.

Randy, Brett, and Rosetta came back with food and a heap of blankets and the five of them went upstairs to the empty apartment. Casey spread out a blanket on the floor like they were going to have a picnic. Angela struggled to see how Casey, who looked like a grunge goddess, could possibly be dating such a bona fide adult as Brett with his well-pressed preppy clothes, but from the way Brett looked at Casey, his adoration of her was obvious.

The five of them sat on the floor telling stories and

laughing like long-lost friends. Casey wanted to know all about the things Angela had done as a little kid, and Rosetta was more than happy to chime in with embarrassing stories about Casey. Randy and Brett's main contributions were to laugh at the right moments, and they did that quite well.

Eventually, the truth came out about how a ghost hunt had led Angela to Casey, and as she and Randy told the story, Angela couldn't tell if Casey's expression was one of disbelief or concern or fascination.

"See that, Casey," Rosetta said, when they had finished their tale. "Runs in the family, like I always told you." She turned to Angela. "Casey was terrified when she first starting getting messages from the spirit world. Thought she was losing her mind."

"So y'all both have it, too? The gift?" It was as Calliope had said, Angela thought. Her supernatural ability had been passed down from her mother.

"Oh yes, runs in the family," Rosetta said.

"When it first happened to me, I thought it was a sign that I was mentally ill, like my mother," Casey said. "It was Rosetta who taught me how to deal with it. There are ways to shut it off."

"And ways to learn to use it," Rosetta said, nodding.

"I've been learning from a medium on St. Nabor," Angela said.

"I'm sorry, what's happening?" Brett asked.

"Oh, they're bonding over their shared ability to talk to ghosts," Randy said.

"Have you all been drinking when I wasn't looking?" Brett asked.

"I have a question," Randy said. "If y'all can communicate

with spirits, then y'all know all of this," he pulled the brochure from his pocket, "is bogus, right?"

Rosetta shrugged. "People like it."

"If more people could communicate with ghosts, they'd understand that there is nothing fun about hearing a spirit speak," Casey said. The Greeks, with their understanding of frightening spirits who only spoke after drinking an offering of blood on the banks of the River of Ocean, had a better sense of what ghosts were like than any modern ghost hunter.

"Randy is a ghost investigator," Angela said. "That's how we met."

Angela saw Brett catch Casey's eye and raise an eyebrow, which at first Angela interpreted as disbelief, but then he said, "What'd I tell you? There's more than meets the eye in this life."

"Did Ryan's spirit ever talk to you?" Angela asked quietly.

Casey sighed. "I didn't really believe Rosetta that the voices in my head were ghosts until Ryan died. And then he started talking to me. The meditations Rosetta taught me couldn't keep him out."

Angela's eyes were rimmed with tears.

"He wanted you to keep me?"

Casey nodded.

"And you didn't listen."

"I was alive. I had to make choices in this world, not in whatever space he exists in now."

Angela wiped a hand under her nose and then said, "Do you still hear him?"

Casey shook her head. "For a long time, I used alcohol and drugs to keep myself numb. When you're numb, the dead leave you alone. Then I came here and I made a choice to be part of the living. I don't talk to ghosts. Not his or anyone else's. Even if I wanted to, I don't have anything of his anymore. There's no connection."

"You have me," Angela said.

Casey opened her arms, and Angela fell into them in an embrace that was twenty years in the making.

"He watches over me," Angela said, as she pulled away. "I know he does."

Somehow Angela managed to bring up the topic of wanting to meet Casey's family, which caused a moment of awkward silence, before Casey explained that her mother had also recently died, and then Rosetta dragged Casey off into the kitchen where some tense whispering took place, before the two of them came back and sat down, looking grim and subdued.

Angela listened to Casey explain the possibility that she had inherited a BRCA1 genetic mutation that would dispose her to certain types of cancer, and that if she had inherited it, she might have passed it on to Angela, too. The fact that the end of her quest involved more bad news struck Angela as hilarious, and she started to giggle as Casey finished her explanation. Her giggles turned to laughter, which turned to gasping, uncontrollable cackling, and everyone was staring at her like she'd lost her mind, but if she didn't laugh, she was definitely going to cry. It was honestly like she was cursed. After a few minutes, her laughter subsided, and she apologized.

"It's okay, there's no right way to react to news like this," Casey said gently.

"There's probably a wrong way," Angela said, and she stifled another giggle.

"Yeah, it's not really that funny," Casey said, but she smiled.

"Does it ever get easier?" Angela asked.

"What?"

"Life."

"Not in my lengthy experience," Rosetta said.

Eventually Rosetta announced that she had to go make sure everything was all set at the festival and Brett helped her up while she complained about how old ladies weren't meant to sit on hard floors. As she turned to go, she said, "And Angela, I'm very sorry dear, but actually there aren't any rooms at the inn, so I hope it's not too inconvenient for you to stay here. Free of charge, of course. I'll send your bags over."

"She's interesting," Randy said, after Rosetta had gone.

"I like her," Angela said. She liked that she was related to such a feisty woman. Rosetta was her aunt. Her great-great aunt. She and Rosetta were linked. Just as she and Helen and Marilyn were linked. She'd grown up on a small island, and far away Rosetta and Casey were on another small island. Marilyn was on the island of Manhattan, and Helen—well, she wasn't on an island—but it was the same idea. There were invisible bridges between them all, and now the bridges had been made visible, and the world had become so much smaller and so much bigger all at once.

As the night wore on and they all began to yawn, Brett suggested they use the blankets Rosetta had sent over to make the floor into a bed, but it wasn't as if any of them were going to sleep anyway. All night, they talked and laughed and cried and laughed some more. Angela felt like she'd been reunited with a long-lost sister. She'd always wanted a sister. She couldn't think of Casey as her mother any more than she could think of Ryan as her father, but that might be okay. What she needed was family, and she had found it here.

In the wee hours of the morning, Angela closed her eyes and offered up a prayer of thanks for all the moments that led her to that cold, gray October day in Maine, and for her big, crazy, unexpected family. It was as if, at twenty years old, she'd been reborn. A new life was beginning for her, full of adventure, full of love, full of laughter.

In the morning, Casey lay on her side watching this beautiful, sleeping woman who was her daughter. They had stayed up nearly all night, but Casey wasn't tired. She'd never felt more awake in her life. She was so happy that she could hardly trust her emotions. Something was going to go wrong. Something always went wrong. The universe did not give her happiness without snatching it away.

She knew now she had to go get the genetic test, otherwise she would spend every day waiting for the sickness to begin. Now she could understand how knowing her risks could bring peace of mind, and beyond that, could help her make sure her life was long and full and healthy, because she had so much to live for. She rolled over and snuggled into Brett and her eyelids began to droop when she heard the door of her apartment open.

The next thing she knew, Bentley's wet, slimy tongue was on her face, and Rosetta was standing over her, saying, "We aren't done yet!"

Of course. One last day. She had to get up and make coffee and muffins and spend one more day behind the counter at the Beach Plum Café. Today the last of the guests would leave and the next chapter of her life would begin.

"Let the kids sleep," she said, pushing Bentley off and getting up. What strange words to come out of her mouth. Let the kids sleep. She'd never been happier to have an early wake up after a sleepless night.

THE END

Acknowledgments

I am indebted to so many people who helped me in the process of writing and publishing this book.

First, my kind friends and family who read earlier versions: Stephanie Monahan, who patiently read several drafts and who keeps me sane at our weekly writing sessions; my mother Dorothy Vanaskie, the best first-reader and cheerleader a girl could ask for; my sister Laura O'Neill, who found time in her truly insane schedule to read and offer feedback; Caitie Huppert-Dwyer, who always knows how to reassure me in my moments of doubt; and Michael Smith, whose literary expertise I value.

Second, my devoted proofreaders: My father Thomas Vanaskie, my proofreader since high school; and Laurel Dile-King, a friend, mentor, and sharp-eyed reader.

Third, all of the people who supported my Kindle Scout campaign. Although Kindle Scout did not choose my book for publication, your generous support in nominating my book and in sharing the news with your friends made that effort feel positive, encouraging, and productive.

Last, but certainly not least, my husband Todd and all the family and friends who patiently put up with the ups and downs of dealing with a writer. The process of making a book is an emotional roller coaster, and one I couldn't survive without the best of friends. Particularly, Shannon, Kristen, Lisa, Glynis, Dina, and Sarah—thank you for believing in me even when I don't believe in myself.

About the Author

Diane V. Mulligan is the author of three novels. This is her most recent work. Her first novel, *Watch Me Disappear* (2012), was a finalist in the Kindle Book Review's Best Indie Book Awards in the Young Adult category in 2013, and her second, *The Latecomers Fan Club* (2013), was named a 2014 IndieReader Discovery Award winner. In 2015, she released a brief guide book to self-publishing called *The Sane Person's Guide to Self-Publishing*.

Made in the USA
Charleston, SC
16 February 2017